JOHN RAIT

PUFFIN CANADA

ONCE EVERY NEVER

LESLEY LIVINGSTON is a writer and actress living in Toronto. She has a master's degree in English from the University of Toronto, where she specialized in Arthurian literature and Shakespeare. She is the author of an award-winning urban fantasy trilogy for teens that includes the novels *Wondrous Strange* (winner of the Canadian Library Association Young Adult Book Award and Ontario Library Association White Pine Honour Book), *Darklight,* and *Tempestuous.* Visit Lesley online at www.lesleylivingston.com.

ONCE EVERY NEVER
Lesley Livingston

PUFFIN
CANADA

PUFFIN CANADA

Published by the Penguin Group

Penguin Group (Canada), 90 Eglinton Avenue East, Suite 700,
Toronto, Ontario, Canada M4P 2Y3 (a division of Pearson Canada Inc.)
Penguin Group (USA) Inc., 375 Hudson Street, New York, New York 10014, U.S.A.
Penguin Books Ltd, 80 Strand, London WC2R 0RL, England
Penguin Ireland, 25 St Stephen's Green, Dublin 2,
Ireland (a division of Penguin Books Ltd)
Penguin Group (Australia), 250 Camberwell Road, Camberwell, Victoria 3124,
Australia (a division of Pearson Australia Group Pty Ltd)
Penguin Books India Pvt Ltd, 11 Community Centre, Panchsheel Park,
New Delhi – 110 017, India
Penguin Group (NZ), 67 Apollo Drive, Rosedale, Auckland 0632,
New Zealand (a division of Pearson New Zealand Ltd)
Penguin Books (South Africa) (Pty) Ltd, 24 Sturdee Avenue, Rosebank,
Johannesburg 2196, South Africa
Penguin Books Ltd, Registered Offices: 80 Strand, London WC2R 0RL, England

First published 2011

1 2 3 4 5 6 7 8 9 10   (WEB)

Copyright © Lesley Livingston, 2011

Manufactured in Canada.

Library and Archives Canada Cataloguing in Publication

Livingston, Lesley
Once every ever / Lesley Livingston.

ISBN 978-0-14-317795-1

I. Title.

PS8623.I925O53 2011   jC813'.6   C2011-901642-7

Visit the Penguin Group (Canada) website at www.penguin.ca

Special and corporate bulk purchase rates available;
please see www.penguin.ca/corporatesales or call 1-800-810-3104, ext. 2477 or 2474

For Ward

"Bog bodies."

Clare Reid turned from watching the parade of suitcases trundling past on a baggage carousel at Heathrow International Airport to gaze in bemusement at the slender, raven-haired seventeen-year-old girl standing next to her.

"Excuse me?" she asked, pitching her voice so that she could be heard over the drone of conversation and unintelligible PA announcements in the crowded terminal.

"Thirteen of 'em." Allie McAllister spoke without looking up, her nose buried in the glossy pages of a guide to the British Museum. "Perfectly preserved corpses from the first century. They're on display and we're going to get to see them."

"Al ... why do you delight in tormenting me?" Clare asked.

"I'm not tormenting you. I'm generating fun and fascinating summer itineraries for you. This one's for when we go to the museum."

"'Fun' and 'fascinating' and ..." Clare counted on her fingers, "... 'museum.' Huh. Which of these things doesn't belong?"

Al grinned. "You know as well as I do that sometime within the next forty-eight hours, Maggie is gonna haul our collective butts through the doors of the Hallowed Halls of History no matter how much you kick and scream in protest. *I* am simply planning ahead."

Clare smiled wanly and shook her head. Typical Allie McAllister, Girl Genius. As usual, Al had applied keen-eyed analysis to a looming problem situation and was already working out a solution. Clare had to admit, though, Al had Maggie pegged.

Maggie—Dr. Magda Wallace—was Clare's aunt. A highly respected, world-renowned professor of archaeology, special projects consultant to the British Museum, and—for the duration of the summer—the functional equivalent of Clare's truant officer while her orchestra-musician parents continent-hopped on a world tour with the Symphonia Internationale.

Clare pushed away the brochure Al was waving in front of her face. "You actually want to spend precious minutes of our last summer vacation before final year hanging out with dead dudes."

"Don't knock it. Vampires and zombies are very hot right now."

"First of all, vampires are *un*dead. And zombies are ... ew."

"So that leaves bog guys."

Clare smiled indulgently at her best friend since grade three and turned back to the luggage conveyor. No sign of their bags yet, so she looked instead at her watch and frowned through the mental calculations necessary to set it to UK time.

"This whole time-difference thing wigs me out," she muttered.

"It should," Al said, tucking the museum pamphlet into the pocket of her neoprene computer bag. "We've lost hours. Actual time loss."

"What?" Clare blinked, startled by the notion. "No we haven't."

"*Tempus fugit,* pal." Al shrugged.

Clare stared at her blankly.

"Time flies."

"That's stupid."

"It's true." Al pointed skyward. "The entire time we were up there, hurtling through the sky, confined inside a pressurized metal tube, events of the world took place all around us that we were fundamentally, chronologically detached from. It's like time travel."

Clare stared at Al for a moment. "You watch too many movies," she said and punched her on the shoulder.

Turning back to the luggage-go-round, Clare yawned and stretched, keeping one eye open for a glimpse of her hot-pink tartan suitcase. She'd slept through almost the entire flight over from Toronto and now felt stiff and dehydrated—and like her head wasn't screwed on quite right.

"Who's picking us up?" Clare asked. Maggie hated driving in the city, so Al had told Clare not to worry about it and made alternative arrangements for them on her end. "It's not that creepy chauffeur dude your mom had the hots for last time we were in London, is it?"

"Nope." Al snaked between two older men in suits and nabbed her sleek black suitcase from the conveyor belt. "When Mumsy's not on this side of the pond, we don't rate a limo."

"Charming," Clare said over her shoulder, lunging for her own overpacked bag as it tumbled down the chute. She hefted it off the belt and the two girls made their way through the terminal to the arrivals pick-up driveway.

"Milo's got a car. He told me he'd be waiting for us."

"Great. Milo the Übergeek." Clare groaned, trying to remember the last time she'd seen Al's cousin. It had most likely been in close proximity to a reference library or a Star Trek convention. "Seriously—how does somebody with glasses that thick even qualify for a driver's licence?"

"Dude. Harsh." Al grinned. "You haven't seen him in, like, five years."

"Your point being?"

"I think Milo's kinda cool."

"You think Math-a-lympics are cool. You are an unreliable source."

The last time Clare had seen Milo the Mastermind he'd been about fourteen years old and practically a poster child for dorks everywhere, with floppy yellow bedhead hair and Coke-bottle lenses in thick black frames sliding down a nose perpetually buried in grad-school-level textbooks. Brains the size of planetary gas giants ran in the McAllister family genes.

Not that Clare, by comparison, was stupid—not by any stretch. In fact, Clare and Al both came from families brimming with high-functioning intellectuals and artists. It was one of the things that had brought them together when they'd first met in grade school. It had provided an initial foundation for their friendship. As they grew older, though, it had become increasingly apparent that—whereas Al was a chip off the ol' family mental block—Clare's potential genetic propensities had failed to manifest. Or skipped a generation. Or something. Despite an IQ that fell well within the "gifted" range, Clare had consistently defied her parents' expectations and grown up to become—as she'd been told time and again by teachers and tutors and guidance counsellors—average.

Oh, how she hated that word.

It wasn't that Clare didn't *try* to pay attention, it's just that she was easily distracted by shiny things and boys. Shiny things like the sleek silver BMW convertible parked beside the curb in the arrivals lane. And boys like the lean-muscled, golden-haired god leaning against it.

"Milo!" Al shouted.

Clare looked around. "Where?"

"There." Al pointed and waved.

And the blond Adonis with the smokin' hot ride waved back.

"THIS THING IS AWESOME!" Al enthused as Milo steered with practised ease through what to Clare seemed wrong-side-of-the-road traffic from the wrong side of the car. "I can't believe they gave you a Bimmer for a company car."

"Sweet, huh?" Milo grinned at his cousin. "I totally lucked out on this gig."

"Oh please, Mi," Al snorted from the front seat. "OS practically begged you to come work for them. They probably got all drooly on their ascots when you said yes."

"OS," as Clare understood from the conversation, was short for Ordnance Survey—the national mapmaking agency of Great Britain. At nineteen, Milo was the youngest employee of the venerable company; they'd hired him, Al had explained, to work summers when he wasn't in class at Oxford. He did "topographical vector cartography something-something ..." Clare had lost the thread of his job description about halfway through. Something to do with making digital maps. And computers. Of course.

"You should totally apply for an internship, Allie," Milo was saying. "I could give you a reference and you'd be a shoo-in no problem ..."

While the two cousins chatted, catching up, Clare sat in the back of the car surreptitiously analyzing Milo's profile and trying to reconcile it with her memories of him as a boy. It wasn't easy. Actually, it was impossible. Nothing about him fit that picture—not the wavy, wheat-gold hair or the broad shoulders or the lean-muscled, lightly tanned arms, not the strong square fingers lightly gripping the steering wheel or the long legs in the faded, fitted jeans that stretched out under the dashboard ...

"Clare?" Milo half-turned around and Clare got the impression he'd already said her name more than once.

"Hm?" She sat up, startled.

"I said 'How about you?'" Milo turned back but Clare noticed that he kept glancing at her in the rear-view mirror. Probably trying to decide if she was ignoring him or just not that bright. "What are your plans for after graduation?"

Plans? What plans? The very thought of life post–high school made her blood run cold. "Oh, you know ..." She shrugged. "I'm sort of weighing my options at the moment ..."

"Cool." Milo nodded as if he understood. He'd probably been buried under the weight of his options, whereas—not that she was going to tell him this—Clare's were feather-light. "Hey. Do you ladies want to do a little sightseeing tomorrow?" he asked. "I can take a bit of time off and show you around if you want."

Clare's heart leapt for a brief instant ... and then plummeted off a cliff into free-fall. That just wasn't going to happen. At least, not until she'd convinced Maggie through a few weeks of intensely good behaviour that she was worthy of an un-supervised day pass. "I ..."

"Thanks for the offer, Mi," Al interjected. "But Clare's kinda under house arrest while we're here."

"Excuse me?" Milo said, one dark gold eyebrow raised.

Al proceeded to explain—in Technicolor—about the house party debacle that had led to Clare's exile: the now-legendary disastrous weekend when word of a two-day parental absence at the Reid household had leaked out on Facebook. Al regaled Milo with party highlight anecdotes while Clare sank deeper into the BMW's leather bucket seat and wished she were dead. "And then some guy I've only ever seen while walking past detention hall threw up in the front hall closet. And on the dog. And then—get this—somehow he manages to throw up in Clare's mom's baby grand piano!"

And that, on top of everything else, was the unforgivable act that sealed Clare's fate. Never mind the dog.

Al glanced back over her shoulder at Clare's face and tried to stifle her giggles. "Sorry, pal. But you have to admit ... it was fairly epic."

Milo was laughing, although Clare was fairly certain it was polite laughter. In the rear-view mirror his blue eyes flicked up and his reflected gaze met hers. "So," he said wryly. "Party girl, huh?"

"Oh. Yeah ... nonstop." Clare lowered her gaze so that she wouldn't have to actually see the look of superiority she *knew* would be there in his eyes. Maybe, back home in Toronto anyway, a guy who looked like Milo wouldn't necessarily have been out of Clare's league: she'd generated occasional passing interest from one or two of the school hotties. But a guy who *thought* like Milo? Forget league, it wasn't even the same sport.

"Hey," he said, "nothing wrong with that. Go crazy. Live a little before you die, right?"

Right. Before she died of embarrassment. Or, if her aunt had anything to say about it, boredom. *See?* Clare thought. *There are at least two options for you to weigh. Go crazy.* Well, it was going to be a long summer. She just might.

2

Shopping at Harrods. The Millennium Wheel. Shopping on Kensington High Street. A river cruise on the Thames. Shopping in Soho. A picnic in Hyde Park. Hell—she'd even have settled for snapping pictures with the unsmiling guards outside Buckingham Palace and shopping at a tacky souvenir stand. But no. Clare's first day in Swingin' London Town and here she was ... at the museum. Al had been dead on.

Nothing interesting was ever going to happen in Clare's life ever again.

"So. Bog bodies?"

"You're kidding." She turned and glared balefully at Al. "Are you still fixating on that?"

"According to the guide it's the first time the exhibit has been made public. It's a recent archaeological find and it was hugely significant—thirteen perfectly preserved corpses discovered in a peat bog in Norfolk. They've never found a mass sacrificial site like this before anywhere!" Al bounced on the balls of her sneakered feet. "C'mon. It'll be interesting!"

Clare amended her prognosis: nothing *she* considered interesting was ever going to happen in her life ever again. She didn't have her cell phone—she'd forgotten it back at Maggie's—and so couldn't even distract herself with a game of BubbleXplode (all social media platforms having been locked out by her parents after the Facebook debacle). She leaned against the base of a marble statue, staring with unseeing eyes at the grandeur of the British Museum's Great Court.

"You've got me there, Al," she sighed, pushing a hand through the tumbled waves of her light golden-brown hair. "Nothing more fun than spending an afternoon hanging out with swamp remains."

"Bring on the bog zombies!" Al cheered.

"This is why we don't get dates, y'know."

"Is *that* why?"

Clare knotted her arms across her chest. "I can't believe you never told me about Milo."

"Are you still fixating on *that*?"

"You were totally holding out on me."

"I was not!" Al protested. "I *told* you he was cool."

"Yeah, but you never told me he was *hot*," Clare muttered. "So. Very. Hot."

Al laughed out loud at the look on her best friend's face, her voice echoing through the vast, majestic court like birdsong. Clare pushed away from the statue and began to wander aimlessly, scuffing her feet on the polished floor as she went. Sunshine poured down through the vaulted ceiling of glass and steel latticework, illuminating the marble statuary and the gleaming stone curves of the Reading Room.

Clare remained determinedly unimpressed by the spectacle. She'd been there before on visits with her aunt, and for all the dent it made in her attention the museum might as well have been a Walmart back home in Canada. Except that a Walmart would have had makeup counters and a magazine rack. And would therefore have been an *infinitely* better waste of time, in Clare's humble opinion.

She felt a stab of homesickness.

Already? Bad sign ...

A whole two months away from home was already starting to look like an unending purgatory of waiting around in elegant marble foyers for Maggie to take care of Matters Intellectual. Spending summer vacation in London hadn't been Clare's idea, but then again her choices *were* rather limited as far as that went. Fending for herself had *not* been presented as an option: she could either spend two months under the ever-watchful eye of her aunt or she could accompany her parents on tour. Which would have meant spending all her time in concert halls and hotel lobbies. Both Clare and her parents had viewed *that* prospect with almost exactly the same bleak level of enthusiasm.

Stupid Facebook party ...

At least the London deal had been sweetened by the fact that Al had convinced *her* mom to allow her to spend the summer with her nice, responsible, reliable cousin in England, too— thereby effectively accompanying Clare into exile. Unlike Clare, Al had actually jumped at the idea of spending the summer in Jolly Olde. *She*, certainly, could use a break from her home life, which mostly consisted of getting endlessly picked on by a gaggle of older brothers or blithely ignored by her elegantly eccentric mother, who spent most of the time in her art gallery (gin martini clutched tightly in one fist, latest in a series of avant-garde "artiste" boyfriends clutched tightly in the other).

Of course, having now renewed her acquaintance with the aforesaid "nice, responsible, reliable" *scorching-hot* cousin, Clare was rethinking her prospects. She wished Milo had been a little more persistent about the sightseeing idea, but apparently he was honouring her house-arrest situation, and so Al had turned up at Maggie's townhouse solo that morning. Of course, Maggie had gotten frothy at the mouth with the merest suggestion of letting the girls loose on their first day anyway, hence the museum foray. When she wasn't doing fieldwork, Maggie worked on contract for the institution and had for years. Clare's mom had once joked that Maggie spent so much time at the museum they should just set up a cot and a hotplate for her in one of the unused display cases.

Clare turned on her heel and continued to wander aimlessly.

Al tripped along beside her, the fringe of her midnight-black bangs bobbing above her wide-set blue-grey eyes. "Back to our present dilemma. We're stuck here until Mags is done. So we might as well go in search of something horrifying to keep us occupied." She dug through her bag for the illustrated guide. "According to this, that means either a touring exhibit of ancient South American fertility idols, or the bog dudes. Your choice. Or"—she jerked a thumb over her shoulder at where Maggie was standing heads-together with a tall, sharp-featured woman in a crisp white lab coat—"we can tag along with your aunt and the freaky curator lady for some really gripping chat on pottery shards and radio-carbon dating. Whaddya say? Maybe it will inspire you to follow the Perfesser into the old family trade."

Clare shuddered at the thought. It wasn't that she didn't have a deep fondness for "the Perfesser," as Al called her. But she dreaded the thought of becoming anything the least bit like her. Or like the head of British Antiquities, Dr. Ceciley Jenkins, the "freaky curator lady." It was Dr. Jenkins who'd scheduled the meeting with Clare's aunt that afternoon.

"Girls!" Maggie barked from across the hall. "Come meet Dr. Jenkins."

Dr. Jenkins, as far as Clare could tell, seemed to have been produced by the very same Lady Archaeologist 3000 machine that had spat out her aunt. She'd camouflaged her potentially attractive features with an almost identical starchy-updo, no-makeup, lab-coat fashion sense.

"We went to the same school together, once upon a time," Maggie said. "Can you believe it?"

"I *really* can," Clare murmured under her breath.

At her side, Al stifled a giggling fit. Barely.

"Dr. Jenkins recently became a full-fledged curator!" Maggie beamed benevolently and prodded the girls forward. "Say hello, now."

Clare waggled the fingers of one hand in wan greeting. Al choked out a "hiya."

"Er—hello ..." Dr. Jenkins said, eyeing them as if they were a couple of soda cans unearthed at a Mesopotamian dig site. The curator's manner was stiff and formal, and she smiled as though profoundly unused to the gesture. The result was sort of evil-clown grotesque. It was painfully obvious that Dr. Jenkins was deeply ill at ease in the presence of anyone too young to have qualified for a doctorate. "It's, uh, it's very nice to meet you ... Alice, Clarinet."

Clare rolled an eye at her aunt. *"Clare,"* she muttered. Maggie knew better than to give out her full stupid name. *Stupid musician parents* ...

"Urm ... we might be a while, Maggie," said Dr. Jenkins. "I need your opinion on several aspects of the new exhibit installations ..."

Casting her eye around the Great Court, Maggie spotted a group of teenagers milling about in front of two tour guides. "Girls, why don't you go and join the Summer School Enrichment Tour," she suggested, the tone of her voice conveying the misguided notion that this activity was to be considered "cool."

Proudly defiant in her uncoolness, Al brightened up immediately.

Clare, on the other hand, tried to silently indicate to her aunt that she'd rather spend an hour or two in the museum gift shop jamming unsharpened souvenir pencils up her nose.

Somehow, Maggie didn't get the hint. "Ceciley, would that be all right?" she asked the curator.

"Oh! Oh, of course it would!" the good doctor exclaimed with ill-concealed relief. She turned to Clare and said, in the kind of tone usually reserved for new puppies and the bribery of misbehaving eight-year-olds, "It's the Ancient Europe Tour, Clarinet, and there's a display of *bog* bodies as an added bonus!"

"So I've heard."

"Nothing more fun than bog people!"

With that, Al doubled over in uncontrollable laughter only partly disguised as a coughing fit. Clare gave her aunt a peck on the cheek—whispering that Maggie owed her one, *big* time—and resigned herself to her fate.

THE TOUR GROUP shuffled like a many-sneakered millipede from room to room, display case to display case, peering at coins and pottery shards, beads and rusted blades, broken glass bottles and gap-toothed ivory hair combs—all that remained of long-ago daily lives. Now priceless artifacts.

But to Clare's glazed-over eyes nothing in those cases could compare with the stuff on display in Harrods department store. A couple of the glass boxes in the Ancient Britain room contained polite little paper notices informing visitors that artifacts had been removed while the gallery was under renovation. Frankly, Clare couldn't see how that made the exhibit any *less* interesting.

It had been such a major disappointment when she'd first discovered that charmingly dishevelled, quip-slinging, adventure-loving archaeologists were *totally* the creation of some Hollywood executive's fevered brain. Mystical artifacts and quests for priceless treasure, more of the same.

"Could this stuff possibly be any more boring?" she muttered, earning a disapproving glance from a white-haired security guard who sat on a little folding chair by the entrance to the room. Drinking tea.

Oh yeah. Definitely a hotbed of action, Clare thought. *I expect a treasure heist any second now ...*

It was about half an hour into the tour and even Al had long since tuned out the guide's nasally drone. The two girls dawdled far behind the throng of keener students as they entered the Special Exhibits room, where the lights were dimmer than the rest of the museum and a banner proclaimed SPECTRAL WARRIORS: BOG BODIES OF THE NORFOLK BROADS.

Aha. So this was the object of Al and the curator's gruesome enthusiasm.

The bog guys.

"What's a 'broad'?" Clare asked Al. "I mean, other than the standard definition."

"It's what they call a bunch of wetlands around Norwich. Rivers and swamps and marshes. Come on. Let's check this stuff out." Al tugged her by the sleeve farther into the shadowy room.

A field of chest-high plinths topped with environmentally controlled, clear Perspex boxes about the size of coffins stretched from one end of the room to the other. Clare peered with idle curiosity into the first box, unable at first to make out what was in it. A plaque on the wall bore the words CLAXTON MAN—and identified the contents of the display case as the first of thirteen bodies discovered by a bunch of turf cutters a few years earlier, and named, apparently, after the tiny town perched at the edge of the soupy bit of real estate in Norfolk under which it had been discovered.

Clare's eyes wandered past the rest of the text and focused instead on the accompanying photo—an artist's reconstruction of what the dead guy might have looked like back in the day: young, with dark reddish-brown hair tied back from a noble-looking face. *Good bone structure,* Clare thought. With a cool haircut and some styling he might have even passed for cute.

She turned back to the case and leaned over, almost pressing her nose to the glass in suddenly acute, totally morbid fascination. The remains looked nothing like the young man in the picture. Nothing like a man at all, really. More like saddle leather that had been cut in a pattern and sewn together in the vague shape of a human being—and then discarded in a rumpled heap like a Halloween costume on the first of November. Clare could see that his head still had hair on it and that there was stubble on his cheeks and chin. She stared and stared, intrigued in spite of herself. The quality of preservation was fairly astonishing, actually. She could even make out the remains of a fox-fur armband that circled his left bicep, just above the elbow, and a thin rope cord that had been tied around his neck above a simple, decorative metal ring he wore like a collar. He had a small gold hoop in one ear and around his wrists were intricately designed matched cuffs made, apparently, of silver—although it was hard to tell. They had long since lost their sheen.

Clare was still staring when she noticed that her reflection in the glass seemed to have grown a second head. Al had come up behind her and was gazing at the bog man with detached curiosity.

"See? I told you," she murmured. "Creepy. Definitely creepy."

"I dunno." Clare shrugged. "Looks kinda ... peaceful."

"How peaceful can you be when you've been stabbed, bludgeoned, strangled, and thrown into a bog to die?" Al turned and looked at Clare, who stood blinking, her mouth hanging open. "That's what the sign says." She straightened up and pointed at the plaque.

"Oh." Clare struggled for a moment, groping for a witty rejoinder, and then gave up. There wasn't much she could say to that. She glanced back at the reconstruction photo and thought that the eyes of the face in the picture looked sad. She shivered a little and turned back to where Al had circled around to the other side of the glass case. She was staring with keen eyes at the morbid remains and glancing back and forth between that and the brochure in her hand.

"Maybe you're right, though," she continued. "Maybe they didn't feel a thing. According to this, archaeologists found traces of ergot in their digestive tracts."

"Which is?"

"Toxic slime mould."

"Ew."

"In small quantities, it produces hallucinations," Al read. "What the ancient Druids would have considered to be powerful mystical 'visions.' But it has to be ingested in the right quantities, otherwise it just causes horrible, screaming-painful death."

"Sounds delightful." Clare looked down at another one of the leathery bodies and wrinkled her nose. "But why go to all the trouble of getting these poor suckers all hepped up if they were just gonna off them?"

Al shrugged. "Apparently, there's a theory that these guys weren't just run-of-the-mill sacrifices, but an elite class of warriors that were ritually killed on the eve of a major battle so that they could become kinda like ghost warriors."

"Wouldn't it have made more sense to keep your best fighters alive so they could actually, I dunno, *fight* for you?" Clare asked dryly.

Al shrugged. "Their spirits were supposed to mystically empower the troops, I guess."

"That's stupid."

"War's pretty stupid in general, if you ask me," Al said, continuing to thumb through the display descriptions in her brochure. "Ooh! It says you can still see the marks of a tattoo on this one's arm ..."

"You know," Clare said as they wandered from case to case looking at the grim displays, "more and more, I have the sneaking suspicion that you actually truly dig all this mouldy old stuff."

"Did you just pun?" Al looked at her in surprise.

"What?" Clare blinked. "No!"

"I just thought—'dig' ... never mind."

"Totally unintentional. Let us never speak of it again."

"Aha!" Dr. Jenkins's voice made Clare and Al jump. "Here you are—and I see you've found old 'Pete Marsh' and friends!"

The girls turned and stared at the grinning archaeologist, who bestowed upon them a cheesy, exaggerated wink.

"That's what we in the trade like to call the bog men." She chortled a bit to herself and said, "You know—it's a pun! Because it was a *peat marsh* that ... well. You get the gist."

"You see?" Clare murmured to Al. "Punning *bad*."

"Right." Dr. Jenkins clapped her hands briskly, fished a pair of "Visitor" security passes with little metal clips on them out of her lab-coat pocket, and handed them over to the girls. "Put these on and come along down to Restoration Room D when you've had your fill of the boggy men, girls. Clarinet, your Auntie Magda is a wonder. We've only a few more installation details to go over and then we're finished, so don't dawdle ... Ta!"

"Pete Marsh?" Al wondered aloud in Dr. Jenkins's wake. "Holy crap. That's the best a bunch of intellectuals could come up with? I am *so* disappointed."

Clare glanced over her shoulder at the spirit warriors' remains. Suddenly it felt to her as though the temperature in the room had plummeted—like a shadow racing over the face of the sun. She shivered and pulled Al by the sleeve. "C'mon. Let's ditch the bogloids. This whole room is starting to give me the creeps."

Somewhere in front of them the guide warbled something about a fifteen-minute film presentation on corpse-preservation techniques. Al's mouth quirked in a lopsided grin. "If you insist," she said. "Even *I* have limits to my eggheadery."

RESTORATION ROOM D was a great, vaulting subterranean chamber filled with row upon row of industrial metal shelving units filled with numbered bins and boxes of artifacts that Clare could identify only as "unidentifiable." In her earlier visits with Maggie it had been the same—smelling of dust and just about as interesting.

Except this time.

Even Clare was forced to drop her jaded, world-weary stance upon entering the room. There were things laid out on the tables that actually looked like ... *things*. Bits of chariots, an ancient bronze cauldron with a huge dent and a piece missing from the rim, lengths of chain, and faces carved in stone. There was even a helmet with two cone-shaped horns sticking out of either side. And in the middle of the biggest table lay a smallish shield—about half as tall as Clare. It was roughly rectangular with rounded corners and looked as though it was made out of a single sheet of bronze. Three circular bumps, two smaller ones at either end and a large one in the middle, were swirly and decorative and inlaid in places with the remains of bits of coloured enamel. And there were thick, ornately decorated neck rings—Clare remembered from the tour that they were called "torcs." On the same table as the shield was one particular neck ring that even Clare had noticed in the museum brochure. It was called the Snettisham Great Torc, and it *was*, she thought, pretty great. Gleaming and gorgeous, intricately decorated, the torc looked to be made out of hundreds of strands of twisted precious metal that ended in two heavy, swirling loops. It was almost as thick as Clare's wrist.

Al gasped. "Is that *gold*?"

It was. And it was staggeringly beautiful.

"What's all this stuff doing out in the open like this?" Clare asked.

"Oh, it's quite safe." Dr. Jenkins bestowed one of her awkward, patronizing smiles on Clare. "We've top security around here, you know."

Clare stared at the curator. "Phew," she said flatly. "I *was* gonna lose sleep ..."

Dr. Jenkins tilted her head and frowned.

"The museum is almost done revitalizing the Ancient Britain exhibit," Maggie intervened, shooting her niece a warning look. "We're repositioning some of the artifacts and giving the Snettisham Torc its own separate display plinth. The pieces are here to be cleaned before being replaced." She steered Dr. Jenkins over to a table in an alcove covered in architectural drawings. "We'll be done in a moment, girls. Now, you know the rules ..."

Clare rolled her eyes at Al and together they moved closer to the table to get a better look at the ancient swag. It must have been an almost mystical feat to have created an object so exquisite by hand, Clare mused. She actually felt affected by its beauty and shook her head in wonder, a little surprised with herself.

It wasn't just the torc, though—all the artifacts looked ancient and very out of place in the brightly lit room. The fact that a computer sat in a corner on a rolling cart only added to the incongruity, as did the blond, moustached security guard hovering by the far door. The very modern-looking gun strapped to his hip heightened the effect. Evidently the stuff on the table was worth an awful lot more than just its "historical value."

Clare had been around her aunt long enough to know the rules where antiquities were concerned—most of which started with the phrase "NO TOUCHING" and ended with the phrase "NO TOUCHING" and usually included the admonition "UNDER ANY CIRCUMSTANCES" and the word "EVER." But with Maggie and Dr. Jenkins on the other side of the room happily engrossed in egghead chat and the guard posing like a gun-slinger at the OK Corral and basically ignoring anything as non-threatening as a pair of seventeen-year-old girls, Clare couldn't help herself. She couldn't tear her gaze away from the shield, away from its lustrous bronze surface, and the need to touch it came as a sudden, overwhelming compulsion. A distant buzzing started up in her ears, like faraway voices heard through walls. Almost without thinking, she reached out her hand. She laid a finger upon one sinewy curve, tracing the raised design ...

And the world around her began to fall away.

3

The restoration room went dim and shadowy as though a thick midnight fog had rolled in, and Clare suddenly felt as if she was falling forward. There were flares at the edges of her vision as though fireworks had gone off behind her eyes and it seemed to her as if—where she had touched the cool gleaming metal of the shield—her hand had passed right *through* it. She could feel the blood pulsing in her veins and hear the whispering of those far-off voices ... then there was an electric crackle, bright and sharp as though she'd been hit by lightning or stuck her finger in a light socket. Her whole body began to tingle and she felt as though she was coming apart like a cloud of fireflies scattering. She squeezed her eyes shut, and when she opened them again, nothing was as it should have been.

She was outside and it was deep night. All around her was darkness. She could smell the odour of damp vegetation and wet mud, and the sound of rushing water made her half-turn to glance over her shoulder. As her eyes adjusted to the lack of light, Clare realized she was standing on the bank of a broad expanse of a mighty river flowing past, a wide black ribbon under the pale light of a thin crescent moon. She heard the sound of low voices and turned the rest of the way around ...

And froze.

Standing right there, only a few feet away, were the darkened shapes of two men, one huge and bearlike, the other just a bit taller than Clare, with a lean athletic build. They had their backs to her and Clare couldn't make out their features, but they both wore what looked like long, heavy cloaks. They spoke to each other in low tones. Clare strained to hear what they were saying, but the words were unfamiliar and she realized they were speaking some other language. Suddenly the big man lifted his muscle-corded arms high above his head, and Clare saw that he held an object that was shockingly familiar. It looked exactly like the bronze shield in the restoration room. Only *this* one looked brand new.

She gasped aloud and the younger man's head snapped around. Clare felt her heart skip a beat—even in the dim wash of light from the crescent moon, he was strikingly handsome. His hair was a deep, reddish brown and his dark eyes looked almost black in the moonlight. His gaze tracked back and forth, as though he was looking for the source of the sound she'd made without being able to actually see her. He took a step forward, and in a low, musical voice, uttered a single, questioning word.

Her *name.*

In almost the very same instant, Clare heard the harsh call of a raven ring out in the night air—and suddenly she found herself back in the brightly lit room in the museum. She glanced wildly about to see how everyone else was reacting to the strange, startling occurrence ...

Mr. Rent-a-Cop still posed.

The doctors still chatted.

And Al was staring at her, open-mouthed.

Clare's heart was pounding madly in her chest. She shivered and hugged her elbows tightly, motioning Al over with a jerk of her head. "Did you *see* that?" she whispered, her breath coming in shallow gasps.

Al's eyes were the size of dinner plates. "See *what*?" she answered in a shaky murmur. "See you flicker like a broken TV
set and *fade out of existence*? Yeah. Yeah—I saw that. What's going *on*, Clare?"

Clare glanced over one shoulder at the huddled archaeologists and then over the other shoulder at the guard. She and
Al could have been in another dimension for all the attention they were being paid. And then Clare thought about what
had just happened and a chill raced up and down her spine—
maybe she *was* in another dimension. Or had been—a second
ago ...

"Clare?" Al was about to lose it.

"Shh!" Clare tugged Al by the sleeve over behind one of the
tall shelves. "What did you see?"

"I told you! You ... *flickered*!" Al's hands did a spazzy little
dance in front of her face like caffeinated butterflies. "And
then you went kind of hazy-looking ... and then you freaking
disappeared. You touched that shield thing and 'zot'! How did
you *do* that?"

"I don't know."

Al looked as if she'd bolt from the room any second.

"I *don't*!" Clare sputtered a bit desperately. She lowered her
voice again and pulled Al closer. "All I know is, one second I'm
standing here and the next everything's all tingly and sparkly
and ... and dark. There's a crackle of lightning and then I look
around and ..."

"And *what*?"

"And I'm standing on a riverbank in the middle of nowhere,
at night. And there are these guys ..."

"What guys?"

"I don't know. They weren't speaking English. One of them
was big—like *huge*—and holding that shield thing." Clare's
gaze drifted back to the table where the artifacts lay. "It looked

like he was about to throw it in the river. But the other one ... was young. And ... and ..."

"And *what*?"

"Gorgeous." Clare swallowed convulsively. "And he said my name. He looked at me—well, not quite at me—and he said ... *Clarinet*."

"Clare ..." Al had gone milk-pale and was starting to look really angry. "This *isn't* funny."

"Do I look like I'm laughing?" Clare whispered back urgently. "Have you ever known me to make up a story like *that*?"

"... No."

"You said I disappeared. You saw it yourself."

"You did. I did. Seriously, Clare ... *what's* going on?"

"I don't know." Clare looked down at her hand—where her fingertips still tingled—and then back up at Al. "Okay—here's the deal. You keep a lookout and make sure I don't get in shit from the curator or my aunt. Or Robo-Cop. I'm going to try that again."

"Are you deficient?" Al hissed.

No. She was curious. Frantically, terribly, *intensely* curious. For the first time in ... well, for the first time in a long time. Maybe the first time ever. But that guy. He'd said her *name*. And she had to know why.

In her ordinary life, surrounded by extraordinary people, Clare had never really taken much of a chance with anything important. Everyone she knew—everyone in her family, Al, Al's family, Maggie—they were all so ... so effortlessly competent and accomplished. So she'd learned at a young age not to risk doing anything too complicated. She could handle failing. She just couldn't handle failing spectacularly. As a consequence, nothing particularly interesting had happened in Clare Reid's life for a very long time. Nothing ... cool. Nothing to make her extraordinary.

But now, with that single flash of *weird*, everything was different. Maybe she was special. Or maybe she was just crazy.

"You're crazy," Al said.

Well, there you go.

"What if you disappear completely? What if you don't ... you know ... rematerialize? I can't believe I just *said* that!" She shook her head fiercely. "What if you're gone for *good*?"

Clare took a deep breath. "Then you're gonna have a better story than boring old party shenanigans to tell when you get back home to Toronto, aren't you?"

Al glared at her best friend stubbornly and shifted slightly so that she was standing in front of the table, between Clare and the artifacts. Excitement was bubbling up in Clare's chest at the thought of doing it again. Whatever it was she'd actually done. This was ... *definitely* special. She knew that much. She could sense it. Was it normal? No. Explainable? Absolutely not. At least, not yet. And that—surprisingly—appealed to her somehow.

She pegged Al with a tight stare. "Look. You're the scientist. Aren't you the tiniest bit curious about what just happened?" she asked.

"Clare ... you *disappeared*." Al emphasized each syllable of the word. "'Curious' doesn't quite cover it. I'm not curious. I'm freaked. I'm very seriously freaked."

Clare was too, if she was going to be honest with herself. But for maybe the first time in her life she wasn't going to let that stop her. Despite Al's frantic, whispered protests, Clare stepped around her and approached the table for the second time with a kind of giddy anticipation. The image of the auburn-haired young man swam up before her mind's eye. She felt her heart thump in excitement ... and then lurch with apprehension.

Hey, she silently encouraged herself, *why let mind-numbing fear keep you from doing something so incredibly boneheaded it would give Mikey the Linebacker at school pause for thought?* She steadfastly ignored the fact that Mikey also liked to throw himself off his garage roof. For fun.

Come on, Clare ...

What was it Milo had said to her the day before?

"'Live a little before you die,' right?" she murmured to herself. He'd also said, "'Go crazy'..."

Clare smiled then in spite of her fear. Maybe the super-hot egghead had a point. Things seemed to be working out well enough for him, after all. In keeping with thoughts of Milo and in the spirit of scientific curiosity, Clare decided to conduct a control experiment on this second attempt. Instead of placing her hand on the bronze shield again, she surveyed the assortment of artifacts laid out on the table. A brush of her fingertips along the teeth of a carved-bone weaving comb did nothing. Neither did a plain bronze drinking bowl produce any effect. Chariot bits and an iron cauldron hook yielded similar non-results.

Al stood staring at her with her arms crossed tightly, and Clare started to feel a little ridiculous, surreptitiously fondling all that historical junk. But then she put her hand down on the great golden Snettisham Torc.

At least when it happened *this* time she was half expecting the sudden shift in reality—but it still didn't make it any less shocking to find herself suddenly ... wherever it was she found herself.

WHICH, IN THAT MOMENT, was definitely *not* the restoration room.

Just like the first time, all around her was darkness. But she had no idea if it was the same night or a different one.

Clare tilted her head and stared up into a sky that, save for a pale haziness all around her, was shatteringly clear and spattered with an astonishing number of stars, brighter than she'd ever seen them, even on camping trips. The crispness of the air made it feel like early autumn, and it would have been a truly beautiful night—but in the distance, there was fire. And screaming.

She gasped and felt her lungs burn from the acrid smoke that drifted toward her. With her heart fluttering crazily like a tiny, terrified animal's, she stared at the lurid orange glow just over a near rolling hill. She tried to concentrate. Tried to catalogue and memorize every detail of the world into which she'd tumbled—just like Alice down a rabbit hole—so that she could tell Al when she got back. *If* she got back. But back from where?

Clare looked down to see her hand still held out in front of her as if she were still touching the gleaming golden neck ring. Slowly—oh *so* slowly, so as not to break her focus, she lowered her arm to her side. A giddy, fearful thrill ran through her when she didn't suddenly rematerialize back in the fluorescent-lit workroom. She took a tentative step forward.

... And then dropped behind a big rock so she wouldn't be seen. The very same auburn-haired young man as before came suddenly careening over the hill in what looked to be some sort of chariot. And he was heading at breakneck speed down a path that ran right past her.

In a ... chariot? Clare blinked dumbly. *Okay. I'm not so sure this is a "where am I thing" anymore ... I think this is a "when am I" thing!*

As it got closer, Clare saw that the chariot was really more of a wicker-sided racing cart, built for speed and drawn by two sturdy, lathered ponies. The driver was definitely the same guy she'd seen the first time. He was bare-armed and lean-muscled, with skin that showed sun-bronzed even in the moonlight, and he stood with legs braced wide to steady himself as the two-wheeled cart jounced over the uneven ground. He wore a sleeveless tunic with breeches laced tight around his calves and his feet were bare. A simple silver torc encircled his neck, and from his belt on either hip hung a dagger and a short, broad sword with a leaf-shaped blade.

He must be some kind of ... warrior, Clare thought.

A warrior, maybe, but he was no brute. He was strikingly handsome in a wild, dangerous way. His long auburn hair was tied in a tail at the nape of his neck, the bones of his face were elegantly sculpted, and his eyes flashed with fierce intelligence. Clare tore her gaze away from the young man's face long enough to notice that on the floor of the cart, tucked between his straddling legs, was something that looked like a large bundle of cloth. The shapeless thing bounced heavily as, with a sudden, violent curse, the driver hauled the reins back on his steaming charges and the wheels of the cart jumped the rutted track. Pulling the whinnying ponies up short, the charioteer was just in time to avoid crashing headlong into another chariot that came screaming around the bend in the track to meet him.

The young man vaulted over the wickerwork side of his cart, calling out a word—a name? Only it wasn't hers this time.

This time, it was the name of the terrifying creature at the reins of the other cart.

Clare had thought she'd seen female fury before. Like the time the permanent-detention headcase three rows over from her in biology class had Krazy-Glued an entire dissection lab's worth of dead frogs to the principal's Lexus. To Clare, the expression on Ms. Henderson's face was what pure wrath looked like. She'd been *so* wrong.

Pure wrath was the woman in that chariot.

With eyes rolling white like those of the horses pulling her cart and hair a wind-wild tangle of fiery red, the woman leaped to the ground before the wheels had stopped spinning and pounded down the last few yards of the track to meet the other driver. Words that Clare could not understand spilled from the young man's lips—questioning, angry words, from the sounds of them—and the woman answered him in a harsh crow-call of a voice.

Clare stared unblinking at the scene, fascinated, with the knuckles of one fist jammed against her mouth to keep herself from making any noise. She couldn't take her eyes off the young charioteer. He couldn't have been more than a few years older than Clare was—nineteen, maybe twenty—but there was a fierce intensity about him that made her think he was more than just a chariot driver. And there was *obviously* something more to the woman than met the eye. A regal quality blazed through the rage that twisted her features into the mask of an avenging Fury. Under other circumstances, when she wasn't so angry maybe, the woman would have been striking to look at. Not necessarily beautiful—with her strong, angular features, *handsome* was probably a better word, but not at the moment. At the moment, she was *seriously* pissed about something. Clare wondered what on earth could possibly have driven her into such a colossal freak out.

And then the woman turned around.

Below the tangled mass of her auburn hair, the material of the woman's shirt—a kind of long, belted tunic—had been completely torn away in the back. By the dim light of the sickle moon and stars, it looked as though thick black tar stained her torso from shoulders to waist. It took Clare a moment to realize what the stains really were. Blood. The woman was covered in blood. The vicious lash marks from what even Clare could identify as a brutal whipping criss-crossed her pale flesh and blood stained the back of her long skirt all the way down past her knees.

As he surveyed the ravaged landscape of the woman's back, the charioteer spat out another string of words—awfully impolite ones, from the sounds of them—and Clare was close enough to see that bright tears filled the corners of his eyes. But the woman merely lifted her proud head and held up a hand. Then she turned her palm face-up. Wordlessly, the young man reached into the folds of his tunic.

Clare gasped, her heart suddenly hammering, as he drew out a massive gold neck ring. It looked like the *very same one* she had touched in the museum. The woman smiled grimly and took the torc, bending the ends out slightly so that she could slip it around the strong white column of her graceful neck and settle it on her collarbones. She looked as if she'd always worn it. With a nod of thanks the woman turned back to her own chariot, but then she froze. Her gaze drifted toward the blanket-wrapped bundle on the floor of the young man's cart.

She asked the charioteer a single, soft-voiced question.

He hesitated, a riptide of emotion distorting the handsome features of his face, but then—as if in answer—he stepped aside and gestured, his shoulders sagging in what looked like a kind of defeat. From behind the rock Clare craned her neck, watching as the woman strode past him and leaned down to push aside the folds of the heavy woollen blanket.

There was a moment of utter stillness. Silence. And then a high, thin sound spiralled out from where the woman stood, tearing through the fabric of the night air. The cry built to an ear-shattering howl and the red-haired woman fell to her knees, raising her fists to the night sky and throwing back her head. The grief that poured from her throat was like the cry of a wounded animal.

Clare looked back at the chariot. She wished she hadn't.

The folds of the blanket, now thrown aside, had concealed the crumpled form of a teenage girl maybe a year or two older than Clare herself. With only her face and one bare white shoulder exposed, the girl looked as though she could have been asleep; dark eyelashes feathered upon the clear, pale skin and a cloud of long, deep auburn hair pillowed her head.

But from the way her limbs sprawled under the blanket, awkwardly propped up against the sides of the chariot, it was clear that the girl was *not* asleep.

As she stared at the dead girl in the cart, a profound awareness descended upon Clare—her careless actions back in the restoration room had landed her in a very dangerous place. It was a realization that was dramatically reinforced when she suddenly felt the small hairs on the back of her neck rise.

A shiver went all the way up Clare's spine and she turned her head very slowly ...

To find herself staring into a pair of wide blue eyes.

4

The blue-eyed girl crouched in the long grass behind the rock, less than a foot away. She looked to be about the same age as Clare, but the similarities ended there. There was a distance and a depth to the girl's gaze that spoke of having seen and lived through things Clare couldn't begin to imagine. She wore a cloak and a calf-length belted tunic of deep green wool. Her hair was strawberry blond, long and wavy, but it was tangled into knots where it had escaped from a thick plait. There were fresh, deep scrapes along one of her arms and the shoulder of her sleeveless tunic was torn. Tears ran down her cheeks and her pretty face was flushed with exertion. Her breath came in panting gasps.

And she stared right through Clare as if she wasn't even there.

The girl's blue gaze was instead focused sharply on the path and the two charioteers. Her mouth worked silently for a moment and then she whispered the word *"Tasca."* Her voice broke on a sob and she raised a hand as if reaching out toward the unmoving girl in the cart.

Clare jumped back, startled. But she wasn't fast enough to evade the girl's reaching hand and, as her fingertips connected with the space Clare was already occupying, there was a sudden crackling in the air like a strong electrical discharge.

As the girl gasped and flew backward. Clare felt as if she'd been hit by lightning—a much bigger bolt than the one that had sent her there—and the night all around her grew subtly brighter, almost as if she'd turned up the contrast on a TV screen. Sounds suddenly seemed louder, too. She could hear crickets and the scurrying of small animals in the grass—and the laboured, raspy breathing of the blond girl in front of her who was shaking her head back and forth, her eyes squeezed shut. When she opened them again a moment later they went almost perfectly round in shocked surprise.

And they were focused on Clare's face.

"Clare!" she whispered. *"Rho ddiolch i Andrasta!"*

Clare! Thank Andrasta!

The moment froze in time. Clare's mouth worked sound-lessly as she tried to form some sort of reply to the words she heard in her head—different from the ones she'd heard with her ears.

Her name. She had said Clare's name.

Suddenly the girl turned her head sharply as though hear-ing a noise from somewhere behind her. When she turned back, her gaze was full of fear.

"Helpa fi, Clare! Maent yn fy hela ..."

Please help me, Clare! They are chasing me ...

"What?" Clare blurted finally in response, her voice a star-tled whisper. "Who ..."

The girl opened her mouth to reply but a sudden shadow blotted the moonlight from her face. A large, rugged hand clamped tightly over her mouth and Clare skittered backward as the looming form of a man, dressed in a bronze helmet and armour, rose up behind the girl and grabbed her cloak—yanking her back behind the rock, out of sight of the path.

The girl whimpered, but the sound was almost com-pletely muffled by the soldier's calloused palm. The man and woman on the track with the chariots would never hear it.

Clare watched helplessly as the girl thrashed about wildly, her hands struggling at a brooch that fastened her cloak around her neck. As the man tried to drag her away she made one wild lunge directly at Clare.

Clare shook off her paralyzing terror and tried to grab the girl's flailing limbs. Tried to help somehow. But the soldier cracked the girl sharply on the back of her skull with the butt end of his sword hilt and she went limp, eyes rolling up into her head.

Clare cried out in protest, but the soldier ignored her as if she didn't even exist. Or wasn't even there ...

With a glance in the direction of the redheaded woman and the chariot driver, the soldier threw the girl's slim body over his shoulder like a sack of grain and loped away, running silently through the long grass toward the dark edge of the forest and away from the river track.

The girl's cloak lay upon the ground. Clare plucked at the material as if trying to convince herself that what she'd just seen had really happened. Fear and confusion clutched at her and she stayed crouched down, frozen and unsure of what to do. But the young girl was pretty obviously in a *serious* heap of trouble and Clare couldn't help feeling that it was somehow all her fault. If she hadn't been there—hadn't distracted the fleeing girl and stopped her in her tracks—she would have made it to the riverbank. To the young warrior and the ferocious-looking woman, either of whom might have been able to help her ...

"Help!" Clare shouted suddenly, leaping up and shouting, waving her arms wildly in a desperate attempt to attract the attention of the pair on the path. But the woman had already leapt back into her own cart and, with a crack of the reins, the pair of chariots thundered off down the path, away from the distant smoke and fire. Clare pounded down the track in their wake, hollering and flailing her arms to absolutely no effect, the dust thrown by the chariot wheels burning in her throat.

They didn't hear her. They hadn't seen her.

Clare slowed to a jog finally, the sound of her own laboured breathing almost drowning out the sudden harsh call of a raven, startled from its night perch into flight. She bent over, hands on her knees, dizzy. Sparks flared behind her eyes and the world tilted on its axis.

"WHAT HAVE I *DONE*?" Clare gasped.

"You tell me. Then we'll both know." Al's voice still managed to convey tightly wound sarcasm in a fierce whisper.

Clare blinked.

Sudden starbursts faded from her vision and Al's pale, frightened face, framed by the dark fringe of her hair, bent into focus inches from Clare's own.

"Oh *shit* ..." Clare shook her head and glanced around the restoration room. The overhead neons seemed painfully bright after the darkness by the riverbank. She was dizzy and felt as though she were still a bit transparent. She was also, she noticed, shaking like a leaf.

"Clare?" Her aunt's voice floated over to her from behind a row of metal shelving—that is, if something that stern and prickly could float. "You aren't *touching* anything, are you?"

With an almost audible twang Mall Cop's steely gaze snapped over to where the two girls stood. Al composed herself enough to give him a bored *"as-if-we'd-touch-that-dusty-old-stuff"* glare. Satisfied, he went back to his recruiting-poster stance, eyes empty of all emotion except perhaps a wistful longing for mirrored sunglasses to complete the look.

"*Gawd*, no, Mags," Clare replied, trying to clamp down on the warble in her voice. "There's history cooties all over that stuff."

"That's my darling angel." Maggie's voice dripped weary sarcasm.

Clare heaved a sigh of relief and turned back to Al.

"'Oh *shit* ...'?" Al parroted Clare's sentiment of moments before. "*Where* did you just go? And *how* did you do that? And *what* exactly is going on? Clare?"

Clare put a hand to her head, feeling shaky.

"*Clare?*"

"Look—can we just shelve the 'Allie McAllister, Girl Investigative Journalist' thing for a second?" she hissed.

Al's mouth snapped shut, a hurt expression clouding her eyes.

"Sorry. I'm sorry." Clare took a deep breath. "Mags?" she called. "Going to the cafeteria ..."

"All right, luv," Maggie called back. "If you're not there when I'm done, I will have to murder you."

"Deal. Bye." Clare grabbed Al by the wrist and they bolted from the room.

"Why are we going to the cafeteria?" Al asked as they ran.

"To get away from Officer Friendly and the Brainiac Twins," Clare said over her shoulder without slowing down. For some reason, she found that running just at that moment made her feel better. Her sneakered feet pounded down the echoing corridors, Al following noiselessly in her wake.

AL BLINKED. For the first time in what was probably five minutes. Give or take. Since Clare had started talking, really. She blinked again. "Okay." Her voice was quiet. Calm. "I give. Tell me where the hidden camera is. And how you did the disappearing thing. I get it. I've been punk'd. Very good. Very funny. Rich."

Clare's tone was just as quiet. Just as calm. "Al? I understand that this a little weird. And more than a little out of character for me." She leaned forward over the table, clasping her hands in front of her, her stare boring into Al. "I also just experienced what I can only describe as a paranormal phenomenon to which you were the sole witness, and I'm pretty sure that if you don't stick with me on this one I'm gonna start screaming like a freak any second now. *Okay?*" Clare smiled tightly and tilted her head, waiting.

"Um."

"Okay?"

"Okay."

"Okay." It was Clare's turn to blink. *"Seriously?"*

"Yes." Al nodded solemnly. "Okay. I believe you. Tell me again what happened and we'll figure this out, Clare. Together."

The tension flowed from Clare's shoulders.

"You're a peach, Al," Clare gasped with relief. "What would I do without you?"

Al didn't bother to answer. Of course, neither of them could imagine a situation in which that circumstance would ever arise. Clare and Al had been inseparable almost since the day they'd met, the only two new kids in the entire third grade of an upper-crust private school in Toronto's swanky Rosedale neighbourhood that didn't exactly have a tradition of rolling out the welcome mat for misfits and newcomers. After only a week the girls had decided—most solemnly—to pledge eternal loyalty to each other as blood sisters. To that end, they had spent almost an entire afternoon joined at the thumb with an elastic band after they'd pricked their flesh with a safety pin to draw forth drops of blood, which they pressed together to ensure everlasting sisterhood.

Clare's mom had been apoplectic when she'd found the girls in the garden, giggling and purple-thumbed, and had shrieked at them about the dangers of "blood-borne pathogens" and "infectious microbes." Al's mother, on the other hand, had thought it a "sweetly arcane ritual worthy of the bygone romance of the Byronic age."

Al's mom is certifiable, Clare thought—not for the first time— as the incident flashed through her mind. But as flaky as Mrs. McAllister may have been, her daughter was a font of pure analytical thought and Spock logic. She revelled in math problems and puzzles.

Well, this *is one hell of a puzzle,* Clare thought as Al leaned forward, hands clasped, unconsciously mirroring Clare's posture. Heads bent together over their untouched soft drinks, they picked apart Clare's experience one more time and in minute detail. Eventually Clare called a halt to Al's forensic questioning.

"Maggie's gonna come looking for us any minute now," she sighed and checked her watch. "Huh ..."

"What?"

She turned her wrist so that Al could see the digital display face. It was dark.

"You need a new battery."

"I put in a brand-new one two days before we left."

Al frowned. "Didn't you say that you felt a jolt—like an electrical shock—when you disappeared?"

"Yeah ..."

"And again when that girl touched you? The blond girl?"

Clare nodded.

"I wonder if *that* had anything to do with it. I mean ... maybe you shorted out your watch. At any rate, I'd say it's tangible proof that something definitely happened to you."

"Maybe ..." Clare thought about that for a moment. It's not as though she'd ever paid attention in science class, but it seemed plausible enough.

"You said she called you by name?"

Clare nodded. "She called me 'Clare.'"

"Right. Unlike the dude, who called you 'Clarinet.' Or maybe just said some word that *sounded* like it. And you said you didn't think he could see you."

Clare shrugged. "I don't know. I don't *think* he could. But it sure sounded like he said my name. How do these people know my name, Al?"

Al frowned, concentrating. "Beats me. You said the girl definitely saw you. Talked to you. But in a different language? How could you understand what she said?" Al worried away at the details of the incredible story the same way she approached complex problems in algebra.

Clare shook her head slowly. "I seriously don't know. It was like my *ears* heard one set of sounds but my *brain* heard another. It doesn't make any sense!"

"No—no, it kinda does." Al held up a hand, thinking. "My Gran speaks Irish Gaelic. Mostly when she's pissed off at something, so, y'know, a lot. But me? Not so much. Thing is, I know most of the words and stuff and so I totally understand her most of the time and I don't even register that she's speaking in another language. It's like I kind of auto-translate in my head."

"Right." Clare nodded. "Except I don't know any words in ... whatever that was."

"Yeah, well, yesterday you didn't know how to time-travel. But you said you didn't understand the language when it was just the chariot-people talking. That it wasn't until the *girl* spoke that you understood. And that was after she *touched* you. You said you felt another shock when that happened and that things got brighter. And louder. Maybe that has something to do with it. Maybe you formed some sort of ... I dunno ... spatial-temporal link with this girl."

"Maybe ..."

"There's obviously some kind of a connection between the two of you."

"And chances are we'll never figure it out." Clare sighed in frustration. The whole thing was starting to give her a headache. "I wish I knew what happened! I mean—she really seemed like she was in trouble. And then there was the other girl in the chariot ... and that *woman*."

"And the tasty charioteer, don't forget."

Clare ignored Al's salacious grin. Sure—cute guy should've trumped. But she frowned, remembering the whole scene. "Jeezus, Al," she murmured. "You should have *seen* this chick. I don't how she even stayed standing. I've never seen so much blood ..."

"Do you remember what the other driver called her?" Al was still very keen on info-gathering. "I mean, can you remember what it sounded like?"

Clare shrugged. "I don't know. Most of what they said to each other sounded like dogs barking under water."

Al rolled her eyes. "Work with me, here, will ya?"

"I can't remember."

"*Try*! Maybe we can find some information on her."

"Oh—what?" Clare threw her hands up. "Like we're gonna just go look her up and she'll be some famous queen or something? That's like everyone who thinks they had a past life was Cleopatra or Guinevere. Al, that woman was probably just some peasant who'd had her village attacked. A nobody on the wrong side of some barbarian raid or something."

"Not from the way you described her she wasn't." Clare had forgotten for a moment that Al was the type who actually *read* the textbooks on the history-class syllabus. "And you said the guy gave her that gold neck thingy. Do you honestly think your average peasant got to parade around in that kind of swag? She had to be somebody important. You must have heard her name! C'mon, *Clarinet.* Think!"

The "Clarinet" goad worked. "Boo-something," Clare muttered.

"Boo?"

"There was this one word he said and it seemed like a name. And it definitely sounded like Boo-something—"

Al hauled Clare to her feet without another word and dragged her out of the museum's eatery. At the heart of the British Museum, in the centre of a spectacular glass and iron canopy that spanned the sky above the Great Court, stood the Reading Room. A circular structure, it functioned as a library that had served more great minds throughout history than the girls had had hot dinners. It contained a fabulous wealth of information, both in book form and electronically, and it was to the computer terminals that Al led Clare at a pace just slow enough not to get them harassed by the attendants.

Al sat down at one of the terminals and started typing furiously into the library's searchable database. She tried different search terms: *chariot, flogging, whipping*—those last two brought up a slew of blocked sites, forcing Al to rethink her strategy— *red hair,* and *torc.* Then she tried combinations, along with the beginnings of what Clare had thought might have been a name. She experimented with a variety of spellings, hoping to get a hit. "Boo ..." she muttered under her breath as her fingers tap-danced away. "B-o-o? ... unlikely ... B-u maybe? No. B-o-u? ... B-o-u— Holy crap!"

Clare shushed her as the librarian's head bobbed up and swivelled in their direction.

"Boudicca!" Al blurted, ignoring the gesture.

Clare froze. *"Boudicca ..."* she murmured, a whisper of sound. The sound of the name she'd heard uttered by the chariot driver. Al had played *pin-the-name-on-the-raging-redhead* and scored a bull's eye on her very first try.

Al began scrolling rapidly through the text of an encyclopedic entry. "I was *so* right," she muttered excitedly. "That was no freaking peasant you stumbled on."

"Almost got run *over* by ..." Clare amended dryly. She waited impatiently. Finally she snapped, "Hell's bells, Al, who on earth *is* this 'Boudicca' chick?"

"Was." Al pointed at the screen, beaming with quiet triumph.

Clare peered over her shoulder at the webpage. There were a few academic-looking paragraphs of text and a grainy picture that looked like an ink drawing of a long-haired, heavy-set woman with angry eyes wearing a fanciful, Brunhilde-like breastplate. Clare snorted. "That's totally *not* who I saw."

"Yeah, and I'm pretty sure she didn't sit for a Sears Family Portrait back in the day." Al rolled an eye at her. "It's an artist's rendition."

"I *know* that ... What does it say about her?" Clare wasn't sure she wanted to know.

Al's gaze flicked back and forth as she scanned the information on the screen. "You're not gonna believe this."

"What?"

"Well, smart-ass ..." Al pointed at the screen. "It says right here that your mystery lady *was*—"

"No." Clare had a sudden feeling she knew what Al was going to say.

"In fact—"

"No." She didn't want to hear it.

"A famous queen—"

"Shut *up.*"

"Just like Cleopatra."

"Or Guinevere ..."

"Just like that." Al grinned. But as she turned back to the screen and kept reading, the grin faded from her face. "Except with a lot more bloodshed."

"Blood ..." Clare frowned, remembering the cruel lash marks on the woman's back and shoulders. "Yeah ... what exactly was this chick the queen *of*?"

"This." Al gestured vaguely about the room with one hand while continuing to click away with the other.

"Queen of the Library?"

"Funny. Try Queen of *Britain*." Al's eyes never left the screen.

"All of it?"

"Well, a chunk of it, at least." *Click, click, click* ... Al paged through article after article, giving Clare the Coles Notes version as she went. "This was back in the first century AD and Britain was like a whole bunch of counties all ruled by different Celtic tribes. Boudicca's tribe was called the *Iceni* and she ruled from a place that—in later years, once the Romans took over—was called *Venta Icenorum* ... I don't know what the Iceni called it. Anyway, it says here she was married to some guy named Prasutagus and had two daughters. Prasutagus was what they called a client king to the Romans, who were busy invading and taking over the country one tribal territory at a time."

"What does that mean?"

"It means that, instead of getting conquered and enslaved, he paid Rome tribute and they basically let him keep the appearance of still being a king."

"So he was like a puppet."

"A live puppet, yeah. He made the deal and kept his head on. Apparently Mrs. Prasutagus wasn't very happy about it."

"Boudicca."

"Yeah."

"The queen."

"Yeah. She was definitely a queen."

"Okay, okay." Clare reluctantly gave in. "Whatever. I don't need her life story. I just want to know what the hell a *queen* was doing bombing down a lonely river path in a chariot late at night, whipped half to death, with no king, no bodyguard, and only one hot dude and a dead chick for company."

"Not sure." Al kept right on reading. "But if this Roman historian guy, Tacitus, is even half-right I'm guessing it had something to do with her inciting her tribe to 'Rebellion Against the Armed Might of Imperial Rome.'"

"Wow." Clare knew enough history to know that Imperial Rome had indeed been mighty. And heavily armed. She also knew enough to know that, back in the day, those guys had conquered pretty much the whole of the civilized world. With swords and sandals. She tried to imagine what it would take to make someone rebel against that kind of power. Clare shouldered in closer to Al to get a better look at the screen. "What else does it say?"

"Well ... it says here that she was a—"

"Clarinet!"

Both girls jumped at the sound of Maggie's sharp, annoyed tone.

Clare's aunt was bearing down on them from across the Reading Room floor like a ship in full sail. "Honestly—the single most unlikely place in this whole building where I'd think to find you and here you are. I've been searching everywhere. The next time you run off like that, young lady ... *oh, good lord!*" Maggie stopped short, her eyes bulging huge over the rims of her half-specs as she gazed at the images on the screen. "Is it the End of Days? Is that actual *history* you're reading about?"

"Uh ..." Clare blanked on a good comeback. "Yes?"

Al was quicker on the draw. "I have a summer school assignment." She rolled her eyes in feigned boredom. "Clare was just humouring me—don't worry, Perfesser, she's still normal."

"I'm assuming by 'normal' you mean still utterly untouched by intellectual curiosity. Well, thank Heaven, I suppose. I haven't a notion as to what I'd tell your parents ..." As always, the sarcasm dripped in jolly gobs from Maggie's words. "All right, girls. The installation consult is taking a bit longer than expected. Clare, if I give you cab fare, can you and Alice man-age to find your way back to the flat?"

"No!"

Maggie's eyebrows shot toward her hairline. "No?"

"I mean, yeah. Of course we can," Clare amended. "But it's okay. We don't need cab fare, Mags."

"You don't."

"No." Clare turned and gave Al a look. "Al was going to call her cousin to come get her, and I'm sure he can drop me off on the way. Right, Al?"

"Uh ... right."

Maggie eyed her niece with thinly veiled skepticism. "No detours, no stopovers, no 'retail therapy,' no random shenani-gans?"

"None of the above." Clare drew an X over her heart.

"All right then. I'll be home in time for dinner. Shall I pick up a curry on the way?"

"Sure. Make it butter chicken and I'll love you forever." Clare stood and gave her aunt a hug. "You're the best, Mags."

"I know, dear." Maggie patted her fondly on the back and turned to leave. "Stay out of mischief, you two," she said over her shoulder as she went.

With a sigh of relief, Clare turned back to find Al staring at her, her head tilted to one side.

"What?"

"Nothing. I'm just impressed by your ability to multitask," Al mused, a half-smile ticking at the corner of her mouth. "With everything that's happened to you today, you've still got Milo on the brain."

"I figure it this way," Clare said dryly, plucking Al's cell phone up off the table and handing it to her. "Now that I've crossed 'Paranormal Phenomenon' off my life-experience to-do list, I might as well start working my way up to 'Close Encounter.'"

Al laughed. "Are you saying my cousin is an alien?"

"I'll let you know when I get close enough to find out."

Clare grinned at Al, but a chill crawled uncomfortably up her spine. Only a determined effort kept her gaze from straying back to the picture of the warrior queen who, even in that artist's rendition, glared so fiercely out at the world, a wrath-filled Fury, frozen forever in time.

5

"So it's Celtic, and it's called the 'Battersea Shield' ..."

"Yes."

"But they found it in the Thames River?"

"Mm-hm."

"Then why—"

"Because they found it in the part of the Thames that runs through Battersea."

"And when—"

"*Clare*. Dear." Maggie straightened up abruptly from her task. "Alice's cousin didn't give you any drugs, did he?"

"What? No!" Clare jumped back, startled, from the work-table where she'd been leaning on her elbows, eating the remains of their takeaway dinner straight out of the foil container and peppering Maggie with questions. She hoped she wasn't blushing too furiously at the mere mention of Milo. Clare was still inordinately pleased with herself just for having managed to form complete sentences in his car on the way home. Geeks were not supposed to make her feel weak in the knees. And they certainly weren't about to start supplying her with illicit substances, if that's what Maggie was implying.

"I was just wondering, duckling ..." Maggie shrugged and returned to dusting the pottery shards she'd laid out on her table.

"What on earth would make you think something like that?" Clare asked.

Maggie lifted her gaze over the rim of her glasses. "You *do* realize that you are in my work room, don't you?"

"Yes."

"And that you have been here for *some* time?"

"Yeah."

Maggie put down her brush and straightened up, the arch of her eyebrow creeping skyward.

"Mags—"

"*And* that, during this extended tenure in what you have hitherto referred to as 'the Basement Apartment in Downtown Deadsville,' wherein you are normally loath to set one dainty purple-painted toe, you have asked a series of questions of, dare I say it, a decidedly *academic*—albeit grammatically suspect—nature."

"Yeah, but—"

"Insofar as I am aware, your intellectual life has up to this point remained unsullied by queries regarding the nature of ancient archaeological artifacts."

"But—"

"I've also never observed any particularly keen interest on your part in the veracity of noted historical chronicles. Or, as you so eloquently put it, 'that Tacitus dude's story about the bitchin' redhead queen-chick' ..."

"I don't really talk like that, you know," Clare muttered. "And I was just wond—"

"I smell a rat."

"We *are* in a basement ..."

"Clarinet." Maggie's eyes sparkled fiercely. "What in the name of St. Helen's holy underpants are you up to?"

"It's nothing. I *swear!*" Clare protested hotly as Maggie's eyes glittered some more. "I just ... I saw some stuff today that made me curious, okay? That's all." She pouted a bit for dramatic effect. "After all ... you're always telling me to open up my 'TV-addled' mind, y'know. I thought you might be *happy* ..."

Direct hit. Sunken battleship.

Maggie's stern expression melted and she stepped over to Clare, enveloping her niece in an only slightly awkward embrace. "Oh, my—oh I *am*! Clare, my dear, of course I'm pleased."

"Uh ... good." Clare returned the hug with a pat on her aunt's shoulder. "Cool."

"It's just that you've seemed—well—altered since this afternoon." Maggie held her at arm's length and peered into her face with genuine concern. "Are you certain you're all right?"

"I'm fine, Mags." Clare nodded solemnly. "Really."

"You know you can always come to me if you have a problem, duck." Maggie squeezed her shoulders gently and then turned briskly back to work. "*Real* problems, mind. I'd rather not hear sordid details about fashion gaffes or runny mascara or the uckiness that is 'the teenage boy.'"

"No sordid uckiness. I promise."

She bid her aunt a good night and headed out of the basement workshop. At the top of the stairs she absently stuffed her hands in the front pockets of her jeans—and gasped at the feeling of cold metal pressing against the palm of her hand. The sensation cut through a sudden, dizzying vertigo that threatened to send her plunging back down the stairs to Maggie's lair. The house wavered and blurred like mist all around her and Clare felt herself starting to fade out of existence, just like back in the museum.

Before that could happen—before she felt the lightning-bolt jolt that would send her once more hurtling through time—she jerked her hand out of her pocket and out of contact with whatever was in there. Clare gripped the banister as the walls around her resolidified and the sensations of smoke and sparkling dissipated.

A cold sweat sprang up on her brow.

Panting like a scared animal, she ran through the kitchen and up the stairs to her room. Slamming the door, she pushed the bolt lock closed. Then she stripped off her jeans and hopped about with her feet caught in the pant legs, pulling one sock half-off in her haste. Wide-eyed, she grasped the jeans by the cuffs and held them upside down over the bed. A gentle shake and the metal object that Clare had felt in her pocket tumbled out and onto the pastel meadow of her floral bedspread.

"Oh God ..." Clare moaned, stricken. "I'm a kleptomaniac ..."

She sank onto the bed and stared down at a round metal brooch decorated with the same kinds of swirling patterns that had adorned the bronze shield and the great golden torc in the museum.

"Great." Clare snatched up a chiffon scarf that was hanging off her bedpost and threw it over the brooch as if covering up evidence. "Now I'm a freak *and* a thief."

AL'S CELL PHONE rang straight through to her voicemail.

"Al, it's Clare. Call me back. Now!"

Less-than a minute later she called back again. "NOW!"

Three minutes of hard staring at her phone did nothing to increase Clare's incoming call ratio. An added five minutes of pacing produced less than fruitful results. Al was obviously incommunicado. Maybe screening her calls. Probably having a good chuckle with Milo over Clare's pathetically dorky behaviour—

She almost jumped out of her skin when the phone rang.

Clare lurched across the room, knocking it off the side table and under the bed. She had to dive for it before it went to voicemail. Lying half under the bed, spitting at a dust bunny stuck to her lower lip, she shouted, "Hello! Al! Hello!"

"Clare?"

"Yes!"

"Stop shouting." It was Al. Rock solid, cucumber cool. Clare had never doubted her for a second. "What's going on? In your message you sounded like you were being attacked by rabid badgers."

"Nothing so recreational," Clare snorted. Then she poured out the details of finding the brooch and how it had almost sent her on another inexplicable time trip.

"Maggie is going to murder me when she discovers I've gone all sticky-fingers on her. My mother already has her half-convinced I'm some kind of juvie just because of that stupid party ..."

"Whoa, whoa, whoa!" Al's voice crackled with cell-phone hiss. "I don't think you stole anything."

Clare blinked at the phone for a second. "Hello? Brooch?"

"Look, Clare, I'm telling you," Al said. "I was watching you the whole time—well, that is, when I could actually *see* you—and you didn't touch anything even remotely broochlike."

Clare had stopped listening. *"Oh God ..."* she moaned, certain of impending doom.

"Clare ... *Clare*! Get a grip." Al's voice finally penetrated Clare's panic fog. "Jeezus. You're gonna sprain something."

"Okay. I'm okay." Clare struggled to keep from hyperventilating. Al's reasoned tone helped. A little. *"Oh God ..."*

"Describe the brooch to me."

"Uh ..." Clare hesitated. She didn't even want to pull aside the scarf that covered the thing.

"You don't have to touch it," Al coaxed. "Just *look* at it. Tell me what it looks like."

Clare reached out, gingerly snagged a corner of the scarf, and jerked sharply, pulling the cloth away as if a venomous tarantula hid beneath. She was almost surprised to see that the object was really very pretty and not the least bit threatening.

Just a little open circle of gleaming bronze, the ends flaring out as they came together—not quite touching, interrupted by a hinged, straight pin that cut across the diameter of the circle. "It's ... uh ... it's round. Ish," she said.

"'Ish'?"

"Yeah ..." Clare peered even more closely. "Not totally round, but close. Like a broken circle ..."

The whole of the design, she went on, was accented with twisting, knotted lines and a deep red stone was set at the top of the curve. Clare's words trailed off as she looked closer and closer.

"You there?"

"Yeah. Yeah ... I'm still looking. Hang on ..." Clare leaned in further, intrigued now in spite of herself. Up close there was nothing to be afraid of, it seemed. Not that she was going to *touch* it or anything.

"Can you tell what the design is? Does it look like anything or is it abstract?"

"Um ... well ... there's these bits that curl around and stick out like ... uh ... oh, I get it! Those are wings. It's a bird. I mean, it looks like a bird that's been all kind of stretched out and rolled up and tied into a spirally knot like a pretzel."

"A pretzel bird?"

"Yeah ... kinda. I think the stone is its eye ..."

"You're lousy at description. Look—take a pic and message it to me."

"Hang on." Clare aimed her phone's camera at the brooch and with a few clicks sent off a picture to Al.

After a moment Al's voice came back on the line. "That," she said quietly, "is cool."

"It's very cool," Clare agreed. "I *stole* something very cool. From the British *freaking* Museum."

"No, you didn't."

"*Why* do you keep saying that?"

"Because it's the truth." That tone of utter assurance again. "There was nothing like this on the table. *Nothing.*"

"Well then how—"

"I have no idea. All I know is that, wherever you got that thing? It wasn't from the restoration room."

CLARE GOT UP and went to the bathroom to splash some water on her face.

She and Al had promised to meet the next afternoon. Al said she had something to show Clare that would put things in perspective, but she wouldn't say what. She'd made Clare promise not to do anything stupid until then.

However, Clare quibbled silently to herself, *she hadn't specified* what *that stupid something might be ...*

Padding back into her bedroom, Clare changed into a pair of yoga pants and a tank top that she could move in easily. She added a warm, fleece-lined hoodie—just in case—and slid her feet into her favourite high-top sneakers, lacing them up tight. If she'd had anything made of bulletproof Kevlar she would have put that on too, she thought, remembering the muscle-knotted arms of the thuggish soldier and the wicked-looking sword strapped to the belt of the handsome chariot driver. She shook her head and glanced up to make sure she'd locked the bedroom door. And then, holding her breath, she reached out to take the brooch in her hand ...

Sparks crowded around the edges of her field of vision and, just as before, Clare felt suddenly, giddily, light as a feather on a breeze. Every inch of her skin tingled and she braced herself for the impending jolt that would send her travelling through space and time. But the shock still took her breath away when it hit. The walls of her room wavered and then disappeared altogether in a haze of flickering ruby light, and Clare found herself spinning out once more into a void of darkness.

6

Before she could see anything, Clare heard a tiny metallic clanging sound—*ting, ting*—like the tolling of a miniature bell.

As her eyes adjusted to the dimness she found herself sitting cross-legged on a hard-packed dirt floor in some kind of hut with rough stone walls and a sloping thatch roof. A long wooden workbench stood in front of her. She grabbed its edge and hoisted herself up, peering through the dusky air ... and froze. Less than two feet away hunched the figure of a man silhouetted by the fiery glow of what looked like a forge. He was built like the icebox in Maggie's kitchen, not overly tall but almost rectangular, with thick muscles, a great bullish head, a wild red tangle of hair, and a beard that looked as though it had been routinely singed in places. He wore a belted, sleeveless leather shirt laced up the sides and marred in places with dark scorch marks. His hands were monstrous things, meaty and almost pawlike, but as Clare watched, fascinated, his great thick fingers manipulated a tiny hammer and needle-nosed tongs with delicate precision.

With a final *ting, ting, ting* the smith laid down the hammer and lifted his gaze.

Clare briefly contemplated heart failure.

She dared not even blink, hoping that—as before, with the girl on the riverbank—he wouldn't see her. She thought she'd faint when his eyes narrowed and he stared pointedly in her direction. She started to stammer a greeting or an apology or an explanation or *something* ... but clamped her mouth shut as the smith heaved his considerable bulk off the stool and came around to her side of the table. He reached for the leather curtain covering a little window set in the wall right behind her and Clare dove out of the way, crouching behind a basket of logs near the forge. She exhaled a silent breath—he pretty obviously couldn't see her. He stood at the window, cocking his head this way and that as though listening intently. Clare wondered if he'd *heard* her.

He reached up, leaning on the windowsill with his brawny arms, and suddenly Clare was struck by a sensation of familiarity. She knew him. She'd seen him before ... on the riverbank! That was it. His had been the massive, shadowy form that had held the Battersea Shield above his head, ready to heave it into the depths of the river.

Clare crouched there, silent, until finally the smith dropped the window curtain, stretched mightily, and circled back to perch on his stool and return to his work. After a few cautious minutes, Clare's curiosity got the better of her. She crept on silent sneakers back to the workbench and took up her position opposite the smith, craning her neck to see what it was he worked on with such focused purpose. Just then he lifted the thing up between his square, blunt fingertips, admiring it in the ruddy light of the glowing coals. Clare felt her eyes go wide when she recognized what it was.

The brooch.

Only it was missing something: the "eye" of the bird, as Clare had begun to think of it. Instead of a wine-red jewel set at the top of the brooch there was just a round empty space. The smith murmured to himself, too low for Clare to hear, and reached for a leather pouch sitting on the workbench. He opened it and withdrew five little square packets made of sueded leather, folding each one open on the table.

Clare whispered a silent "Oooh ..." as she saw the piles of sparkling stones contained in each tiny package: amethysts and polished pink coral beads; shiny, faceted black jet; winking, deep-blue sapphires; and a glittering pile of garnets that shone a deeper, richer red than rubies. The smith rested his thrusting jaw on the knuckles of one fist and poked at the gems with the tip of a finger, contemplating them by the light of a tallow candle in a clay dish. Clare moved closer and closer until she was barely inches away, resting her elbows on the workbench and gazing down at the pretty things.

She waved a hand cautiously between the smith's face and the stones. He didn't even flinch—just went on muttering to himself, pushing the gems around and separating out a few from each pile.

Clare observed the process minutely.

Now he was toying with just two stones—a creamy pink coral bead and a sapphire. He placed first one and then the other in the empty space in the brooch, considering each for a long moment before tapping it out onto its suede square. He left the sapphire in for a long time.

What about the garnets? Clare thought. *Why isn't he looking at them?*

The man frowned, contemplating the blue stone in the setting. He hunched his shoulders and rubbed his hands over his face, scrubbing at the corners of his eyes. Clare looked at the curled and blackened length of the candlewick and thought, *He's been at this a long time ... he looks really tired.* Which, of course, must be why he was missing the obvious choice.

When he stood to stretch again and went to the door, opening it to inhale great lungfuls of evening air, Clare took the opportunity to nudge the weary craftsman's inspiration. A flawless, wine-dark garnet that looked to be just the right size was nestled in the pile. Scarcely daring to breathe, Clare reached for the brooch and tipped the sapphire out onto the workbench. Clumsy in her haste, she pricked herself on the sharp end of the clasp pin and hissed in pain. A single bright bead of blood welled up and fell from her fingertip into the empty setting. Clare gasped and glanced back to where the smith still stood by the door. He was still staring out into the night, lost in thought. And so, quick as a wink, Clare plucked up the red gem and placed it in the sapphire's stead, leaving the brooch in the exact same spot. She snatched back her hand, sucking on her fingertip, and retreated from the table just as the smith returned to his work. He stared for a moment at the brooch with unseeing eyes ... and then the shadow of a frown creased his broad, sooty brow. He lifted the brooch with its red stone toward the candle flame and peered at it, a light growing in his eyes, dousing the confusion there. Finally, he put the brooch down and gazed around the room.

Clare stood like a statue against the wall, her pulse pounding loudly in her ears as the man's unblinking stare seemed to pause and sharpen as it swept over her. A long, tense moment later, he shrugged slightly and began folding up the other precious gems into the little suede squares. Clare moved closer again to watch as he fixed the stone—the stone *she* had chosen—into its setting, tapping down a collar of bronze with a tiny hammer to hold it in place. He had just finished the job and was polishing the finished piece with a soft cloth when the door swung inward.

Clare caught her breath when a familiar figure stepped over the threshold. Up close, in the confines of the tiny, stuffy hut, the young charioteer was even more handsome than when Clare had first seen him. Maybe it helped that his features weren't pulled tight with rage and grief. Or maybe it was the way the light of the glowing forge played along the planes of his face and the contours of his muscled arms. The way it gleamed in the auburn waves of his hair.

"Connal," the smith said and the two men clasped each other by the wrist.

Connal. Clare silently rolled the name around in her mind, savouring the sound of it. *His name is Connal ...*

The young man raised an inquiring eyebrow at the smith, who stepped aside and nodded at the worktable. In the light cast by the fires of the forge, the finely wrought metal of the brooch gave off a deep rosy sheen. Clare waited impatiently to hear the charioteer's—Connal's—assessment. He stared at it closely, not touching it, for a long moment. Finally he straightened and lifted his gaze to the smith's face.

"Mae hwn yn brydferth, Llassar ..." His voice floated over to Clare, and again her mind translated so that she understood the words: *"This is beautiful, Llassar ..."*

The smith inclined his head slightly, a quiet, steady pride evident in the gesture. Clare felt herself smiling a bit at the compliment. She knew the red stone had been the right one to choose.

"It is perfect," Connal said in a voice of low, smoky music. "Do you remember the one you made for Princess Tasca? Was it only two years ago ..."

"I do, lad," the metal smith answered, his voice deep and booming like ocean surf pounding against distant cliffs. "Her brooch bore the shape of the Lark."

Tasca! Clare thought. *That's the name that girl said in my other ... uh— vision? Visitation? What* do *I call these things, anyway?*

"Aye. That was a fine and lovely piece. But Llassar ..." Connal looked up at him again, his gaze sparking with obvious excitement. *"This ..."*

The burly smith stood silently, his unblinking stare fastened on the brooch.

"The Raven." Connal's voice was full of reverence and a kind of savage excitement.

Aha! thought Clare. *I was right—it is a bird!*

"Ah, Comorra ..." His voice dropped to a wondering murmur. "The Goddess Andrasta has touched the princess, Llassar."

Comorra, Clare thought. *The girl on the riverbank—if the brooch was made for her, her name must be Comorra.*

"She has."

"There is strong magic in this, Llassar," Connal said, gently picking up the brooch and holding it in the palm of his calloused hand.

"Aye." Llassar nodded, one corner of his wide mouth quirking up beneath the red tangle of his beard. "There is."

Connal's eyes snapped up. "Blood magic?"

Clare looked at the red dot on her fingertip and shivered. *Blood?*

Llassar nodded, but his expression was troubled. "The queen would have it so. She worries about the girl. She wanted a strong talisman for her. For my part, I do not wish for her to need such protection. But she has a point—Andrasta's path is not an easy one to tread."

"No, Llassar, it isn't. But it is a good one." Clare heard uncertainty in his voice. But then he smiled and handed back the brooch. "Your skills as both a master smith and a master Druid are beyond compare."

He's a Druid? Clare thought. *What's a Druid? Wait. Al said something about mystical visions and Druids ...* Clare had always thought of Druids as sorcerers or ancient holy men. Wizards. Okay—who was she kidding—she'd never thought of Druids in her life before. She had no concept of them beyond a vague, Gandalf from *Lord of the Rings* sort of mental picture. Or maybe Merlin. Old dudes with beards and pointy hats. Llassar the smith wasn't that old, but he certainly had the beard happening. She couldn't see hats of any description anywhere, though.

From under the shadows of his heavy brow, Llassar's eyes gleamed. "Well, from one Druid to another, let me tell you this: I heard Andrasta's voice in the fire, Connal."

Wait. What? The young hot guy is a wizard, too? Clare drastically reconsidered her stereotype.

Connal's dark eyes glinted in the light of the forge. "She *spoke* to you?"

"And more. Just now I felt a presence ... guiding me ..."

Clare felt herself blushing, thoroughly embarrassed that Llassar should think so. She really hoped she hadn't pissed off some kind of higher power with her goddess impersonation. "Just trying to help," she whispered.

Connal's head snapped up.

Clare held her breath as he turned his head slightly, his eyes narrowing as his gaze swung in her direction.

No way, Clare thought, panicked. *Dude—you couldn't hear me when I was yelling like a maniac on the riverbank!*

He drew his sword so quickly that Clare jumped, jamming her shoulder painfully up against a wooden shelf holding hammers of assorted sizes. Llassar's eyes went wide at the sight of the rattling tools. Clare stiffened in alarm as Connal moved cautiously around from the other side of the workbench, sword held at the ready, firelight gleaming on the blade.

The warrior moved like a panther, mesmerizing and deadly. He was barely six feet away now and Clare had nowhere else to go. Connal's eyes scanned what to him was empty space as if trying to peer through heavy fog.

Another step.

Behind him, the big Druid smith had gone uncannily still, watching Connal as he swept the air in front of him with his blade. Clare tried desperately to reach inside of herself for that tingling, sparking sensation that told her she was on her way back to her own world. Nothing. She didn't even know what it *was*, exactly, that caused her to shift back and forth, but she knew now with a sinking feeling that it wasn't anything she had control over. She'd been so stupid to try this again. What had she been thinking? She was cornered and about to have her invisible self run through by a very visible sword.

This has got to be a nightmare, she thought wildly. But she knew it wasn't. As Connal took another step forward she closed her eyes tightly and wondered what that cold iron blade would feel like when it sliced into her.

Then she heard a great, flapping, shrieking commotion.

Clare's eyes flew open as an enormous, screeching raven suddenly burst through the leather curtain covering the window and beat its wings against the hot, thick air of the hut. Llassar and Connal dove for cover as the creature skreeled in fury and swooped in tight circles above their heads, firelight gleaming in its red eyes.

Clare threw herself back against the wall, away from the slashing talons and great black beak, and felt her insides turn to fireworks. As a rack of iron tongs came crashing down around her, Connal's gaze fixed again on where she stood, invisible to his eye. He snarled and dove forward, evading the angry black bird and thrusting his sword straight at Clare's heart.

She gasped as the point of the blade struck sparks off the stone wall behind her—and felt herself shimmer away to nothing, as if she were campfire embers and smoke on a breeze. Clare Reid found herself once more falling through space. And time.

THE SOUND OF HER PHONE screeching brought Clare halfway back to her senses.

That's annoying, she thought dully. *I should change my ring tone ...*

It seemed as though it had been going on for a long time, and that it was all tangled up somehow with the sound of the raven's high-pitched shrieks. Eventually the phone stopped ringing and then, a few moments later, started up again. Clare groped groggily for the thing and hit the answer button. "H ... hello?"

"I *knew* it!" Al's voice was accusatory. "I knew you'd try again."

"Uhn ..."

"Tell me something—should we have a special classroom designated next semester for *raging idiots* or should we just lock you by yourself in the closet?"

"Uh ... hi, Al ..." Clare blinked at her phone for a second, unable to form a coherent thought. She looked down into her open palm and saw that it was empty. An instant of panicked searching was all it took, though, to find the bronze bird-shaped brooch beneath a fold of the crumpled scarf on her bed. She breathed a sigh of relief and draped the scarf over it again, careful not to touch the brooch itself.

"You touched the brooch, didn't you?" Al scolded. *"Didn't you?"*

"Uh ..." Clare winced sheepishly. "Maybe. A little."

"Well, what *happened*?" Al was almost sputtering.

"Al ..." Clare took a deep breath. "I didn't just touch it."

"What?"

"I saw it."

She could almost hear Al blinking with confusion. "You saw *what*?"

"Al ... *I saw the brooch*. Back *then*. Hell—I saw the guy who *made* it! I helped him pick out the stone and everything!"

"You *what* ...?"

"Uh."

"Clare?"

Clare took a deep breath and told Al the whole story. When she was done all she could hear was the odd static blip from her cell. "Al?"

"There are only two words for this situation." Al's voice was a little breathless. "In. Sane."

"Ya think?"

"What actually possessed you to switch the stones?"

"Well, uh, he was looking at the wrong ones."

"How do you know that?"

"*Duh*—I have the damn thing sitting on my bed. Besides, the sapphire just didn't have the same punch. And I do know how to accessorize, do I not?" she added dryly.

"You know something?" Al mused. "I'm not sure if you just screwed with history or if history just screwed with you."

"What are you talking about?"

"I mean, you might've just thrown a monkey wrench into the whole space–time continuum!"

"The who?"

Clare could almost hear Al shaking her head. "The space–time continuum—do you watch *any* TV? You could have already sent the entire universe careening out of whack. I mean, sure. It's all theoretical. But even the smallest alteration in the past could *potentially* cause the universe to split into alternate realities. Or collapse in on itself. Or alter the course of history dramatically. It's like a domino effect. You might've changed *history*, Clare—"

"I did not!"

"We might not even be in the *same universe* anymore." Al was on a roll. "This could already be a *parallel existence* we're in now!"

"Oh, come *on*!" Clare protested. "It was one itty bitty gemstone! No wrenches, no monkeys, and I seriously think Mr. Blacksmith would have figured it out himself. And anyway, the brooch had a red stone in it when I found it in my pocket and that was before—well, y'know, after—I switched it so doesn't that *prove* the universe remains unaltered?"

There was only the soft hiss of static for a long moment as Al went silent; either contemplating Clare's hypothesis or—more likely—staring at her phone in bemusement.

"Besides," Clare continued, "the dude just thought it was a flash of inspiration from whatsername."

"Whatsername?"

"Yeah. Another one of those Celtic names I have a hard time remembering."

"You seemed to remember this Connal dude's name just fine," Al noted.

"Oh, shut up," Clare muttered. She frowned, trying to conjure up the sound of the name in her head. *Andrasta* ... the name whispered across her mind. She blinked. *Andrasta* ...

"Uh ... Al? Do you have internet access?" Her voice sounded a little hollow in her own ears. *Andrasta* ...

"Uh-huh," Al said. "Why? Don't you?"

"Maggie doesn't have wireless and I'm not gonna start using her computer—she knows I don't do the research thing. Just Google the name 'Andrasta' for me, will you?"

"Okay. Why?"

"That's whatsername's name," Clare explained. "I just remembered it. From the way they were talking about her, I think she was a goddess." *Or something ...*

While she waited, Clare jammed the phone between her ear and shoulder and folded the scarf around the brooch. Then she dug around in her luggage, which she still hadn't unpacked, and found a lone pink pompom sock—*why did I pack a lone sock?*—and stuffed the wrapped brooch into it, folding the entire neat little bundle into the inside pocket of her shoulder bag.

The click of Al's keyboard sounded over the line. "A-n-d-r ... here it is ... Andrasta. Oh you're so right! Andrasta was a Celtic war deity—and the patron goddess of the Iceni tribe," she read out in a scholarly tone. "Her name means the 'Invincible One.' She has the ability to travel the pathways between the worlds as both a messenger and a harbinger. She 'ferries spirits to and fro' between planes of existence—she sounds kinda like a Norse Valkyrie if you ask me—and she is closely identified with the raven as a totemic animal ..."

"Yeah, I got that part." Clare remembered what Connal had said about Comorra's being chosen by the Raven.

"It is thought ... Holy *crap*, Clare!"—Al's pedantic tone evaporated in a sudden flash—"listen to this! It is thought that *the British warrior queen Boudicca* may have prayed to the Raven Goddess on the eve of her battle against occupying Roman forces. Rituals involving this goddess may have included human sacrifices ..."

"Ew." Clare shivered, thinking gruesome thoughts.

Al read on: "It is also possible, however, that Andrasta can be linked to the more peaceful Gallic goddess, Andarta—"

Clare shook her head, remembering. "I don't think so."

"What?"

"That last part." She was remembering the look on Connal's face as he beheld the raven brooch. "I don't think this Andrasta chick had very much to do with peace."

"Well, you might have a point there." Clare could hear the sound of rapid mouse clicks. "There's more on her here. Stuff about blood curses and magic and sacrifices ... Also—I did a little background check earlier on Ms. B., and I gotta tell ya, she had quite the rep ..."

Clare jumped just then, hearing Maggie's footsteps on the creaky wooden staircase. The last thing she wanted was for her aunt to start asking questions—*more* questions—and getting suspicious. *More* suspicious. "Tell me tomorrow," she interrupted Al. "I gotta go."

"Promise you won't do anything *else* stupid?"

"I promise," Clare crossed her heart, even though Al couldn't see her do it, and said, "I won't do anything *else* stupid. Tonight."

"Okay then. And remember we're meeting up tomorrow."

"I know. I'll be there." Suddenly Clare was overcome with the urge to sleep. "G'night, Al."

"Hey Clare?"

"Yeah?"

"Milo wanted me to tell you he says hi."

"Wh—"

"Pleasant dreams, Freak Girl." Al chuckled and hung up the phone.

7

"Wow."

"Yeah. She's something, huh?"

Clare nodded slowly as she stood, mesmerized, staring up at the monument. "It even kind of looks like her. A little."

"It does?" Al asked.

"Well ... no. But there's *something*. Something of her, uh, her spirit, maybe ...?" Clare expected Al to mock her for the New Agey sentiment, but she just looked back up at the massive bronze figure in the chariot looming high above them against the bright blue London sky. It also loomed high above a seriously tacky souvenir stand—stuffed to the awning with plastic Bobby hats and plushy Union Jack bears and foil balloons—but somehow the statue's dignity remained wholly intact.

Across the Thames, the observation pods of the giant Millennium Wheel rotated serenely. All around them people and vehicles bustled to and fro in a noisy stream of humanity. But it faded away to background noise for the two girls standing beneath the shadow of grandeur cast by that queenly figure, frozen in the moment of a thundering charge.

This was what Al had insisted that Clare meet her to see. She had come across a reference to it in her internet searches: the great bronze statue of Boudicca that stood on the banks of the Thames next to Westminster Bridge and the Houses of Parliament. Commissioned by Prince Albert in the nineteenth century, Thomas Thornycroft's sculpture depicted its subject as a commanding, unbowed figure. Arms raised high, a slender spear gripped in one strong fist, Queen Boudicca stood straight and proud on the deck of a scythe-wheeled chariot drawn by a pair of rearing stallions, two young girls crouched behind her. One of the girls was hunched in a protective posture, arms pulled in to herself, as she peeked solemnly out from behind her mother's flowing cloak.

But it was the other girl that Clare couldn't take her eyes off. Her clothes, like those of her sister's, were dishevelled and loose, torn to the waist, her young body exposed. Frozen forever in time, she gripped the side of the careening chariot with one fist and craned her neck trying to peer forward, past the charging horses, as if to see what was coming. As if she could somehow see into the future and wanted to meet her fate with eyes wide open, no matter how awful it might be.

And Clare had the immediate sense that it had, indeed, been awful.

"Comorra ..." she murmured.

Al regarded her silently for a moment. "And the other one must be Tasca, right? The ... uh ..."

"The dead girl I saw?" Clare shivered a bit. "I suppose."

"C'mon," Al said, tugging on Clare's purse strap. "It's a gorgeous day and I didn't bring you here so you could spend it feeling all mopey about something that happened over two thousand years ago. I just wanted you to see the statue. You know ... for a little perspective. Now let's go get something to eat."

Clare followed reluctantly, glancing back over her shoulder as if the long-dead queen and her daughters had cast a spell that would take some effort to shake off. The girls bought a couple of kebabs from a hole-in-the-wall kebab shop and set out along the pathway beside the river, strolling along until they came to a bench overlooking the smooth expanse of dark water. Maybe Comorra had strolled along this very river—maybe the very same stretch of riverbank—all those centuries ago ...

"Al?"

"Yeah?"

"What's happening to me?"

Al was silent for a long moment. She tore open a bag of crisps and threw a few of them to a squabble of pigeons, her brow creased in thought beneath the dark fringe of her hair. "I honestly don't know, pal," she said eventually. "This takes a bigger brain than mine."

"Great," Clare sighed. "I suppose, in that case, I'm doomed."

"No you're not." Al grinned suddenly. "What time is it?"

Clare checked her watch, but—of course—the display was still fried. She'd put it on that morning out of habit. Instead she pulled out her cell phone, which had probably escaped similar electronic death by virtue of Clare having forgotten it at home when they'd gone to the museum. She checked the screen. "It's just after five. Why?"

"C'mon." Al stood and headed back in the direction they'd come from. "He usually likes to work for an hour or two after everyone else has gone home."

"He who?"

"Milo. His office is only a few blocks from here."

Clare stopped short in the middle of the path. "No. Way."

"Look—he's the biggest brain I know."

"Yeah, but—"

"If *he* can't figure out what's happening to you, no one can."

"Yeah, but—"

"D'you wanna solve this or not?"

She did. She really, really did. But the thought of telling Milo that she, well, that she was some kind of freak, made

Clare queasy. Of course, the mere thought of seeing him again cancelled the queasy out. Nearly.

THE LATE-AFTERNOON SUN was pouring through the tinted floor-to-ceiling windows in the high-tech, open-concept space that served as the London office of the Ordnance Survey. The quiet hum of a bank of processors behind a glass partition was the only sound they heard as the receptionist let them in through a set of tall double doors on her way out. The place was deserted except for a corner workstation where Milo, a pair of oversized headphones clamped over his ears, stared fixedly at a slowly rotating graphic on the high-def monitor. His long fingers danced over the ergonomic keyboard and sections of the spidery, spinning graphic filled in with variegated shades of green and brown and blue ...

"Milo," Al called. *"Milo!"*

Clare picked up a paperclip and an elastic band from a supply tray on a nearby desk, bent the little piece of wire and shot it across the room. It pinged off the back of Milo's head and he jumped a bit and turned, his look of annoyance melting into a surprised smile.

"Clare!" he said. "Hi!" And then, "Hey, Allie ..."

He took off the headphones and shook his hair out. The dark blond waves fell just over the top rim of his stylish-cool glasses, catching the sunlight and haloing his face, highlighting his fairly spectacular bone structure ... *Oh boy,* Clare thought, still trying to reconcile *this* Milo with the one she'd once known as a puppyish, slobbery little boy in Superman jammies and cape.

Nope. Does not compute ...

Maybe, she thought, *this* Milo was a by-product of the same paranormal forces that had sent her spiralling back in time the day before.

Heh. Maybe I changed history.

Clare was amused by the possibility for a brief instant. Then her amusement turned to a stomach-clenching anxiety. What if she *had*?

Milo stood and stretched, his lean-muscled physique show-ing through the thin material of his T-shirt, which had a pic-ture of a despondent stormtrooper hunched over a beer in a bar with the caption *"Those* were *the droids I was looking for ..."*

Okay ... maybe she *hadn't* altered the timeline. Milo was ob-viously still a nerd. He'd just morphed into a hot nerd.

"So, Clare de Lune." He grinned at her as he reached over and flicked the screen to sleep mode. "To what do I owe the unexpected pleasure of this visit?"

"Did he just call me crazy?" Clare murmured to Al out of the side of her mouth.

"It's a song," Al murmured back. "It's a compliment. Go with it. I'll explain later."

"Uh ..." Clare was lost.

At the moment, all she really wanted to do was stare at Milo. Maybe flirt charmingly. She wasn't sure. And she *really* wasn't sure how to broach the subject they'd actually come to discuss with Al's cousin. It was the stuff of sci-fi novels and movies. But then again ... that stuff was sort of Milo's forte, wasn't it?

"Milo ... you're a geek, right?" Clare blurted out. She felt her cheeks flush in mortification. *You moron!* she cursed herself silently.

But Milo just cocked his head and grinned a lopsided grin. "Top of my class at Nerd Academy, yeah. Midi-chlorian count's off the chart."

Out of the corner of her eye, Clare saw Al roll her eyes—whether at her or at Milo, she wasn't entirely sure. She blinked at Milo in confusion.

"Sorry," he said. "Jedi in-joke."

"Mi ... we got a situation." Al got straight to the point. "Could use some help."

Milo frowned faintly, curiosity colouring the expression, and pushed two rolling chairs toward them. "I'm all ears, cuz."

"You *used* to be ..." Al snorted.

"Yeah, and you used to be all buck teeth and Batman band-aids. Times change." He laughed and it was a clear, warm sound. "What's up, ladies?" Milo perched expectantly on the edge of a worktable as the girls sat and exchanged hesitant glances.

What if he didn't believe them?

Wait, Clare thought, *what if he does?* What would that say about him?

Regardless, it was too late to turn back, she realized. Al had already started to speak. Hesitantly, at first. But then, as she got into the story, she became more and more assured and animated. She spilled the whole strange, sorry tale out to her cousin, who sat very, very still, listening. Clare kind of wanted to crawl under a rock.

"Are you okay?" Milo asked eventually. Clare heard the question as if it came from a great distance.

"What?"

"Are you okay?" he repeated. He was crouched in front of her chair, although Clare didn't remember him moving—she'd been lost in the memory of what had happened. Milo's long hands were clasped loosely in front of him and he stared up at her.

Great. He thinks I'm certifiable.

"I'm not crazy," Clare said, her voice a dry whisper.

The ghost of a smile touched Milo's lips but his eyes remained locked on her. "That's not what I asked. Are you *okay*?"

"Mentally or physically?"

"Both. You sound like you've had a pretty big shock, Clare." His voice was soft and soothing. The kind of voice you'd use to talk someone off a ledge or calm a skittish horse.

Clare turned a flat stare on him and crossed her arms over her chest. "You don't believe it happened."

"I didn't say that ..."

"But you don't. Why would you? Why would anyone? *I* don't—and I'm the one it happened to. This is stupid. Al—can we go now, please?" Clare could barely look at Milo with his cool, compassionate, appraising gaze, his head tilted slightly to one side ...

Big brain at work, Clare thought. *Analytical. Probably trying to decide whether to call in the paramedics or a mental health professional.*

"Al?" Clare pushed her chair back and stood.

"Wait—Clare. Don't go." Milo got up and put a hand on her arm.

"Why? You're busy and I'm crazy. Obviously. This is just a waste of time."

"Hey now." Milo smiled down at her. "I don't think you're a waste of anything. And I don't think you're crazy. But I also don't know what to tell you. What you're telling me is ... well. It's impossible. You know?"

Clare glared stubbornly up at him. "Yeah. I know."

"But something happened to you. And"—Milo's smile faded and a frown ticked away between his brows—"there's only one way I'm going to be able to help you figure out what that something was."

Clare swallowed noisily in apprehension.

Milo's fingers tightened as he gently squeezed her arm. "Can you ... show me?" he asked quietly.

"Show you what? The brooch?"

"Show me what you can *do* with the brooch."

"Empiricist," Al snorted. "Oh ye of little faith."

Milo's gaze flicked over to his cousin above the rim of his glasses. "If you hadn't seen it with your own eyes, would *you* believe Clare's story?"

Clare looked back and forth between them while Al hesitated.

"Um." Al blinked rapidly.

"Thanks, pal," Clare sighed.

"Well ...?" Al shrugged helplessly.

"Fine." Clare unslung her shoulder bag and set it down on the desk with a thump. She reached into the side zipper pocket, fished around for the pompom sock, and tossed it onto the desktop. It landed with a dull clank. Al and Milo both flinched a little at her cavalier treatment of what was probably a priceless—and mysteriously powerful—artifact, but Clare just crossed her arms over her chest again and stared back and forth between them. She wasn't feeling particularly reverential. "Put a nickel in the cup and the monkey dances. I'll do my little magic trick for you if that's what it takes."

"I ... hang on a second." Milo put his hand on her arm again, and his grip was a little less gentle this time. "I don't want you to do anything dangerous—"

Clare shrugged off his touch and resolutely reached for the sock. She tugged at the scarf and the brooch spilled out, spinning in a little circle before coming to rest. The red stone winked at Clare in the light and she felt her mouth go dry. Beside her, Milo had gone very still.

The anticipation building in Clare's chest was like a bubble expanding, pushing against her lungs. Making it hard to breathe. She could almost feel the firefly tingles along her arms even before she touched the brooch.

She reached out her hand ...

"Wait!" Al yelped. "On second thought, I don't think you should do this." Her dark brows knit together. "Why not just leave it alone? It's done. Past. *Literally.* I mean ... what are we trying to accomplish by having you go back there? Uh, then."

"*I'm* trying to prove a point. Empirical evidence, remember?"

"This is stupid. I don't need to see you do it again and I don't care anymore if Milo believes us or not. Sorry, Mi ..." Al took a step toward Clare. "I just don't think it's worth the risk."

"Aargh!" Clare huffed in frustration. "*You're* the one who suggested we come here. And aren't you the least bit curious about it all? About how I can do this? *Why* I can do this?" She knew it wasn't just proving a point to Milo that had made her want to touch the brooch again. Clare's heart was thumping with excitement at the mere thought.

"Sure." Al nodded. "I'm curious as hell. Also? Vaguely terrified."

"Allie's right," Milo said quietly.

"I am. Wait—I am?"

"Sure. You're absolutely right to be afraid. I mean ... every time Clare takes one of her supernatural sightseeing jaunts, she risks altering the space–time continuum, yeah?"

"Well, yeah," Al nodded. "That's what I tried to explain to Clare earlier."

Clare rolled her eyes. "Here we go again ..." she muttered. "I did *not* throw a wrench at the monkey."

Milo raised a questioning eyebrow in her direction.

"Clare doesn't watch any of the sci-fi channels back home," Al explained. "The inner workings of the universe are a mystery to her. She watches MTV."

"That's not all I watch!" Clare protested. "I like game shows, too." She glanced at Milo as his other eyebrow crept up. "And ... um ... *Star Wars?*"

Milo's expression grew pained.

"Wait! Trek! Star *Trek.* I think. Whichever is the one on TV ..."

Al shushed Clare into silence before Milo started to actually sputter. Cute he may have been, but his geek flag still flew high and proud over his tousled blond head, it seemed. Clare made a mental note to bone up on *Dr. Who.* Not that she even really knew what that was. She'd just heard Al mention it enough to know it was nerd high art.

"Stop trying to sidetrack me. I'm doing this."

"Okay, okay," Al said. "Just promise you're only gonna go there and have a look around this time. A *quick* look. You're not gonna try and, y'know, change the course of history or anything."

"I promise."

"You're not gonna *touch* anything ... you're not gonna *talk* to anyone."

"No touching. No talking."

Clare understood Al's eminently sensible concerns. But she also couldn't resist the urge to try again. It was an adventure. It was secret, thrilling, maybe even a little dangerous ... but it was also more than that. Much more.

"I *know* why you're doing this," Al said pointedly. "You think you're responsible." She had an uncanny way of reading Clare's thoughts sometimes.

"Pff." Clare avoided Al's gaze. "You know perfectly well that 'responsible' is not a term frequently used to describe me."

"I think what Allie means," Milo said, leaning back on the edge of the table and staring intently at Clare, "is that you think you were somehow responsible for that girl getting captured by a Roman soldier. But the last time you went back, the brooch she was wearing hadn't even been finished. Your trips don't necessarily follow a linear timeline. And I think you think that if you keep going back then maybe you'll somehow find a way to get to that girl before the soldier does. You think you can help her. Don't you?"

Clare's eyes dropped to the brooch on the table.

"I do not," she said.

"You do too," Al said quietly. "It's a noble sentiment."

Clare rolled her eyes. This was getting to be a bit much.

"It *is*. It might also be a dangerous one." Al shrugged. "Just sayin'."

"Al ... I know you've done more research." Clare picked up the empty sock and plucked idly at the pompom. "What happened to Comorra? What does that Tacitus guy say?"

"He doesn't." Al shook her head. "And most other historical accounts are generally either inconclusive or contradictory."

"But?"

"But, from everything I've read so far ... I'm thinking it probably wasn't good."

"That's what I'm afraid of." Clare threw the sock on the table and gazed down at the elegant, intricate shape of the raven brooch—its wings, its jewelled eye. "Llassar—the blacksmith guy—said that this was powerful magic. Protective magic. I helped him *make* the thing. And if I can use it to help that girl, I think I kinda have to, y'know? At least I have to try."

"I guess I can't argue with that," Milo said quietly. "We should let her try, Allie. We don't have any right to stop her."

Al turned a suddenly fierce glare on her cousin. "Tell me that again if she doesn't come back."

Clare reached out her hand toward the brooch. Al went stiff with tension beside her and Milo leaned forward, watching intently. Clare's fingertips brushed the cold, smooth surface of the brooch. Her blood fired icy-hot in her veins ... and the world winked out.

8

It had never actually occurred to Clare what it would have meant to live in a world that existed before the invention of the light bulb. It meant DARK. And SCARY. And it suddenly made sense why those horrid old fairy tales meant to scare the crap out of young girls and keep them from wandering away from home almost always took place in the depths of overgrown, lightless forests. As Comorra's world coalesced around her once again Clare took a look around, waiting for her eyes to adjust from Sunny London Afternoon to Murky Ancient Forest at Midnight (likely infested with virgin-devouring ogres—or, at the very least, a lascivious troll or two).

Clare thought she could hear the sounds of howling in the far distance, only it didn't sound like any wolves she'd ever heard on nature shows. She shivered, wondering what on earth could make such an eerie noise.

She took a step forward, out from behind a tree. She had rematerialized at the edge of a clearing in the woods, a meadow ringed with soaring oaks, with the sky overhead an endless black and spattered with stars. A crescent moon cleared the tree tops, and by its pale wash of light Clare saw that a ring of immense stones stood in the middle of the clearing, a man-and-a-half high each. Between the stones bladed pikes had been stuck in the earth, stabbing up at the darkened sky and draped with colourful banners bearing the stylized images of animals, stretched and knotted, fantastical and intricately beautiful.

In the centre of the ring stood a lone, rough-hewn stone larger than the rest, about ten feet high and five wide. Kneeling in front of it was a cloaked and cowled figure. As if sensing Clare's sudden intrusion, the figure stood and spun toward her, pushing back the deep hood to reveal her bright, strawberry-blond hair and pretty face.

"Comorra!" Clare gasped.

The girl's bright blue eyes went wide and she stumbled backward until she stood with her back against the stone. Her gaze took in Clare's appearance—from the strappy, metallic-hued sandals she'd worn that day to the sparkly, beaded-butterfly details of the adorable, time-travel-impractical sundress she'd plucked out of her closet. It was a little early in the season for something so summery, but it was a cute outfit and Clare had been secretly pleased to see Milo's eyes light up when he'd first seen her in his office.

Of course, to someone from first-century Britain, it probably didn't read the same way. It probably made her look like ...

"Tylwyth teg," Comorra whispered.

Yeah. A *faerie*. Or something like that, anyway.

Clare auto-translated the words as the other girl said them, just as she had before, somehow understanding that the translation wasn't exactly ... exact. But it was close enough.

"Disgleirwen," Comorra murmured, dropping her head in a respectful bow. "I did not imagine I would be so honoured as to have one of the Good People here this night ... Have you come to grace this ritual with your goodwill?"

"Shining One." That's kind of nice, Clare thought.

"Uh ... yes." Clare went with the suggestion. Cautiously. "Yes, I have ..."

Comorra cocked her head. "Your words ... they sound so strange. And yet I understand them." Her eyes widened as if she'd just realized that she'd spoken out loud. "I mean no offence, Shining One!"

"Oh, seriously, none taken!" Clare assured her.

"I have never seen one of your kind before. I wasn't sure if the stories Connal told me were true."

What about on the riverbank? Clare thought to herself. *You saw me then.*

But after a moment it occurred to Clare that *that* "then" might not have happened yet. As Milo said, she wasn't necessarily travelling through time in a linear fashion, and so this might be one of those "before" trips. Just like her visit to the blacksmith's hut when he'd been making the brooch— a brooch Comorra hadn't even owned yet, which had later ended up in Clare's pocket, and which Clare had then used to take her to the moment of its making ... *Ouch,* she thought. The whole thing was giving her a headache. It was like one of those word problems in math class crossed with that broken telephone game. *If a brooch travelling through time leaves the first century at point A and a girl travelling through time leaves the twenty-first century at point B, then how many purple monkey dishwashers does it take to get to Carnegie Hall ...?*

"Shining One?"

Comorra's voice broke in on Clare's knotted thoughts. The Iceni princess *did* look a tiny bit younger than the first time Clare had seen her. Maybe only a year or so—her face just a touch rounder, hair a little shorter ...

"Is something wrong?" she asked.

Clare realized suddenly that she was frowning at the girl. She wiped the scowl from her face and smiled. "Call me Clare, okay?"

Comorra's eyes went even wider. She looked as though she was trying to figure out how to respond correctly to such an invitation from a ... well, from an Otherworldly being. Somehow, maybe just from the way she'd said it, Clare recognized the significance of the "tylwyth teg" to someone like Comorra.

Comorra looked as though she desperately wanted to continue the conversation, but the distant sounds of howling—which Clare now recognized as coming from human throats and *celebratory* rather than meant to strike terror—were not so distant anymore. It sounded like the biggest, wildest party ever—and it seemed to be heading their way.

I have to get out of here, she thought.

Except she didn't know how.

Right. Damn ...

Clare knew that if this trip followed the same parameters as the last ones, Comorra would be the only one who'd be able to see her, probably because they'd come into physical contact. Still ... she was a little worried by the young Druid, Connal, who'd been able to *sense* her presence in the blacksmith's hut. Maybe he just had exceptional hearing. Heard her breathing. Or her heartbeat. Something ...

The sound of the approaching revellers was now shaking the leaves on the trees, and Clare could see the orange glow of torches reflecting off the forest canopy.

"Thank you for the gift of your presence at my sword ceremony, Clare," Comorra said.

"Oh, uh ..." Clare struggled for something appropriately mystical and significant-sounding for a ... a sword ceremony. She remembered Llassar and Connal saying something about how Comorra had been chosen by Andrasta. The Raven Goddess ... goddesses and faeries hung out together in Celtic cosmology, right? She hoped so ...

"The Raven sends her best," Clare said. *That ought to work.*

Comorra's eyes sparkled fiercely and Clare suspected that it had, in fact, been *exactly* the right thing to say.

"But I'd really love it if we could keep my presence here our little secret. My ... magic keeps me hidden from all but those to whom I choose to appear. And, tonight, that's just you." Clare glanced over her shoulder as the first of many cloaked figures appeared at the edge of the clearing, dark shapes picked out in shadow and flame. "Okay?" She put a finger to her lips.

Comorra mirrored the gesture with a conspiratorial smile. Then she twitched the hood of her cloak up and spun back around to resume her kneeling pose in front of the standing stone.

Clare ducked behind the stone, trying to melt into the shadows and slow her breathing. A dozen men and women carrying flaring torches stalked out from beneath the oaks and took up stations at points all around the standing stones. Some beat out complicated rhythms on drums played one-handed with short, flared sticks, and some sang. A handful of young children followed in their wake and began to dance in time to the drumming, weaving an intricate circle around the middle stone—and coming perilously close to where Clare stood frozen, scarcely daring to breathe. But none of them seemed to notice her there. It seemed that Comorra really was the only one who could see her. Still, she tried to make herself as small and flat as she could.

People continued to file out from under the trees, some pounding sword hilts on shields and stomping their feet in counterpoint to the drumming, and soon the whole clearing shook with the vibrations. The crowd was a visual riot of braided and styled hair, garishly patterned, finely woven cloaks, and the clash and jingle of beautifully crafted gold and silver jewellery. Clare couldn't decide whether the combined effect of so much extravagant finery on display was barbaric or exuberantly rich and sophisticated. One thing was certain: the artistry involved in all the weaving and dying and smithcraft on display went far beyond anything she'd expected a bunch of hut-dwelling tribal yahoos to have mastered. Her ideas, if she'd had any to begin with, of what life must have been like in the ancient world were being radically rewritten. The people crowding all around her were ... impressive. She hadn't been expecting that.

As the great clamour rose to a tremendous crescendo Clare felt battered by waves of sound and had to cover her ears with her hands. But just when she thought she couldn't take it anymore a sudden, shocking silence descended on the grove. Clare took a chance and peeked around to see what had caused it. And into that stillness walked—well ... *talk* about impressive.

The sea of revellers parted and into the centre of the stone circle walked Boudicca, Queen of the Iceni. The queen shimmered with gold and amethyst. Deep red garnets hung from her ears and flashed on her fingers and a delicate, braided silver torc encircled her neck. The sword strapped to her waist was, in contrast, plain and workmanlike—battered, well-used, and freshly sharpened.

At her side strode a tall man who was obviously a king. His long, dark blond hair was held back by a circlet of red gold and he wore a flowing robe girdled with a heavy belt made of linked copper lozenges that held an ornate ceremonial sword to his hip. His chin and cheeks were clean-shaven, but the braided ends of his flowing moustache reached almost down to the line of his strong jaw. His profile, lit by torch flame and silhouetted against the dark of the forest, was regal—handsome and striking—and around his neck he wore a thick golden torc.

The Snettisham Torc.

Boudicca turned to address the gathered throng in a clear, ringing voice that carried up and into the waiting shadows of the night. "Tonight, the rising moon of Beltane Eve marks the start of my daughter's sixteenth year. Tonight, she sheds the skin of childhood to become a woman. Tonight she becomes a warrior!"

Comorra stood and threw back the cowl of her cloak, turning to face her tribe with a look of fierce pride on her pretty face.

From the opposite side of the clearing Princess Tasca came forward, smiling broadly at her younger sibling. Clare felt her heart clench at seeing Comorra's sister alive. The older girl's cheeks were flushed and her eyes sparkled with excitement. Clare had a hard time reconciling that with the image of her lying crumpled and lifeless on the floor of Connal's chariot. She too wore a blade hanging from her belt—smaller and more slender than her mother's, made to fit a more delicate hand and a wrist not yet corded with years of strength and use. She carried something wrapped in snow-white doeskin, which she presented to the queen. As Boudicca threw back the leather wrap Clare stepped out from her hiding place and, unnoticed by the crowd, craned her neck to see what it had concealed.

It was another sword. Polished to a gleam and almost pretty, it looked as though the hilt was made of bronze, with a leaf-shaped, dark-grey iron blade. Alongside it lay a tooled leather sheath that hung from a jewelled leather belt.

"Comorra." The queen buckled the sword belt around the girl's waist and then took the blade from its bed of white leather. "I give you your sword."

Simple as that.

Comorra's slim fingers reached out—hesitating a moment—and then grasped the sword by the hilt. Its blade was short, no longer than some of the daggers worn by the men, and yet Comorra handled it with grace and assurance. The blade sang as it whipped through the air. Then, with a flourish that was only a little showy, Comorra spun the blade in her palm and slid it home in the scabbard at her side as if it had always belonged to her. Her mother smiled and Princess Tasca beamed with pride at her sister.

Then Comorra's father stepped forward.

Clare watched Boudicca's expression alter in the nearness of her husband's presence. Suddenly she was no longer just handsome ... she was lovely. Soft and glowing as a girl in the throes of a first love. The look was fleeting, but it made a powerful impression on Clare.

The king began to speak. "In the world I would make for you, my daughter, you would need never unsheath the blade your mother gives you." He turned and gestured. With a start Clare saw the young Druid, Connal, step forward. In his hands he held a little carved wooden box. The king reached up to unfasten the plain, utilitarian pin that held Comorra's cloak closed at her shoulder and replace it with the ornament from the box—the very same brooch that had sent Clare spiralling through time to this world.

"I fear this is not such a world," the king continued. "But I am comforted. The Raven Goddess watches over you, Comorra."

Comorra's glance flicked over to where Clare stood watching. Clare put a finger to her lips again, terrified that the princess might call her out, but Comorra simply nodded, smiling ever so slightly, and turned her eyes back to her father.

"May she keep you ever safe."

Clare grinned as Comorra exclaimed with wonder at the intricately wrought ornament. The Iceni evidently revered beautiful things, and of course the brooch was exquisite. Catching the light from the ring of torches, the garnet sparkled dramatically in its setting. At the front of the crowd, near the royal family, Clare saw Llassar grow tall with pride. She herself felt a certain giddy thrill to see the princess so pleased.

But then a shiver ran down her spine. She turned to see Connal *staring* at her—or rather, at the space she invisibly occupied—a faint frown on his brow. Clare found that she was holding her breath as his piercing gaze swept back and forth through the space where she stood.

But then Comorra smiled at him and his expression cleared. He gazed at her with obvious and abundant affection, and Comorra returned his look with one of her own that was halfway between bashful and smouldering.

Whoa, Clare thought. *She's seriously crushing on him ...*

Clare could hardly blame her. Connal was, to put it mildly, rock-star gorgeous. The young Druid's chestnut-brown hair was shot through with deep red highlights that gleamed in the torch fire. And like many of the other men, he wore almost as much ornamentation as the women. Gold glinted at his earlobe and a silver torc shone at his throat. A long grey cloak was thrown back over his shoulders, revealing a finely woven tunic fitted smoothly over the contours of his muscled chest, and buckskin trousers were laced tight around his calves above his bare feet.

Connal moved with an animal's sliding grace as he stepped toward the princess. "I speak for the Druiddyn to convey their blessings upon you, Comorra, and my own. Your father speaks truth when he says Andrasta holds you in her hands." He touched the jewelled brooch on her shoulder, and Clare could have sworn she saw Comorra shiver with delight. "You are beloved of the Raven. Your mother has called upon the goddess to protect you and she has answered. That is all the protection you should ever need."

"It should be indeed, Connal." Comorra grinned and then glanced at her mother. "But as my mother would no doubt agree, I will keep my sword close, just in case!"

They all laughed at that, with Boudicca's harsh mirth ringing out above the other voices like the cry of a carrion crow. Then everyone who had swords drew them from their scabbards and thrust them into the night sky, as if they would tear it open to bring daylight pouring forth.

It seemed that the brief ceremony was all the formal solemnity the Iceni could take. They rushed forward and surrounded the royal family, hugging and pounding on backs until the whole thing began to look like a rugby scrum. Comorra and her family were swept out of the grove in the direction of some kind of feast, Clare guessed—judging from the mouthwatering smells of roasting meat wafting toward them from that direction.

As quickly as it had filled up, the clearing emptied out, the whirlwind of revellers vanishing beneath the shadows of the trees and leaving only their whoops and hollers in their wake. Clare sagged against the rough stone, giddy with the contagious excitement of the Iceni. Lightheaded, she closed her eyes for a moment and tried to steady her breathing and slow her rabbit-fast heart. It worked—right up until the moment she felt the ice-cold edge of metal brush against her shoulder. Clare yelped and ducked as her eyes flew wide and she saw Connal lunging around the corner of the standing stone, sword sweeping the air before him. The young warrior grabbed for the space where Clare stood invisible, and the palm of his hand slammed against her shoulder, spinning her around. There was a lightning-bolt electric shock—just as when she'd first made contact with Comorra on the riverbank—and Clare saw Connal snarl and jerk back. But the jolt didn't deter him for long, and suddenly Clare found herself pinned to the standing stone, held motionless there by Connal's forearm ... and the sharp sting of his sword blade against her collarbone.

"They say that the kiss of cold iron is death to the tylwyth teg," he hissed into her ear. "But I think it would take more than just a kiss. You threaten my princess at your peril, Otherworlder ... You will not take her away to your hidden realm."

"I'm not!" Clare sputtered desperately. "I wouldn't!"

The warrior shook his head as if trying to shake sense into her words.

"I'm not here to hurt her—I want to *help* her! Comorra—"

"You will not speak her name!"

Clare could feel the rapid pounding of Connal's pulse where his wrist pressed against her skin and she wondered, through her terror, if he was anywhere near as afraid of her as she was of him.

"You have no power here," he said. "Return to your own world!" He reared back with his sword as, above their heads, a raven screamed in the night, the sound harsh in the darkness.

Clare squeezed her eyes shut—and felt herself shimmer out of existence. She heard Connal's astonished gasp as his blade plunged down toward where she stood ... an instant too late.

HIS EYES ARE REALLY BLUE ...

They were also full of amazement. And concern.

Wait a second ... where ... when am I?

Clare was flat on her back on the floor of Milo's office, staring up into his blue, bespectacled eyes as he bent over her, gently shaking her by the shoulder. Al peered over his shoulder, frantically calling Clare's name, her voice harsh and cawing.

"Why ... why am I on the floor?" Clare asked.

"Because you collapsed!" Al exclaimed.

"You disappeared ..." Milo's voice wasn't exactly tense, not like Al's, but it did sound hoarse. Almost as if he'd forgotten how to use it. Or was too startled by what he'd just seen to remember how to make his throat muscles work properly. "You *actually* vanished."

"And then you reappeared," Al added helpfully. "And *then* you fainted."

"Oh ..." Clare struggled to sit up.

"You didn't pass out the last time." Al crouched on the floor in front of her. "What happened this time?"

"I don't know." Clare had never fainted before. Then again, she'd never almost been *stabbed* before. Fear of imminent death must have just plain overwhelmed her. She put a hand to her forehead—it was clammy with sweat.

Milo jumped to his feet and stalked over to the watercooler on the far side of the office. After a moment he brought Clare a little paper cone full of cold water. She gulped at it thirstily. Her mind was a tumbled mess of images and impressions ... darkness and howling and ... Connal's sword, descending on her where she stood, shoulders pressed into the unforgiving stone ...

"Oh shit ..." Clare shied away from the memory of the torch-light glinting on that blade.

"Okay." Al blinked, peering at her intently. "See ... that's what you said the first time this happened. Were you on the riverbank again, Clare? Did you see Comorra?"

"Riverbank, no. Comorra, yes."

Milo helped her climb shakily to her feet and sit down. Clare took a deep breath, finished the water in the paper cup, and crumpled it into a ball. Then she told them everything that had happened.

"I thought we agreed on no touching. No talking. No mon-keying with the time stream!"

Al was cross and agitated. Clare wondered what kind of sci-fi conjecture had passed between her and her cousin while she'd been gone. "I'm sorry. I didn't do it on purpose. Does the British Empire still stand?"

"Very funny," Al said sourly.

Milo had gone a little pale, Clare noticed. And quiet.

But at least he seemed to actually believe her. Hard to deny what had happened, she supposed, when she had shimmered out of existence right before his very eyes.

There's your proof of paranormal activity, Hot Stuff, she thought. *Logic your way out of this one.*

Al blew a long breath out and sat down, having seemingly exhausted her store of nervous tension. "So that's how she got the brooch, huh?" she said eventually. "I guess it must have been pretty important to her."

"Yeah," Clare nodded, lost in thought. *And she gave it to me for a reason ...*

Her gaze slipped over to where the raven-shaped ornament sat innocuously on a nearby desk. Milo reached out a hand for it and Clare and Al both tensed. He closed his fingers around it ... and nothing happened. Milo didn't disappear. He didn't even flicker. He held the brooch out to Al.

"Thanks, no."

"C'mon, Allie," he urged. "I want to know if it's just Clare."

Al hesitated for a moment and then, lips pressed into a tight line, she snatched it from his hand. Nothing. Al let out another long breath and turned to Clare. "Guess you're the Chosen One, pal."

Clare was distinctly uncomforted by the sentiment. They sat together in uneasy, contemplative silence—until Clare's cell phone jangled noisily and scared all three of them half to death.

"Oh, for the love of ..." Clare grabbed it out of her bag and checked the display. "It's Maggie. She'd better not be checking up on me," Clare muttered and slapped the phone to the side of her head with a flat "Hello."

Al and Milo listened to Clare's monosyllabic responses and watched as the blood drained from her face. Clare *knew* the blood was draining from her face because she could feel herself growing cold, starting with the top of her head.

"Clare?" Milo asked when she finally hung up. "Are you okay?"

"No. I don't think so ... no ..."

"What did Maggie say?" Al asked, frowning.

"She's at the museum," Clare murmured.

"Wow. Shocker."

"With the police."

"Uh?"

"What?" Milo's voice was sharp with concern. "Why?"

"She said there'd been a ... there was a ..." Clare felt as if she was about to start hyperventilating. "There's been a theft."

"She *said* that?" Al asked. "What ... when ... who—"

"Allie, shh." Milo reached out and took Clare's cold, limp hands and held them, squeezing gently. "What else did she say?"

"Um ..." Clare's fingers clenched convulsively around Milo's.

"Can you tell me?"

She nodded, staring at Milo with unblinking eyes and breathing in rapid, shallow little sips of air. "Uh ... that was it. That was all she said. Just that something had been stolen. From—uh—from the stuff in the restoration room. She wants me to meet her at the museum." Clare's knees felt weak and her stomach lurched at the thought of facing Maggie. That kebab earlier suddenly seemed like a terribly bad idea.

"Did she say who, uh, *what* was"—Al swallowed noisily—"stolen?"

Clare shook her head. Then panic took hold. "I thought you said I didn't take anything! Jeezus, Al!"

"You didn't ..." Al didn't sound so sure anymore.

"Allie?" Milo looked at her.

"She didn't!" Al turned on him, regaining her adamant stance. "I *know* she didn't. I swear to God! I didn't see that brooch—*it wasn't there!*"

"Well, then we don't have anything to worry about."

"We?" Clare looked at Milo and blinked.

"You." Milo shrugged. He turned and went back to his desk, taking out a set of keys from a drawer. "C'mon. I'll drive you." He grabbed the brooch, wrapped it back up, and locked it in the drawer. "No sense wandering around the museum with anything that could potentially make for an awkward situation."

"I didn't steal it." Clare looked at him.

"I believe you."

The girls turned to stare at each other silently for a long moment.

"I'm dead," Clare said bleakly.

"Come on." Milo nodded toward the door. "You're not dead. And I'm not about to let anyone kill you. Now let's go find out what's going on."

9

"**S**it down, girls."

Clare and Al glanced nervously at each other. Milo was waiting for them in the museum's Great Court. They'd decided it was best not to gang up and rally to Clare's defence before they knew if she actually needed defending.

Maggie waved them toward a couple of hardbacked chairs in a corner of the curator's office. She was positively crimson with rage as she gripped a sheet of paper in one hand so tightly that it creased around the edges of her fingers.

"This. Is. Intolerable."

Clare swallowed.

"What on earth would make anyone think they had a right—*any* right—to take something that quite simply and by all rational argument does not *belong to them*?" Maggie's voice skirled upward. "Not only that! *This* theft is a crime against history. A crime against humanity! The artifacts in this building are a legacy meant for all. Not just scholars. *Everyone!* The lofty and the common alike. Everyone can come to this institution and gaze upon its contents and be amazed. But *only* if those contents are not bloody stolen away and—God knows—probably sold on the black market to some crackpot recluse who runs around naked late at night in a private vault stacked with

Nazi-looted Monets and crates full of smuggled tribal fertility goddesses—"

"I didn't mean it!" Clare blurted, unable to withstand any more of her aunt's frothing tirade. "I swear I won't sell it to a naked crackpot!"

"What ...?"

"Uh ... I ... won't sell it to a crackpot?"

"Sell *what*?" Maggie's righteous anger dissipated into a cloud of confusion in the face of Clare's baffling outburst. "Good Lord, Clare, I don't have time for games."

"No. Of course." Clare backpedalled furiously. "Sorry."

"The torc is an irreplaceable piece of history. Worth far more than its weight in gold, which is substantial."

"The ... torc?" Clare and Al exchanged confused glances.

"The Snettisham Torc." Maggie rolled her eyes. "Oh for the love of— The great big shiny gold necklace thingy that was sitting on the table in the restoration room yesterday. Surely even *you* must have noticed that?"

"I noticed it ..." Al squeaked.

"There, yes, you see?" Maggie turned back to Clare.

"Uh ... okay ..." Clare's mind raced. Of *course* she'd noticed the "great big shiny gold necklace thingy." She'd probably even left a fingerprint on it. It had sent her hurtling back through time! But now that she realized Maggie wasn't accusing them at all, Clare started to calm down. "Right. The torc. And it's what now?"

"Stolen." Maggie's glare was positively baleful. "Were you listening—even a *little*—when I told you why I wanted you to meet me here instead of back at the townhouse?"

"Uh ..." The phrase "stolen artifact" must have set off Clare's inner auto-pilot back in Milo's office.

"I surrender," Maggie sighed and threw her hands in the air. "The television wins. Your mind is mush beyond reclamation. Clare, I'm going to have to stay late today to help Dr. Jenkins and the police with the investigation, and I'll most likely have to come in early tomorrow, too. It's getting on, I haven't shopped for the groceries, and I didn't want you roaming the city all evening without food or money. I thought perhaps you could wait for me and eat in the museum's cafeteria ..."

The girls shuddered in tandem. The museum's "wrapped sandwiches" tasted far more of "wrap" than "sandwich." And anyway, food was the last thing on either of their minds. As gently as she could, Clare took her agitated aunt by the wrist.

"Mags?" she said. "Look. Don't worry about me, okay?"

Maggie's normally calm, cool, unflappable exterior seemed to be on the verge of crumbling. Clare had never seen her so upset, and it made her think there was something going on here. Something *else* going on. She gave her aunt's arm a little shake.

"I know this is important, Mags. And I know that my mother probably has you convinced that I can't tie my own shoes without triggering a minor apocalypse somewhere in the world or altering the flow of history"—*Okay,* Clare thought, *that last one is maybe a little too close to the truth*—"but I can totally fend for myself while you take care of this. Without incident."

Maggie smiled wearily in something approaching gratitude. Her eyes, Clare noticed, were red-rimmed. She patted Clare's cheek and, without another word, went over to where her purse sat on a table. She fished around in it and pulled out a bank card.

"The PIN is your birthday, duck—month and day," she said and handed it over.

Clare blinked at her, surprised by that somehow.

Maggie brushed it aside. "I didn't figure anyone would ever guess that."

"Probably not." Clare recovered herself and grabbed the card before Maggie changed her mind.

"No trips to Aruba, please. And scout's honour you'll at least *try* and keep from burning London to the ground."

"I'll at least try. Scout's honour."

"And, oh yes! Not *one* word of this to *anyone*. The police are keeping this matter strictly under wraps for the moment. Now keep in touch and off you go," Maggie said, already turning her attention back to the matter at hand.

Clare and Al looked at each other and headed into the outer office. Suddenly its door flew open and Dr. Jenkins burst in, flapping like a penguin in a pencil skirt as she hurried past.

"Well, there'll be no help from that high-priced security firm we hired!" she squawked at Maggie in the other room. "They can't even contact the guard. Gone on vacation, he has. To the Turks and Caicos—some bloody beach resort with no bloody phones—won't be back for three bloody weeks! I *thought* he looked like the surf-bum type ..."

The girls moved back toward the inner office so they could hear what was going on. Clare peered around the half-open door.

"What about the cameras?" Maggie dodged a bit to the side to avoid the curator's flailing arms.

"They show nothing. Nothing!"

"How can that be?"

"They've been rigged—the digital files and their backups of that day are both gone—replaced with a repeating loop of an empty restoration room. The night guardsman never suspected a thing." Dr. Jenkins rubbed her temples feverishly. Strands of reddish-brown hair had escaped her tight bun and were sticking out comically around her ears. "I really wish thieves would stop watching caper films. They get far too many ideas."

"Not 'they' ..." Clare watched as her aunt's expression darkened. *"Him."*

"Him, who?"

"Morholt." Maggie almost spat the word.

"Don't be ridiculous," Dr. Jenkins said sharply. "He's dead."

"I beg to differ. He's very much alive."

"Oh Magda, really! Those rumours are just that. Rumours."

"No, Ceciley, they're not. I know Stuart Morholt."

"*Knew* him. In university, Magda. So did I—in case you've forgotten—but that was a very long time ago and every insane whisper you've heard about him since is just mad storytelling. Bunk. He was a liar and a fraud and a two-penny con artist and mischief-maker. You *know* he drank himself unconscious and burned to death in a fire on one of his silly 'spiritual retreats' over four and a half years ago."

"What if he didn't?" Clare's aunt sank wearily into a chair, her hands still twisting the sheet of paper. "I never believed that. I think he's been lying low and biding his time until he could steal something like the torc to use in one of his arcane rites."

"Oh now, really!" Dr. Jenkins scoffed. "Surely you don't truly believe all that Druid nonsense. For heaven's sake, Magda—"

Clare went cold at the mention of the word "Druid." Al leaned forward, straining to catch every word.

"—It's farcical, I tell you. All that posturing of his back in the day. Claiming to be some sort of Celtic mystic, for heaven's sake! It was all just to get the skirts to swoon over him. I'm sorry to say, he was girl-mad. And I think that you—"

"He wasn't girl-mad. He was power-mad."

Dr. Jenkins just shook her head. "Professor Wallace, honestly. I'm surprised at you."

Maggie shot to her feet, eyes blazing. "Really, Ceciley! Are you? You may have chosen to forget that night in the Midlands but I never have. I remember it as if it were yesterday and I remember the look in that poor young man's eyes. We made a terrible mistake and we all share the blame, but Stuart Morholt—"

"I don't care to discuss the distant past," Dr. Jenkins said stiffly.

"You're a fool if you think to underestimate Morholt. A *bloody* fool!"

"Magda!"

"You didn't really know him, Ceciley," Maggie continued. "You didn't know him the way I did. And you didn't get *this* in your email inbox today!" She slapped the paper down on the tabletop.

Dr. Jenkins blinked, picked up the crumpled sheet, and began to read. Her eyes grew wide behind her glasses. "This ... this can't be real."

"You'd better just hope not."

Suddenly, from behind Clare and Al a pair of uniformed policemen appeared and stalked past them into the inner office and closed the door behind them, effectively shutting the girls out from what was becoming a truly gripping conversation.

"Who the hell is Stuart Morholt?" Al murmured.

"I have *no* idea," Clare said. "But I think we should find out."

"Oh yeah."

"D'you think this theft thing is a coincidence?" Al asked quietly as they walked through the Eastern Gallery on their way down to the Great Court.

Clare rolled an eye at her.

"Yeah. Me neither."

Clare's initial relief at not being the actual target of Maggie's wrath was fading and she was beginning to feel a gnawing anxiety. The whole thing had started out as some kind of crazy adventure, but it was as if she'd gone from playing with matches to lighting a raging bonfire: just what she'd promised Mags she wouldn't let happen.

10

Milo pushed his glasses up onto his forehead and rubbed the bridge of his nose, gears evidently whirring away in the vault of his skull. They'd talked the matter half to death the night before after leaving the museum, but apparently Milo was still running his cerebral analysis programs. Clare wondered if he'd slept much. And then blushed furiously at the thought of him lying in his bed not sleeping. Thankfully, he didn't seem to notice the sudden rush of colour to her cheeks.

"Okay. So," he said, going over the sequence of events for the umpteenth time. "Nothing else on the table—nothing except the torc and the shield—made you ... you know ..."

"Zot," Al chimed in helpfully.

Clare plucked a trio of malt-vinegar-soaked fries out of the newspaper cone in Milo's hand and folded them into her mouth. "Can we please come up with a cooler term for what I do?" she said. It was Saturday morning, and the OS offices were deserted. They'd come back to retrieve the brooch— Clare had been feeling distinctly uneasy without it, and so Milo had agreed to fetch the thing, but only after picking up fish and chips on the way. Apparently, his brain didn't do so well on an empty stomach.

"'Zot' doesn't work for you?" Milo smiled faintly.

"I like 'zot,'" Al said. "It's very genre."

Clare glared.

"Okay. Okay." Al put up a hand. "Not 'zot.' So ... what do you want to call it then?"

"I don't know," Clare muttered, thoroughly embarrassed that they were even having this conversation. "Never mind."

"No," Milo said, his expression thoughtful. "No, Clare, you're right. You should have a proper name for this. It's a gift, after all. A talent. And it's yours. You should call it whatever you want."

"But I don't know what it is," she said, looking back up into his eyes. It helped enormously that Milo was actually taking her seriously. It helped her be less afraid. A little.

"Well ... what does it feel like when it happens?"

What *did* it feel like? It tingled. And burned—like cinnamon or ginger—a hot, sweet spice that she could taste and feel. Like fire in her veins. Then everything around her would spark and sparkle, flare sun-bright with that lightning flash that made her whole being feel as if it were made of fireflies ... and then she would flicker away into star-spattered darkness ...

"It ... I ..."

Milo waited patiently.

"I ..." It was almost a whisper when she said it. "I shimmer."

"Shimmer?" Milo nodded encouragingly. "You shimmer?"

"Yeah."

"I like 'shimmer,'" Milo said, grinning.

"I like 'zot,'" Al muttered.

Milo ignored his cousin. "'Shimmer' it is then, Clare. But whatever you want to call it, there has *got* to be something particular to those artifacts—a specific mechanism of some kind."

"Mechanism?" Clare frowned, picturing something mechanical.

"A trigger."

"Oh. Right. So what do you think that is?"

"Pfft." Milo waved his hand in the air. "I dunno. Magic?"

And there it was.

The M word.

Apparently it had just kind of slipped out, but Milo's mouth snapped shut the second it did, his scientific sensibilities shocked to their square roots. Because it suddenly seemed that, up until that point, Milo and the girls had been pretty actively avoiding uttering *that* particular word.

"Heh heh." Al shifted nervously. "Yeah ... magic."

Milo's frown deepened. "Honestly? I'd be more comfortable with quantum physics. But yeah. Kidding aside, I think we pretty much have to go with magic on this one."

Clare hugged her elbows in tight to her body, a chill chasing up her spine to her scalp. "When Boudicca and Llassar used the word 'magic,' I was really kind of hoping it was, you know, just a figure of speech."

"Not really looking that way," Al murmured.

"Which would make me a *total* freak."

"Yup." Al nodded in thoughtful agreement. "Or maybe not. I mean, maybe it's not you. Necessarily. What we need to figure out is what the *actual* event trigger is here. Is this 'supernatural phenomenon'—I call it that *only* for lack of a better descriptor and, under the present circumstances, in lieu of a clearly defined system of nomenclature—is this phenomenon an inherent psycho-physiological occurrence exclusive to *you*? Or is it a function of some mystical property intrinsic to the artifacts themselves?"

"Al, you're talking like a grad student again. It makes me want to knock you over the head."

Milo stifled a grin. "Put it this way: Are you the shimmer-*er* or the shimmer-*ee*?"

"Oh. I kind of think it might be a little from column A, a little from column B."

"You mean a bit of both?"

"Right. See—and I know this is going to make me sound like some kind of New Age touchy-feely weirdo, but these things—the brooch, the torc—they're not like, you know, toasting forks. Not everyday stuff. And not stuff that's ... public, either, if you know what I mean. Like, I get *nothing* from the bowl or the comb or the cauldron hook." She moved her hands in little circles in the air. "But Boudicca's torc, Comorra's brooch—those things are special. They're *possessions*. In the most personal sense, it seems to me. There's ... I don't know ... *feeling* there. A connection."

"Okay." Milo shifted and leaned forward. "I'm with you so far. But what about the Battersea Shield? How much emotional investment can you have with a piece of armour?"

"Well," Clare said, "a *lot* of emotional investment maybe. If you lived back then, your life kind of depended on your equipment, didn't it? Wouldn't you develop an emotional attachment to a favourite sword?"

"A sword, maybe. A shield? Seems a bit of a stretch," Milo said. "I don't think most shields even made it through an average battle intact. They just got hacked to pieces and discarded."

Clare blinked at him, and he shrugged a bit shyly and reached for his Pepsi.

"I watch the History Channel ..."

At least he's a well-rounded geek, she thought.

Al was chewing thoughtfully on a mouthful of breaded haddock. "Milo's right. And, anyway, from everything I've read on the subject, archaeologists all agree that the Battersea Shield isn't really a shield at all."

"But it is something ... special maybe." Milo said. "Is that what you're thinking? That it was something more than just an Iceni objet d'art?"

"Yes! That's my point, exactly!" Clare nodded vigorously. Al and Milo's enthusiasm for solving the puzzle was infectious. "I mean, I don't think I could, like, brush up against a Neolithic soup pot and get hit with the mojo. But certain things—important things—*that's* what seems to set off the shimmering. And when I saw Llassar and Connal about to throw the shield in the river on my very first trip, they didn't look like they were just taking out the trash. They looked like they were doing something *important*."

"Like a ritual." Milo turned his sky-blue gaze on Clare and smiled. "Okay. I'm impressed."

"By what—the flawless logic of my deductive reasoning?" Clare preened.

Al snorted in amusement. "That—and the fact that you used the word 'Neolithic' in a contextually proper fashion."

"I wish I could go back to the museum and try again with something else," Clare said. "But things are probably a little on the jumpy side around there, what with the whole theft thing."

"Right," Milo said. "The other angle of the puzzle. The worrying angle."

"Yeah, I'd really like to get to the bottom of that one," said Clare anxiously. "I mean, what if there's someone else who can do what I do?" She stared at the gleaming brooch where it lay on her scarf on Milo's desk. "What if *that's* how they stole the torc?"

"We don't even know what exactly it *is* that you do, Clare." Trust Milo to caution her against leaps in logic.

"Right." Clare reached over and pilfered another french fry and popped it in her mouth. "What I really don't understand," she continued, licking her fingers, "is this: there was, like, a king's ransom in that room, all laid out on the table like a Sunday buffet. And the only thing missing is the torc. I wonder why the thief took just that one piece?"

"Portability, is my guess," Milo said. "Dude couldn't very well have just walked out of the museum with the Battersea Shield tucked under his arm ..."

Clare looked over at him. His T-shirt du jour was pale blue with a faded vintage Superman crest on it that stretched nicely over the muscles of his chest. Milo hadn't shaved that morning and the blond stubble just at the corner of his mouth glistened with a faint shine of chip grease. She wondered what it would be like to kiss the lips of a slightly prickly, salt-and-vinegar-flavoured geek god ...

"Do I have something in my teeth?"

"Hmm?"

"You're staring."

"Oh! ... No ... just thinking."

"Right." Milo's expression shifted to something between subtle amusement and shyness and he ran a thumb along the line of his bottom lip.

Clare looked away, feeling her cheeks redden again. "I mean ... what you said about the shield makes sense, but there was other smaller stuff laid out in the room, too. Why go to all the trouble for just one piece of hardware when you can go full-on kid-in-a-candy-store?"

"I think he took the torc for the prestige factor." Al wolfed down her last bite of fish. "Art thieves are weird. They can crack into a vault full of priceless stuff and walk back out again with nothing because it wasn't quite the *right* stuff. I've heard my mom tell stories like that of gallery break-ins."

"Your mom hangs out with a whole lotta nutjobs," Milo said as he wadded the now-empty newspaper cone into a ball and lobbed it into a wastebasket. Then he stood, walked over to his workstation, and flung himself into the chair behind his computer terminal.

Al shrugged. "Yeah, Mumsy's a cracker-magnet. No argument. Nevertheless, my point stands. And let's face it—the torc was the absolute star of the Ancient Britain collection. It was about to get its own display case."

"Kind of makes it seem like the thief was thumbing his nose at the museum," Clare reasoned.

"Sure does." Al nodded. "So this Morholt guy Maggie was talking about. You've *never* heard his name before?"

"Nope."

"Because the way the Perfesser was talking about him ..."

"I know," Clare agreed. She'd heard it too: both *what* Maggie had said about the guy and the *way* she'd said it. "I gotta say, I'm intrigued. Also? Slightly disturbed."

"Yeah."

"Stuart Morholt," Milo piped up suddenly, gesturing at his computer screen. "Arch-Druid of the Order of the Free Peoples of Prydein. Scholar, Sage, Sword of Righteous Truth."

"Pardon?" Al turned to him.

"Also—according to another, less public-relations-driven website—Criminal, Crazy, Con-artist Extraordinaire."

"What's Prydein?" Clare asked.

"A really old name for Britain. Pre–Roman invasion."

"Oh."

"What site are you on, Mi?" Al squeezed in behind him, peering over his shoulder.

"The mighty Wikipedia led me to these two in particular." He pointed with one hand and mouse-clicked with the other. "The first one is the official site of the aforementioned Free Peoples—looks like a bunch of weekend LARPers to me—and this one: something called 'wacko-whackers.com.' It's like a de-bunker kind of site. They seem to have vastly differing opinions on your man Morholt."

"Wait, what's a LARPer?" Clare asked.

Al and Milo exchanged an indulgent glance.

"Live Action Role Player," Al said with only a touch of con-descension in her voice.

"Ah."

"Weird ..." Milo murmured. "According to both these websites, Stuart Morholt is definitely dead."

"Not if he's stealing stuff from the museum, he's not," Clare snorted.

"Dr. Jenkins said he was dead, too," Al said.

"Yeah," Clare nodded, thinking back over the conversation. "But Maggie sure didn't agree with her on that point. And there was something else they were talking about that just sounded weird ... about a trip to the Midlands with Morholt when they were all students and something terrible happening. Something Maggie said she'd never forget."

"Well ..." Milo pointed at the screen. The three of them stared at the information, mesmerized. "It says right here that Stuart Morholt, 'a known fugitive wanted for various acts of theft and destruction of property,' was killed in a fire. That was almost five years ago."

"So ... what the hell?"

"What the hell, indeed," said a voice from over Clare's shoulder—right before she felt the chill of cold metal pressing against the base of her skull ... and heard a noise she'd only ever heard on television or in the movies.

The unmistakable *chck-chck* sound of someone cocking the hammer of a gun.

11

Milo swallowed nervously.

Al stifled a gasp.

And Clare suddenly forgot how to breathe.

"What ... the hell ... indeed," the voice repeated with languid amusement. The voice was male, older, dulcet, with an upper-class Oxford-ish accent. And, Clare hoped, the product of her hyperactive imagination. Still, she thought she should check.

"Al, Milo ..." Clare asked quietly, "is there a guy with a gun standing behind me?"

Milo's jaw tightened and he nodded. Al, wide-eyed, just said, "Uh-huh ..."

It wasn't the response Clare had been looking for.

The man chuckled. "What your inarticulate little friends mean is 'Yes, in fact, there is an impeccably stylish gentleman standing directly behind you, holding a vintage, silenced Walther PPK just below your ear—and yes, before anyone asks, that *is* the same gun used by the Connery-era James Bond—and it is quite capable of making mincemeat of your pretty little brainpan.' They might also add, if they were very clever, that this gentleman strongly warns you against pulling any teenage *'girl power'* bravado crap and instead suggests you

do exactly what he says in order to avoid an untimely and—
it's safe to imagine—sloppy demise."

Clare swallowed the knee-jerk sarcastic retort that was on
the tip of her tongue and asked, politely, "Could I at least ask
what you want from us? Uh, please?"

"I happen to think you could be a very useful little creature,
my dear," he replied. "A girl who can disappear into thin air
would, to my way of thinking, be a marvellous help to me in
my ... pursuits."

Clare went ice-cold from the inside out. "I'm not really looking for work." Her voice was barely above a whisper.

"Too bad. Work just found you." His tone slipped effortlessly from convivial to *don't-mess-with-me* and back again. "I find
myself very much intrigued with your disappearing act."

"What if I say that I don't know what you're talking
about?"

"Having observed your little magic trick firsthand I'd say
you were lying. Of course, initially I wasn't sure if I'd really
seen it or not. But then I checked the museum security record-
ings after I'd absconded with them and it seemed my eyes did
not tell a lie. Now, how's about you do me the same courtesy?"

Clare remained silent.

"Tell me about the vanishing act, my dear." The pressure
eased behind Clare's ear, and from the corner of her eye she
saw the barrel of the gun swing in the direction of Al and
Milo, who now stood paralyzed in the middle of the room. "Or
I will shoot your friends where they stand."

"No—wait!" Clare yelped.

"Yes?"

There was a sheen of perspiration on Milo's brow. Al had
gone a shade of whitish grey and looked as if she might pass
out.

"I'll tell you," Clare said quietly. "I'll tell you everything."

She heard the sound of one of the tall stools over by a work-table scraping along the floor and sensed the man behind her settling himself to sit on it. Clare turned around slowly and got her first good look at him. His face was tanned and chiselled, handsome in a severe kind of way under a thatch of dark hair only just beginning to silver at the temples. Mid-forties, Clare figured. About the same age as Maggie ...

Clare had a sudden flash of insight. She didn't care what the internet said and she trusted Maggie's instincts. She knew who this was. Stuart Morholt. Self-professed Lord High Muck-a-Muck Druid. And suddenly she understood how he knew what she could do. He had *seen* her vanish. He looked much less dorky without the cheesy blond moustache and wig under the guard hat, but it was definitely the same guy who'd been standing guard in the museum.

"Well. If it isn't Officer Friendly," she murmured.

"Beg pardon?" He raised one charcoal-coloured eyebrow.

She had to give him credit for not giving away the game back in the restoration room. Then again, since he'd been there to steal the torc, staying cool had been his only option.

She cleared her throat nervously. "Mr. Morholt, I presume?"

He looked mildly surprised that she'd deduced his identity without prompting, but all he said was, "In the flesh. And not nearly as dead as some would like to think." He nodded graciously toward Milo's computer screen. "But I do thank you for your interest in my present state of well-being. Now. On to matters of more import." He eyed Clare keenly, his gaze minutely appraising. "Tell me your story, Clarinet Reid."

He knew her name. Her full, stupid name. And he'd called her by it. Seeing as how he had a gun, she let it slide, this once. But she wondered just exactly how well Stuart Morholt really knew her aunt Magda.

He was still staring at her, unblinking. "Tell me how you disappear."

"I *don't* disappear."

Stuart Morholt sighed impatiently and swung the pistol toward Al again, who whimpered.

"No! I mean, I—I don't *just* go invisible!" Clare stammered. She felt tears of frustration welling up behind her eyes. "Jeezus. I'm gonna tell you what really happens and you're not gonna believe any of it. Then you'll shoot us and we'll die and this sucks!"

"Try me." The self-professed Druid's voice was surprisingly gentle. Inquisitive.

Clare blinked hard, stubbornly willing back the waterworks.

"Trust me on this one, Miss Reid," Morholt continued. "You'll have an easier time convincing me than you would your auntie Magda." He laid the gun down in his lap and took his finger off the trigger.

Clare found it marginally easier to talk without the flat black eye of the gun barrel staring at her. "I don't just disappear," she said again, her voice hoarse, almost a whisper. "I ... go elsewhere. Else*when*, really. I go back. In time."

"Back?" Morholt's voice was carefully neutral. "Back in *time*, you say?"

"It happened for the first time with the Battersea Shield in the museum. That's what you saw on the security tapes. I just touched it and, uh ..."

"Zot," Al murmured.

Morholt frowned. "Zot?"

"Yeah," Al said nervously. "We haven't really come up with a scientific term for it yet."

"Yes we have!" Clare protested. "I thought we were going to call it 'shimmering.'"

"That's not really scientific," Al said obstinately.

"Oh—and 'zot' is?"

"Ladies ..." Morholt pinched the bridge of his nose as if he felt a sudden headache coming on.

"I just think 'shimmer' sounds more fantasy than sci-fi—"

"And didn't we already decide that this thing I do is *not* science-based?"

"Ladies ..."

"Yeah, but—"

"Look. It's my thing. Milo even agrees that—"

"Ladies!" Morholt slammed the gun onto the tabletop and the girls jumped. *"Please."*

Clare swallowed apprehensively as the gun swung back up toward her. After a tense moment, Morholt waved it in a motion that indicated she should continue with her story.

"Right. Um. I touched the shield and, well ... suddenly, there I was—standing on a riverbank in the dark and right in front of me were these guys wearing cloaks, and one of them was holding up a shield—"

"The Battersea Shield? Was it the same one?" Morholt leaned forward.

"Maybe. I'm not sure ..." Clare's spine tingled and her hands went cold at the memory. Of course it had been the same shield. She'd been sure of it. Pretty sure. She just wasn't going to tell Morholt that. "And then I came back. The first time was only a few seconds."

"And the second time? I saw it on the tape. With the Snettisham Torc. You touched the torc and you disappeared—you went back—a second time." Morholt leaned forward again. "Did you see anyone? Were there people that time?"

"Yeah, there were people," Clare snorted. "I only saw Boudicca. How's *that* for people?" Out of the corner of her eye she caught Al giving her a warning look. But Clare was feeling a little reckless. And angry. She didn't like bullies and Stuart Morholt was exactly that. A bully with a gun ...

"Boudicca." Morholt breathed the name like a sacred word in a prayer. "Did *she* ... is the Great Torc *hers*? Is that who it belonged to?"

Over Morholt's shoulder Clare saw Milo's expression turn cautionary too, and decided that a bit of backpedalling might be in order.

"I don't know," she said. "I didn't see it."

Morholt raised an eyebrow.

"What?" Clare crossed her arms over her chest and stared defiantly. "I *didn't*. It's not like I was taking *notes*, y'know. There was a *lot* to look at!"

Morholt stared back, unblinking, for a long moment. Then he seemed to come to a decision. He reached over and plucked Comorra's brooch from the table. Clare held her breath, half expecting him to disappear just as she had—he *was*, supposedly, a Druid—but nothing happened. He frowned at the ornament, perhaps having expected the same thing himself.

"All right," he said finally. "Perhaps, Miss Reid, you'll pay better attention if you have a bit of incentive. Would the knowledge that your friends' lives depend on the quality of your observations improve them somewhat?" With the flick of his thumb, Morholt flipped the brooch through the air like a coin in Clare's direction. She staggered backward, almost falling over a computer service cart, but still couldn't stop herself as her right hand instinctively reached out and caught Comorra's brooch. Her other hand came down on a laptop sitting on the cart, which exploded in a miniature fireworks burst of electrical disruption. Amid a shower of sparks and the smell of burning circuitry, the Ordnance Survey office—and the world outside its windows—winked out once more.

12

The first thing she noticed was the screaming.

Terrific, Clare thought. *Do they ever* not *scream around here?*

But then she realized that, like the other time, the sound wasn't exactly screaming. More like ... *keening.* Eerie and raw, the open wound of sound carried on the wind. It was as though it issued from a multitude of throats—a dissonant symphony of grief that raised the hackles on the back of Clare's neck and made her want to turn and run blindly into the night.

I wonder if I'll ever materialize in broad daylight, she thought, fighting down the urge to flee. As her eyes adjusted to the gloom, Clare took in her surroundings. She was standing underneath the shaggy, overhanging eaves of a thatched roof. Just to the right of her head was a window—a roughly square opening cut in the thick earthen wall, covered from the inside by a soft leather curtain that was drawn aside just enough to let Clare peek in. She stood on the tips of her toes—and saw Comorra, illuminated by the flickering red light from a glowing charcoal brazier, head bowed over something she held in her hands. Her hair was unbound and fell in a rippling wave of rosy gold over her shoulders and down past her waist. Clare saw that what Comorra held in her hands was the raven brooch. She watched as the princess lifted it to her lips and whispered a few words. Then she kissed it and pinned it to her cloak, tears running in tracks down her cheeks. Comorra dashed the wetness away with the back of her hand and, throwing back her shoulders, stalked out of Clare's line of sight.

From outside, beyond the curve of the house wall, Clare heard the sound of a door creaking open and then slamming shut. She inched forward and caught a glimpse of Comorra's bright hair as the princess headed down a dirt path that led to an open space in the midst of what appeared to be a settlement of some kind. The clearing looked as though it could double as an open-air market in the daytime. From her vantage point Clare could see people streaming toward it in groups of two and three, most of them striding purposefully as if something important was about to happen. And yet the gathering had a distinctively un-festive air. The faces of the men and women were set and serious. Grim, even.

In the distance Clare could see that surrounding the settlement was a wall—a timber palisade of tall, sharpened stakes. *This must be Venta Icenorum.* The capital of the Iceni territory. She blinked, surprised that she'd remembered the name of Boudicca's village—the Roman name, anyway. Details from Al's info-dump sessions had actually lodged in her brain. Now *that* was a first.

Clare followed Comorra at a distance, moving as silently as she could and keeping to the shadows beneath the shaggy thatch overhangs of the scattered roundhouses. There were more of them than she'd expected. It was more like a town than a village. The houses ranged in size from large garden sheds to a huge structure with a soaring, conical peaked roof that looked as though it was some sort of great feast hall. As she darted from house to house, hiding in the shadows, Clare wondered what the dwellings looked like on the inside. She hadn't been able to make out any details, peering through Comorra's window, but she suspected that the squat little huts were probably full of ratty animal furs and straw and smoky

fire pits. Suddenly it struck her that this might be the same village where she'd found herself earlier, in Llassar's forge hut.

Clare slowed as she approached the edge of the crowd.
Stragglers were still coming in and the last thing she wanted to
do was accidentally bump into a stray Iceni warrior. Especially
considering the fact that, beneath their flowing, checkered
cloaks, all the men carried swords. Most of the women did,
too—and they looked just as capable of wielding them.

As she crept closer to the gathering, Clare saw that it was
one particular group of women who were the source of the
hackle-raising, ululating cry that had frozen the blood in her
veins. They stood stone still with their arms raised to the sky,
heads back and mouths open, the sound of their frenzied
keening like the very edge of madness.

At the centre of the gathering stood the commanding figure
of Queen Boudicca. Her now-familiar crown of flame-coloured
hair flowed down her back and shoulders like a shimmering
cape, its waves capturing the light of dozens of flaring torches carried by the tall, proud men and women surrounding
her. She stood beside a pile of stacked logs, intended, Clare
thought, for a huge bonfire. Then she saw the body that was
carried through the crowd on a bier and lifted up onto the top
of the pile.

A swollen, sickly-looking moon shone down, casting the
scene in a yellowy-blue pall. Clare gazed at the man who lay
upon the funeral bier and felt her jaw drop open in shock and
dismay. It was none other than the king. Boudicca's husband.
Comorra's father. Clare wondered how he had died.

And then, in the next moment, she wondered whether *she*
might expire in a similar fashion—perhaps on the point of a
sword.

"Do not move," said a voice in the darkness.

Clare turned slightly to see the handsome young warrior
she'd come to know as Connal snarling at her, the blade of

his naked weapon gleaming in the pale moonlight. He jabbed the sword at her, forcing her to step back. Clare's shoulders jammed up against the earth-and-wicker outer wall of a house and she skittered sideways along its curving contour. When she suddenly came to a doorway she tripped over her own feet, tumbled backward through the leather flap that curtained the opening, and landed on a soft, thickly woven rug. Clare gasped and scrambled to her knees, trying to steady herself. By the light of a dozen flickering lamps she could see that the rug beneath her was intricate and colourful, a sophisticated piece of craftsmanship. Blinking up through the tangle of hair that curtained her face, she saw that the one-room roundhouse was elegantly furnished. A pair of low, backless couches faced each other across a central fire pit where the coals of a small, neatly banked fire glowed. On the far side of the room was a raised sleeping platform covered in cushions, a gleaming-white brushed sheepskin rug, and several tasselled woven throws. A pair of windows was set into the curving wall, covered in tacked-down leather curtains, and bunches of dried herbs hung from the rafter, perfuming the air of the hut with delicate, spicy fragrances. All in all, it was cozy and well-kept. Stylish even. A candidate for a feature spread in *Better Huts and Gardens*.

Clare took it all in during the few seconds she had before hot-body Druid-boy had her up off the floor and pinned flat to one of the couches with a sword at her jugular. Again.

"Aren't you going to get tired of doing this every time you see me?" she asked in a hoarse rasp, fear constricting her throat.

"Perhaps I should just kill you and not have to worry about it."

Not exactly the response Clare was looking for. Then again, if he was going to kill her outright he would have done that already. Maybe there was a level of respect—or fear—for whatever he thought she was. If so, she could use it to her advantage.

"That would be an overreaction on your part. An unnecessary one," she said, trying to keep the quaver out of her voice. For good measure, she added the old B-movie standard line, "I come in peace," leaving out the *Take me to your leader* part. Prasutagus wasn't taking appointments anymore, obviously, and she really didn't want to be whisked off to Boudicca just then.

"You come in stealth. Again. During an occasion of grief."

"Last time it was an occasion of celebration, wasn't it?" Clare countered.

"Your kind are drawn to ritual."

"Not really. I've never liked weddings or funerals and I only went to the school formal because I found a killer dress—"

The word "killer" was probably a poor choice, considering. The blade edge pressed harder against her throat and Clare felt a sharp pain followed by a trickle of blood seeping down toward her collarbone. She couldn't control the whimper that escaped her lips.

"Please!" she pleaded, her voice breaking. "I'm not here to hurt anyone! Please let me go ..."

The young man's eyes narrowed and he stared at her intently for a long moment. Then he pushed himself away from the couch to stand before Clare, sword held at the ready should she try something. What that something could possibly be, she had no idea. Clare had never in her whole life felt so entirely helpless. A sword pointed at her in the past, a gun pointed at her in the present ... it was maddening. It was crazy. How had things gotten to this point?

"Why are you here?" said Connal warily.

Clare sat up and pressed her hand to the wound on her throat. She could feel it was shallow—barely more than a scratch—but blood still seeped through her fingers, warm and sticky. "Isn't that something you should ask a guest *before* you attack them?"

"Are you guest, or intruder?"

"I came to find Comorra."

"That is what I was afraid of."

"I'm a friend of hers!" Clare bristled at the flatly hostile expression on Connal's face. She *had* actually come to think of herself as the Iceni princess's friend.

"And so you came to pay your respects to her father, the king, as he lay upon his funeral pyre." The skepticism was heavy in his voice. "Just as the Roman soldiers stand there even now, defiling our ritual, hovering like carrion crows to pick over the carcass."

"I didn't know the king was dead."

"Did you not?"

"No."

Connal eyed her with simmering suspicion. "You are not a spirit of this place."

"How do you know?" Clare bluffed defiantly.

He laughed grimly and shook his head. "You remind me of the Roman girls I have seen in the governor's villa, with their bright, airy garments and glittering beads and sandals. Tell me—did the conquerors bring their own sprites and spirits with them from their cursed land across the sea? Along with their soldiers?"

"What—wait a minute. You think I'm one of the bad guys?"

"I do not know what I think. I only know that I have never seen one of the Fair Folk of *this* land. And I am Druiddyn."

"And I guess that makes you super special," she said bitterly. "I thought you were supposed to be peaceful and smart. The guys with the brains—not the bullies. I guess I was misinformed."

Yet Clare was actually starting to get the impression that, whatever else he might be, Connal wasn't in fact the same kind of bully that, say, Stuart Morholt was. It didn't seem as though he actually wanted to hurt her. Only that he was fiercely protective of his people. Of Comorra. Well ... so was she. So there.

Clare stood—carefully, slowly—and moved past the young Druid to push aside the curtain at the door of the hut. Comorra stood on one side of her mother, weeping silently. On the queen's other side stood Princess Tasca, sobbing unashamedly.

"His name was Prasutagus," Connal said quietly from close behind her.

"I know."

"He was a good man. May his shade find the peace he lost in his life in the Land of the Ever Young. And the honour he once had."

"What do you mean 'once had'? He lost it?"

"You see the men in the shadows under the tall oak?" Connal pointed past her to a group of five Roman officers in what looked like full ceremonial dress, armed to the teeth with weapons. "*They* are the reason that our king is dead."

"Did they kill him?"

Connal hesitated, his face darkening. "We Iceni used to call him our eagle. He was so fierce and golden and we were more than proud to have him as our king. But when the Romans came, bearing eagles of their own so bright that the sun turned them to fire, the king's spirit seemed to weaken. He had seen the other tribes go down to the Roman *spatha* and *gladius*. He had seen the mighty Caradoc of the Catuvellauni tribe to our west turn rebel. And then he saw that rebellion crushed, and Caradoc brought low and taken away across the sea in a ship. In chains. And so, when the time came and the Roman Emperor Claudius set out to tame the Iceni, the king folded his wings and sat upon his perch and let the emperor make of him a pet." Connal's frown deepened. "It broke him, I think. He just seemed to grow small and weak. It was not long before the fever took him ..."

Connal's voice drifted away and Clare turned to see his expression go stony with cold rage. She followed the line of his gaze and saw that the group of Roman officers was approaching Boudicca where she stood by the bier. Across the empty space, the head of the Roman representatives locked eyes with the queen for a long moment. Clare watched the queen's knuckles grow white as she clenched her hand into a fist. Then the Roman spoke. From so far away Clare couldn't hear what he was saying, but she saw Boudicca's shoulders stiffen and the crowd around her shift uneasily.

"What's going on?" Clare asked, her voice almost a whisper.

"I do not know ..."

Suddenly Boudicca turned on her heel and stalked over to where the king lay. The crowd went utterly still as she reached up and, prying the ends open, slipped the great golden torc from off the king's neck. Clare heard the sharp intake of Connal's breath as she did so. Boudicca thrust the golden neck ring high into the air where it gleamed dully in the moon and torchlight. Then she strode toward the Romans and, with exaggerated gestures, offered it to the officer in charge.

"You honour us with your presence on this occasion of joyful sadness," she said in a deep, harsh voice like the call of a crow. Somehow, the way she said "honour" made it sound like an insult. She thrust the torc at him again. "Take this—*paltry* an offering as it may be—as a token of our friendship to your Claudius from Prasutagus's queen, who reigns after him. A gift for Rome on the occasion of my husband's death. From one ruler to another."

Even from that distance, Clare saw the Roman flush beet-red beneath his helmet. The queen continued to hold the king's neck ring out to him, the muscles of her arms taught beneath her pale skin. After a long, exceedingly uncomfortable moment, the Roman took the torc, bowed perfunctorily to the queen and, pivoting on his sandalled heel, led his men down a path that led away from the town, their armour rattling like tin cans as they went.

Connal's expression, when Clare turned to look at him, was exceedingly grim.

"Um. What just happened there?" she asked hesitantly.

"I think Boudicca just started a war."

Clare opened and closed her mouth. She didn't understand what he meant by that, and even if she had, she really didn't know what she would have said—especially when Connal had no way of knowing just how right history would prove his guess to be.

With a look of disgust, Connal gazed down at the sword in his hand and sheathed it in the hanger at his belt. *Well ... that was progress,* Clare thought. At least it seemed he wasn't thinking of killing her outright anymore. She turned back to the door to see Comorra dart forward and place a sheaf of herbs and flowers on the shield covering her father's chest. Then Boudicca took a torch from Llassar and thrust it into the logs. The pitch-soaked wood caught almost instantly and flared, casting a lurid orange illumination over the macabre scene. The flames began to lick at the edges of the dead king's cloak and soon he was engulfed in their fiery embrace.

The whole tribe burst into a frenzy of mourning, the women tearing at their hair and howling, the men beating on their shields and shouting cries of grief at the sky. Boudicca's rigid stance finally seemed to crumple a bit. Her shoulders slumped and her daughters hugged her tightly from either side, as if they knew she might fall if they didn't. The three women stood there, clinging to each other, an island in the middle of the whirling, wailing sea of Iceni.

Clare blinked rapidly as tears of sympathy spilled down her cheeks. The Iceni didn't seem to think it was embarrassing to weep openly. Or even unmanly. Clare saw more than a few big, hairy tough guys sobbing like babies, tears running into their beards. Eventually, the grieving Iceni began to drift away up toward the great hall perched on the top of the hill, where Clare could already hear wildly beautiful, spine-chilling voices raised again in keening song. Finally, the last of the people left the clearing and Boudicca and her daughters stood alone by the funereal bonfire.

Clare let the curtain fall and turned away, her heart aching. She knew how this whole story was going to play out. She knew that what she'd just witnessed was the beginning of the end of the Iceni as a free people. The end of a way of life for the tribe. It made her unexpectedly, ineffably sad.

"You weep," Connal said quietly. She'd almost forgotten he was there.

Clare brushed the back of her hand over her cheeks and sniffed. "Yeah. So what."

He crossed the space between them and put a finger under her chin, lifting her face upward. He wasn't that much taller than she was, but he was so close she had to crane her neck to look into his eyes. He smelled of pine needles and fresh-cut herbs and clean air. Another tear spilled down Clare's cheek as she stared up at him. He caught it on the end of his finger and touched it to the tip of his tongue—as if to make sure the tears were real. "I did not think the Fair Folk wept."

"I guess you thought wrong."

Clare felt her heart start to hammer in her chest. Of course it was in fear, she told herself. It had absolutely nothing to do with the extreme proximity of the tanned and muscled, wildly handsome young man cupping her face in his hand.

He was close enough that even in the dimness she could tell the colour of his eyes—rich, dark brown—and make out the intricate, swirling patterns on the tiny gold earring he wore. Her heart pounded even harder.

Almost as if he'd heard it, Connal touched the pulse point under her jaw. Then his fingertips traced a path down her throat, opposite to where the searing sting of his sword had made her bleed, and he flattened his palm against her skin just above the neckline of her summer dress. She waited, breathless, as he cocked his head, listening to and feeling the pounding of her heart.

"Your heart beats as mine does. Your blood flows beneath your skin. And yet you are not of this world."

"Not ... exactly," Clare whispered, her mouth gone sand-paper dry.

"But you are very beautiful." Connal moved his hand up to her hair, running his fingers through the golden-brown waves. He closed his eyes and took a deep breath. "You smell like flowers," he said.

I smell like Pantene Pro-V Extra Volume, Clare thought faintly. But she didn't think that would translate into Iceni.

Outside, in the distance, she could hear Prasutagus's funeral pyre begin to crackle loudly.

"Connal ... that's your name, isn't it?" Clare needed to break the tension of the moment somehow. She just might snap if she didn't find a way to make him back off a step or two. Saying his name out loud seemed to do it.

"How ..." he almost asked the question. But of course Clare was a creature of magic and mystery for him, and so why shouldn't she know his name? She didn't tell him that it had been plain old eavesdropping. He bowed his head a little. "Aye. That is what I am called." Then his eyes flicked back up to her face and a small smile tugged at one corner of his mouth. "May I be so bold as to ask what I should call you? Perhaps if we became better acquainted—if I knew your name—I would be less inclined to thrust a sword at you the next time we meet."

Uh ... Clare blinked. *Is he* flirting *with me?*

Not that it mattered—whether he was or not, Clare already felt herself answering his smile with a shy one of her own. "I'd like that," she said. "My name is Clare. Clarinet, really."

Dude, said a small, disgusted voice in the back of her mind. *Telling him your full name? I don't even know you.* She silently told the voice to shut up. Even though she might have secretly agreed with it. She certainly didn't recognize herself as she stood there making small talk with a guy dressed in buckskin who'd just drawn a sword on her for the second time. But then, Clare wasn't used to a lot of what had happened to her in the last few days. And Connal was absolutely magnetic. Probably why she couldn't seem to move away from him ...

But when he reached a hand out to touch the floaty material that gathered in a ruffle down the front of her dress *(in curiosity, sure, but still—hands!)* Clare shook herself out of her trancelike state and spun around, intending to walk briskly toward the door. She needed space. She needed air.

Connal put a hand on her shoulder and she froze in her tracks. It wasn't his grip that stopped her—it was gentle—it was the mere fact of his touch. "Come by the fire, Clarinet. Please."

No. No no ... Fire was not air. Fire was farther from the door. Farther from the air Clare so desperately needed.

"Please," he said again, leading her unprotestingly—*why* wasn't she protesting?—back toward the couch by the little sunken fire pit. "I have been terribly inhospitable and I have hurt you. Let me make amends. I do not want the Fair Folk angry with me. I do not want *you* angry."

"I'm ... I'm not ..." Clare murmured. She wasn't what? Angry? Well ... maybe not anymore. When he'd first attacked her, sure. But that was pretty understandable. And really, for a first-century barbarian in a savage, untamed land, Connal was being pretty civilized at the moment. She watched as he stoked the fire back to life and swung a small cauldron on a metal arm over the flames. Then he crushed a handful of herbs from the bunched sheaves hanging from the rafters into a shallow bronze bowl. He fetched a clean scrap of cloth from a basket, tore it in two, and pressed a strip of it to the cut on her neck. It came away stained bright red and Clare felt a little queasy at the sight. Connal folded the scrap of linen carefully and set it aside. Then he poured warm water from the cauldron over the herbs in the bowl and soaked the other piece of cloth in the infusion. A soothing, medicinal fragrance filled the little room.

Clare realized that her eyes were closed when she felt the heat from the wet cloth seeping into her skin and heard Connal murmuring words in a sing-song chant under his breath. She caught the gist that they were an incantation of sorts—a healing spell of some kind—and it reminded her that she was sitting in front of a Druid. A magician. A sorcerer. It made her curious.

"How did you know?" she asked as his hands moved deftly along her skin. "In the grove that night—Comorra's celebration—how did you know I was there?" She opened her eyes and found him staring at her intently, as though he was trying to read a sign written in a foreign language. "I thought Comorra was the only one who could see me."

Connal dropped his gaze and shrugged, frowning faintly. "I do not know. I am Druiddyn and we are trained to be sensitive to the spirit world. I just … felt your presence. As if there was someone standing in a crowd—someone I knew—who was staring at me."

Clare felt a shiver run up her spine. *Freaking Druids …*

"I've only ever felt that sensation once before," Connal mused quietly. He shook his head and smiled at her. "Never mind. There. The bleeding has stopped."

Clare knew what other time he was talking about—the night in the forge when Llassar had finished making Comorra's brooch. She remembered Llassar maybe sensing her, too—but not in the way Connal had. She decided not to mention it. She didn't want Connal to think she spent all her time lurking around unseen in the Iceni village.

Connal reached for a small jar of something pungent and dabbed it on her neck. "This," he said, "will help it heal without scarring."

"Oh ..." Clare hadn't thought of that. How was she going to explain this to Maggie? That she'd cut herself shaving?

Connal laughed at her expression. "Unless you *want* a scar."

"I really don't." She laughed a little too. Explaining a mark on her neck would be the least of her worries when she got back. If she got back. She'd been gone for a long time, it seemed ...

Her gaze drifted to the small metal bowl in Connal's hands. It was decorated with the same sort of swirling patterns that Clare recognized from the shield, the torc, and Comorra's brooch. He handled it carefully, she noticed. As if it were special. Powerful. Her neck barely felt sore at all anymore. Almost like magic.

"That's pretty," she said, pointing to the bowl.

"Thank you." Connal inclined his head. "I made it."

"Oh!" Clare was surprised at that. "You mean you're a metal guy, too? Like Llassar?"

Connal's gaze snapped up to her face. "You know the master smith?"

"Uh ... I know *of* him." She should really watch just how much she said.

"I'm not surprised that word of his talent has reached even to the lands of the tylwyth teg. He is among the most talented of the Druiddyn artisans ever to have lived," Connal said reverently. "His skills at melding magic and metal are legendary. He was sent here by our order to serve Boudicca. Just as I was. We are both bound to her in loyalty and service for as long as the queen lives."

"You're not from around here?" *Me neither,* she thought silently.

"I was born a prince among my own tribe, the Dyfnient, in the mountains far to the west of here. A beautiful place, shrouded in mist and secrets."

He must mean Wales, Clare thought. Her aunt had always described it as being something out of a storybook.

"May the sword and flame of Rome leave their lands forever untouched."

"Why did you leave?"

"I showed an aptitude. With both metal and magic. So the Druid of my tribe sent me here. To learn from two masters. Llassar taught me how to shape metal and Boudicca taught me how to use it. And they both taught me how to use magic. How to call down the gifts of the goddess Andrasta."

Boudicca? A Druid? A sorceress in her own right? Al had left that part out of the history lesson.

"I thought all Druids did was gather mistletoe and sing poetry and make potions. I didn't know they ever really got their hands dirty."

Connal laughed curtly. "Oh ... we are quite capable of, as you say, getting our hands dirty. And bloody, if need be."

He reached out a hand—a very gentle hand—to brush the hair away from her shoulders.

"Although I prefer to keep my hands clean," he said as he ran his fingertips down her arms and lifted her hands toward his face. He turned them over in his own, running the pad of his thumb lightly over the lines of her palms as if divining her future. "Like yours. So clean and smooth ..."

Clare held her breath as he raised her hand and pressed it to his cheek, which was rough with stubble. His nostrils flared and she wondered if he could smell the perfume she'd put on that morning. She wondered if he liked it, if he could ...

"You have no calluses. Your hands have never held a sword, Shining One," he murmured as he turned his head, almost as if he would plant a kiss on her wrist. "Are you not warriors in your world?"

Suddenly the leather flap curtaining Connal's door was pushed aside and Clare felt her heart leap into her throat. Connal was startled too, but they both relaxed in the next moment as Comorra ducked through the door. The princess pulled up short in surprise at finding the young Druid with such an unexpected house guest. In such close proximity. Comorra's eyes were bright with weeping and they flicked back and forth between Connal, who still held Clare by the wrist, and Clare.

"Comorra!" Connal rose swiftly and held out a hand for her, drawing her over by the brazier and sitting her down on one of the low stools. "Come. Sit down. I think you know my guest?"

The princess nodded at him, her eyes never leaving Clare's face. "I missed you at my father's farewell, Connal ..."

"It's my fault," Clare said. "I wanted to visit you again, Comorra. I had no idea it was such ... bad timing. I sort of accidentally surprised your Druid friend here and we had a bit of a ... misunderstanding." She gestured at her bandage. "But it's all cleared up now."

Comorra's gaze flicked to Clare's neck wound and then over to Connal, who'd gone to fetch a small earthen jug and mugs. The tense set of her shoulders relaxed a bit.

"I'm really sorry about your father."

The princess ducked her head and nodded silent thanks as Connal poured out some kind of thick, foamy drink into the cups. He gave one to the princess and held one out for Clare. But as she reached out to take it, inside her head she heard a cry so sharp it caused her actual pain.

"Milo!" Al's voice cut through her mind.

Simultaneously, she heard the cry of a raven outside the window.

"Damn!" Clare exclaimed as the cup dropped through the space where her hand had been only a moment before, spilling its contents on Connal's rug. "Sorry ..." Her apology faded into the darkness as, right before the astonished eyes of Comorra and Connal, she shimmered out of existence.

13

"**M**ilo!" the raven's voice echoed, harsh and angry in her ears.

No ... that's Al's voice.

Clare's head spun dizzily.

When the disorientation seeped away and she opened her eyes, Clare was cautiously pleased to find that—in *her* world—the sun still shone through the wall of tinted windows, the sky was still blue, and London was still there. Apparently she had managed yet another successful shimmer into the past and back again. All without altering the timeline. At least, not appreciably. Everything seemed normal and exactly as she had left it.

Well ... not exactly everything.

For one thing, there was a large scorch mark on the carpet where the laptop had had a meltdown. The smell of burning synthetic fibres hung in the air and a sputtering fire extinguisher lay on its side on the floor. Clare would have to remember to be careful around electronics when shimmering in the future, she thought in the seconds before she realized the other thing that was different.

Milo was lying face down on the floor, with Al and Stuart Morholt facing off over his unmoving form. For a brief moment Clare started to panic, thinking Milo was dead—that

Morholt had shot him—all while she'd been busy heavy-breathing over someone else in the far-distant past. But then she saw that his chest was definitely rising up and down as he drew breath and she went weak-kneed with relief. And guilt. Not that she thought—in any reality, or any timeline, no matter how far-fetched—that she had any kind of shot with Milo. Still ...

Clare turned to Al, who stood rigid, hands balled into fists, glowering at Morholt. "Did Milo pull teenage 'girl power' bravado crap after I left?" Clare asked.

"Yeah," Al said sourly. "He did. And then Ninja Assassin here karate-chopped him."

"It was judo." Morholt rolled his eyes. "And I'm not about to apologize for taking corrective behaviour against an impulsive young fool. There's a time and place for gallantry. That was neither."

"You sonofa—"

"Language, Miss Reid." Morholt tutted. "He'll live. Let's see if you two can manage the same feat." He glanced at the smouldering laptop and his lip twitched. "Interesting. It seems your ability throws a mean electrical charge upon activation. I dare say you'd short-circuit just about anything you came into contact with that had a live current running through it. You're a veritable walking thundercloud, my dear." He smiled at his little joke. "Something to keep in mind for our future jaunts, eh?"

"What exactly do you mean by 'our future jaunts'?"

"In good time. Now. Let's have some answers. Where did you go and what did you see?"

Clare felt her jaw clenching. She didn't want to tell him. Sharing the intimate details of Comorra's father's funeral with someone like Stuart Morholt ... well, it just seemed like a further betrayal of the princess. And her grieving mother,

Boudicca. *I could lie,* Clare thought. *Make up the details. Fudge the truth ...*

But Morholt's eyes narrowed at her as Clare hesitated, and she knew that, with his knowledge of the ancient Celtic world, he would probably see through any lame-ass story she could make up.

"What did you *see*?" he asked again, less gently this time.

Clare took a deep breath and told him everything.

WELL ... SHE MAY HAVE left out a few of the less important details about a certain flirting Druid. Still, once Clare got into the telling of the tale, even Al seemed to forget her righteous indignation and listened, rapt.

"There's one thing I don't understand—why did she give the Romans Prasutagus's torc?" Al wondered when Clare had finished. "And why did your Druid pal say she'd started a war by doing that?"

"It was an insult," Morholt murmured, half to himself.

Al raised an eyebrow. "A big, shiny, gold insult?"

"On such an occasion," he explained, "it should have been the Romans bringing Boudicca gifts. By giving *them* one instead, she was pointedly drawing attention to that breach of etiquette and respect. And by making it a gift of such richness, of such significance, she was adding insult to injury. In the eyes of the Iceni, Rome and their emperor would have lost face—hugely—because of it. And even though it may not have been the Roman custom, that officer surely would have understood Boudicca's intentions in the context of Celtic tribal traditions. He would have been perfectly well aware that she was flouting Rome's authority and sending a message that she, as queen, would not be as biddable as her husband before her."

Clare shook her head in admiration. "Wow. That was pretty ... um ..."

"Ballsy?" Morholt said dryly. "We are talking about Boudicca here."

"Yeah. I guess that was the word I was looking for." She sat down on the edge of the desk, feeling suddenly exhausted from everything she'd been through in the last few hours. "Are we done here? You got your in-depth report about what life was like back in the day. Can't you just leave us alone now?"

"No ..." Morholt's expression had started out thoughtful. Now it looked as if he was hatching a nefarious plan. Clare felt her stomach clench in apprehension. "No," he said again, "I don't think I'll be doing that."

"What?"

"I shall require your services, Miss Reid."

"What?" Clare gaped at him. "After all that? Look—you know now that I don't have some kind of power of invisibility, so you know I'm no use to you."

"We shall see about that. Let's go." He motioned Clare toward the elevator.

"I can't go anywhere," she said. "Because whatever it is you want from me, I can't shimmer without Al."

"Oh please. Do you think me a fool?"

"You don't want to know what I think of you," Clare muttered sourly. "Believe me or not, I don't care. Irregardless, I can't do my little magic trick without her."

"'Irregardless' isn't a word, you ridiculous girl."

Clare just glared at him.

"Fine," Morholt sighed. "Then I guess you're both coming for a little ride."

Shit. That wasn't what Clare was hoping for. She was hoping that she could stall him and keep him at Milo's office long enough for Milo to regain consciousness. Three against one and they might have had a chance.

"What about Milo?" she said desperately. "I ... uh ... I need him, too!"

Morholt snorted. "Your lying skills need almost as much work as your vocabulary. I'm willing to hedge my bets with your little sidekick, but I'm afraid Prince Valiant stays here." He walked over to a desk and picked up a packing tape dispenser, tossing it to Al. "Wrists behind his back," he commanded, gesturing to the unconscious Milo. "Bind his ankles, and a piece over his mouth for good measure, please."

Al did as she was told—she was smart enough to know that they were pretty short on options to the contrary. When she was done, Morholt gave the binding job a cursory glance and rolled an eye at Al.

"A predictably shoddy job. Don't worry. I didn't expect cellotape to hold him for long. Just enough for the three of us to get reasonably long gone." Morholt scribbled with a Sharpie on a piece of letterhead. Clare read the words as he wrote them:

You're smart enough to know that calling the authorities would be a very, very bad idea. The well-being of your lady friends depends on your good behaviour. So behave.

Cheers, S. M.

"Long gone?" Clare asked as Morholt tucked the note in the collar of Milo's T-shirt where he'd be sure to find it on waking. "Long gone *where*?"

"You're both coming for a little ride." He pointed to Comorra's brooch where it lay on the desk. "Wrap that up and bring it along," he ordered Al. "And let's not dawdle."

Clare and Al hesitated, the seriousness of the situation sinking heavily upon them. They were being kidnapped. At gunpoint. Clare swallowed and felt herself grow pale.

"Oh, go on," snarled their abductor. "I'm not going to shoot you. *Yet.* But please don't think for a moment, ladies, that I will put up with any further crap from either of you. The car is in the garage. Now, mush, you two."

Al wrapped the raven-shaped pin back up in its sock and stuffed it in the side pocket of the messenger bag she carried. Then she fell into step beside Clare as Stuart Morholt marched them toward the elevator, down to the deserted parking level, and over to a sleek, silvery-grey car.

"Wow," Al said. "Choice ride, Evil-doer."

"A limited-edition Bentley Mulsanne. And yes. It *is* rather choice."

Morholt pressed the button on a key fob as they approached and the engine started up remotely with a sonorous growl. The car was elegantly muscular, with a distinctive snub-nose front grille and long, sweeping lines along the body. It sported gleaming chrome detailing, ominously tinted windows, and—the girls soon discovered—a roomy trunk, good for hauling antique furniture, stolen artifacts, or two kidnapped teenagers.

"WAS I SEEING THINGS back there, or was that a cut on your neck?"

"It was. Has it stopped bleeding?"

"Looked like it." Al wriggled around in the dark confines of the trunk, elbowing Clare in the head as she shifted and squirmed. "What happened?"

"I got a little too close to my friendly neighbourhood Druid," Clare said, gingerly touching the side of her neck. *Way* too *close, actually.* She felt herself blushing at the memory and thought she could actually feel Al's stare intensify. "Anyway. Not really the issue at the moment. How are we going to get out of our present predicament?"

"We could start banging really loudly on the trunk lid," Al suggested.

Except that Morholt suddenly began blasting rap music at an insane volume—no doubt to mask any attempts the girls might make at attracting the attentions of passersby. Besides, they could tell that he was driving fast enough that no one would have time to notice. He'd probably planned a route with the least traffic stops just in case. Seemed like the type. The fact that he hadn't duct-taped them or tied them up meant that he was pretty sure there was no way they could escape. However, that didn't stop Al from blindly exploring every inch of the inside of the sedan's generous trunk.

"Tire iron," she muttered, "bolted down ..."

Clare shifted her butt as Al's hands patted around.

"Emergency road kit ... okay, some of this could be useful ..."

She could hear Al rummaging through the kit, but she couldn't imagine what it could possibly contain that would prove useful. A tire gauge and socket-wrench set still weren't going to make them a match for Morholt's firearm. But it seemed to provide a nice distraction that kept Al from freaking out. Clare wished she felt the same.

"Nice bluff back there, telling Morholt you needed me to help you shimmer." Al pitched her voice over the thrumming bass coming through the car speakers.

Clare shrugged as much as the close confines would allow. "Wasn't."

"Er." Al stopped rummaging. "What?"

"Well ..." Clare shifted around so that she was facing Al, even though she couldn't see her in the darkness. "I don't so much need you to *go* as to *get back*. I think. That's my, you know, working hypothesis. Maybe."

"Okaaay." Al sounded skeptical, but willing to explore the possibility. "What makes you think that?"

"Did you shout out Milo's name just before I shimmered back last time?"

"Um, I think so." Al paused, remembering. "Yeah. Right after Mr. Ninja took him out. Just a natural reaction, I suppose ... Why?"

"Because I *heard* you. Only you sounded like a bird."

"You're kidding."

"If I could glare at you sardonically right now, I would," Clare said dryly. "That is not something I would likely make up, is it?"

"Good point."

"And I've started to realize ... there's *always* a bird. A raven. It's what brings me back. I think it's you. Your, um, spirit? Or something. You're like my anchor to the present, I think."

"Wow. A raven, huh?"

"Yeah."

"Quoth me—'Nevermore.'"

The girls both laughed a little. It sapped some of the tension out of the situation and for that Clare was grateful. Al really was the best kind of friend.

"Hey Clare ... remember what you told me Llassar said about 'blood magic'? And how you'd pricked your finger on the brooch?"

"I thought about that maybe having something to do with it. But it's not like we're related, Al."

"No, I know. But remember when we did that stupid 'blood sisters' thing when we were kids?"

"Yeah." Clare snorted. "I remember. My mom almost killed us and our thumbs nearly fell off."

Al laughed again. "Yeah. It was dumb. But maybe that single drop of blood meant something more than either of us realized at the time."

Clare thought about that for a moment. It *had* only been a single drop of blood that had fallen onto Comorra's brooch, too ... "You really think so?"

"I don't know. It's just a theory. But whatever happens, I guess I just wanted you to know that it's always kind of meant a lot to *me*, anyway. I'm not sure I'd cope very well without you around."

"I feel the same way, pal."

"Okay. Just remember that when you're shimmer-tripping, okay?"

"I promise. Just remember to keep bringing me back."

"I will. And then, if we get out of this mess—"

"We *will* get out of this mess. I promise you that, too. Stuart Morholt has no idea what he's gotten himself into."

THE BENTLEY FINALLY rolled to a stop and the *thump-thump-thump* of the stereo speakers fell silent. Footsteps, then the opening of the trunk and a shaft of blinding late-afternoon sunshine as Al and Clare blinked up at Stuart Morholt and his gun. He motioned them out and the girls unfolded themselves, clambering stiffly onto the cracked cement floor of a dilapidated, saggy-roofed warehouse that slouched on the banks of the Thames. They could see the river and a seedy stretch of industrial neighbourhood through the gaping shipping doors at the far end. The building itself looked as though it had been abandoned sometime before the Beatles hit it big. It was empty except for a series of sturdily built plywood-walled container rooms with slide-bar locks on the outside and bare-bulb light fixtures that cast ghastly yellowish shadows. The place smelled of diesel and machine oil and the rotting-vegetation funk of overgrown river weed.

Morholt led them deeper into the warehouse. When he reached the last locker he stopped and pointed the barrel of the PPK at Al's messenger bag that held her super-sleek laptop. "Leave that," he said curtly. He'd already confiscated their cell phones when he'd locked them in the trunk of the car.

Al reluctantly unslung the strap from across her body and lowered the bag gently to the cement floor. Clare knew it was killing her to do it. Al was never more than five feet from her computer at any time. Even when she slept.

Morholt pointed at the locker. "Get in. I've got an errand to run. Contemplate your futures while I'm gone. Scream your heads off all you want. There's no one in a ten-mile radius to hear. Cheerio."

With a nasty grin, he shut the door and the girls heard the slide-bar lock slamming home against its fittings with a bang like a judge's gavel falling, sentencing them to doom. They shivered together at the sound of Morholt's expensive Italian loafers striding back the way they came, the jungle-cat purr of the Bentley starting up, the slam of the car door as Morholt got in ... and then the car fading into the distance as the modern-day Druid drove off.

THE GIRLS HAD been quiet for almost half an hour, listening for any sound that Morholt had come back. For the last few minutes Al had been crouched down on all fours, peering through the crack under the door of their little prison cell. Finally she sat back and turned to Clare.

"Friendship with you is not dull." Al smiled wanly. "Have I ever mentioned that?"

"Sorry."

"Never mind." Al stood up and undid the clasp of her belt. "I think I might have figured a way to get us out of here." She held up the belt—it was made of plain black leather and it fastened by hooking a single claw on the back through one of the holes in the leather. The buckle was a silver disk with an X-Men insignia on it. She'd bought it at a comic book convention.

"You're going to call the X-Men to come rescue us? I hope it's one of the cute ones and not the big fuzzy blue guy ..."

"We don't need mutants to save us."

"We don't?"

"Not with your wicked-ass magic and my mad super-spy skills, we don't." Al grinned and dropped down on all fours again. The gap between the bottom of the door and the floor was about an inch—plenty of room to slide the belt under. Al began the tricky job of manoeuvring the hook of her belt so that she could snag the strap of her messenger bag and gently—oh, so gently—drag it over closer to the locker. She sweated and swore for what seemed an eternity until she could just reach and grab the strap of the bag with her finger-tips. "Excelsior!" she muttered as she dragged the bag right up to the outside of the door and rolled over onto her back, panting with the effort.

"Al? Even if you could get your computer out of the bag, I don't think it'll fit under the door—"

"Don't need the computer," Al grunted as she rolled back onto her stomach. After a bit more swearing and scrabbling she shimmied back away from the door and held up Clare's pompom sock triumphantly.

Clare was unaccountably relieved to see the cloak pin again. "But how would—"

"Look," Al explained. "When you touch the brooch, you go ... but the brooch stays here. When you come back, you come back to where the brooch is. The test of my working theory is this: you touch the brooch, you zot—"

"Shimmer."

"Shimmer. After you're gone, I slide the brooch under the door, you un-zot—"

"Un-shimmer."

"Un-shimmer *outside* the storage container. Get it?"

Clare felt a grin spreading across her face. "This officially makes you the best sidekick ever. You know that, right?"

"Okay ... see, how come *I'm* the sidekick? I'm the one with the plan!"

"Yeah, but I'm the one with the superpowers."

"Good point."

Clare suddenly grew serious. "Al ... what if something happens to you while I'm gone?"

Al shook her head. "It won't. But, y'know—don't *dawdle*." She shook the brooch into her palm and held it out. "After you *shimmer*, count to one hundred. Meanwhile, I'll get the brooch outside the container. Then we both concentrate hard on bringing you back." Al paused. "Worth a shot?"

"Hand it over." Clare glanced around, making sure she wasn't near anything electrical this time. "Here goes nothing ..."

14

Clare hadn't planned on materializing in a sunlit, frost-crisp meadow directly in the path of a galloping horse kicking up clouds of sparkling ice-fog as it thundered directly toward her. The creature loomed huge in her field of vision, the size of a tank and just as terrifying. As the ground beneath her shuddered Clare screamed and threw her arms up in front of her face. The horse's piercing whinny shattered the cold air and it reared back, pawing at the air and almost taking Clare's head off.

"Whoa!" the rider shouted, sawing on the reins. "Whoa, Meryn!"

Clare risked a glance between her upraised arms as the rider pushed back a hooded cowl and a cloud of strawberry-gold hair tumbled out around her shoulders.

"Clare!" Comorra exclaimed. "Hush, Meryn ..." She leaned forward to pat his steaming neck, trying to calm him down. Clare saw now that the horse was barely more than a sturdy pony, not the thundering juggernaut she'd imagined. Meryn danced nervously and snorted, clouds of vapour pouring from his nostrils. Comorra backed him up and turned him side-ways so that she could look down at Clare—who stood there in her sundress and sandals, feeling exposed and silly and chilled to the bone.

"Hi," she said, trying to sound casual. And as though she'd meant to materialize in front of the princess's horse like that. "Long time no see. Or maybe not. I'm never sure ..."

"Shining One," Comorra said as she swung her leg over her mount's back and slid to the ground. She looked at Clare closely and tilted her head. "You are shivering!"

With nimble fingers Comorra undid the raven brooch that held her woollen mantle and swept the cloak around Clare. As it settled warmly on her bare shoulders, Clare couldn't help sighing with relief. The cold had been something of a shock after her shimmering and its usual fiery sensations. At least it was daylight out for once.

"Do you not have early frosts in the Otherworld?" the princess asked her wryly.

Clare smiled. "I know I'm not exactly dressed for the weather. I never really know what to expect when I come here." She thought of the last trip—and the handsome young Druid who'd been there to 'welcome' her with a sword in his hand. "Or who ..."

"Did you mean to find Connal instead of me?" Comorra's voice, musical and low, said one thing while Clare heard another. She was getting used to that phenomenon, but was beginning to wonder if she could get used to Comorra herself. The princess was remarkably straightforward. Blunt even. "You desire him," she said. "Don't you?"

"Ex*cuse* me?" Clare squawked. "Where on earth did you get *that* idea from?"

"In his house, the night of my father's farewell. I saw the way you looked at him."

"What—wide-eyed with terror?"

"He made you blush."

"He makes *you* blush, too, Princess."

Comorra blinked at Clare, her expression carefully neutral.

"Oh, come on! He's not exactly hard on the eyes, you know. I have a feeling he has that effect on most girls with a pulse."

Comorra allowed herself to return Clare's grin and shrugged a bit shyly. "I used to think Tasca would have him. But ... I do not think he feels that way about her and ... I have dreams now of my own." She tilted her head at Clare in an almost birdlike fashion. "Do you know that *you* are sometimes in my dreams, Clare?"

"I am?"

"In them, we meet on the bank of the Great River. There is smoke and screaming and Connal and my mother are there with chariots. And my sister ... is dead." Her gaze went cloudy at the memory of the dream. A dream that Clare knew was certain to become a reality. "Were you really sent to me by Andrasta? Are you my protector?"

"Uh ..."

Comorra's blue eyes squeezed shut as the memory of the dream images washed over her. "Tasca will not die. It is only a dream, is it not?"

"I ..." Clare absolutely did not know what to say. Her heart went out to the girl. And she shrank from the knowledge that what Comorra had glimpsed was, in fact, a scene from her future. A wave of guilt washed over her at the thought. Comorra's premonitory dreams were—she instinctively knew—*her* fault. The girl had seen something she'd not been meant to see and it had been because of *her.*

"Clare?" Comorra repeated, her voice melodic, the cadences almost haunting. Her pale blue gaze washed over Clare like a searchlight, self-possessed, wise beyond her years. "In my dream, Shining One, a Roman finds me. And takes me. But before he does so—I always give you *this.*" She held out the brooch that had fastened her cloak closed around her neck.

Clare stared down at the bronze raven. It seemed to stare right back at her.

"I put it in the pocket of your breeches," Comorra said. "Just before everything goes dark."

Clare felt her eyes go wide. *So that's how it got there!* she thought. *I was right. I'm not a klepto after all—yay, me!*

"I know it is only a dream," Comorra continued, "but this brooch is yours, now—truly—if only you will beg Andrasta on my behalf to keep my sister safe."

Clare groaned inwardly. She didn't need to hear Al and Milo lecturing her about the dangers of monkeying around with the time stream to know that she couldn't accept Comorra's gift. Offering. Whatever. Because if she *did* there'd be no way for Comorra to give it to her in the future. Which of course, for Clare, was the past. But if she was in the past now, did that mean it was in her future as well? Her brain started to knot in the way it always did when she contemplated the matter. If she took the brooch, would it mean she'd be stuck in the past with no way to get home? She wasn't willing to risk that chance.

The eye on the pin seemed to wink at her.

Clare's mind raced. How could she get Comorra to keep the brooch without offending her or telling her what would happen in her future—an admission that would surely have other, equally dire consequences?

"Uh ..." She stopped and tried to imagine what Al might say. "That brooch was made for you, Comorra, um, Daughter of Boudicca." It was harder than she thought. Then she remembered the words exchanged by Connal and the smith. "The fire spoke its shape to Llassar. It is the gift of Andrasta. It is ... oh, hell. Look. Why don't you just hang on to it? I think that's probably what would make Andrasta the happiest. Y'know?"

Comorra glanced down at the brooch and back up at Clare. Then she smiled a little. "Thank you, Shining One."

"Please. It's really just 'Clare.'"

"I have always heard that the Fair Folk were hard, tricksy bargainers. But you are kind. And, in truth, I do not wish to part with it. It has been my favourite thing ever since Connal first pinned it to my cloak at my Warrior Making."

"That wouldn't have anything to do with Connal now, would it?" Clare grinned. "There—see? Now you're blushing!"

Comorra ducked her head, but she was smiling now and the haunted look had left her eyes.

"You know ..." Clare said, reaching up to scratch behind Meryn's ear as the pony nuzzled at her shoulder. "Before I met Connal, I always thought Druids were just a bunch of grumpy old men."

"Don't let my mother hear you say that!" Comorra laughed. "She is Druiddyn, too! But I will grant you that, in some tribes, they are. Perhaps the Iceni are just very lucky."

Clare wished that were the case, that she could tell Comorra about what was in store for her people. She wished she could tell her to just pack up and head for the hills. "Luck" wasn't in the cards for them. Clare thought it might be a good idea to try to change the subject, but just then another rider appeared at the far side of the meadow.

"That is Macon," Comorra said, shading her eyes. "One of my mother's chieftains."

Clare hoped desperately that she'd remain invisible to him—for surely Comorra couldn't readily explain her presence there. But as he approached there was nothing to indicate that he'd noticed anything out of the ordinary.

She ducked behind Meryn's flank. "I'm not here, okay?" she said to Comorra. "Remember how I told you that my magic hides me from the sight of most mortals? I'd like to keep my presence here quiet if that's all right with you."

"Of course." Comorra vaulted onto Meryn's back and smiled down at Clare. The princess seemed delighted at the idea of an invisible companion. "Our secret. I promise. I would never betray a friend." She turned back toward the approaching rider, her grin faltering as she read the expression on his face.

"Macon," she greeted him as he slowed his horse to a walk. "You look to be the bearer of unhappy news."

The man pulled his horse to a stop and inclined his head in a gesture of respect. Despite the chill his cloak was thrown back over his shoulders, and Clare saw the designs of an intricate tattoo circling the bulging muscle of his upper arm. She knew a couple of guys back home at school who fancied themselves rock stars and would've killed for wicked ink like that.

"Princess," Macon said. "Your mother has been called to Londinium. She's being feasted at the Roman governor's *mansio*. The invitation has been extended to you and your sister as well. I'm to gather an honour guard of chieftains and we are to make ready to depart in the morning."

Comorra nodded and shifted her horse a little in front of Clare, as if to hide her from Macon's sight. Not that she needed to—his roaming gaze had passed right over Clare without seeing so much as her shadow in the frost-whitened grass.

"And who, exactly, is it that wishes to entertain Queen Boudicca in Londinium?" Comorra asked. "I have heard that the governor himself has gone to stamp out the flames of rebellion among the western tribes."

"He has." Macon nodded, chewing on the corner of his moustache. "The Legions have gone west again in an attempt to impress upon the tribes just how much better off they would be toiling under the gilded sandals of the imperator than they are now, living as free men. And yes, Seutonius Paulinus will be riding at the head of that column."

"Then who—"

"The Emperor Nero's envoy, Seneca, lodges in the governor's *mansio* in Londinium these days."

"Seneca?" Comorra frowned. "The moneylender?"

"Aye." Macon's tones were shaded with disgust. "The same. That man is a menace—one of Nero's slick-tongued bottom-feeders, with his hands in the imperial purse."

"I have heard mother say that he makes her almost long for the days of the old emperor, Claudius," Comorra said. "What does he want with us?"

"Only a friendly supper, according to the invitation," Macon snorted. "Which was, in reality, more of a summons. He's here under the emperor's orders to ensure that proper tribute will continue to flow now that Prasutagus is gone. But I've a nasty suspicion that he'll do more than that."

"Mother will know how to handle the Roman," Comorra said firmly, chin lifted.

"Aye, sweeting." Macon smiled down at her with genuine affection. And, Clare thought, a hint of sadness. "Your mother knows a great many things. But with your father half a year dead now, the carrion crows are gathering at the edges of our land. Boudicca will have a fight on her hands before too long if she's not careful. I have the uneasy feeling that Seneca's here not only to safeguard tribute, but to call in the king's old debts. And I've no doubt there'll be rather more interest lumped on top of them than there should be by rights."

"What will happen to us?"

"If Boudicca doesn't pay, Rome may decide to find her in default. And then they will come with their soldiers and simply take what they want to call the debts even." Macon's eyes clouded with anxiety and his mount, sensing its rider's mood, shifted nervously and whickered. "It was a dangerous road your father put us upon when he politicked with the race of men who perfected the art of double-dealing."

Clare had forgotten the cold as she listened to talk of things that were far beyond her frame of reference. And Comorra seemed to have forgotten Clare as she mulled over Macon's news.

"I must go and find Tasca," Comorra finally said. "We will have to dress with care on the morrow ..."

"Aye," Macon agreed grimly. "Don't forget to wear your swords." Then he wheeled his mount around and galloped back across the meadow, the horse's hooves kicking up sparkling puffs of ice crystals.

Clare realized with a start that she'd been fascinated by the talk of political intrigue—the very thing that had made her eyes glaze over in school. She also found it interesting—and somehow deeply gratifying—that Macon had spoken to Comorra not as a child or as a girl, but as an equal. She couldn't imagine most of the adults in *her* world speaking like that to her ...

And, more than anything, she was proud of the fact that she'd actually understood what they were talking about. Al's crash course in Iceni–Roman relations had really paid off—

Al! she suddenly remembered.

Okay, thought Clare, *I should go now. Now would definitely be a good time to go ...*

Comorra turned and held out a hand to Clare. "I must leave now, my friend."

"Oh. Yeah. Me too, actually ..." Clare scanned the skies distractedly, hoping for a glimpse of dark-feathered wings. Nothing. Had she heard the call of a raven earlier and ignored it? Was Al in trouble? How long *had* she been gone? "Wait!" she said as Comorra took up the reins. "Your cloak."

"Keep it, Clare." Comorra smiled down at her. "You need it more than I do."

"Not where I'm going," she said, handing it up. "I hope."

Comorra tilted her head quizzically but reached out her hands for the cloak. "Go gently then, and return again in friendship, Shining One." With that, she put her heels to Meryn, who broke into a swift trot and headed back toward where Clare could see a slow, lazy spiral of cooking smoke from the village spiralling up into the pale blue sky. Clare watched Comorra go and then turned in a full circle, rubbing her bare arms for warmth, scouring the skies for her raven. When a shadow in a stand of oaks at the edge of the meadow finally caught her eye, she hobbled over toward the trees, trying her best not to break an ankle on the uneven ground. In her strappy sandals, Clare's feet were almost numb with cold.

The raven sat hunched and quiet on a low-hanging branch. It rolled a grey eye at Clare as she stood beneath the tree looking up at it. It looked ... grumpy.

"Al?" Clare said, feeling slightly ridiculous.

The raven ruffled its feathers in irritation and opened its beak. *"Skreeee ..."* it croaked.

"Oh, come on. I'm sorry. I got a little distracted. Call me home, will you?"

The raven launched itself off its perch, circled once in the air, and uttered a harsh, imperative call. With great relief, Clare felt her blood ignite as her vision started to tunnel and the glare of the autumn sky dimmed to red and black.

AS THE SPINNING AND SPARKLING of her shimmer-trip faded and the world around her bent itself back into shape, Clare almost shouted for joy. The rusted, peeling walls of the abandoned old warehouse solidified around her and she realized that she was *outside* the storage locker! She'd done it!

"I did it!" she gasped.

"You dawdled," Al answered from inside the locker.

"I didn't!" Clare protested. "I—"

The sudden sensation of Stuart Morholt's stupid *stupid* James Bond gun-barrel jamming up against her skull—again—made her want to cry.

"Crap," Clare muttered.

She heard Al sigh wearily. "Told ya."

"Are you gonna get tired of doing that anytime soon?" Clare asked over her shoulder, utterly deflated. Defeat snatched from the jaws of triumph—that's what *this* was ...

"No. But then again, I won't have the opportunity," Morholt answered coldly. "Next time I'll just shoot you straightaway."

"That strikes me as shortsighted on your part, Stu." It had to be obvious, even to Morholt, that she was far too exhausted to be frightened just then. She walked a few paces forward and collapsed, shivering, on an old upturned milk crate, ignoring Morholt and his Walther PPK utterly. After a moment he lowered the pistol, looking as though he suddenly felt a bit silly for pointing it at a seventeen-year-old girl who apparently had no fear of it. Or him.

Morholt bent and picked up the brooch where it lay on the floor. "My. What a clever little girl you are, Miss Reid. And don't call me 'Stu.'"

"Get stuffed. *Stu.*"

The knuckles on Morholt's gun hand went positively transparent and his handsome face flushed purple with rage.

"Helloooo ..." came Al's muffled voice. "Sidekick in peril in here."

Clare sighed. "You can't possibly be in any more peril in there than you would be out here, Al."

"Yeah? There's a rat in here. A big one."

"I'll bet the one out here's bigger."

"You really are related to Magda, aren't you?" Morholt snarled. "Apple, tree. Not falling far."

Clare glared sourly at him as her teeth began to chatter.

After a staring contest he was clearly destined to lose, Morholt shook off his sports coat, draping it over Clare's shivering shoulders.

"Well, whaddya know," she muttered, clenching her jaw. "Chivalry ain't dead. Thanks. You're all heart."

"Don't push me, Clarinet. I really *don't* have a great deal of compunction about making your existence particularly uncomfortable to get what I want. That said, you're not much good to me with pneumonia."

"What is it I *am* good for, Mr. Morholt?" Clare looked up at him and pulled the jacket closer around her. It smelled subtly of high-end cologne.

Morholt reached into an expensive-looking black leather briefcase—the objective of his "errand," Clare surmised—and pulled out what looked like a cigar box. For really nice cigars. The rosewood lid radiated an antique sheen, and when Morholt lifted it the ambient light in the warehouse disappeared into the midnight folds of a rich, indigo velvet cloth. Wrapped in that cloth, which he tenderly folded aside, lay the Snettisham Great Torc, gleaming softly.

"I want the rest of *this*," he said quietly.

"This?"

"Boudicca's hoard. Her treasure."

"You've lost me."

Morholt knelt down in front of Clare and stared directly into her eyes with a fevered glare. He began to speak in a low, reverent, storyteller's voice. "Once Boudicca realized that she faced ultimate defeat by the juggernaut of Rome, she drank poison. Her loyal chiefs spirited her away. They hid her dead body in an unknown grave that she'd had prepared in advance for just such an eventuality. Her final resting place has never been found. But she was, in all likelihood, buried with a wealth of gold and riches that would make the museum's current collection seem flea-market paltry."

"Especially since you nicked the best piece yesterday." Clare gestured at the Great Torc.

"And I want the rest of it." Morholt's eyes glittered. "I want the gold that Boudicca was buried with. All of it. And you're going to tell me where it is."

"And, again, there you lose me." Clare huffed with frustration. "Because y'see, Stu, I don't know where Boudicca's grave is."

"But don't *you* see, Clarinet?" Stuart Morholt smiled an icy smile. "Boudicca does."

15

Clare stared at Stuart Morholt. What a totally creepy thing to do. What a *brilliant* totally creepy thing to do. Through her he could glean firsthand knowledge of treasure troves that hadn't even been discovered yet. That might never be discovered. It was an archaeologist's dream.

Still, the thought of using her newfound gift to conduct what was, essentially, a scouting mission for a grave-robbery was positively stomach-turning to Clare. She had to stall.

"I won't do it. Not unless you let Al out of the storage locker."

"No."

So much for stalling.

"No more bargaining, Clare. Miss McAllister's welfare is only your concern, insofar as she won't *have* any welfare if you don't behave."

"Then at least let me back in." Clare crossed her arms across her chest and waited, set and purposeful.

"Why?"

She fingered the sleeve of Morholt's jacket. "Tweed really isn't my style. Before I go back I'm going to need to switch clothes with Al. I almost froze to death this last time."

"Right. This last little unauthorized time."

"Unauth— Oh, get *over* yourself!" Clare spluttered. "Who do you think you are?"

"I think I am the last of a long line of very powerful mystics, Miss Reid, and you would do well to remember that. I am the closest thing to Boudicca living today. I am a Druid. I am—"

"You are delusional!"

Morholt's lip lifted in a sneer. "You wouldn't say that if you knew what I knew. If you'd seen what I am capable of. I'd tell you to ask your aunt Magda about it, but I'm sure she'd tell you it was all nonsense. She's in denial and has been for years. Not that I blame her, of course. Fear is the hiding place for the weak-minded."

Maggie? Weak-minded? *Definitely delusional,* Clare thought. "If you're so all-powerful, what the hell do you need me for?"

"Don't you understand? That is the very nature of my gift— the thing that has brought us to this juncture. The Fates have tied the threads of our destinies together, my dippy little time-tripper, so that I may further my ends. You are meant to be my window into the past. A tool to use as I see fit to further my aims of restoring the Celtic peoples of this isle to their former glory!"

"You think?"

"Don't you?"

It was weird. Stuart Morholt didn't actually *look* insane ...

He smiled at Clare coldly and moved toward the storage locker. With a twist and slide of the bar lock, he swung the door wide and gestured her in like a maître d' at a fine restaurant. Clare walked past him, shrugging out of his jacket as she went.

"Make it quick," Morholt said. "We've got work to do, my young apprentice."

"Oh super," Al said dryly from where she stood, jammed as far into a corner of the compartment as she could get. "Now he's talking like a Sith Lord. Clare, please tell me you won't go over to the Dark Side."

"Not unless they have cookies," Clare said as the door closed behind her. Morholt waited outside as the girls went about the business of switching clothes, trying to avoid looking in the direction of the opposite corner where a rat the size of an Alsatian hound perched on the rim of an empty barrel.

"It won't stop staring at me," Al said. "It showed up while you were dawdling and now it won't stop staring at me." As swiftly as possible, she pulled Clare's flimsy sundress on over her head.

"I *wasn't* dawdling and, you know, that actually looks cute on you. You should wear florals—"

Outside, Morholt pounded on the door. Clare slipped her arms into Al's many-pocketed, military-style jacket and said, "Hold your shorts—we'll be out in a minute. Jeezus."

"I'm getting just a little sick of him," Al muttered.

Clare pushed the door open but remained standing in the locker. "Al's not staying in here with Ratzilla. I wasn't kidding when I said I needed her. She's my anchor to the present. My homing beacon. Don't ask me how—it's magic. But it means I need her rabies-free and able to concentrate. Like it or lump it, Stu. Let her out. Or else I. Don't. Go. Back." Clare jammed one tightly balled fist on her hip and stood with her feet apart. "But hey, you're a clever guy. Good luck finding Boudicca's tomb all by your own damn self!"

Morholt glared at her and his gun started to drift up again.

"And, in case you hadn't worked *this* one through, Mastermind?" Clare snarled. "Shooting one or both of us will do absolutely zip to further your cause."

"You know ... it'd almost be worth it just to shut you up." Morholt begrudgingly stepped aside to let Al out. "Alas, not worth as much as that treasure hoard."

SURPRISINGLY, Morholt began to treat Clare with some small degree of respect. They actually had a reasonably snark-free discussion of Clare's shimmering abilities, dissecting the details of where and how she had turned up in the past. It seemed that it usually—at least, after those first fluky tries in the restoration room—corresponded vaguely to a proximity to whichever object she used as a trigger and, in some way, to whatever she was thinking of at the time she shimmered.

Clare had to admit that she was kind of looking forward to shimmering again. And, with Morholt approaching it in an analytical, game-plan kind of fashion, she was almost able to forget his ultimate nefarious purpose. The dude had been an archaeologist at one point, she gathered as he talked. He and Maggie had known each other. Worked together. And maybe more than that ... but Clare's mind had veered sharply away from making any further connections on *that* score.

When she felt close to ready, Clare asked Morholt to spread out the velvet cloth on the upturned milk carton and lay the gleaming, golden neck ring in the centre. As she neared the torc she almost thought she could feel the thing pulling her back into the past before she even laid her hands on it. It seemed a much stronger trigger than the other artifacts. Stronger even than Comorra's brooch.

Morholt instructed Clare to concentrate on trying to appear sometime close to the end of Boudicca's life, but Clare had a different idea. Instead she would concentrate on Boudicca as she had first seen her—when Connal had handed her the golden torc on the riverbank. Right around when Comorra was taken by the Roman soldier. Maybe, Clare thought, she could get there in time to do something to save her. Or at least let someone know what had happened so that they could maybe help her ...

Something. Clare knew that this was in no way any kind of exact science. Or exact magic, rather. It was more like directed dreaming—she could try her hardest to influence an outcome, but she didn't really understand the mechanics. She just had to hope for the best.

"This might take more than one trip," she said as she kneeled on the concrete floor in front of the torc. She pushed up the sleeves of Al's jacket and wiggled her fingers like a magician about to perform a magic trick—only without the "trick" part.

Morholt shrugged. "Yes, well. We've got all the time in the world now, don't we?"

"What if I can't exactly get an audience with the queen?" Clare tried to keep her nerves under wraps while stringing Morholt along. "Any bright ideas, Stu?"

"I'm sure she's not the only one who knows where she'll be buried with her hoard. You're a clever thing—keep your eyes open. And your ears." Morholt smirked. "Maybe not your mouth, so much."

Clare chose not to dignify that with a response. Instead she turned to Al. "Any pointers from Research Central?"

"You want *pointy*?" Al murmured, head down over her laptop, scrolling through more of her Boudiccan research. Her voice was tight with tension. "How about swords? And spears? Maybe some sharpened stakes? Especially if you happen to land smack in the middle of the Iceni rebellion. A plethora of pointy, that's what you'll get." Al tended to hyper-quip when she was nervous.

Morholt peered over her shoulder at the computer screen.

Al glared up at him indignantly. "Do you mind? I'm trying to work. And, by the way, your lair tech is sadly lacking. The wi-fi here at Casa de Villain sucks."

Morholt rolled his eyes and wandered off, pulling a cell phone from his pocket and tapping on the screen.

"What happened after Boudicca's flogging, Al?" Clare said, tying back her hair and making sure Al's borrowed sneaker laces were done up tight in double bows, just in case. She felt like a covert-ops mission commander getting briefed by the team field specialist. "Gimme the Coles Notes."

"Let's see ..." Al's fingers danced over the keyboard and scroll pad as she called up offline versions of the research she'd done the night before. "Just the third-period highlights, right? The king—Prasutagus—dies. Rome calls in all his debts plus big-time interest. Boudicca responds with a cheery 'sod off' or words to that effect. Rome, as you know, considers that uppity and has Boudicca flogged."

"Yeah. I know. I saw the scars." Clare shuddered at the memory.

Al nodded. "Well, our redheaded girl rebels and sends out a call for all the oppressed tribes in the surrounding kingdoms to come join in the fun. Her war party, which was really more like a massive mob, burns three cities—including London—to the ground. Except, of course, it was called Londinium back then and they were really more like towns than actual cities. Anyway. Boudicca and her army rampage mightily and are only stopped when the governor—"

"Seutonius Paulinus?" Clare interrupted. "I thought he was off campaigning against the tribes in the west."

Al glanced up, startled. "Uh, that's right, O Freshly Knowledgeable One. How did you ...?"

Clare waved it off. "It's not like I met him, or anything. I just, y'know, heard talk. And I happened to be sort of paying attention at the time. And *not* dawdling."

Al's jaw drifted open in amazement. Clare could hardly blame her. Every time she thought—actually gave *real* thought to the things she was doing and seeing—she felt pretty amazed too. When she wasn't scared pants-less.

"Go on, Al."

"Okay ... uh ... Boudicca is stopped by this Seutonius Paulinus guy only when he rallies virtually every available legionnaire he can get his hands on and rushes back east. He manages to crush Boudicca's far superior numbers due to strategic superiority and the unbeatable discipline of the Roman army." Al frowned, peering at the information on her screen.

"And thus began the systematic repression and debasement of the true peoples of this isle that, to this day, there has yet to be made a reckoning for," Stuart Morholt murmured as he walked back over to them. There was a faraway, fevered look in his eyes.

Clare and Al exchanged a glance and Al turned back to her screen. "Okaaay," she continued after a few moments, "our esteemed kidnapper does kind of have a point. This Paulinus guy was a machine. No wonder he thrashed the Iceni. He wasn't just off 'campaigning against the tribes in the west,' Clare. He was staging an assault on the Druid stronghold on the island of Mona, torching sacred oak groves and slaughtering Druids wholesale. It was a surgical strike aimed right at the heart of the spiritual foundations of the Celtic tribes. Jeez ... this guy was brutal. And smart. Boudicca really didn't have much of a chance."

"I don't know," Clare said, feeling the sudden, irrational need to defend the long-dead queen. "It seems to me she accomplished something no one else could have."

"Well, if by 'accomplish' you mean providing an all-you-can-eat buffet for a skyful of Andrasta's ravens, then yes, I guess she did."

"It sounds as though you'd rather the Iceni had just rolled over and let the Romans have their way."

"I didn't say that."

"And you wouldn't," Clare said softly. "Not if you'd seen what they'd done to Boudicca and her daughters in the first place."

Al didn't have anything to counter that. She gave Clare a long, grave look instead. "Good luck, pal. I'll be waiting here for you when you get back."

Clare nodded, not trusting herself to speak, and stretched out her hands toward the Great Torc of the Iceni Queen. She shivered as she traced her fingertips along the torc's contours. The warehouse around her went dim and sparkly, flashed with lightning, and then faded to black as Clare heard Boudicca's voice inside her head.

"Andrasta," the voice whispered. *"Andrasta, hear my cries ..."*

16

War horns brayed in the air.

Drums beat and men and women howled out for blood as they beheld their queen, her body torn by Roman whips, holding in her arms the lifeless form of her eldest daughter, Tasca. Boudicca stood spear-straight and stone-still on a platform made from a large provisions cart. She was flanked by Macon and Connal. Clare saw that his handsome face was twisted with emotion—she couldn't tell whether it was anguish or rage.

A crowd of Iceni warriors surrounded the cart. Most held flaring firebrands that made the blackness surrounding the queen leap out behind her like a wind-blown cloak of shadows, or—Clare thought, shivering—the wings of an enormous raven. Boudicca's face was a death-white mask, rigid with rage and streaked with blood and grime. The brilliant mantle of her hair was a wild and tangled skein that caught and held the light like fireflies in a net.

It looked to Clare as though the scene playing out before her was taking place very soon after she had first seen Boudicca on the riverbank. Enough time must have passed since then for word of Boudicca's flogging to have spread like a plague among the Iceni. Clare spun around in a circle, surveying her surroundings. She stood just beyond the edge of the crowd that was gathering to hear Boudicca's words. Men and women, all of them armed with swords or spears or bows—some already painted with the spiralling blue designs that the Iceni wore into battle—streamed by her without so much as a glance. Clare was grateful for the veil of magic that rendered her invisible to all those she hadn't actually touched. Or maybe it was the other way around. Maybe the magic made her real only to those whom she did touch ...

Suddenly a burly, long-haired warrior wearing a checkered cloak and carrying an enormous two-headed axe went rushing by—within a foot of passing through what to him would have seemed empty space. Clare deked out of the way. However the magic worked, suddenly appearing out of thin air to a guy like that couldn't be good, and so she headed for a stand of trees on a bit of high ground about thirty yards off. The vantage point would give her a good, safely distant place from which to gather intel, even though she was pretty sure this time-jump wouldn't give her any clues to Boudicca's grave site location. When she reached the trees she froze: someone was there, off to one side, crouching in the shadows. And Clare could feel their eyes on her.

She swung around—and let out her breath in a sigh of relief. "Comorra."

She was alive! Ever since Clare had witnessed her capture by the Roman soldier on the riverbank she'd feared the worst for the princess. But Comorra's tunic was torn and the hem of her skirt was in tatters. A blossoming purplish bruise shadowed her cheek and blood seeped from one of her nostrils. Although her eyes were empty of emotion, tears ran down her cheeks, leaving gleaming white trails in the dirt that smudged her pale skin.

"Comorra?" Clare knelt down beside her and put a hand gently on her shoulder. "Are you all right? That Roman ... The soldier. Did he ...?"

Comorra held up the little sword Clare had seen her earn on the night of her Warrior Making. The sharp edge of the blade gleamed red in the moonlight. "He tried."

Horrified, Clare put her arms around her. "Tell me, Clare," Comorra murmured in a soft, small voice. "Can you fly?"

"What?" Clare relaxed her hug a little and looked down at the princess who huddled against her like a poor wounded bird. Clare smoothed Comorra's hair with one hand while she gently pried the sword from her white-knuckled grip with the other. "What do you mean?"

"I have heard that there are those of the tylwyth teg who can grow wings and fly if they wish ... can you fly? Like Andrasta? Like her ravens?"

Clare felt a chill run up her spine at the mention of the goddess. "Uh ... sort of. I guess. Not on my own I can't, but we—in my world—we have ... um ... great big chariots with wings. They take us places. But I don't think that's what you mean. I did try hang-gliding once, two summers ago ... that was pretty cool."

Comorra tilted her head at Clare, not understanding.

Clare gestured with outspread arms, trying to put the experience into words that the Iceni girl could understand. "It's like strapping on a big pair of wings and jumping off a cliff into the wind. It picks you up and you soar. Just like a bird ..." Clare remembered the experience vividly. The sheer terror and the absolute, exhilarating freedom of it.

"It sounds wonderful." Comorra smiled a small, dreamy little smile.

"Yeah," Clare nodded. "It was pretty cool. I guess that's the closest I've ever come to really flying."

"I've dreamed of that ..." Comorra snuffled a bit and shook her head. "Of finding some way to take wing and soar above all this. Ever since the Legions came to this island, all I have wanted to do was to find a way to fly up into the sky. Where I would be so far away that I couldn't even tell which army was which. And it would no longer matter to me." She scrubbed at her face with a corner of her sleeve, wiping away the tears and most of the dirt. When she looked up at Clare she seemed to come back to herself and smiled a wan but genuine smile. "Is that silly of me, do you think?"

"I don't think so. But, then, I can be pretty silly sometimes, so I'm probably the wrong person to ask."

Comorra laughed a little.

"Besides, silly's not so bad."

"No." Comorra turned her head and gazed through the trees to where her mother's harsh, strident tones rang through the air. She was accompanied by a chorus of steadily rising shouts and cries from the gathering throng. "But *that* is ..."

"Yeah. *That* can't be good." Clare frowned, already knowing the outcome.

"War is never good." Comorra shook her head sadly. "Despite what my mother would say."

The girls watched as battle chariots and a few fast-running men and women split off from the fringes of the throng, heading in all directions.

"Where are they going?"

"To the other tribes. To gather as many of our people as will come to fight the Romans."

"Comorra, what exactly happened in Londinium?" Clare asked. She knew what Al had told her. What the history books said. But she doubted it was the whole story.

"We went to the governor's *mansio*. It was a trap. Seneca goaded my mother into refusing to pay any of the king's debts by heaping ridiculous amounts of interest on top of them and then calling her honour into question. She would have paid back the original loans—she *would* have! But what Seneca wanted ... it would have paupered us as a tribe."

"This Seneca guy sounds like a creep."

"He is a loathsome toad. When we arrived, he was toying with my father's torc. My mother had given it to the Romans on the night of my father's funeral. He dangled it from his fingers as though it were a worthless bauble and then, later that night, he put it around the neck of one of the serving girls. She giggled and pranced around in it like a fool. Seneca told her that it suited her—like a collar for a good dog."

"And your mom didn't just kill him on the spot?" Clare was aghast. She could only imagine the kind of humiliation the proud queen would have felt—or maybe that had been the idea. Maybe Connal had been right when he'd told her that by presenting the torc to the Romans, Boudicca had probably started a war. Seneca's actions had most likely sealed the deal—and maybe that had been the queen's intentions all along.

"My mother would not brook such an insult, of course."

Right, Clare thought. *Of course* ...

"We tried to leave, but when we got to the courtyard the Roman soldiers surrounded us. They took my mother out into the public square and ..." Comorra squeezed her eyes shut but then opened them again after a moment, as if willing herself not to cry. "They chained her to a post and they flogged her."

Clare winced. She remembered what Boudicca's back and shoulders had looked like. It hadn't been any kind of punishment at all. It had been torture, plain and simple, for the sick amusement of a bunch of decadent Romans. And it had been a message to the Iceni. One that had backfired rather spectacularly.

"Mother didn't even cry out," Comorra said with pride and awe. And horror. "Then everything turned to chaos. The Roman citizens—and even some of our own people—went mad with blood lust. They cheered each stroke of the whip. Now I understand why the Romans have the coliseum in Rome. They are a vicious people ..."

"How did you guys get away?" Clare asked.

"There were also those in the mob who were loyal to Boudicca. Those who had been loyal to Prasutagus, too. Some of them rebelled, protesting the treatment of the queen. They set fires, broke through to where my mother was chained, and set her free. Connal went in search of Seneca's serving wench so that he could take back my father's torc."

Clare preferred not to contemplate how he'd achieved that. She preferred to think he'd simply asked politely. She doubted it ... but she refused to give it any further thought. There were some things that she wished to remain blissfully ignorant about. But at least she knew now how Connal had come to possess the torc he'd handed back to the queen that night.

"My mother's chiefs fought to get past the gates to our chariots," Comorra continued. "Many of them fell. I escaped with Tasca, but we got separated in the madness. I tried to go back but the soldiers ... they were merciless. They cut our folk down like wheat as they fled. And so I ran."

"Down to the river," Clare murmured. "I know. That's when we first met."

Comorra looked at her in vague puzzlement.

"I mean—that's when we first met *tonight*. By the river."

The princess nodded. "And when that soldier caught me and tried to take me back to Londinium ... I fought."

"I guess you won."

Comorra shook her head a little. "He lost."

"I'm so sorry."

"For what?"

"For not being able to help you."

The two girls sat there for a long moment, silent amid the rage roaring through the night just beyond the shelter of the trees. But eventually Clare noticed that Comorra seemed to have gone utterly limp. And where her arm rested against

Comorra's ribs, she felt something wet. Warm. When she pulled her hand away it was sticky with blood.

"Oh God! You're hurt!" Clare eased the girl back against the trunk of the tree. "Why didn't you say something? Wait here—I'll get help!"

Comorra's head nodded forward and she looked as though she might faint.

"Hang on," Clare pleaded. "Just ... hang on until I can bring help!"

She leapt up and ran, breaking from the cover of the trees and standing on the lip of the little rise, waving her arms over her head.

"Help!" she shouted. "I need help over here!"

The men and women rushing past ignored Clare as if she wasn't even there. Which, of course, she wasn't. Just as she had tried to attract Boudicca and Connal's attention when Comorra first got into trouble, Clare was useless. Helpless.

No. Not this time. She was not about to let Comorra bleed to death just because she wasn't supposed to exist in that time. Clare's mind spun. If she suddenly appeared to one of the frothing-mad mob members she'd likely get cut down. Frantic, she started to run. In the near distance, she could see the hunched shapes of the thatch-roofed houses of the town. Maybe one or two stragglers were left in Venta Icenorum that she could approach for help.

She slowed when she saw a familiar figure stalking past one of the buildings just outside the town. It was Llassar—the Druid blacksmith—the one who was responsible for everything that had happened to her in the last few days. He had a bulky travelling pack slung on one shoulder and his long cloak flapped in his wake. The singed tangle of his hair and beard wreathed his broad face like a mane and Clare saw the gleam of a sword hilt at his side. The master smith walked with long, loping strides, and Clare had to really sprint to catch up with him.

She ran down the little hill and through the yards surrounding the stables—and when Llassar paused for a moment to shift the weight of his pack, she made her move. Clare lunged down the path and slapped the palm of her hand flat against the huge man's burly chest. It was like sticking her finger in an industrial-wattage light socket. She flew through the air on contact and Llassar flew in the opposite direction, a look of extreme shock and surprise on his sun-browned, soot-stained face.

"Mighty Cernunnos!" he swore, as he landed hard on his hip in the dust. He shook his head and looked around, his gaze suddenly snapping up to zero in sharply on Clare's face. His breathing was quick and shallow but he moved slowly, warily, as he got back up to his feet. His eyes never left Clare's face as he backed up a step and moved his hand to the hilt of his sword.

"Please," Clare said, holding out her hands, palms up. "Please, Mr. Smith—Llassar—please don't be afraid. I am ... shit. What the hell did she call me again? Oh, right! I am *tylwyth teg*."

Llassar's eyes went saucer-wide and his nostrils flared, giving him the look of a startled muskox.

"I am a friend of Princess Comorra."

"Comorra ..."

"I was there the night you made her brooch. The raven pin with the red eye."

Llassar gaped at Clare open-mouthed.

"The stone. The red stone. Remember? I helped you choose it. Not—I mean, hey, you were really bagged that night—not that you wouldn't have probably picked that one anyway, I just gave you a nudge. I'm Clare. Clarinet. At least that's what Connal calls me but, I mean, it's really just 'Clare' and ..." She was babbling, she knew, but she had to make him understand before he either ran for the hills or ran her through with his sword. "... and I'm here because I need your help."

"Andrasta's wings," Llassar whispered. He stood perfectly still. And then, after a long moment, he took a tentative step toward her. "You ... you are *real*." His voice was full of wonder. "I thought Comorra had been fooling with me ..."

"She *told* you about me?" Clare was surprised. Comorra must have trusted the blacksmith a lot.

He nodded his head slowly, his eyes never leaving her. "She did. I didn't believe. That is, I wasn't sure. But I can see you, too!"

He reached out with one huge, square, dirty-nailed finger toward Clare. As he touched her cheek another electric-shock crackled in the air—only tiny this time, like carpet static in a dry house. He touched her hair and her forehead and then poked a bit at her shoulder.

"Dude." Clare rolled her eyes. "I'm *real*."

Llassar tilted his head. Growing up, Clare had had a beagle named Reggie that used to do the same thing when she talked to him—as if he could understand what she was saying, but just had to listen very carefully. She couldn't blame Llassar— she'd had to do that too at first. And some of her words doubt- less didn't translate into the Iceni tongue. Clare made a mental note to stop using expressions like "dude."

"I never really—I mean—I thought ..." Llassar stumbled over his words, searching, it seemed, for the right thing to say to a being from the Otherworld. "I fear you have chosen an ... awkward time to visit the House of Iceni." His gaze went to the distance where Boudicca still stood riling up the locals. But then he turned back to Clare and held out his hands, palms up in a sort of formal greeting. "Forgive me my crude behaviour, Shining One. And welcome."

"It's just 'Clare.' I'm not really all that shiny at the moment. But, y'know, whatever ..." Clare sighed. This was getting *way* too complicated. Now there were *three* people who knew of her existence, and all the while Milo's voice repeatedly echoed through her head: *"Don't monkey with the time stream!"*

"Clare ..." Llassar rolled the sound of her name around his mouth.

"That's me. Good ol' Clare, monkeying with the time stream," she groaned. "Oh, God ..."

"Which god do you speak of?" Llassar's gaze grew sharp with interest. "Are you their messenger? Are you sent by Andrasta? Do you travel her ways? Do her bidding?"

"Uh ..." Clare stammered, "I ... can't really say."

"I understand." Llassar nodded. "The Fair Folk must keep their secrets close."

These people take all this paranormal stuff way *too well,* thought Clare. But in their world it had probably been an awful lot easier to believe in the supernatural than it was for people in the twenty-first century. She suddenly had an inappropriately hilarious mental picture of bringing Al's laptop with her on the next trip: *"Behold! The power of Google compels you!"*

Too bad that shimmering fried electronics. And first-century wi-fi probably sucked worse than it did back in Morholt's warehouse ... *Stop. You need to focus.*

"Comorra is hurt," Clare said, grabbing the burly smith by the hand and leading him back to the little hill. "She's bleeding and needs help."

"The princess!" Llassar exclaimed, his pace quickening. "Where is she? Is she all right? We thought the Romans had captured her."

"Yeah, uh ... they did." Clare squirmed a little inside, thinking of the part she had inadvertently played in that capture. "She got away."

They reached the stand of trees where Comorra lay, her breathing shallow but steady. The princess opened her pale blue eyes when Llassar knelt beside her, her pain-clouded gaze registering dull surprise.

Clare shrugged. "If you can't trust a Druid ... who can you trust?"

"Your faerie *is* real, Comorra." Llassar smiled gently, moving her arm away from the rent in her tunic so that he could examine her wound.

"Of course she is real! I am too old for imaginary playfellows, Llassar." Comorra smiled back, trying to muster up a teasing tone. She looked older—far beyond her years—and in her eyes was the weight of unsought wisdom. "Would that I were not ..."

The Iceni princess gritted her teeth and hissed in pain as Llassar pulled away the fabric that had stuck to the gash along her ribs. Clare grimaced in sympathy and swallowed against the slightly sick feeling at the sight of the blood.

"It is a long cut, but not deep," Llassar said. "Not *too* deep, anyway. I think I shall have to practise my needlecraft upon you."

Llassar got a shoulder under Comorra's uninjured side and Clare supported her on the other. His travelling pack kept getting in the way, though, so Clare offered to carry it for him. The smith hesitated, but after another glance at Comorra he handed over the lumpy pack. Clare sensed something familiar in its oblong contours, but she shouldered the awkward thing and followed in Llassar's wake down the darkened path toward the little roundhouse the princess called home. The way was deserted—the entire tribe, it seemed, had gathered in the field beyond the town to hear their queen speak.

Clare and Llassar made Comorra as comfortable as possible on the sleeping platform in the thatch-roofed hut. She looked around as the Druid bent over a brazier, heating a small bronze cauldron that sat on a metal tripod above the coals. Like the inside of Connal's hut, Comorra's was tiny, but more cozy than cramped. It was neatly arranged with sumptuous tapestries— rich hangings and cushions and rugs. The furnishings were mostly wood, decorated with intricate, knotted carvings. In the corner a small hanging loom bore a half-finished length of brightly checked green and gold cloth.

Llassar rummaged around in a basket of sewing and weaving supplies and returned with a small spool of finely spun thread and a long bronze sewing needle. Then he went back to the fire and added some kind of powdery substance from a pouch at his belt to the heating water. It smelled the same as the concoction Connal had used to treat her wound—a sharp tang like pine and lavender. Clare sat by Comorra's head and held her hand as Llassar washed the wound with the hot, scented water.

"The herbs are cleansing," he explained to Clare, "and they will help to numb the flesh surrounding the wound."

But Clare could tell from the way Comorra gripped her hand that it didn't numb it enough. She doubted very much that *she* could have put up with the pain of the slim bronze needle sewing her flank shut, but Comorra barely made a sound as she sucked air through tightly clenched teeth while the Druid smith worked.

After he was done his needlepoint, Llassar took a thin length of plain woollen cloth and began tearing it into strips to make bandages to cover Comorra's stitches. He had just tucked in the last bandage and was returning the cauldron to the fire when the leather flap that curtained the doorway was suddenly, violently ripped aside. Clare almost went into cardiac arrest as Boudicca stormed into the room.

She scrambled to get out of the way as the flame-haired warrior queen crossed the floor of the tiny hut and knelt beside her daughter.

"Comorra!" Boudicca's husky voice cracked with emotion. "One of the chiefs told me that he had seen Llassar carrying you this way. Oh, my dear one—I thought the Romans had you prisoner still ..." A cloudy frown darkened the queen's brow. "You are hurt."

"I'm all right, Mother."

Boudicca stared into her daughter's eyes for a long moment. "Yes," she said finally, as though she had looked for—and found—a strength in her daughter that she hadn't necessarily known was there until that moment. "You will be, I think." She took her daughter's hand gently in her square, calloused fingers. "Comorra ... your sister is—"

"I know." Comorra's eyes brimmed with pain and loss.

Boudicca gathered her into an embrace, careful of the bandages she wore. Llassar eyed the queen's own wounds and began to tear more strips of cloth.

Watching silently from her place in the corner, hidden from the queen's eyes, Clare's heart hurt as she thought about the night that Comorra had tried to barter her brooch so that Clare would watch over Tasca and keep her safe. She wished there had been something—anything—she could have done. But, really, there wasn't. Not then, not now.

I'm just a girl. A girl who could travel through time. But still, when you got right down to it, just an everyday, average girl. Clare used to hate the thought of her averageness. But at the moment it seemed to be a lot less complicated and dangerous way of life. The best thing—the *only* thing—she could do now was to leave Comorra and her mother to grieve in private. And so, as the fierce queen rocked her only surviving child gently in her arms, Clare shared a glance with Llassar and then slipped out the door into the night.

17

Clare headed toward the trees, lost in thought, the toes of Al's borrowed purple sneakers scuffing along in despondent rhythm. She was just under the canopy of sheltering boughs when Connal caught up to her. Somehow, she wasn't surprised to see him there.

She nodded at him in wordless greeting and they walked awhile in silence. A short way from Comorra's house they came to a small hidden garden next to the banks of a little meandering river, barely more than a brook, that splashed through the trees near the timber wall that encircled the town. It was remarkably peaceful. The moon had risen high into the sky and its pearly light fountained down through the leaves, sparkling in the ripples on the water and the dew upon the grass. Clare stumbled in exhaustion and Connal steadied her with a hand on her arm.

"You are weary," he said. He unclasped his cloak, spreading it on the ground near the water's edge and bidding her to sit.

"Thanks," Clare said, sinking down gratefully. Her legs felt like jelly. Having come that close to Boudicca was like falling into the zoo enclosure of a Bengal tiger. A really pissed-off Bengal tiger. Clare's adrenalin had spiked through the top of her skull and now she felt lightheaded.

"What brings you to visit the Iceni this time, Clarinet?" Connal asked softly.

Clare raised an eyebrow. "You still think I have an uncanny way of showing up at inopportune moments, don't you?"

Connal glanced sideways at her. "It is ... an unsettled time among my people right now. Dangerous."

"I know. Believe me." She didn't mean to snap, but Clare was getting a bit tired of everyone questioning her motivation. "I didn't exactly plan it, but I'm kinda glad I showed up when I did. If I hadn't, Comorra might still be lying out in the forest bleeding to death."

Connal's eyes went wide with alarm and he started to get up. Clare put a hand on his arm.

"She's fine. Llassar patched her up and Boudicca's with her now. I'd give them some space if I were you."

A look of intense relief washed over Connal's features as he sank back down beside Clare. He squeezed his eyes shut for a moment and murmured to himself, "I was so afraid she had fallen to the same fate as Tasca ..." Then he opened his eyes and looked at Clare. "The Iceni owe you a great debt of gratitude, Clarinet. Thank you."

"Hey. No problem. I'm just ... just glad I was in the right place at the right time."

The darkness seemed to settle upon them like a heavy velvet cloak. If Clare ignored what she knew was going on all around them in the rest of the village, she would have said that it was almost tranquil. "Are you thirsty?" the young Druid asked, reaching into the satchel that was slung across his shoulder. He brought out a drinking cup made of polished horn and dipped it into the silvery stream.

Clare nodded her thanks as she took the brimming vessel and tipped it to her lips. She *was* thirsty. Her mouth had been so dry from fear that the cold, clean brook water, even with its slightly metallic tang, went down better than an icy can of

Coke. She savoured it, along with the relative stillness of the night away from the mad crowd. Away from the blood and horror and gathering doom. The quiet of the moment and the steady, calm companionship of the young man sitting next to her were wonderful.

Connal seemed to feel no great need to force conversation or to ask her any of the thousands of questions about her that must have been buzzing around his mind. She was thankful for that. In the distance the faint, angry sounds of the gathered tribe rose and fell like surf, too far away to be heeded. But also too close to ignore.

"What happens next?" Clare asked finally.

Connal shrugged. "If the tribe agrees with Boudicca—and I cannot see how they will not—then we go to war. It is as simple as that. And as complicated."

"Oh."

"The goddess Andrasta will paint her limbs with woad and wash her hair in blood and hitch twin ponies of smoke and shadow to her war chariot. The fiery trail from her wheels will scorch the sky and the world will burn."

"Uh ... that's a euphemism, right?" All this talk of Andrasta as if she were a real person—or entity, at least—had made Clare almost believe that such a thing might happen.

Connal uttered a little, mirthless laugh.

"Do you know of war in your world, Clare?"

Clare nodded. "Yeah. Unfortunately. It sucks."

Connal smiled and shook his head. "You have a succinct way of putting things—even in your strange language. War does indeed 'suck,' as you say."

"Connal ... can't you talk to Boudicca? Can't you change her mind?" Clare ignored the voice in the back of her head that yelped *Are you insane? You can't just try and change history like that!* Knowing what she knew, she would have felt like a jerk not to try.

"This is *our* land, Clarinet. The Romans will have it over Boudicca's dead body."

"You got that right," Clare murmured. It hurt her just to think about it. "Connal, talk to her. You're a Druid. Isn't she supposed to listen to guys like you?"

"The only one the queen ever really listened to was Prasutagus."

"That's just great!" Clare threw up her hands in exasperation. "He's dead!"

"Aye," Connal interrupted her. "He is dead. And he might *not* be if *he* had listened to *her*."

Clare blinked at the young Druid in confusion. "You've lost me."

"What I told you the night of the king's funeral wasn't true. I didn't know the truth at the time, but ... the king did not die of a broken spirit, Clarinet. He did not die of illness or accident." Connal reached into the pouch at his belt and held up a small, dry bit of something that looked like a piece of bark. "He died of *this*."

"What is it?" Clare began to reach for it without thinking.

Connal pulled it away before she could touch it. "It is a kind of mushroom. The Roman is a clever animal, you see." He smiled mirthlessly. "And somehow, in small amounts, dried and crushed to powder, *this* found its way into the many jugs of rich red wine that the Romans gave to the Iceni king as a measure of their 'friendship'! How unlucky for Prasutagus that he had a taste for wine."

"Oh ..."

"And how unlucky for the Romans that Boudicca would never touch it." Connal's grin faded. "The only thing that she would ever drink was good stout beer made by her own craftsmen ... and *that* predilection will cost the Empire dearly. Llassar hasn't told the queen yet, but she suspects."

"How does Llassar know?"

"We Druiddyn are trained in the art of healing—a consequence of which is that we are also trained in the darker arts of harming. We must know the one to effectively bring about the other, sometimes." Connal's eyes were cold as he returned the poisonous fungi to his pouch. "This poison is subtle, effective ... and leaves only a slight discolouration at the back of the victim's throat. Llassar discovered it as he was preparing the king's body for the pyre." His handsome features clouded at the memory. "But that is what this war is all about, Clarinet. The Empire would take that which does not belong to them and they will do it by any means necessary. War, treachery, politicking, it does not matter to them. There is no honour in that, and no honour in them, and *no honour in us* if we let them! Even though I know well that we will lose in the end."

"Why do you think that?"

Connal shrugged, staring off at where the tribe had gathered and the torches burned. "The Iceni are a warrior people. Rome is a war machine. We fight with all the passion in our souls. They fight with none. What Boudicca doesn't understand is ... *that* is why they will win."

"And when the queen loses ..."

"She will die." Connal was matter-of-fact.

"So over Boudicca's dead body it is then, huh?" Clare said, her tone bitter.

Connal shrugged again. "And mine."

"Wow. That's thinking positive."

He smiled sadly at her. "I know my fate, Clarinet. It is tied to the queen's. I can no more escape my death than I could have escaped my birth. It is my destiny."

Connal's casual disregard of his own impending doom made her want to weep with frustration.

"Why does the thought of my death upset you so, Clarinet?"

"Because I ... you're ..." Clare couldn't exactly come right out and say that, among other things, his death would be a pointless waste of a total hottie, but she also couldn't help thinking it.

His eyes narrowed, glinting with a subtle mirth. "It does upset you, doesn't it?"

"Of course it does!" Clare protested, her cheeks growing hot. "I mean ... death is just bad and stupid on principle. Especially if it's pointless!"

"But you are one of the Fair Folk, Clarinet." Connal leaned close to nudge her with his shoulder. "We have always been told that the dwellers of the Otherworld do not give much thought or care to the mere mortals of this realm."

He was teasing her. It was *so* not fair. Clare began to feel a bit flushed.

"Yeah, well," she muttered, "you're not exactly the kind of mortal I would ever refer to as 'mere' ..." The sparkle in his gaze seemed to have effectively shut down Clare's internal editor function. She was still talking and couldn't seem to stop. "In fact," she heard herself say, "you're probably the un-merest mortal I've met in a long time. See ... uh ... 'mere' as a word—uh—adjective, I think, doesn't really quite cover it where you're concerned. You know—you as a mortal. You have a lack of mereness. What's the opposite of mere? Never mind. Not important."

"Clarinet?"

"Yes?"

"Are you all right?"

"Yes. And also, if it's okay by you, I'd like to shut up now ..." *Or possibly just go somewhere and swallow my own face.* She could feel her cheeks turning brighter and redder as Connal began to laugh. She was grateful for the darkness.

It took Clare a long moment of sustained embarrassment to figure out that he was laughing *with* her, not *at* her. She started to laugh then herself.

Connal leaned back on one elbow and regarded her. "Are you really from the Otherworld, Clarinet?" he asked.

Clare snorted, caught up in the moment. "No. I'm really from Toronto. Normally. I guess at the moment I'm from Londinium. Except now we call it London."

"Now?" Connal tilted his head quizzically.

"Uh—*then*. Never mind. Forget I said that. You probably wouldn't believe where I come from even if I could somehow manage to explain it to you. Which I can't. Or you'd just laugh at me. Because it's complicated. *I'm* complicated. I'm a complicated girl."

"I like complicated girls," Connal said and smiled again.

It should be illegal to possess a smile that devastating, Clare thought.

"And I promise not to laugh," he said.

Clare sighed and hugged her knees. Was there any harm? Seriously. If Connal told anyone else her story they'd probably just label him the village idiot and ignore him. Besides, the Iceni were about to become far too preoccupied to worry about her. Time-stream monkey outrage notwithstanding, it would be nice to share her secret with him ...

"Okay," she said. "Here's the deal: I'm not from the Otherworld, but I am from *an* other world. Strictly speaking. In space and time, at least. I'm from the distant future." She paused and waited for his reaction.

"I see." Connal smiled, pretty obviously trying not to be patronizing. "And what is that, exactly? The *'diztan-fee-you-chur.'* I do not know that place. Is it an island?"

"You have got to be kidding me." Clare blinked, mildly put out that her revelation hadn't provoked a more dramatic response. "How come you can understand everything else I say?"

"I do not know. I understand the meaning of most of your words, even if the sounds are unfamiliar. But *that* word—it has no meaning for me. It is only a sound."

"It's two words," Clare frowned. "Distant *and* future."

"Ah!" Connal's face lit with sudden comprehension. "But 'distant' pertains to space, Clarinet. 'Future' pertains to time."

"Well then, what do you call two thousand years from now?"

"Irrelevant." He shrugged. "A dream."

Could it be? Clare wondered. Could it actually be that these people had no actual concept of the far future? Of the progression of history beyond that which—as Connal said—pertained only to them?

"Well that certainly gives new meaning to *Carpe diem* ..."

Connal cocked his head, his expression turning wary. "Do you speak in the tongue of the Roman?"

"What—Latin? Oh yeah. I guess." Clare grimaced at the unintentional faux pas. "I mean ... no. I took it for half a semester in grade ten and totally flunked out. That's about the only thing I remember from that class, and it's just an expression that managed to survive into my era. Sorry. No offence."

"I have heard the words before—from the Roman traders that hawk their tawdry wares in the market stalls at Camulodunum—but I do not understand them. What does 'carpe diem' mean?"

"It means 'seize the day.' Live for the moment." Clare smiled ruefully. "You know—tomorrow may be too late and you may never get another chance to do something that you really want to do."

"A Roman concept I can understand," Connal murmured. "And appreciate."

And then he kissed her.

Clare felt her eyes go wide, but after a moment, she kissed him back.

"Carpe diem," he whispered against her lips as his hands wrapped around her shoulders and he pulled her toward him, gently but with determination. Clare felt her own arms wrapping around his neck and then his hands were in her hair, tangling in her gold-brown curls and holding her face close to his as his lips pressed against hers. Connal smelled like fresh air and moonlight and woodsmoke and fresh green growing things. He tasted like brook water. Clare felt as though her skin was on fire everywhere he touched her.

It seemed, as kisses went, you really couldn't beat a first-century Iceni Druid in a secluded, moonlit grove.

It would have been nice if they hadn't had company.

But even with Connal's hands cupping the sides of her head, Clare heard the sharp, hissing intake of breath from over her shoulder. She broke from the kiss and turned in time to see Comorra, bandaged and bloodied, swaying slightly on her feet. She drew her sword from her belt. There was a wild, dangerous look in her eyes.

Clare scrambled to her feet and dodged backward as Comorra lunged at her, the blade of her sword whistling through the air in a deadly arc.

"Hey!" Clare exclaimed. "What the hell?"

"He is not yours!" Comorra snarled, slashing once more with the blade.

"Comorra!" Connal cried out. "Stop!"

Clare ducked again, the blade narrowly missing her cheek. Comorra had her non-sword arm wrapped around her torso, as if trying to hold herself together. If she hadn't been wounded, Clare had the suspicion that she'd probably already be missing a vital body part or two.

The princess came at her again, but this time Connal was able to get around her and wrap her in a tight bear hug, confining her arms to her sides. She struggled weakly against him, tears of rage and hurt streaming down her face.

"She cannot have you, too," Comorra wailed weakly. "She has taken too much from me already."

"What?" Clare shook her head. Suddenly the Iceni words weren't making any sense to her. "What are you talking about?"

"I know," Comorra said. "I know now. What you are ... You are a thief of souls come to take those dearest to me."

"Okay. You are delirious and suffering from blood loss. Obviously."

"Thief!"

"Connal ... what is she talking about?"

"I came to find you," Comorra's voice choked on a half-sob. "To *thank* you. I thought you were my friend. I truly did. But now I know."

"Know *what*?"

"You were there the night my father burned." Comorra spat the words as an accusation. "You are here now that my sister is dead. You watched as that Roman took me away on the riverbank and you did nothing."

Clare had a sick feeling in her stomach. Really ... how must that have looked to Comorra? "I couldn't!" she protested. "I didn't know how—"

"But you knew we were going to Londinium—you were there when Macon told me of it. Did you skulk there too, watching as they whipped the flesh from my mother's back? My mother will go to her death soon and I will lose her." She half-twisted in Connal's grip, her expression wild and anguished. "I cannot lose you too, Connal."

"You *won't*," Clare said emphatically.

"So say you. When you are here"—she strained against Connal's hold on her—"trying to steal him from me even now. I told you. I *told* you I wanted him. And yet here you are with him. Will you take everyone from me who I love?"

A crushing weight of betrayal fell down on Clare as if from a great height. Comorra certainly had a point. She had known that the princess was smitten with the hot young Druid prince. She'd known that. And still she'd kissed him. Without a thought for the feelings of the girl that she'd come back in time with the express purpose of saving. How screwed up was that?

"I am tired of losing." Comorra sagged back into Connal's arms. The fight seemed to go out of her and he turned her gently around.

"Little bird," Connal said gently. "You have not lost. You have not lost *me*. You are not well. Come, let me take you home."

Comorra straightened, shrugging off his arm and lifting her chin. "I am well enough. Strong enough. Choose, Connal. And then come to me when you will. If you will."

She turned and walked back toward the roundhouses of the town.

Clare took a few steps in her wake. "I should probably talk to her," she said. "Explain things. Explain that she didn't really see what she thought she saw ..."

Oh? said a dry voice in her head. *So what really did just happen here, then?* Clare wasn't sure. She knew that her heart was still racing and that it wasn't entirely because Comorra had attacked her. It was because Connal was standing there, close by her, in the moonlight. And she could still feel his kiss on her lips.

"I think maybe you should go," Connal said. He shook his head, a weary expression on his face. "It was nice to think that, for a moment, I could forget what was to come. I could forget myself. It was foolish of me. My priorities are my people. My princess and my queen ... and the fulfillment of my destiny."

He turned and looked at her, and for a moment Clare was struck with a powerful sense, not of déjà vu, but of familiarity. With the planes of his face so sharply outlined in moonlight and the shadow of stubble on his cheeks and chin, he looked older. Sadder. He looked like—

Overhead a raven cawed harshly.

Like someone she'd seen before ...

Somewhere.

Fireworks went off behind Clare's eyes. She cried out the young Druid's name, but that world was already gone. Faded back into shadows and mist.

"WHO ON EARTH is Connal?" Stuart Morholt peered down at her as she rematerialized.

Clare felt faint. But it wasn't just the effects of shimmering. Or having had a sword drawn on her. She'd suddenly realized exactly who on earth Connal was. And what, exactly, his sacrifice would be. Her mind flashed back to the image on the plaque beside the display case in the British Museum. Connal's self-professed destiny was to become a Spectral Warrior of the Norfolk Broads.

Connal the Druid and Claxton Man were one and the same.

18

"I can't. I can't go back there again. You don't understand. It's not a nice place. They don't think like rational human beings! Connal's chipper as hell about skipping off to his grim fate and Comorra drew a *sword* on me. After I helped her out of the forest and everything!"

"Sounds like she wasn't really thinking all that clearly, pal," Al said. She was transcribing the details of Clare's visit into a database that they could cross-reference for tomb clues. Morholt had allowed her to stay out of the storage locker as long as she could make herself useful. "I mean, imagine what that kind of trauma does to your thinking processes. Not to mention the blood loss. Somebody probably should have made sure she'd stayed in bed."

"Yeah, well Llassar was probably a little preoccupied with stitching Boudicca back together ..."

The image of Comorra charging at her with a sword swam up before her mind's eye again. Clare shook her head violently. "Screw it. I'm not going back. You can shoot me if you want. I can't do it."

Morholt straightened up from where he'd been perched on a broken chair and went over to his briefcase. Clare figured he was getting his gun so that he could threaten her again, but instead he pulled out a bottle of water and handed it to her. "Here," he said, his tone soft. "Drink."

Clare gulped thirstily. It tasted flat and chemical compared to the spring water she'd shared with Connal in his horn cup, but she was parched. Exhausted. Morholt seemed to know it. He sat down again opposite her and leaned his forearms on his knees.

"I am sorry this is difficult for you."

"Please do not get all Stockholm-syndromey on me, Stu. I don't think I can handle compassion coming from you just at the moment."

"You think me mad." He cocked his head, gazing at her intently. "Or possibly evil?"

"I think *that's* giving you too much credit." She finished the water and handed him back the empty bottle. "Right now, I just think you're a plain old garden-variety thief."

"Even after you've seen the power of the Druiddyn? Experienced it firsthand? *Tasted* it?" That feverish light sparked in his eyes again.

Okay. Maybe he was a *little* mad ...

"Don't you want to see this through?" he asked, his stare boring into her. "Don't you want to know if you're right about Connal?"

"No!"

"You know, there have long been rumours. Stories of a blood curse that would be cast upon those who disturb the grave of the queen."

"And so you want to disturb it. Good plan, Stu."

"Only because I happen to think that you, my dear, with your otherwordly talents, are the only one who could do so without bringing that curse to bear. And at the same time, it could answer all your questions. Aren't you the least bit curious about the mysteries of Boudicca's ultimate end?"

Was she? Of course she was. So far she was the only person living who knew what had really gone down with the legendary queen. She exchanged an uneasy glance with Al, who bit her lip but remained silent. Clare knew perfectly well what her thoughts were on meddling with history—but she also knew that Al was in some ways just as conflicted as she was. Her scientific curiosity demanded to be satisfied even while her pragmatic self counselled her to leave well enough alone.

"You are, whether you like it or not, a part of her mystical legacy, Clarinet," Morholt pressed.

"I *so* am not!"

Morholt raised an eyebrow.

"You're an idiot," she said.

He raised the other one.

"You *really* believe all this 'curse' bull?" Clare shook her head. "I take it back. You're not just a thief. You're an *insane* thief. You are bonkers, Mr. Morholt. Certi-freaking-fiable! I mean—I'm the one actually doing the time travelling and *I* don't believe it!"

"Yes, well. I am also one of those rare souls who put stock in those things that are not readily explained by the mundanities of science. Things like the Lost City of Atlantis and shaman spirit guides and voodoo and curses. It's why I'd never steal anything from the Tutankhamun Collection. And—speaking of blood curses, I wouldn't go near the Hope Diamond, either."

Al snorted. "As if you could. I've seen it. It's sitting in the Smithsonian behind three inches of bulletproof glass!"

Morholt's eyes glinted at them. "You've really never heard of me, have you?"

"Sorry to disappoint." Al glared sourly at her captor. It seemed to Clare as though she was taking the whole getting-a-gun-pointed-at-her thing rather badly. Good for Al.

"I will admit that surprises me a touch. Especially coming from you, Miss Reid." Morholt glanced at Clare and chuckled dryly. "I'd always rather fancied that your aunt Magda might have fallen into a habit of mentioning me often. And with great fondness."

"The first time I ever heard your name was yesterday. And I wouldn't say her reaction was 'great fondness.' More like seething rage."

"Dear old Magda." Morholt picked up the gun again and toyed with it absently.

Clare decided to change the subject. "Hey ... Why does everyone think you're dead?"

Morholt put the gun back down. "Because it suits my purposes to have it so."

Clare stared at him until he clarified.

"The authorities tend to stop hunting you once they think you're dead."

"Why were they hunting you in the first place?" Al asked.

"I have a fondness for antiquities." His smile slid back into place. "And explosives. I have ideals. And I have an extreme distaste for the Establishment. These things tend to dovetail nicely every now and then."

"Maggie never thought you were dead," Clare muttered.

The smile wilted a bit on his face. "Your aunt is, among other things, keenly intelligent. More's the pity that she and I did not ultimately see eye to eye. I still miss her sometimes ..."

"Oh *whoa!*" Al exclaimed suddenly, rearing back from her computer. "Did you know—well, I'm pretty sure you *don't* know, 'cause I discovered this myself—but did you know that Boudicca's army butchered *seventy thousand people* during her colossal freak out? How pissed do you have to be to do something like that?"

Clare thought again about the sight of Boudicca as she had beheld her daughter, Tasca, dead on the floor of Connal's chariot. "Pretty pissed."

"I'd have to agree with that assessment," Al murmured. "Did you also not know that there's a buried layer of ash *three inches thick* under London that's all that was left of the city after this chick was done with it?"

"Gee," Clare said. "Just the kind of thing that would make my aunt giddy as a schoolgirl."

Al raised an eyebrow. "I can't even imagine that."

"I can," murmured Morholt.

Clare shuddered once and chose to ignore the implications of that statement. She sat there silently for a moment, her thoughts drifting back—not to Boudicca or even to Comorra, but to Connal—and she realized with a sinking feeling that Morholt was going to get his wish. She was going to go back.

"I'm going to go back."

"What? Why?" Al gaped at her in astonishment. "I thought you just said—"

"I did. Apparently I was wrong." Clare checked to make sure her shoelaces were tied tight and pushed the curls that had escaped her hair elastic back off her face, securing her ponytail tighter.

Why are you doing this? she asked herself. Did she want to see Connal one last time before he met his gruesome end? She remembered the grisly display at the museum and her heart ached to think of him dying like that. Maybe she just wanted to know why he'd ended up that way. And ... maybe she wanted to stop it from happening. Clare shook her head sharply.

Time monkeys. Angry, angry time monkeys.

She remembered what Connal had told her about being able to sense her before he could see her. How he'd said it had felt as if someone he knew had been staring at him. Maybe, Clare thought, it was because—in her world—they already *had* met. Sort of. In the museum. He'd just been dead for two thousand years and lying in a glass case ...

"Clare?" Al's voice was small and worried-sounding. "I know you're gonna go through with this whatever I say, so ... I just want to say this: keep your head down. Roman archers used to set fire to their arrows before shooting them."

Terrific, thought Clare, *flaming arrows*. Just another typical Saturday night in the life of Clarinet Reid, Girl Average. As Morholt and Al watched, she approached the cigar box on the crate once more and crouched down in front of it. She ignored the whispering voices in her head—the ones that beckoned her on and the ones that warned her away—and flexed her fingers as if she were about to play a concerto on her mom's piano back home. Then Clare reached out to touch Boudicca's golden torc ... and tried very unsuccessfully not to think about fiery death raining down from the sky.

THE SKY WAS ABLAZE, but thankfully not in the way Clare had feared. She stood for a moment and marvelled at the beauty and brilliance of one of the most spectacular sunsets she'd ever seen. She had shimmered onto the raised hump of land where the great hall of Venta Icenorum stood: Boudicca's hall. Clare wished Al hadn't told her that after Boudicca was defeated the Romans would raze the village, knocking down the roundhouses and the thatch-roofed hall. They'd build their own squared-off, regimented Roman town there as a constant reminder to a conquered people of just how conquered they were.

Clare sighed. A little knowledge was a depressing thing.

In the distance she could hear voices—mothers calling children, men hailing each other—and the muted cacophony of livestock being tended to before nightfall. It seemed as though she'd shimmered into a quiet, ordinary evening. Clare walked over to one of the few windows set high in the curving wall of Boudicca's hall, pulled herself up by the sill, and peered inside.

So ... not an ordinary evening, then. She swallowed against the sudden tightness in her throat. Boudicca stood in the centre of the hall where a roaring fire blazed. She was alone except for the company of her daughter, Comorra. Who was pleading with her.

"You cannot do this!" Comorra said, crouched on a low stool and staring up at her mother with desperate eyes. "Mother!"

"I can and I will." Boudicca reached into a wooden chest at her feet, selected a pair of spiralling gold arm rings, and slipped them up her well-defined upper arms. Beneath a long pale wool cloak swept back over her shoulders, the queen wore a sleeveless white tunic that was richly embroidered along its borders and belted with more gold. Her hair gleamed in the firelight, trailing down her back in twin plaits fastened with gold, and dark-red stones shimmered at her ears and on her fingers. They reminded Clare of drops of blood. It was obvious that Boudicca was dressing with a great deal of care that evening. "It is necessary."

"I will hate you forever. I will never forgive you."

"In time you will understand." Boudicca picked the great golden torc out of her jewellery chest next and slipped it around her neck.

"I won't." Her daughter glared up at her. "I *won't* understand."

"Comorra. Andrasta watches over you. I need her to watch over *all* the Iceni. You know as well as I do that the Raven will give her favour only when blood is spilled. When a life is given freely. It is his destiny. It is why he is here."

Comorra slowly rose to her feet. "I love him, Mother."

A shadow flashed across Boudicca's face and Clare sensed that the queen was thinking of her own lost love. Prasutagus.

But Prasutagus was dead. Murdered by the Romans who were now trying to steal her land and sell her people's legacy into slavery. Her expression turned stony once more. "Then honour his sacrifice."

Boudicca turned and swept out of the room. Comorra sank down beside the fire pit, wrapped her arms around herself, and wept bitterly.

Clare waited until the queen was well down the path. There was a biting chill in the air and she shoved her hands into the pockets of Al's jacket. And that's when she got an idea. A wild, ridiculous brainstorm that—if she was luckier than she had any right to be—might just save the day. Or at least a Druid.

Once she could no longer see Boudicca's fiery hair in the distance Clare counted to ten. And counted to ten once more. Then she went around to the front and shouldered open the heavy oak door, slipping into the shadowy hall. The smell of roasted boar and spices and beer wafted all around her. It seemed as though there'd been a feast of some kind recently.

A farewell party for the soon-to-be spirit warriors, maybe? *Nice,* Clare thought. *More like a last meal for the condemned.*

"Are you here to gloat?" Comorra's voice cut through the smoky gloom.

"Nope." Clare crossed the rush-strewn floor and crouched beside the princess. "I came here to apologize. And maybe help you if I can."

"Help with what?"

"Well ... correct me if I'm wrong, but isn't your mom on her way to go sacrifice Connal to a goddess before she marches down to Londinium to start a great big ol' war?"

Comorra nodded. Her pretty face was blotchy and tear-stained, blue eyes full of misery. "Connal has been chosen as a gift for the goddess. A spirit warrior." She drew a shaky breath. "He will die the triple death at the head of twelve other chosen warriors. With their sacrifice, Boudicca will beseech the goddess to aid us in our plight."

Thirteen sacrifices. Thirteen glass cases in the museum. "I thought so," Clare said grimly. "There's a bog not too far from here, isn't there?"

Comorra nodded. "A sacred place. It is neither land nor water. It is where the Druiddyn sometimes perform their rites."

If you could call murder a "rite," Clare thought. She remembered what Al had said about the way the bog victims had died: stabbed, bludgeoned, garroted, and thrown into a marsh for good measure. Well, she'd be damned if she let something like that happen to Connal.

But it has happened, said a voice in her head. The one that she usually had an argument with. *You know it's happened. You saw the remains. You can't change that.*

Couldn't she? She could certainly try.

Time monkeys be damned, Clare thought grimly. *Connal is worth the continuum chaos. I hope ...*

"When is all this supposed to happen?" she asked Comorra.

"At the rise of the full moon tonight."

"It won't do any good, you know. Boudicca will still lose this war."

Comorra looked at her, a slight frown on her face. "How do you know that?"

Clare thought of the macabre, petrified skin suit that was all that was left of Claxton Man in the museum. "I just know is all. So, in light of that colossal futility, I'd like to try and keep this whole sacrifice thing from happening. Would you like to help me?"

"You would do this so that you can have him for yourself? Or are you at odds with Andrasta?"

"No." Clare didn't want to explain how she didn't exactly hang out with goddesses on a regular basis. And yet she didn't want Comorra thinking that Andrasta was going to take care of this whole mess if the Iceni just crossed their fingers and sacrificed a baker's dozen of their people. "Look, Comorra, I don't want Connal. I mean, he's really something. But he's not *mine*. And you were totally right back when you tried to kill me. I mean, not about the killing part. I'd rather you didn't do that again. I mean you were right that I shouldn't have been snogging your guy. Especially because I knew you liked him. But that kiss ... it didn't mean anything. It just sort of happened. And I'm sorry."

Comorra ducked her head and nodded once, sharply. "Thank you. But I don't see how it matters now. He's not mine either." Her voice broke on a choking sob. "He never will be. He'll belong to the goddess after tonight."

"Is there any way we can stop it?"

"The only thing I can see preventing the sacrifices is if the goddess Andrasta herself were to appear before my mother and forbid it."

Clare felt a wolfish grin spread across her face. "That's kind of what I was hoping you would say."

Comorra's expression conveyed just how likely she thought the odds of that happening were.

"Oh ye of little faith," Clare said, giddy with fear and excitement at the thought of what she was about to try to do. She glanced at the sky, turning now from vibrant shades of orange and red to dusky purple as the sun sank behind the horizon. "When is moonrise?" she asked.

"About three hours from now."

"Then come on. We don't have much time."

"To do what?"

"To turn you into a goddess."

SHEER AUDACITY. That's what Al would call it. No ... Al would call it sheer stupidity. And she'd be right. Except that Clare had Al's help—and *that* was going to make all the difference. Because in the pocket of Al's jacket were two magnesium mini-flares, a box of strike-anywhere wooden matches, and a handful of chemical glowsticks from the emergency road kit of Stuart Morholt's Bentley.

The jacket Clare now wore.

Score.

THE CLOAK WAS long and voluminous and dyed a dark indigo that was almost black. It sported a deep hood and dragged on the ground behind Comorra when she tried it on.

"It was my father's," she said.

"I don't think he'd mind you putting it to good use," Clare replied.

With the hood up, in the darkness of the forest, it would completely obscure the princess's features. It would do nicely.

Comorra wore a pair of fine, soft kid-leather riding gloves. Clare silently marvelled at the workmanship and clever stitching that rivalled any pair she'd ever tried on in a department store back home. She'd been so ignorant. How had she ever considered these people to be barbarians? Well—except for what they were about to do to Connal. *That* was pretty barbaric ...

Comorra still wasn't entirely convinced that what they were about to attempt wasn't some kind of dire affront to her deities. "This sounds like a dangerous path. What if Andrasta becomes truly angry?"

"As opposed to just plain neglectful?" Clare muttered as she threaded a remarkably finely spun length of thread through the eye of a large bone needle. "Seriously, Comorra—what exactly has she done for you, lately?"

The princess looked a bit shocked at that. "She is a goddess," she protested, although it sounded a bit half-hearted. "Her will is inscrutable."

"Yours isn't." Clare motioned for her to hold the edges of the cloak out like wings and got to work with the needle and thread. And with the glowsticks pilfered by Al. "Maybe the goddess is waiting for you to take matters into your own hands and deal with the situation. Maybe she wants you to stand up for yourself and do what you think is right. Either way, Connal's most likely going to die horribly if you do nothing. Call that the will of the goddess, or the disappointment of the goddess, or the 'Oops, I just wasn't paying attention' of the goddess. But believe me, whatever Andrasta's opinions on the matter, unless we stop it it'll happen."

"You keep saying that, but how can you be so sure?"

"I've *seen* it, Comorra. You have to trust me on this."

"But what if the sacrifice *will* help us win this war?"

"It won't." Clare recalled Al's bleak statistics on the Boudiccan rebellion. "Like I said, I've seen that, too. And I'm sorry. The Roman army will conquer the Iceni."

Comorra squeezed her eyes shut against a wave of emotion that swept over her.

"Hey," Clare said as gently as she could. "Look. Maybe it isn't the greatest situation to be in, but maybe this way you can at least do something to help some of the Iceni survive. You and Connal."

"What do you mean?"

"I mean run. Hide. Go into the west—go back to Connal's tribe and help *them* fight." Clare struggled to remember something Al had told her about the Roman conquest of Britain. About the fact that, in the western and northern reaches of the island, some of the Celtic tribes had remained free. "In the mountains, Comorra, the tribes of Britain might stand half a chance of avoiding total annihilation. But not here. Not any-more. I think your mom knows that. Standing and fighting is suicide. I think she's just planning to take as many of them down with her as she can when she goes."

Comorra was silent for a long time. Finally, she looked Clare square in the eyes. "Tell me again what I must do."

19

Connal stood on a rise of land, motionless as a statue. The bodies of twelve other men lay face down at the water's edge.

Clare felt her heart sink. Given the way Comorra had raced her little chariot she'd been sure they would arrive in time to save them all. But Boudicca had begun the ritual ahead of schedule—sacrificing the other men just before moonrise. All except Connal, who was to be their leader in death. That the baleful, unblinking moon-eye would bear witness seemed an honour to be reserved for him alone. The others had died in darkness.

Comorra had pulled her chariot to a stop well away from the open space that stretched between the woods and the margins of the peat bog where Boudicca was performing her ritual murders. Ranks of blue-painted warriors, some of them with hair and moustaches stiffened to fearsome points, stood on either side of a wooden platform that had been built out over the brackish swamp for just such a purpose. Clare wondered fleetingly just how often they threw people into the oil-black, evil-looking bog. Were there more bodies down there, lying buried beneath the thirteen "Spectral Warriors" the archaeologists had already found? Maybe not. Maybe the sacrifices were made only when things got out-of-control desperate. Or maybe Boudicca had been the first one to do something that drastic.

Clare surveyed the gathered Iceni. There were probably a hundred men and a handful of battle-hardened women at Boudicca's side, all armed to the teeth. A field of swords and spears waved in the air like wheat.

Clare suddenly had second thoughts about the wisdom of her plan. But it was too late to back out now. She couldn't—not after everything she'd done to convince Comorra. The two girls were hidden on the far side of the gathering, near to the edge of the slough but far enough away to remain unseen, and Clare was trying to figure out a way for them to get close enough. But then Comorra tugged on her sleeve and drew her farther away still. Clare was about to ask her where she was going when the princess stopped and pointed to the bog's edge. A fishing skiff—a small, flat-bottomed boat—bobbed gently on the scummy surface of the water. A long pole lay in it that it would suit their purposes nicely.

Comorra motioned Clare to climb aboard and then cast off the single line, pointing in the direction they should go. Clare pushed the pole against the mushy bottom of the bog and the skiff glided silently into the marsh.

In the darkness, with Comorra swathed head-to-toe in the black cloak and Clare invisible to the Iceni, they were able to get to within about twenty feet of the ritual stage without being seen. Boudicca's back was to them and she was giving some kind of speech. Twelve pale bodies were slowly sinking into the murky bog. One of them was Boudicca's chief, Macon—Clare could tell by the tattoo on his arm—and she felt her heart clench. In two thousand years that mark would still be visible on his skin.

Comorra stiffened in front of her and Clare peeked around to see what she was looking at. Connal still stood on the shore beside the queen—and now two Iceni warriors stood behind him, holding the ends of a thin rope that circled his neck. One held a knife and the other a short, wicked-looking war club. And yet the young Druid prince stood serenely, facing directly toward where the girls silently guided their skiff. His hair was unbound and flowed over his shoulders in a rich red-brown wave. He was shirtless and barefoot, with a sword belt strapped to his waist and a fox-fur armband tied around one bicep. On his wrists he now wore a pair of ornate, matched silver cuffs—the same ones Clare had first seen on the withered, leathern arms of Claxton Man's remains. Both the bracelets and the gold hoop in Connal's ear gleamed in the torchlight that emphasized the sculpted contours of his chest and arms. Inappropriate as it may have been in that moment, Clare was hard-pressed to tear her eyes off him.

When she did manage it, she saw that Llassar stood between Connal and Boudicca holding a wide, shallow bowl full of ... *Oh, man,* Clare thought, feeling her stomach turn over, *is that blood?*

She wrenched her gaze back to Connal. Swirling, bright blue designs had been painted on his naked torso and face. She looked closer and saw that his eyes were open and slightly glassy. Clare remembered vaguely what Al had said about the traces of ergot—the hallucinogenic compound—found in the digestive tracts of the spirit warriors. Boudicca must have had them drugged as part of the ritual. Or maybe to keep them from trying to run away. She probably hadn't had to use much with Connal, though.

Stupid macho "it's my destiny" crap.

Tough. He was going to have to find another destiny. And she was going to help him—whether he wanted her to or not.

The princess motioned for Clare to stop poling. Standing straight and tall in the prow of the skiff, she reached back with her gloved hands. Clare crossed her fingers and pulled out the necessary items from her pockets for their insane stunt. She'd told Comorra that her "magic" would be frightening, and that she should prepare herself and not flinch or cry out.

Comorra did her proud. When Clare lit the two magnesium emergency mini road flares and handed them off to her, she barely batted an eye as the swamp lit up suddenly like a fairground. Comorra flung her arms wide and held the blinding, spitting, hissing flares up for all the Iceni warriors to see. As she did she revealed the neon chemical glowsticks that Clare had hastily sewn into the inside of the cloak, casting Comorra's shadowy hooded figure in a spooky red light. It was the cheapest of cheap theatrics, but the Iceni believed so thoroughly in the supernatural that the fiery spectacle worked an absolute charm.

"Boudicca!" Comorra called out in a harsh, commanding voice.

The queen's eyes went wide.

"Mighty Queen of the Iceni!" Comorra cried, "I am the Voice of the Raven. I am the Goddess of Battles. Mine is the fire and smoke, spear, and sword."

"Andrasta!" Boudicca whispered fiercely, triumphantly.

On either side of her, battle-hardened warriors gasped and went pale beneath the swirling blue designs of their Celtic war paint. One or two of them looked as though they might actually drop to their knees in fear and reverence. At Boudicca's elbow, Llassar almost dropped his bowl full of crimson liquid as he threw one hand in front of his eyes to shield them from the blinding light of the flares. The theatrics were working better than Clare had dared hope. Just as long as the Iceni queen continued to buy the ruse ...

"Hear me, Boudicca, beloved of the Goddess." Comorra pitched her voice lower and much louder than her normal speaking tones. It echoed in the darkness, ringing out over the heads of those gathered there. She gave a virtuoso performance. "Hear my commands and obey! It is my dearest wish that you spill no more blood this night. I have received your spirit warriors into the ranks of my own and I myself shall lead them. Leave this last alive so that *he* may redden his sword with the lives of the Roman interlopers."

Boudicca cried out, aghast. "But the sacrifice is incomplete—"

"I am sated with the blood of mine own, Queen of the Iceni!" Comorra cried out harshly and raised the blazing silver-white flares higher. "I crave the blood of the enemy! Do not deny my wishes, Mighty Queen. Let this one's life serve to carry my doom to the field of battle. It is my wish!"

With that, Comorra swung around and—just as she'd rehearsed with Clare—handed off the flares and closed her cloak, dousing the light of the glowsticks. The Iceni warriors gasped. Once back in Clare's possession, the flares were just as invisible as she was. In the utter darkness that followed such a blinding light it would appear as if Andrasta had vanished into thin air. Clare quickly doused the flares in the swamp and poled the skiff away, steering it behind an obscuring stand of trees in the middle of the bog. Stunned silence followed in their wake.

"ARE YOU SURE it worked?" Clare asked as Comorra snapped the reins, urging her ponies to a trot. They had made solid ground south of the gathering and circled back around to retrieve her chariot. Clare held the sides of the little wicker cart as it jounced over the uneven ground. Al's pilfered glowsticks and extinguished flares were back in her pockets and Comorra had ditched the cloak over the side of the skiff where it had swiftly sunk without a trace. Now they just had to get out of there—before moonrise drew back the curtain on the Wizard of Oz and exposed the two girls for the goddess-impersonating fakes they were.

"You're sure Boudicca won't kill him? Connal's safe?"

Comorra glanced over her shoulder, a grim smile on her pale face. "Did you not see them? Her warriors? Even if my mother was still bent on completing the sacrifice, they would never have let her. They will not risk angering the goddess. Connal will live to fight another—"

She broke off abruptly and hauled the ponies to a halt, peering into the darkness of the forest far ahead.

"Comorra, what—"

"Shh!" She held up a hand to silence Clare. Then she pointed. Clare looked over the princess's shoulder, straining to see. At first she could make out nothing in the gloom. But then, under the light of the now fully risen moon, she saw it. The glint of metal. Armour and shields. Spear heads.

Romans.

"We have to go back," Clare whispered.

Boudicca was gathered together with her warrior elite, their backs to a swamp in a place that was tailor-made for an ambush. They would be caught totally unprepared. The Romans were intending to end Boudicca's war before she'd even begun to fight it.

"We have to warn them."

Comorra nodded, and guided the chariot ponies toward a wider stretch of track where she could turn them around. The next thing Clare knew they were hurtling back whence they'd come, bent low in the cart to avoid whipping branches.

"How did they know?" Clare asked as they careened through the trees. "How did the Romans know about the gathering?"

Comorra shook her head. "Who can say? Paid off a disgruntled slave, maybe. It doesn't matter. They know." She shot a brief glance back over her shoulder. "Clare ... I'm sorry. About before. About attacking you."

"Uh ... okay." Clare held on tight as Comorra expertly steered the chariot between two towering oaks. "No hard feelings.

Believe me, I wouldn't be here if there were. Is there a reason you're bringing this up now?"

"Things are about to get very dangerous, I think."

Oh? Clare thought. *Like it's been a stroll in the park so far tonight?*

"I will warn my mother and do what I can to help. I just wanted you to know ... if something bad happens ... that I think of you as a friend. A *true* friend." She pulled the ponies to a halt where the trees began to thin at the edges of the bog. Then she turned and gripped Clare by her shoulders. "Find somewhere safe to hide now, Clare. Unless you have any extra magic this night, you must promise me that you will stay safe and let the warriors make war."

"That's a promise you don't have to ask me for twice, Comorra."

The girls hugged briefly and Clare jumped down from the chariot platform. Comorra slapped the reins and the ponies surged forward. The chariot broke through the cover of the trees and, at the princess's shouted warning, the gathering of Iceni devolved into ordered chaos. Now they were preparing to fight.

THE SKY LIT UP with what looked like dozens of miniature meteors—trails of fire arcing through the velvet black. Flaming arrows.

Damn it, Al! Clare cursed silently. *Why do you have to be right about everything?*

The battle was spilling out past the edges of the clearing now, coming ever closer to where Clare crouched, hidden behind a large yew tree. From beneath a rain of fiery Roman missiles and under the glare of a full, baleful harvest moon the Iceni rushed to meet their fate.

Clare kept glancing upward into the night, but in a sky full of fiery death there was no raven to call her home.

Suddenly the tide of battle shifted. Almost too late Clare saw the line of Roman soldiers driving a clotted knot of thrashing Celts straight toward *her* tree. In an instant they were almost on top of her. Clare had to move. *Now!*

She ducked frantically as the blade of an Iceni pike whistled over her head and then dodged to avoid being skewered by a Roman gladius. Then she turned and sprinted for all she was worth. A flaming arrow grazed her pumping arm and slammed into the ground beside her as she ran.

"Stop aiming at me!" she screamed, as terrified and indignant as only a semi-super-powered seventeen-year-old girl could be. "I'm invisible, goddammit!"

What she was *not*, however, was incorporeal. She looked down to see that the arrow had left a black burn mark and a smear of sticky, smoking pitch on the sleeve of Al's jacket. Terrified, Clare poured on a burst of speed. A sheltering stand of elm trees was near—about thirty yards. Maybe twenty ... She probably shouldn't have glanced back over her shoulder.

Because when she turned her gaze forward again, it was only to find herself without sufficient time or space to avoid running headlong into a hard-eyed, scar-faced Roman soldier stepping out from behind a tree. A soldier who seemed surprised to discover himself jolted into the air by the touch of a girl appearing as if by sorcery right in front of his eyes. The shock-contact with Clare knocked him back a good couple of steps before he could recover himself—which he did with alarming alacrity.

Hooray for all that Legion training, thought Clare as the soldier swung his wicked-looking short sword back in a prelude to removing her head. He would have done it, too—if not for the absolutely timely, gloriously *painful* tackle that knocked the wind out of Clare—and Clare out of reach of that deadly swing.

She rolled to a stop some feet away and looked up just in time to see Connal, his teeth bared in a terrifying grimace, spring to his feet after sending her flying. He was still shirtless, and the swirling blue designs of the war paint on his limbs and torso seemed to slide and dance over his skin as he moved. Clare wondered briefly why on earth the Iceni eschewed armour. The Romans had armour—shouldn't they?

And then she realized: Connal didn't *need* any armour. She watched dumbfounded as he dispatched the veteran soldier with a darting feint and a quick, short thrust of his sword. The blade slid between the buckles of the legionnaire's armoured breastplate and sunk in almost to the hilt, as if the man inside were made of butter. The soldier toppled over with barely a grunt, and before he even hit the ground Connal had freed his weapon with a casual kick, the blade making a black and silver arc in the moonlight. In a profound state of shock, Clare absurdly found herself thinking about how graceful the young Druid made the act of killing look.

And then, just for fun, she fainted.

CLARE AWOKE in a dark, leaf-filled hollow, tucked under a mossy outcrop somewhere deep in the forest. She opened her eyes to see Connal crouched motionless in front of her, watching her. A sense of relief washed over her at the sight of him. She was safe. But then she remembered how he'd looked when he'd dispatched that legionnaire—a wide-eyed, wild-haired, whirling tangle of limbs and iron and deadly grace. Suddenly she didn't know what to feel.

Now his sword lay naked on the ground beside his feet. Connal's skin was spattered with blood that looked black in the moonlight. The blue paint on his face and naked chest was smeared now, marring the intricate designs. Clare swallowed nervously and sat up, her side aching from where he'd shoulder-checked her.

"I'm sorry," he said quietly.

"It's okay." Clare grimaced a bit from the pain.

"No. Not that." He shook his head. "Well, yes, I am sorry I hurt you. But that's not what I meant."

"What did you mean?"

"I'm sorry you had to watch me kill that man."

"Oh. Right. That."

"You have not known death before now, have you, Clare?"

She thought about that. Aside from her beloved beagle, Reggie, buried in a corner of the yard back home, Clare hadn't ever experienced death firsthand. She'd certainly never had to *watch* someone die. Or be killed. Until now. Until Connal.

"I thought not. I *am* truly sorry."

She looked at him and smiled wanly, feeling older than she ever had before. Possibly even a little wiser—if that was possible. "Are you crazy?" she asked him finally, finding her voice. "You saved my life, Connal."

"Oh, I am most definitely *not* sorry about that!" he said, grinning a little. Then his expression shifted. "I think, though, that I was only returning a favour, was I not?"

Clare blinked at him. "How did you know?"

"The rest of them couldn't see you hiding behind 'Andrasta' in the back of that boat, Clarinet, but I could."

Of course he could. Clare had hoped he'd been too hopped up on whatever mystical narcotics they'd shovelled into him to notice. She wondered if Llassar had seen her too.

"Don't be mad," she said. "I know you keep saying it was your destiny and everything, but—"

He shook his head. "If it was so, I would be dead even now." He toyed with one of the bracelets on his wrist, his expression thoughtful.

Clare followed his gaze. The matched silver cuffs were works of art—with knotted designs that looked like stylized ravens chasing foxes, or maybe the other way around.

"Those are beautiful," Clare said.

"Boudicca had Llassar make them for me," he said softly, a touch of something that sounded like regret in his voice. "She has had him make ... a lot of things."

"He's a talented guy," Clare said.

Connal nodded. "Llassar's gift is great. His magic, powerful. He is one of the only Druiddyn left I know of who can work the blood magic. The Raven's magic. And although he does not do it lightly, he does it for her. For Boudicca."

"Why do you sound as if that's a bad thing?"

"Blood magic has consequences, Clarinet. Sometimes unexpected ones. But she asks it of him because it is a hard temptation to resist. Especially when one is as wounded in spirit as Boudicca is." Connal shrugged as if there was a heavy weight on his shoulders he needed to shift. "Blood magic offers the pathway to retribution in her eyes. But I fear this war of hers may be one of those consequences. Andrasta—the *real* Andrasta—does not give without taking her Raven's share."

In the far distance they could hear the faint cries of those still fighting and dying in the forest. A look flashed across Connal's face that told Clare he wished he was fighting too. Alongside his queen. Or as her spirit warrior, maybe.

"Connal, I hate to tell you this," Clare said, "I really do. But even when you *did* lead her spirit warriors, it didn't matter. Boudicca still lost."

He frowned at her, confused. "What do you mean—even when I *did* lead them?"

"I mean the Iceni aren't going to win this war. With or without your sacrifice."

"You have seen this? In your ... distant future?"

"Yes. Sorry." She watched a flurry of emotions twist across his handsome face. "But listen, it's not ... they don't conquer everything. I mean, the Romans don't get the whole island. Parts of the west stay unconquered. The Celts fight ... they hide. And in the end, a lot of years from now but in the end, the Roman Empire goes down itself and fades away. And please don't tell anyone that because I'm pretty sure I've already drastically altered history as it is."

"Clarinet. I've never met anyone like you."

"I can believe that." Clare had come a long way from thinking of herself as just an average teenager from Toronto. She laughed a little. "I'm the kind of girl a guy like you only meets once every—I don't know—never?"

"Will you stay and help us fight this fight?"

"I can't. This isn't my world, Connal."

He reached up and put a hand on either side of her face. "But you keep coming back. Something draws you here ..."

A shiver ran up Clare's spine as Connal tilted his head and pulled her closer. Despite the powerful attraction she felt for him, she couldn't help thinking about Comorra and how *she* felt about him. Clare reached up to push Connal's hands away, her fingertips brushing the cold metal of his silver bracelets.

Suddenly the *shiver* turned to *shimmer* and Clare jerked her hand back, startled, as the familiar, electrified jolt of energy flooded up her arm.

"What the hell?" Clare glanced back and forth from her fingertips to Connal's silver bracelet. His wrist cuffs weren't just made by Llassar. They were tied to her, somehow. Specifically. They were shimmer triggers, too—just as the torc and the shield and Comorra's brooch were. Why? *How?*

She stared at Connal, waiting for an explanation. The Druid prince looked wary and, for some reason Clare couldn't immediately fathom, almost *embarrassed*.

"Is there something you should be telling me? Maybe something about what exactly it *is* that draws me here?"

"I ... I'm sorry," he murmured.

"What for?" There was an uncomfortable churning in her stomach. She felt a sense of premonition—almost as if she knew what he was going to say, or that she wasn't going to like it very much.

"The queen is using something I gave her. Or rather she is making Llassar use it—to create talismans to bind your magic to the Iceni to aid us in our troubles."

"What?" Beneath a building sense of dread, Clare was utterly confused. "Bind me how? Connal—I have no idea what you're talking about. But I do know you're scaring me."

"I didn't mean for her to do it and it is my fault because I told her of you. I suppose I just wanted to prove to her that I was worthy. That I had power to help my people. I gave her a cloth—one with your blood on it. From when I cut you."

"My ..." At the mere mention of her blood, Clare felt faint. "You gave my *blood* to Boudicca?"

"You are a creature of powerful magic, Clare," he said as if explaining to a small child. "And the need of the Iceni is great. We need all the magic we can get to call the goddess to protect and guide us."

The goddess. Clare understood now. Boudicca had "dedicated" her to Andrasta just as Connal had been. The queen had made Llassar cast a spell with Clare's blood. A spell that somehow ensured that, two thousand years later, the objects she had enchanted would call to Clare. Just as Comorra's raven brooch had when Clare herself had accidentally bled on it.

Clare almost blew out a frontal lobe trying to figure out which had come first—her shimmering or Boudicca's *enabling* her to shimmer. *Chicken ... egg ... chicken ... egg ...*

What did it matter? It was done and there wasn't anything she could do to turn that particular clock back. Her own existence hurtled on in a linear fashion no matter how profoundly she screwed up reality all around her. And it wasn't Connal's fault. It was hers.

"Blood magic," Clare murmured.

"Blood ..." The raven sitting on the branch above her head seemed to answer back.

Clare closed her eyes—and let the shimmering take her away from Connal and the faraway sounds of Boudicca's war.

20

"**W**hy is there blue stuff on your face?"

Clare took a deep breath and counted to ten before she opened her eyes. "I was partying with Smurfs. I wanted to fit in."

"Sounds like fun. Did I call you back too soon?"

"No!" Clare struggled to sit up. Her muscles screamed at her—it felt as if she'd just run a marathon. "Talk about dawdling—I thought you were *never* going to call me back!"

"I had a few things to take care of first." Al held out a hand to help her up. "Notice anything different?"

Clare was suddenly hit with the fact that she was no longer in a deserted warehouse. She and Al were sitting in a secluded area of a park with birds singing overhead and no sign of Stuart Morholt anywhere. Clare turned back to Al, who was grinning like the proverbial canary-swallowing cat. She'd *done* it. Somehow, while Clare was counterfeiting deities and dodging fiery death from the sky, Al had wrought their escape.

"Okay ... This officially elevates you from sidekick status. How the *hell*?"

"Extreme geekness has its advantages." Al shrugged nonchalantly. "The entire time I was doing my Iceni research and collating your reports for Stu in the warehouse, I was also messaging with Milo."

"I thought the wi-fi there sucked."

"I just said that to get Morholt off my back. I didn't want him suspecting what I was doing."

"Ah."

"Anyway, Milo hit the forums on hack-chat.com for me and—it took a while and probably a boatload of owed favours—but he remotely downloaded a couple of nifty little high-end pieces of software to my machine. The first one turned the Bluetooth capability on my laptop into essentially a frequency transmitter and the second was a key-code sequencer. Morholt's Bentley is one of those cars where everything responds to a keyless remote, see?"

"No."

"So all I had to do was input the make and model of the car and the sequencer just cycled through until it found the right RF and numeric code that, once transmitted, would *unlock* and then remotely *start* Morholt's car and—bingo. Now do you see?"

"No."

"At any rate, we're free. And I now own the title of World Junior Miss Grand Theft Auto."

Clare knew perfectly well that her jaw was hanging open. Wide open.

Al laughed at her expression. "With you gone, I don't think Stu considered me much of a threat. He was on his cell phone most of the time arguing with someone and he just got kind of careless. I made it pretty obvious that I was trying to eavesdrop, and eventually he went outside on the waterfront to continue his chat. So I grabbed the torc, hit the transmitter hack, beat feet to the car, burned rubber, and got the hell outta Dodge."

Clare could tell that Al was trying to be super cool about the whole thing, but her cheeks were bright pink and her blue-grey eyes sparkled fiercely. She was damn proud of herself and probably still scared out of her wits ...

"I can't believe you did all that!"

"Hey. You were gone a long time. I had to amuse myself somehow."

Clare hugged her hard. "Please don't ever *not* be on my side."

"I could say the same for you." Al squeezed her back and then pushed her away to arm's length. "Now let's get to somewhere where we can hail a cab and go back to Milo's place. You can give me your shimmer report on the way!"

IN HUSHED TONES in the back of a boxy black London taxi, Clare told Al everything—from confronting Comorra to disguising her as an angry goddess to the Roman ambush. Right down to the flaming arrows. Al sat rapt, listening to every crazy detail as if she were sitting around a campfire hearing the best ghost story in the world. Which, in a way, it was. All those people were long gone. Comorra was long gone. *Connal* was long gone. Finally Clare lapsed into silence, thinking about what that meant.

Al's voice broke in on Clare's reverie. "He's gonna be really glad to see you, you know."

"What? Who?"

Al just sighed and shook her head.

"What?" Clare said. "What did I do wrong?"

"No—nothing," Al said. "I was just thinking about Milo. I guess you weren't, huh?"

"What? Why would you say that?"

"Well ... I guess it makes sense. I mean, you've got your super-hot Bog Bait waiting for you in the past. And he's exciting and dangerous and ... blue. I'm just feeling a little bad for the guy in the present, I guess."

"Milo? You think Milo ... what? Likes me?" She'd been trying to quietly ignore the possibility; hadn't dared hope that it might be true. Milo had been wonderful to her, of course, but she feared he was too cool for her. And too smart: Al put up with her, but Al was her best friend. Milo would never find an academic slacker like Clare worth expending any serious brainpower on, regardless of how much he had to spare. Would he?

"You really think so?" she asked Al.

Al just rolled an eye at her.

"That's borderline ridiculous, Al," Clare snorted. "Milo doesn't even know me. Not really."

"Milo's been in love with you since he was fourteen years old."

"I ..."

"He told me."

"When?"

"Well ... when he was fourteen," Al said dryly. "The first time. And pretty much on a yearly basis, every time I've seen or talked to him since then."

Clare had to bite her lip to keep from making outraged squealing noises. "Why didn't you ever *tell* me?"

"Because he didn't want me to."

"Why the hell not?"

"Because he knew what you thought of him." Al shrugged. "You thought he was a nerd."

"When he was fourteen he *was* a nerd, Al!"

"In his mind, he still thinks he is."

"Well." Clare threw her hands in the air. "Obviously. And the reason he thinks that, of course, is because he doesn't own a *mirror*."

"Okay, so he's a little insecure. We geek folk tend to get like that."

"He doesn't have to be." Clare shifted around to face Al. "*You* don't have to be. You've been a nerd the entire time I've known you. I hardly even notice your nerdliness now."

"Gosh. Thanks."

"I kid." Clare sighed and shook her head. "I guess I know what you mean, though. And I was probably a total jerk to Milo when we were younger."

"Probably. Although, apparently not enough of one. He's nuts about you, Clare. And if you tell him I told you that, I will kill you dead."

The taxi pulled up in front of the tall glass condominium tower where Milo lived. Al paid the driver and the girls walked into the lobby. Al had her computer bag slung across her body and was carrying the rosewood cigar box containing one of the great treasures of British history tucked under one arm.

"Hey," Clare asked suddenly. "Why didn't we just drive the Bentley here?"

"Oh, yeah." Al grimaced. "I kind of drove into a lamppost once I was far enough away from the docks."

"On purpose?" Clare gaped at her.

"Yup. I figured the police would find it and then maybe they'd try to find Morholt. Even if they don't, the dent in his swanky fender will probably send Stu into an apoplectic fit. And that idea appeals to me *enormously*."

"Why didn't you go to the police after you got away?"

Al laughed. "Mostly because I didn't think they'd believe my story. And even if they did they probably wouldn't have let me hang on to *this*." She patted the rosewood box with the torc inside. "I figured it might not be the greatest thing if you got back from your latest shimmer and found yourself locked in a police evidence vault somewhere. Would've been a waste of all Milo's hacking and my wicked cool super-spy skills."

Right. Clare probably wouldn't have thought of that herself. "Damn." She shook her head ruefully as they stepped inside the elevator. "It's really hard keeping up with you sometimes."

"What are you talking about?" Al punched the button for the thirteenth floor.

Clare shrugged. "I mean, sometimes I just feel really dumb next to you. And Milo."

Al blinked at her silently for a moment. "Clare, no offence, but that's the stupidest thing you've ever said."

"What?"

"Do have *any* idea what you just did? You saved Connal's life and you did it in a *particularly* ingenious way."

"Yeah, but—"

"For as long as I've known you, you've never given yourself enough credit," Al sighed. "You're one of the smartest people I know. You're also one of the bravest. So you're a little reckless. And you can't do math. And you're easily distracted. And maybe you should study a little harder in English class. Oh— and your sense of direction really truly does suck, but—"

"Okay! Okay." Clare held up a hand. "I get it. I'm not a *complete* moron."

"Nope. Not a complete moron. And I'll say it again: you just saved a guy's life."

"A guy who's been dead for centuries. Does that count as ironic? I'm never sure."

"I think it does. But still—think about it. He's dead now, yeah. But not then. And who knows how many years he lived after you and the princess hauled his butt outta that swamp, and how many of the Iceni and his own tribe he actually saved in turn? At least he didn't die for nothing as a victim of Boudicca's madness. At least he was still there to take care of Comorra. Who, by the way, you *also* saved."

Clare frowned, thinking about that as the elevator doors slid open—and Milo almost tackled her to the ground.

"YOU'RE ALL RIGHT," Milo murmured into her hair as Clare stood there, not daring to breathe for fear he might let go.

Al was right. Milo cared about her. Really cared about her. Smart, funny, sexy Milo.

"I've been going crazy with worry. You're all right ..."

"Yup. I'm good," Al said with cheery sarcasm as she stepped around Milo and Clare and headed off down the hall. "Don't worry about me, cuz. Came through unscathed. No problemo. Miss Junior World Grand Theft Auto, here. I'm kind of a genius ..."

Milo loosened his death grip hug—a little—and turned to look after Al. "What's she on about?"

"Nothing," Clare smiled and reached up to where Milo had the shadow of a bruise on his forehead. He must have hit his head when Morholt knocked him out. "I'm glad you're okay, too."

"Oh, yeah." He dropped his gaze, his expression rueful. "Sorry about letting that creep get the drop on me ..."

"Hey, Milo. It's okay. He had a *gun*. I don't want you being a hero and getting hurt, you know."

"Oh." He frowned. "You don't?"

"Well ... not *badly* hurt. No." Clare may have liked the idea that Milo wanted to be a hero for her, but she wasn't about to tell him that. She didn't want him doing anything stupid for her sake.

"Are you really okay?" He tilted her face up so he could look into her eyes. "He didn't lay a hand on you, did he?"

For a second Clare thought he was talking about Connal instead of Morholt. But that was silly. Still, she couldn't get over what Al had said about Clare having ... *feelings* for Connal. She didn't. At least, she didn't think she did.

Right. You always kiss guys you don't care about ...

Milo's face was so close to hers she could have kissed *him* in that moment. His blue eyes behind those black-framed glasses were filled with concern. "I'll kill him if he hurt you," Milo said softly. He sounded as if he meant it. It sounded like something Connal might have said.

"I'm okay," she said. "Really. You don't need to kill anybody for me just yet."

Milo relaxed his grip on her and smiled. "Okay."

Suddenly he seemed to realize that he'd been kind of manhandling Clare. He let go of her and took off his glasses to polish the lenses with the edge of his T-shirt—thereby conveniently avoiding further eye contact—but it was too late. Clare could tell he'd been worried about her. It gave her a warm feeling deep in her chest.

"Come on," he said, a semblance of his usual, easy grin sliding back into place, "I think I figured something out while you were gone."

Inside Milo's apartment the furnishings were sparse: a huge desk, a leather couch, and some chairs. There were also some lovingly detailed scale models of spaceships hanging from the ceiling—the Millennium Falcon and the original-series Enterprise were ones that Clare recognized—several computers, and an entire wall devoted to maps, including a large, full-colour map of Britain stuck with a handful of coloured push-pins.

"I've been racking my brain trying to figure out what the connection was between the shimmer triggers."

"That's easy," Clare said sourly. "It's me and my super-shimmery DNA."

Al and Milo gave her identical looks that would have been comical if Clare had actually been joking. She filled them in on what Connal had told her about Boudicca and the blood magic.

Milo whistled low when she finished. "That's heavy."

"That's *crazy*," said Al. "They think you're, like, some kind of tribal totemic demi-goddess or something."

"Yup." Clare sighed. "When, as far as I can make out, it's just the fact that Boudicca put the whammy on me in the first place that gives me any magic at all."

"Wow. Isn't that kind of like the time-loop paradox in that Heinlein story, Milo?" Al mused.

"I don't even wanna know what you're talking about," Clare said.

"It's sci-fi. About a guy who time-travels in loops and keeps running into himself—"

Clare held up a hand. "Stop. Seriously—I can't even think about this stuff for extended periods. I start to feel like a puppy that chases its own tail for so long it gets dizzy and throws up." She turned back to Milo. "Anyway. Now you know. So how does this new info play into your theory?"

"Perfectly, actually," he said, chewing thoughtfully on his lower lip. "Like I said—I was trying to see the connections. I mean, we know—definitively now—that they're all connected to you, but why *those* particular objects, right? The torc and the brooch ... that's easy. They're symbolic ornaments. Worn, in part, for protection. And, as you said before, they're personal. But the shield?"

"Right. It really doesn't seem to fit the same profile."

Milo held up one finger, his blue eyes sparking with excitement. "Well, in a way, it does. I think it's a symbol, too—a sort of grave marker. But more than that."

"I don't follow you."

"What does a shield do?" he asked.

"It protects things," Clare answered. "People. Keeps them safe. Um ... hidden, maybe? Am I getting warmer?"

"Bang on, in fact." Milo's grin widened. "Is Boudicca still safe and hidden?"

"You mean, in her grave?" Clare shrugged. "I guess— Oh, I see where you're going with this. The shield's magic keeps her hidden."

"Yup. That's my theory anyway. I figure this blood magic stuff acts kind of like the Romulan Cloaking Device on *Star Trek*."

Clare raised an eyebrow.

Milo grinned. "Or something like that. And, at the same time, the shield itself tells us *exactly* where the grave is located. It's like a voodoo doll—a miniaturized version of the thing you've cast a spell on. It's representative. Work magic on the one, and it affects the other sort of by remote control."

"So it hides the grave while pointing out where the grave is."

"Or, at least, what it looks like. Yeah."

Al wasn't convinced. "Mind explaining how you came up with this—might I point out, weirdly contradictory—theory?"

"Something had been nagging me about this so-called shield. The round shapes on it ... their placement ... When we got talking about it earlier, I looked it up on the museum website. And I kept thinking it reminded me of something. I finally figured out what that is."

Al and Clare waited.

"Tumuli."

"Geshundheit," Clare said.

Al snorted, but then something sparked in her gaze. "Wait," she said, staring keenly at Milo. "You're talking about bar-rows." She glanced at Clare and shrugged. "Hey. I watch the History Channel, too."

Milo spread his hands wide and bowed his head like a stage magician. "I speaketh as the Maker of Maps. Dunno why it didn't click right away—it's not as if I spend days looking at the damn things for a living or anything!"

"Aaaand ... you've lost me, eggheads," Clare sighed.

Al walked over to the wall full of maps. "Barrows are heaps of earth—the technical term is 'tumuli'—that are manmade constructs. Most of those barrows are grave chambers. Burial mounds. They're all over Britain." She circled a finger over an area of the map.

"Really, how do you know all this stuff?" Clare asked.

"Like I said. History Channel. Also? There's this thing? Called 'the internet'? You should really look into it. I think it's gonna be a big hit."

Clare rolled her eyes. "Right. I'll shut up now. Carry on."

Milo took pity on her and picked up the explanation. "Like Al said, these ancient tomb barrows are scattered all over Britain—the plains around Stonehenge are lousy with 'em— hundreds of the things, in all kinds of configurations and cluster groupings. A lot of them have been excavated or destroyed by development, but the majority just sit there untouched. I think Boudicca is buried under the one—well, a grouping of *three* to be precise—that conforms exactly to the dimensions of the Battersea Shield."

Now it was Clare's turn to be skeptical. "Let's say you're right. Let's say the shield *is* some kind of Iron Age treasure map. How the hell are we going to find the exact configuration where X marks the spot? You say there are hundreds of these things. And we don't even know where to look."

"Not necessarily," Al chimed in. "I mean, we know where to start ... right, Mi?"

"Right. Let's make the reasonable assumption that Boudicca would have been buried on or near her own stomping grounds."

"Reasonable," Clare agreed. "But we *are* probably talking a pretty hefty chunk of real estate, here, right?"

Al shrugged one shoulder. "Well ... according to my research, the Iceni territory corresponded roughly to what is now modern-day Norfolk. So that's kinda biggish, yeah."

"That's my point." Clare shook her head. "The Roman Freaking Legions couldn't find her tomb. And I'm pretty sure they gave it the old college try."

Milo nodded. "From ground level the barrows all look pretty much the same. Just bumps of land. They would have had no way of knowing which one was hers."

"But you do?"

"Well, yeah." He turned and pointed at the wall. "See, the Romans didn't have *aerial photography.*"

Clare blinked and saw the maps again as if for the first time. "Oh ..."

"Check this out!"

Milo threw himself into the chair in front of one of the computer terminals with what Clare thought was adorably boyish gusto. She found herself doing a compare-and-contrast between him and Connal. The Druid prince was undeniably magnetic. But Milo was ... kind of awesome.

Clare and Al moved to stand behind his chair.

"All I needed was to figure out the shield's dimensions—"

"How on earth did you do that when it's at the museum," Clare asked, "probably under more security than ever?"

Milo grinned, pulled up a search engine, and started mouse-clicking away at light speed. The girls watched as he called up the online pictures of the Battersea Shield from the British Museum's website. His fingers danced over keyboard and mouse and a high-quality enlargement photo of the shield popped up on the high-def screen.

"Cool," Al said. "I'm betting you converted that graphic into a 3D wireframe model the same way you do for an aerial topography shot, right?"

Milo clicked and tapped and scrolled. "Bingo."

"They don't call you Wunderkind for nothing." Al grinned.

"No ma'am, they do not." Milo leaned closer to the screen. "Now ... I can take this vector graphic and use the Heritage

Society Land Monument archives to find a close topographical match. Size, shape, relative placement of the tumuli—the
works ..."

Clare watched in rapt fascination as Milo worked. Image
after image sprang up on the screen and Milo's long, tapered
fingers made them dance as if to unheard music. It was like
watching a concert pianist play. It was also, Clare thought,
weirdly sexy. She had to restrain herself from reaching out
and tracing the contours of Milo's shoulder blades through his
T-shirt as they slid back and forth.

"Bull's eye."

Clare and Al crowded in on either side of Milo and stared
at the results.

"Ordnance Survey Map reference number TL586453." Milo
leaned back in his swivel chair, crossing his arms over his
chest and looking extremely pleased with himself.

"Bartlow Hills ..." Al breathed the name as if it were a
magical incantation.

Clare was thunderstruck.

Images of the Bartlow Hills, a group of three hillocks—
tumuli, as Milo and Al had called them—swam up on the
screen. The middle image rotated at a stately pace, giving
Clare a three-dimensional aerial view of the barrows. She
gasped, astonished at how closely the contours of the land-
marks seemed to correspond with the Battersea Shield. Milo
overlaid a transparent image of the shield on the rotating topography and Clare could see how the high-domed bump, or
"boss" as Milo called it, in the middle of the ancient artifact,
and the two smaller, swirling roundels top and bottom, overlaid the grass-covered humps almost exactly.

"X marks the spot," Milo murmured, calling up an information page on the site as the girls stared at the monitor. "Wanna
know what's even weirder? Those three hills just happen to be
the only ones left out of a whole group of barrows that were

plowed under to make way for an old railway line back at the turn of the century. The three Boudiccan Tumuli—that's what I'm gonna call them—remained untouched when the others were levelled. Almost as if they were—"

"Protected by magic!" Al and Clare exclaimed in unison.

"Right. And nowadays the English Heritage Society doesn't let developers just go around levelling those suckers, so there they sit. I'm willing to bet that our redheaded girl slumbers deep beneath, just waiting to be found."

Clare shivered. "That is not exactly an unchilling prospect."

"Nice use of the double negative." Al elbowed Clare and grinned.

"Thank you."

They could see from the aerial shot of the tumuli that a wooden staircase had been constructed up one side of the highest hill so that tourists wishing to climb to its summit could do so without contributing to erosion. Other than that, the barrows looked relatively untouched.

Queen Boudicca's burial site.

Clare tore her gaze away from the screen and hugged her elbows. In the back of her mind she thought she heard a throaty voice, like the harsh croak of a raven, calling her name. She knew what she was going to do. What she *had* to do.

21

"You don't have to go back again. You *know* Milo's right."
"I know he's *probably* right. I need to be sure."
"Why? So you can go tell Morholt where to dig?"

Clare sighed and looked at Al, who stood between her and the rosewood box. Al only ever got this snappish when she was truly freaked out about something. She wasn't angry with Clare, she was afraid for her.

"No, Al," she said. "I need to be sure so that I can tell Morholt to dig anywhere *but* there. You know he's not going to give up on this anytime soon. And if we know—absolutely know—the exact whereabouts of the tomb, we can do everything possible to protect that place. We just need to make sure it's the *right* place. *I* need to make sure."

"Are you really able to direct your shimmering that closely, Clare?" Milo asked from where he leaned on the edge of his desk, arms crossed over his chest and a faint frown on his face. He wasn't happy about the idea of Clare taking another shimmer trip either, she could tell, but he also hadn't said anything to stop her. She kind of appreciated that. "I mean, do you think you can manage to hit the barrows at the right time?"

"I can try. Hey—the last time, Al said 'flaming arrows.' And what did I get?"

"Yeah," Al muttered. "Really sorry about that ..."

Suddenly Milo was across the room and gripping Clare's arms. Hard. "Listen to me, Clare." His stare seemed to stab through to the back of her skull. "You *listen* to me. I'm not going to stop you from doing this. It's your gift and you have every right to use it as you see fit. I also know that you seem to need to go back there for ... well, for whatever reason. That's fine. But you'd damned well better promise me you'll be careful. You've been luckier than you've had any right to expect, but I don't think you can exactly place your faith in people who see you as some kind of blood-magic vending machine."

Clare stared back into the depths of those blue-sky eyes. Milo was worried about her. Deeply, passionately worried about her. And it thrilled her more than just a little to know that. "One quick trip. That's all this is. And it's the last."

Here's hoping those aren't stupid famous last words. She told herself to shut up and offered a reassuring smile to Milo.

"I promise."

THE FACT THAT Clare *did* sort of wind up in the right place was actually pretty astonishing to her. Maybe she really was starting to figure out how to direct her shimmering. That thought did nothing to comfort her, however, once she realized that she'd rematerialized not just *at* Boudicca's tomb ... but *in* Boudicca's tomb.

As she felt herself growing heavier, more solid than the air around her, Clare realized that the darkness of her in-between-time journey wasn't dissipating. For a moment she panicked, thinking she was stuck—caught between worlds. But then she realized that, although she might not be able to *see* anything, her sense of *smell* was working just fine—and it was telling her that she was underground. Clare breathed deeply, inhaling the cold, earthy air and trying to calm her jangling nerves.

Slowly, as her eyes adjusted, she became aware that she was in a passageway, and that light, dim and flickering, was coming from somewhere in front of her. And sound.

Singing.

Clare moved toward it slowly, silent as a ghost in the gloom of the underground tunnel. She hugged the rough-hewn stone and earthen walls, stepping carefully on an uneven floor puddled with shadows. Up ahead the corridor seemed to widen, and she could make out the shape of an archway leading to a chamber.

Eerie, broken music echoed around her and Clare shivered in apprehension.

Don't panic, she told herself, *you're invisible.*

She reached the mouth of the tunnel and saw that it opened up into a round, domed grave chamber, lit by torches on poles that cast an uncertain, flickering glow—just enough for Clare to make out someone—a man—standing in front of a body laid out upon a stone bier. He was singing. And it was obvious from the tight, strained quality of his rich voice that he was also weeping. But even through the heartbreaking pall of sorrow, Clare recognized the voice.

"Connal?" she whispered.

Instantly, the ragged music stopped in his throat. Connal lifted his head and turned slowly to look at Clare where she stood in the doorway. Beneath a plain woollen cloak he still wore only breeches, a sleeveless sheepskin vest, and a fox-fur armband. His torc was a simple double strand of twisted silver and the matched pair of silver fox-and-raven cuffs still circled his muscle-corded wrists. Blood and dirt covered his hands and arms and dried blood striped his face in rust-coloured streaks. His auburn hair had mostly come loose from his leather tie-back and it hung around his face in tangles. His left arm hung awkwardly, and Clare saw that he bore a shoulder wound that was seeping fresh crimson through a tattered bandage already stained dark.

Clare shifted her gaze to Connal's handsome face; he looked years older than when she'd seen him last. She wondered fleetingly if a great deal of time had passed since her previous trip, but as she looked more closely at him she dismissed the thought. It was really only fatigue and grief, carved into the planes of his face and painted in dark smudges under his eyes, that made his gaze seem a hollow thing.

"Clarinet?" he murmured. "Are you really here?"

"Yes," she said. "I'm here."

In three long strides he had his good arm wrapped around her, so tight she could barely breathe. He clung to her the way a drowning man might cling to a piece of driftwood. He smelled of acrid smoke and earth and iron.

"I thought you would have forsaken me along with the goddess. You tried to warn us. You tried to warn me ..." His voice was choked with anguish.

Clare put a hand up to stroke his tangled hair, shushing him as if he were a hurt child. "It's okay. I'm here. I'm right here."

He shook his head under her hand. "I didn't listen. I should have listened to you. You saved my life ... and now it seems that I live on only so that I might bear witness to the death of everything I ever held dear."

"Connal." Clare pried herself out of his embrace and turned his head so that he would look at her. "What's happened? Tell me."

His mouth worked as he struggled to put grief into words. "The queen is dead."

Clare knew that already. That was why he was here, wasn't it? In her tomb?

"She did not die alone."

Connal stepped away and looked back over his shoulder. As Clare followed his gaze it suddenly felt as though her own heart would crack in two. The body on the bier was not the one she'd been expecting.

"Comorra!" she cried. "No!"

Clare ran to the stone slab where the Iceni princess had been laid out. She was richly dressed in a gown of deep russet, a thin gold torc around her neck and silver bracelets and anklets circling her limbs. Her cloak was held together at the shoulder with a plain, undecorated clasp. Because, of course, she'd given her raven brooch away. To someone she'd thought would protect her. Clare swallowed painfully, her throat closed with emotion.

"Oh, Comorra ..."

A tiny, sad smile lifted the corners of the princess's lips and her small, smooth hands were curved around the hilt of the sword that lay on her breast. The blade gleamed dully in the ruddy torchlight, its edge dinted in places. Had Comorra died in battle? It didn't look as though she'd suffered any mortal wounds, although it was hard to tell in the dimness.

Clare felt the prickling of tears behind her eyes. "What happened?" she asked. "I thought you were going to run away together. How did she die?" This wasn't the way it was supposed to have happened. Comorra was supposed to have lived— to have fled into the west with Connal. That was why Clare had saved him. So that he could save her. So that they could be together.

"Comorra would not leave with me," Connal said. "Not if there was a chance that the Iceni might win."

"But I told her—"

"She wanted to believe in her mother so much. And, in truth, Boudicca's army seemed unstoppable. At first. But the Roman is a patient animal. Seutonius simply waited for her to make a mistake. And then another and another—and then the tide of the battle began to turn. Soon it became obvious, even to Boudicca and the chiefs, that we were facing not only defeat but utter destruction. Our lines—such as they were, there was never any discipline in our ranks—collapsed and it swiftly became a bloodbath. Comorra agreed to run with me then. Only it was too late. It was chaos. Thousands upon thousands dead and dying. We had to climb over the bodies of our own to flee the field."

Clare watched as Connal's eyes tracked back and forth as if he was watching the whole, horrific scene playing out in his head. Her heart broke for him.

"It was madness ..." He struggled to continue. "I tried to stay with the princess, but we were separated in the confusion. The Romans won, of course. Just as you said they would. But it didn't end there. In the days after the massacre they pursued us. Hunting the rest of the Iceni ... Hunting Boudicca. We fled into the forests singly and in pairs. Trying to find our way home ... thinking we could make a last stand." Connal's eyes squeezed shut in anguish. "But we were so few. At last, after three days of running and hiding, I found my way back home. The town was deserted. I made my way to the Great Hall. I knew that if Comorra had made it back alive, that is where I would find her. And I did."

Somehow Clare knew what he would say next. "She wasn't the only one there, was she?"

Connal shook his head, his eyes pools of despair. Tears shone on his lashes in the torchlight. "Boudicca was sitting in her chair in front of the council fire. I do not know how long she had been dead but Comorra found her, a cup of hemlock in her cold hand. As I walked through the doors, Comorra was swallowing the last of the poison that Boudicca had left behind."

"Why would she do that?"

"Grief. Despair ... She was all alone. I should have been there ..."

"Connal—"

"I tried to stop her, but she'd already ..." He closed his eyes and shook his head so hard the tears flew from his cheeks. "A moment earlier—a *moment*, Clarinet—and I could have ... I was too late."

"It's not your fault, Connal."

"It is!" He slashed a hand fiercely through the air. "I never should have let her go into battle. You told me what would happen. I should have tied her to her chariot and taken her into the west whether she willed it or no. I should have died first before she had to see what she saw. It should have been me that drank from that cup. Comorra was ... I ..."

Connal's head dropped forward and his hair curtained his face. Clare felt as though an invisible hand was squeezing her heart. Comorra had loved Connal. And now Clare knew that, whatever had happened between her and the Druid prince, it was nothing in the face of the truth that Connal had also loved Comorra in return. And he'd never told her.

She tried to swallow the painful lump in her throat, but it just wouldn't go away. Tears gathered along her lashes, turning the torch flames to rainbow spangles as she tried to blink them back. Connal mustered a smile and took Clare by the shoulders, gazing down at her.

"I'm sorry, Clarinet ..."

She shook her head. "It's just ... I'll miss her. That's all." That wasn't all. She wouldn't just miss her. She would mourn her. She was supposed to have saved her. She wiped a sleeve across her face. "What will you do, now?"

Connal looked at her with a strange, aching longing in his eyes. And a kind of wildness she'd never seen in him before. He shrugged and turned toward the archway. "What *should* I do?" he said. "I've said goodbye to my princess. Now I must go and bid farewell to my queen. And then ..." He shrugged again and spun away from her, stalking down the darkened passageway as if it were a brightly lit hall.

Clare turned, stopping for one last look at Comorra. Somehow she just couldn't bring herself to say goodbye. She followed Connal through the tunnel and out into what must have been the main burial chamber under the highest of the three hills. And suddenly she knew why Stuart Morholt was so damned eager to discover the whereabouts of Queen Boudicca's tomb.

THE FLAMES OF A DOZEN pitch torches painted the curving walls of the high-domed burial chamber in lurid swaths of light and shadows. Everything had a sheen of orange and red. And gold. There was gold everywhere; an absolute bounty of priceless treasure. Piled against the walls were chests and baskets filled with golden torcs and necklaces, earrings and arm rings, bracelets and belts and brooches. There was silver too, and bronze. Jewels.

More riches, Clare was sure, than even Stuart Morholt had dreamed about.

It was a treasure hunter's dream. And an archaeologist's.

Everything Maggie or Dr. Jenkins would ever have wanted to know about the life and times of an Iron Age Celtic warrior queen could have been discovered right there in that one place.

Weapons and armour lay stacked in neat piles and a dismantled war chariot lay off to one side. Shallow wicker and reed baskets and trays sat heaped with food and wax-sealed wine and beer jugs stood next to drinking mugs and goblets. A chest filled to the brim with rich garments stood next to a wooden crate containing soft leather boots and slippers. There was an ivory-coloured box that looked as though it contained cosmetics or toiletries, and a bronze comb and a mirror lay on top of that. There was even a brazier, provisioned with unused charcoal, and a cauldron that looked a lot like a soup pot. The Iceni must have prepared the tomb for their queen well in advance because it seemed to contain everything that Boudicca could possibly have need of in her next life. Including the companionship of her late husband.

A large slab of polished stone stood alone among the grave goods, on top of which sat a sealed urn decorated with elaborate, swirling patterns.

Prasutagus, Clare thought. *He's here, too.*

On the other side of the chamber, there was another slab of stone. And on it, laid out as if sleeping peacefully, was the body of Queen Boudicca of the Iceni. Clare wondered for an instant why Boudicca's body had not been committed to the flames as her husband's had been. But she already knew the answer: *time.* With the Romans hunting the rebel Iceni, there had been no time for funeral bonfires. Boudicca and Comorra had been buried as they were. Probably Tasca, too, under the third barrow.

She approached the bier hesitantly, as if Boudicca might suddenly sit upright and accuse her, and rightly so, of trespassing. The stone surface was richly draped with furs and the queen lay upon a flowing mantle of her own glorious mane of red hair. Unbound and brushed to gleaming, it reached almost to her knees. Her hands, strong and pale, were wrapped, as Comorra's had been, around the hilt of her sword, whose blade bore the deep grooves of hard-fought battles. The queen's feet were bare and calloused, but gold shone on her wrists and ankles.

And around her neck was the great golden torc.

That makes no sense, Clare thought, frowning. *It was called the Snettisham Torc because it was found in Snettisham.* The neck ring had been discovered stashed in a hole in the ground near the north coast of Norfolk along with a whole bunch of other treasure. But if it was here now, in a grave that had never been discovered, never been plundered, then how was that possible?

Clare looked over to where Connal stood at the foot of Boudicca's bier. His haggard face was like a stone mask, except for his lips, which moved in a silent flood of words Clare couldn't make out. His dark eyes burned as he stared at the queen. Finally he took a step forward and removed one of the two matching silver bracelets that encircled his wrists. He kissed the silver cuff in his hand, and after mouthing another string of unheard words, placed the beautifully wrought ornament on the cold, polished stone at Boudicca's feet.

"It will be my punishment," he murmured. "For serving the queen so blindly in life, my soul will return here after I die to serve her forever in the beyond. For good or ill."

Clare thought he was being a little harsh on himself, but it wasn't the time or place to point that out. Besides, it wasn't as if his spirit was actually tethered to the silver bracelet. It was a gesture, she thought. Nothing more.

He walked over to Clare and held out a hand. "I am finished here and now I will leave this place, Clarinet. Will you come with me? Boudicca's chiefs will come soon to close up the tomb. They will pile rocks over the entrance and cover it with earth and turf. And, with the help of Llassar's enchantments, perhaps the Romans will never find it."

No, Clare thought. *They never will.*

Connal plucked one of the flaring firebrands from its sconce and led the way out of the chamber, Clare following close behind. He led her down a passageway opposite the one they'd come through, into another, smaller chamber that held the body of Tasca, and then out into the chill black night.

Llassar waited with his same bulky travelling pack slung over his shoulder.

"Hey," Clare greeted him. "Mr. Smith."

Llassar blinked at her and then inclined his enormous, leonine head. "Lady Clare," he said. "May the goddess smile upon you."

"Yeah. You too."

"Perhaps one day, again. For now, she turns her face from us, I think."

If Connal was surprised to see that Llassar and Clare knew each other, he didn't register it. In fact, Clare thought, he's not really registering much in the emotion department. She worried about him. He seemed shocky or post-traumatic or something. His behaviour in the grave chamber with the bracelet and Boudicca struck her as odd.

Llassar hefted the pack higher on his shoulder and nodded at it, saying to Connal, "I finished it last night. It will keep her safe. After we close up the barrow, we'll take it to the Great River and offer it to the gods in their domain that they may mark her passage."

Clare recognized now the contours of the bronze shield she'd seen Llassar holding high above his head in her inaugural shimmering. She remembered how it had been that first sight of Connal, the sound of him saying her name, that made her want to explore this world. It seemed like a thousand years had passed since then. In a sense, she supposed it had. "Is that the grave shield?" She nodded at the pack. "Are you guys going to go throw it in the river?"

Connal and Llassar regarded her with mild surprise.

"Hey, look. I'm guessing you cast one of your magic spells on that thing using *my* blood, didn't you?"

The two men exchanged a wary glance. Llassar had the good manners to look vaguely guilty about it.

"Right. Well, so, you shouldn't be surprised that I know about it then. And don't worry. It worked. The grave remains undisturbed."

Llassar seemed relieved, not only that the enchantment, according to Clare, had worked, but that she hadn't wrought some horrible vengeance on him for using her "tylwyth teg" blood in the process.

"Let me ask you something, though." Clare frowned, puzzling. "When you close up the tomb, are you going leave the torc with the queen? The big gold one she's wearing now?"

"Yes!" Llassar said in alarm. "The torc *must* stay with her. It is ..."

"What?" she said with a sinking feeling. "Cursed?"

He nodded his big, shaggy head. "Aye. It was Boudicca's doing. Not just enspelled. But cursed. Blood cursed."

"Damn." Clare put a hand to her neck, remembering the sight of her blood on the cloth Connal had used to clean the wound. *Stupid scrap of cloth ...* "She used my blood in that one, too, didn't she?"

"And her own," Llassar said. "It was a dark spell. An evil spell. I counselled her against it but she would not be dissuaded. Her grief had made her mad. That is why I created the grave shield—so that I could bury her vengeance with her where it would never be found."

Great, Clare thought. *Nice try.* Except that it *had* been found. In a hole in the ground in Snettisham.

Clare took a deep breath and explained, as simply as she could, that in her world the torc was on the loose. The passage of time really did seem an abstract concept to the Druiddyn, but Llassar and Connal seemed to get the gist of it. As she spoke their confusion turned to alarm.

"Connal," Llassar rumbled. "This is ill luck. Clare has only ever sought to help us. For Boudicca's vengeance to be inflicted on her world ... it is not just. Not right."

"You say the barrow remains hidden, Clarinet," Connal said. "Undisturbed. How do you know that? Unless you yourself have found it there?"

"Oh. Yeah." Clare shrugged. "Well, Milo was the one who actually found it. And he's sort of a genius. But like I said, it's undisturbed and we won't tell anyone. In fact, we're actively trying to *keep* it a secret. That's why I'm here talking to you guys."

"Who is Milo?" Connal asked.

"He's ... a friend." Clare blushed and felt ridiculous for it. "He's been trying to help me through all this. Although I'm still not really sure why. All I've done so far is gotten him hit on the head and had a gun pointed at him—"

"The queen's torc must never be worn again, Lady," Llassar interrupted. "You must return it to her barrow. It must lie here with her—or it will carry her spirit out into the world and Boudicca will wreak her vengeance anew. I have seen what my queen is capable of." He looked at Connal. "We both have. It must not happen again."

"How am I supposed to do that?" Clare stared at the smith in disbelief. "Even if I take the torc to the barrow, there's no way to get it *inside* the grave chamber."

"Connal might be able to help," Llassar said quietly, turning to look at the young Druid. "If he is willing."

"Wait," Clare said. "What? He can?" She turned to Connal. "You can?"

Connal looked at the sorcerer smith with a question in his red-rimmed eyes.

"Boudicca meant for you to be her spirit warrior," Llassar said, putting a hand on Connal's shoulder. "But this Shining One kept that from happening."

"Oh ..." Clare grimaced. "You saw me in the boat too, huh?"

Llassar nodded.

"Um." Clare dropped her gaze to the ground. "Yeah. Comorra also had a hand in it. We didn't mean any harm."

"I know. That is why I never told the queen what I saw that night. If Andrasta had wished it so, Clarinet," Llassar said, "it would have been so."

Clare didn't argue.

"I think the Raven Goddess has had other plans for you all along, Connal." His gaze shifted to the silver bracelet the Druid prince wore. "I made those cuffs for you at Boudicca's request, and there is strong magic in them. *Her* magic." He nodded his bearded chin at Clare. "They were to be your talismans, Connal, and through them Andrasta was to give you the gift of walking the spirit ways—just as she opens those ways to Clarinet."

"Right," Clare put in, as if she knew Andrasta personally. Llassar and the rest of her Iceni pals seemed to think she and the war goddess did coffee dates in the Otherworld.

"The spirit warrior ritual was never completed," Llassar continued, speaking directly to Connal. "Your spirit was readied for travel, but it was not released. It is within you still, but it is unbound. Unfettered. It can go forth now ... and then return again. And, once in her world, your spirit can guide Clarinet along another way—along the spiral path that is the unseen road leading into the heart of the queen's barrow."

Clare knew she was staring at Llassar wide-eyed. But, really? Was it so much of a stretch for a Toronto girl who'd been bouncing back and forth in time for the last few days? She turned to look at Connal. There was a wildness still in his eyes, but he'd taken on a look of rigid determination. He nodded once, curtly. Clare got the uneasy feeling that he was agreeing to what Llassar had proposed only because he had nothing to lose.

"You don't have to do this," Clare said.

He shook his head. "Llassar is right. It is Andrasta's will. I will go with you when you return to your world and I will be your guide." He slipped the silver cuff off his wrist and held it out to Llassar. Clare remembered how the talisman had sparked and triggered her own magic when she'd touched it. "Make the magic, Llassar."

"I can," the Druid smith said. "But I'll need help."

"What kind of help?" Clare asked.

Llassar's gaze met hers and, beneath his beard, his mouth quirked upward in a humourless grin. "How good a friend is this … Milo?"

22

"Oh, sure. That doesn't sound like a recipe for disaster at *all*," Al said. And then added, in net-speak, "End sarcasm." Just in case Clare hadn't picked up on it.

Llassar had told Clare what needed to happen if his magic was to work in her world. Clare had conveyed the plan, with all its details and dangers, to Al and Milo. Milo fell silent, mulling the idea, while Al frothed over with proclamations of impending doom.

When Connal had placed his silver wrist cuff in Boudicca's tomb, Clare had assumed it was simply a gesture. Of course, that was before Llassar had enlightened her; otherwise, she never would have guessed that Connal's disembodied spirit was actually tethered to his accessories—one of which was now sitting on Milo's coffee table. It looked innocent enough, but Clare had watched Llassar perform the ritual. She had felt the night air crackle with the power the Druid smith called down and had watched as the cuff began to glow with eerie, eldritch light in the moments before Connal slumped to the ground, senseless. And Clare knew that the bracelet she'd carried back with her through time was brimming with Connal's disembodied spirit—just waiting to be released so that it could play tour guide at Bartlow Hills.

But there was only one way for it to do that.

"Do you have a better idea?" Clare sighed. She shared Al's concerns.

"No." Al sat glaring suspiciously at the harmless-looking piece of jewellery. "But I'm *so* not keen on risking the health and well-being of the only guy in London who will drive us places this summer."

Milo snorted. "Thanks, Allie."

Al waved a dismissive hand at him. "Plus he's my cousin and I love him yada yada. This is a *bad* idea. There cannot possibly be any worse ideas than this one."

"Fine," Clare snapped. "Okay. I know what we're gonna do instead."

"What?"

Clare stood up and pulled on a pair of leather driving gloves that Milo had lent her so that she could handle the silver artifact—and any other shimmer triggers—without risk of coming into contact and setting off a time trip. She put the cuff back in her jacket pocket where Llassar had placed it and turned to Al. "We're going to take Boudicca's torc back to the museum, give it to my aunt, and tell her the whole weird-ass story, top to bottom. And then *she's* going to tell us what the hell to do."

"Okay," Al said. "I give up. You win. That is a much, *much* worse idea."

AL AND MILO had both honestly thought she'd been joking when Clare had made the suggestion back in Milo's apartment. Maggie had thought she'd been joking when she'd started to tell her about the last few days.

None of them thought she was joking now.

But the fact that Maggie thought Clare was being serious didn't exactly mean she was having an easy time wrapping her cerebral faculties around her niece's story. She had tried breaking it down into its component minutiae and focusing on the details one at a time, but that held its own share of problems.

"Wait just one minute, young lady!" Maggie had squawked abruptly at one point in the telling. She shot out of her desk chair and stalked across the room, closing the door to her office and throwing the bolt lock for good measure. "Clare—do you mean to say you've actually *met* Claxton Man?"

"Yes."

"More like 'Claxton Hottie,'" Al murmured.

Clare kicked her under the table. Over in the corner, standing beside a shelf groaning with books and what looked like a real human skull, Milo frowned faintly.

"*The* Claxton Man?" Maggie asked again.

"*Yes.*"

"The *Bog* Man Claxton Man?"

"His real name is Connal—"

"Oh dear ..." Maggie got a bit on the breathy side. "What was he like?"

"Really cute, apparently," Al chimed in.

Clare squeezed her eyes shut. Al seemed to be exacting some kind of penance for Clare's having made time with a dead Druid while Milo got his lights punched out on her behalf. On the one hand, Clare could actually appreciate Al's loyalty to her cousin. On the other, she really wished Al would just shut up.

"Dark smouldering gaze, nice chest, square jaw ..." Al was on a roll. "Soft lips. Occasionally painted blue—"

"Soft ..." Maggie's eyes went window-wide with shock. "Clarinet Imogen Reid! Were you snogging a Bog Man?"

Milo's blue eyes glittered with grim amusement.

"Uh—yeah." Clare glared at Milo defiantly for a moment. She wasn't about to apologize to him. He'd had *five whole years* to declare his affections, after all. She turned her attention back to her aunt. "Yes. A bit. And it wasn't my idea. Also, he was *pre*-bog. But, y'know, thanks for the mental picture ..."

"I haven't even met this boy," Maggie protested weakly, wandering back behind her desk where she wilted down into her chair. Maggie had somehow seized on this one issue and defaulted into parental-substitute mode. "You're not to have boyfriends unless I've at least *met* them ..."

"He is *not* my boyfriend. He is *so* not!" Clare protested hotly. "Look—you can ground me later if you really feel the need, okay—"

"I may just do that."

"—but right now there are slightly more important things to worry about than which archaeological curiosity I've been sucking face with!" Clare glanced over at Milo. "That goes for you, too!"

Clare's outburst seemed to snap Maggie back to reality somewhat. She raked a hand through her hair, throwing one side of her neatly swept updo into disarray. "I just don't know what you expect me to make of all this, Clare. The whole story is ... well, it's ..."

"Mags," Clare said quietly, "Please. I *know* you used to hang around with Stuart Morholt. *He* had no trouble believing any of it. And I have a sneaking suspicion that, deep down, you don't either."

Maggie regarded Clare sharply for a long silent moment, an obvious struggle going on behind her eyes.

"Do you?" Clare asked.

"I ..." Maggie sighed and slumped forward, leaning on her desk. "... No. You're right, Clare. I've ... seen things. Done things. A long time ago."

"You were one of the Order of the Free Peoples of Prydein, weren't you, Dr. Wallace?" Milo asked.

Clare and Al turned to stare at him. And then back at Maggie.

"I was very young. Inexcusably stupid. Also a bit smitten ..." Maggie smiled bitterly. "We were all antiquities students at Cambridge, and—just purely for fun, you understand—a bunch of us formed a little secret club. In the beginning it was just a silly excuse to dress up and have parties in fields. But for a core group of us, it became something more. One time, in second year, we decided to take a road trip to Glastonbury Tor."

"That big hill in the Midlands where they have the hippie music festival every year?" Clare's parents had actually gone to it once, back in the throes of their bizarre musical youth, and she'd seen pictures of them standing knee-deep in mud and paisley polyester at the base of the hill.

"Yes." Maggie nodded. "There's always been a theory—not exactly a scientific one, mind you—that says if you walk the path the right way, you open up a mystical portal to another world."

"I did some recent aerial survey conversions of that area," Milo said. "In overhead photographs you can see ridges in the hillside that wind around in a kind of switchback pattern. Like a maze."

"*Exactly* like a maze." Maggie nodded. "Some people think King Arthur's buried there. Others think it's a gateway to Hell. Or the Underworld." She looked at Clare. "Or the past."

Clare shivered.

"At any rate, there was one young man who was part of our group, and he worshipped Stuart, who treated him as a lackey, of course." Maggie's gaze went unfocused as she began to remember. "There was ... an incident. Stuart performed a ritual he'd discovered in some arcane text with one of the artifacts we'd found on a student dig. The young man—he was just a boy, really, a Romance Languages major—he just ... disappeared. Vanished into thin air right in front of our eyes. We never saw him again."

"Did you go to the police?"

Maggie shook her head. "I'm thoroughly ashamed to say we didn't. I didn't. Stuart convinced us straightaway that we'd be laughed out of the university. Or worse—charged with some sort of crime. So we all agreed to never speak of it again. The poor lad's disappearance was chalked up to a runaway due to academic stress." She sighed, and it was the saddest sound Clare had ever heard her aunt make. "But every year on that date I drive out to Glastonbury. And I can hear him. *Feel* him there. He's not gone. He's just ..."

"Elsewhere," Clare said. *"Elsewhen.* I know. I've been there."

"Yes." Maggie's gaze snapped back to her niece. "And you have a *lot* to answer for young lady, after all this is said and done! What have I always told you about antiquities? NO TOUCHING."

Clare refrained from pointing out that touching antiquities was what Maggie did all the time and, in fact, she'd developed a nicely lucrative little career for herself in the process. "So what do we do, Mags? Do we give the torc back to the museum? Hand it over to Dr. Jenkins? Tell her to increase security by about a billion percent?"

Maggie took her glasses off her head and tossed them on the desk, pinching the bridge of her nose. "I haven't seen Ceciley all day. And frankly, I'm rather disappointed in her. She vehemently denied that Stuart Morholt is even alive—let alone responsible for the theft—even after I showed her the note he left behind. But she knows as well as I do what he's capable of."

"What *is* he capable of?"

"Exploding things, mostly. After the incident at Glastonbury he went a bit off the rails. I mean, mentally. We parted ways—rather acrimoniously—and I haven't had any direct contact with him since. Not until the torc was stolen and he saw fit to send me a mocking little note letting me know *he* was the one who'd stolen it."

"Why'd you guys break up?"

"Because after Glastonbury I decided to leave the whole of that nonsense behind me and concentrate on *real* history and *real* science. No more mystic mumbo jumbo for me. As for Stuart, in the early eighties he became notorious—wanted by Scotland Yard for several instances of what, in today's parlance, would be known as 'domestic terrorism.' He was responsible for blowing up the offices of developers and politicians who were razing sites he deemed of historical significance. Even if they were of no real worth whatsoever to the scholarly community. He once broke into a construction site near Tewkesbury and torched an entire fleet of bulldozers because a road-widening project was going to require the removal of an ancient yew tree that Stuart had decided was once sacred to the Druiddyn."

"Really. How would he know?"

"Oh, it's all arbitrary nonsense. He claimed he was being spoken to from the beyond, haunted by the spirit voice of an ancient Druid. One who demanded the restoration of the greatness of the Celtic Tribes—a true return to the glory of the Island of the Mighty. Honestly. He's completely mad. And when the authorities came close to catching him one too many times, he faked his own death. I knew it wasn't true. I think Ceciley did, too. She's just been in denial all this time. Poor deluded thing."

"What's her connection to him?"

"She was also a member of the Free Peoples back in the day. I always suspected that she only did it because she was rather nutty over Morholt."

"But Stu had his eye on someone else," Al said.

Good lord, thought Clare. *Maggie's blushing.*

"I don't think it's safe to return the torc to the public eye at the moment," Maggie continued, brushing aside the comment. "Dr. Jenkins doesn't take Stuart Morholt seriously, and I don't think she'll believe your story about Boudicca's curse. To this day she denies she was even *with* us at Glastonbury Tor. No. I think we have to risk returning the torc to its rightful owner."

Clare blinked. Honestly, it was the last thing she'd expected Maggie to propose. "You mean ...?"

"I think we must go to Bartlow and walk your Druid's spiral path."

Al was staring openly at her. "I thought you said it was all mystic mumbo jumbo."

"I did," Maggie replied grimly. "But I didn't say it wasn't real."

"MILO?" He'd been silent for almost a full two minutes. Clare could hardly blame him, now that she'd told him exactly what she needed him to do.

She shifted Comorra's brooch from one leather-gloved palm to the other, reassuring herself that she had it with her so that she could leave it with the princess in her tomb. It seemed only right, somehow. Still, Clare was having massive second thoughts about the whole scheme. It was one thing to send herself hurtling through time and space, but another thing entirely to enlist Milo to play host to the disembodied spirit of an ancient mystical warrior prince. It really was asking too much.

"Milo?" she said again. "You seriously don't have to do this if you don't want to."

"Right," he said finally, raising his head and smiling faintly at her. "I remember you saying you didn't want me to be a hero."

Damn. I never should have opened my big mouth. "That's so not what I meant and you know it," she said, frowning up at him. "I just meant you don't have anything to prove to me."

"I know that, Clare."

His eyes were so blue it was almost like staring up into a cloudless sky. Clare found herself getting lost in his gaze.

He grinned. "But maybe I have something to prove to myself. I mean, hey—what kind of self-respecting geek chickens out from an actual paranormal experience? I'd have to turn in my Ghostbusters proton pack *and* my Green Lantern ring. Plus they'd bar me from the San Diego Comic-Con for life."

Clare grinned back. "I love it when you talk nerdy to me."

"Ooh," he leaned down and whispered in her ear, "when all this is over, remind me to read you poetry in Elvish."

"Elvis wrote poems?"

"Can we shelve the canoodling till a later date, guys?" Al suddenly appeared beside them, effectively putting a stop to the nerd-flirting. "I have limited reserve nerve for this mission and I'd rather not have a complete mental breakdown before we achieve our objective."

Maggie finished double-bolting her office door and joined Clare, Al, and Milo in the middle of the room. They had decided that, before heading out to the middle of Cambridgeshire to find the Bartlow Hills tumuli, they would first test whether Connal's spirit could indeed be transferred into Milo's consciousness. Since they wouldn't be able to get into the tomb without Connal's help, they had to find out first if the magic worked.

Clare pocketed Comorra's raven brooch and nervously picked up the silver cuff from the table. She held it out to Milo, who reached out a hand.

"Wait!" Clare said. "For luck ..."

She stood on tiptoes and kissed him lightly on the lips. Before Milo could turn too bright a shade of pink he took a deep breath, plucked the silver cuff from Clare's palm, and slipped it over his wrist. Maggie and the girls watched, horrified, as Milo's eyes suddenly flew wide and he opened his mouth in a silent scream. The muscles of his neck stood out in sharp relief and veins in his temples began to bulge. His hands grabbed for the sides of his head and collapsed forward, landing hard on his knees as he went down on all fours.

"Milo!" Clare shouted and dropped to the ground in front of him.

"Dude ..." He started murmuring like a chant, his body rocking back and forth. "Dude ... dude ... *dude* ... chill ..."

"Milo?" Clare reached out but he flinched away from her.

"Chill ... seriously ... I'm here ... I ..." He wrapped his long arms around his own shoulders, hugging himself as if to keep from flying apart. "I'm right here. Let me drive. Let *me* drive, man ..." Beads of sweat stood out on his forehead. "Dude ... Connal. Chill out, man ... this hurts ..."

Staggering to his feet, he backed into the corner of the office, his shoulders jamming up against the shelves, rattling the skull, and batted the glasses off his face. The girls and Maggie watched, spellbound, as Milo became ... spellbound. His posture altered. So did the carriage of his head and his facial expression—all subtly, but distinctly. Clare could've sworn that, for the briefest instant, his blue eyes actually darkened to Connal's almost-black brown.

"Clarinet ..." Her name rasped out from between Milo's lips in a voice that was definitely not Milo's.

"Connal?"

"Aye ..." He shook the yellow hair from his eyes and stared wildly around the room. At the books and furniture and high, plate-glass windows. At the electric light fixtures and the computer whose screen saver swirled with brilliant colours and patterns. He took a hesitant step forward and looked down at his own feet. At the jeans and sneakers he wore, at his hands ...

at the watch on his—on Milo's—wrist. He fingered the fabric of the T-shirt he wore.

Then he lifted his gaze and peered at Clare as if she was hard to see. "This is the Otherworld?"

"This is *my* world," she said quietly and picked up his glasses, handing them to him.

He put them gingerly back on his face and blinked. Then his gaze shifted to where Al stood, one fist jammed against her mouth so that she wouldn't scream. "You." His voice was lower than Milo's by almost an octave. The words came out as guttural and musical at the same time. "You are ... Allie?"

Al nodded and squeaked out, "I'm your cousin. His cousin. Milo's cousin."

He nodded, his expression turning inward. "Milo ..."

"Is he there?" Clare asked.

Connal nodded and smiled, the muscles of his face tight. "He is. I can see things. Know things. Through his eyes ... his mind ... It is an interesting experience."

"I'll bet," Clare said, and took him gently by the arm. "I'd like you to meet someone." She looked over to where her aunt stood open-mouthed in awe. "Mags?"

Maggie stepped toward the young man who only a moment before had been someone else entirely.

"Connal." Clare took Maggie by the elbow and drew her closer. "This is my aunt, Doctor Magda Wallace."

"The blessings of the goddess fall upon you, Doctor Magda Wallace." Connal's voice was rough, but he inclined his head toward Maggie in a gesture of respect.

"I ... I ... it's very nice to meet you, young man," Maggie stammered, as star-struck as if she'd just met one of the Beatles. Which for an archaeologist, Clare supposed, she kind of had.

"Milo?" Clare shook his arm a little. "Are you still in there?"

He turned to her, and after a moment smiled the ghost of a familiar smile. "Still here, Clare de Lune," he said, his voice sounding far away. "It's a little crowded in here all of a sudden, but yeah ... I'm still here."

"Still in the driver's seat?"

"Yeah ... yeah. I'm still driving. Maybe though, just to be on the safe side, somebody else should take the wheel on the way up to Bartlow." He dug into the pocket of his jeans and tossed the keys to the Bimmer to Maggie. Then he winked at Clare. A wink that could have been Milo's own—or not. It looked as though it took a lot of effort. "C'mon," he said, his face shifting through unfamiliar expressions as he headed toward the door. "Let's go."

23

It was just before moonrise.

Clare, Al, Milo, and Maggie stood in a circle on the platform at the summit of Bartlow High Hill. The land all around them seemed touched with magic that evening. Deep shadows pooled in the contours of the countryside like dozens of black lakes as a big-bellied harvest moon rose, casting a silvery-golden glow on the gentle swells of far distant hills. Milo—Connal, really—turned his face toward the kiss of the moon's light as it lifted above the bowl of the Earth, balancing on the edge of the horizon for a long moment like a tightrope walker on a high wire. Then it lifted free and began its slow and stately passage, sailing across the face of the indigo sky.

Milo closed his eyes, and when he opened them again his blue gaze had been replaced with the Druid prince's dark, haunting—or maybe it was haunt*ed*—stare. He held out a hand to Clare on one side and Maggie on the other. Clare stripped off the driving gloves she'd been wearing and took his hand. Maggie took the other, and then they both held out their other hands to Al, who swallowed nervously before reaching out to close the circle. As the silver cuff on Milo's wrist began to glow Clare was struck by an illusion of the fox and raven coming to life, chasing each other around and around in an endless circle. Milo's lips started to move, mouthing silent incantations in the same way Connal had done in Bouddica's tomb. A sudden surge of electrical energy flowed through them and Clare gasped, closing her eyes against the sensation.

"Look," Connal's voice said after a moment. "See."

Clare opened her eyes. The world around her ...

"It *shimmers*," Al breathed. "Oh wow, Clare ... you were so right."

Maggie and the girls looked out over the transformed landscape that glimmered faintly, as if dusted with starlight.

"Do you *see* that?" Clare said, her voice barely a whisper in the cool night air. "There *is* a path ..."

"There is indeed," said Connal as he dropped Maggie's hand, "but only for those with the sight to see."

Still holding on to Clare, he stepped off the wooden platform and led them onto the sparkling track—a gleaming, phosphorescent trail that wound around the hill. It bent and twisted into spirals and whorls, knotting and writhing like the patterns on the Battersea Shield. Or like the designs on Comorra's brooch. The walkway looked as though it were made of thousands of fireflies, their tiny sparks glinting in the droplets clinging to the dew-wet grass.

Milo's feet moved with unerring certainty as Connal's spirit led them around and around the hill. Every time the path intersected with the modern wooden staircase Connal simply walked through it as if the stairs were an illusion. As if they didn't exist.

Clare and the others followed in his footsteps until suddenly ...

"Claaarrre? Whaaaatt's haaaapeeeniiing ..." Al's distorted voice echoed all around her as Clare glanced wildly about. *Everything* was sparkling fiercely now. Not just the path but the trees and the hills and the night sky. The air itself shimmered and danced as if they stood in a snow globe that some giant hand had just turned upside down. Clare heard Maggie's sharp

intake of breath and then, as quickly as it had begun, it ended. Gone. All the billions of sparkly lights just winked out. It was utterly, completely, terrifyingly dark.

"Clare?" Al whimpered.

"Hang on ..." Clare fumbled for the tin candle and safety matches they'd found in an emergency kit in the trunk of Milo's car, half-buried underneath a bunch of old vinyl records and a cricket bat. But even before she lit the wick, the stale, cold, earthy smell of the place told Clare where they were. The illumination from the thin yellow flame of the candle proved her right. They had done it. And now they stood in the middle of the vaulted central chamber of Boudicca's tomb.

"Okay," Al said weakly, standing paralyzed beside her. "I'm gonna faint now ..."

"Al!" Clare shook her a little. "It's okay—we did it!"

"I know. That's why I'm going to faint."

"Don't be scared." Clare brought the light up between them, the ghoulish shadows it cast undermining her words.

"You're joking, right?"

"No." Connal answered for her. "There's nothing to be afraid of here."

"Now I *know* you're joking."

"Alice," Maggie said kindly, "I guarantee we are the only living things in this chamber. The barrow has been sealed shut for almost two thousand years. There's no one else here!"

"Well ..." A voice echoed off the high stone roof. "No one else except me."

AL MUST HAVE jumped a foot and a half when she heard Stuart Morholt's voice. Maggie used a particularly vibrant swear word, and Clare just hung her head, defeat washing over her.

"I don't believe this," she groaned.

"Oh believe it, my dear Miss Reid," Morholt said, his smile ghastly in the glow of Clare's candle. The gun in his fist gleamed in the light.

"How did you find us?" Clare asked, her voice leaden.

"Yeah," Al said, "how? I totally got away clean from your stupid hideout."

Morholt rolled his eyes. "I *totally* let you."

"What?"

"I put a two-way GPS transceiver in your computer bag." Morholt knotted his arms across his chest, a self-satisfied sneer lifting one corner of his mouth. "I figured that if you could act as Miss Reid's homing beacon, you might as well act as mine. You're such clever things, you two. I gambled that you would eventually find the tomb. As much as she doth protest, I knew that our intrepid time traveller simply wouldn't let it go until she'd found this place." He turned to Clare. "And I vowed that when you did I'd be right behind you. In a somewhat worse-for-wear Bentley, I might add. Don't think I've forgiven you ladies for that."

Clare glared at him. It was frustrating in the *extreme* that he was right.

He winked at her. "Curiosity, meet cat."

"Fine," she muttered. "So that's how you tracked us to Bartlow. How did you follow us down *here*? Mystical GPS?"

"When I said you were clever, I didn't necessarily mean you were smart." Morholt shrugged. "I'm not sure how you managed to work out the exact pattern of the spiral path, but I can tell you that footsteps in wet grass tend to leave a pretty clear impression under the light of a full moon. You left a trail the village idiot could have followed."

"I guess that means you should drop off your 'Idiot' job application at Bartlow Village Council," Clare shot back. "Maybe they're hiring."

Morholt's sneer went a bit brittle. "You little—"

"Stuart, will you for once in your life stop being such an ass?" Maggie burst out. "Just for one moment! *Look* where you are. Where we are. Think about it. This is not a game."

Morholt turned to Clare's aunt, his dark eyes glittering. "I never for an instant thought it was, Magda. That was always *your* failing. Perhaps you'll admit now that science doesn't have an answer for everything."

"Neither do you," Clare said. "I think this *is* all a big game to you. You yammer on about honour and glory and Boudicca's righteous wrath. But I've been there and I've seen what happened and I know some of the people involved. They're not some abstract concept in a history text. They're not just a couple of dry lines written by that whatsisname guy—"

"Tacitus," Al murmured.

"Right." Clare nodded. "The Iceni were people and they hurt and loved and died just like people do now."

"Died and left behind a legacy that should not be lying forgotten in a tomb where it can do no one any good," Morholt said. "I'd wager there is enough treasure here in this one tomb for me to build an empire and dedicate it to the ideals of the forgotten tribes of this island." His voice rose as he spoke, echoing off the walls of the chamber.

Clare wondered if he really was that deluded.

"Which reminds me." He pointed the gun at Al. "Hand over the box."

Al hesitated. But Morholt seemed to have little patience to spare with the girl who'd dented his Bentley. He cocked the hammer back on the pistol with a click that was shockingly loud in the gloom.

"Now."

Al reached into her bag and pulled out the rosewood box that held the torc. She handed it to Morholt, who flipped open the lid.

It was empty.

"What the hell?" Clare gasped.

Morholt pointed his gun at Al's head. "Cute," he snarled. "Where is it?"

"It was there! It was right there! I swear!" Al said frantically.

"It can't be," Milo said faintly. His voice was thin but, Clare noticed, it was his. Not Connal's. "Something we didn't take into consideration. The torc—it's already here. Once we crossed over the mystical threshold into the barrow, both versions of the torc couldn't exist in the same place. I'll bet it's still around Boudicca's neck, because"—he glared meaningfully at Stuart Morholt—"in this timeline here inside the tomb, it hasn't been stolen yet."

"Right you are. An oversight I aim to correct."

"I know you ..." Milo spoke again, only this time it wasn't Milo. The shift was subtle, but Clare recognized Connal's intonation taking over once more.

Morholt raised an eyebrow. "Of course you know me. Or did I jar loose a few neural pathways when I knocked you on the head?"

Connal took a step forward, hands curling into fists. "I know what you are," he said in a low growl. "You seek to take that which isn't yours. You remind me of the Romans."

For a moment Morholt frowned in confusion and his gaze shifted between Milo and Clare—he had no way of knowing that the handsome young computer geek was toting around the consciousness of one of the very people Morholt claimed he'd taken up the legacy of.

The self-professed Druid waved his gun at the real Druid and said, "Back off, hero. All of you. Stand over there," he ordered, motioning them toward the rough stone wall they could just make out in the gloom.

"Milo," Clare whispered into his ear, "can you get a grip on Connal, please? Try to explain the concept of 'gun' to him." She watched as Milo's face contorted through a series of expressions as if he were having a silent argument with himself—which in a way, Clare supposed he was. Then he shook his head sharply and the tendons of his neck seeming to relax a bit. He let Clare guide him toward the wall while Morholt knelt carefully and shrugged out of an enormous backpack. He pulled out a jumbo-sized glowstick—obviously he'd remembered the effect of shimmering on electronics and had made allowances—and with a crack, twisted the plastic tube to activate the chemical luminescence. In the eerie green light Clare got a good look at him. Morholt was dressed head to toe in a black jumpsuit with so many pockets and zippers and snaps it looked as if he'd mugged an eighties hair band and stolen their gear. He wore black leather gloves, military-style boots, and a Batman-worthy utility belt.

As he raised the sickly-green illumination over his head it revealed the true spectacle of the contents of the tomb.

Even Clare—already knowing what was there—was affected by the sight.

On the great stone bier Boudicca's skeleton lay upon a long carpet of red hair, the great golden torc resting on fleshless collarbones that gleamed a pale chartreuse in the green chemical glow. The queen's once-rich garments had been reduced almost to dust and the iron sword that had lain on her breast had rusted away to almost nothing—only the bronze hilt remaining intact in the cage of her skeletal fingers. Everywhere else in the tomb precious stones winked and gold and silver and bronze glowed, but it was the sight of that corroded blade, a warrior sword reduced to brittle shards, that Clare couldn't drag her gaze away from.

Because *that* was what Boudicca had been, first and foremost. A warrior.

Queen, mother, wife, even woman—those things had been secondary. "Diplomat," Clare thought, hadn't even made the list. Instead her fierce pride had won out over everything else—including her need to survive. It had cost her life. And the lives of seventy thousand other men and women, and Clare simply could not wrap her head around that. Comorra dead. Connal wounded and weeping, living broken for the rest of his days—however many more there had been. Londinium burned to the ground. And all for what?

For honour.

For vengeance.

For Andrasta ... Clare flinched at the words that whispered in her mind in the husky voice of the queen. Her glance flew to the bier where the remains of Boudicca lay.

Still dead, she thought, trying to steady herself. Still lying there. Not even a tongue left in her skull that could have spoken those words.

Clare took a deep breath. In the uncertain, goblin-green light the shadows leaped and danced on the barrow walls like giant raven's wings spreading wide on phantom winds. But that was just an illusion. And the voice Clare had heard was just a trick of her overheated imagination. She was sure of that. Mostly sure ...

Stuart Morholt unzipped another compartment of his pack, removed bricks of what looked like modelling clay, and stacked them in a little pyramid.

"Is that what I think it is?" Milo asked in a cracking voice.

"It is, if you think it's plastic explosives." Morholt withdrew a handful of batteries and inserted them into a little black box he pulled from another pocket. A light on its side blinked red and green. Satisfied, he took out the batteries and put them back into the pocket. "Just in case. We don't want any stray zotting to fry my detonator now, do we?"

"Shimmering," Al barked. "And what the-detonator *hell*?"

Morholt chuckled. "I, in my wisdom, foresight, and extreme cleverness, saw fit to bring enough C-4 with me on this little expedition to bring down half of Mount Everest." He patted the bulky pack affectionately. "I'd planned on using it to get *into* the tomb ..."

Clare was agog at the damage he could wreak. "You were going to *blast* your way in here?"

"Yes." Morholt grinned unpleasantly. "But fortunately I had you, Dorothy, to lead the way down the Yellow Brick Road. And so now I'll just use it to get out. I'll pack the original entry with the plastique and kaboom. Under this much dirt, even the local pub hounds won't hear a thing. Then off I'll go into the night, with the richest hoard of treasure this side of the Valley of the Kings!"

"You can't do that! You can't blow a hole in Boudicca's tomb—"

"Oh, stop." Morholt's voice was cold. Hard. "Don't get all self-righteous with me, Miss Reid. How on earth did *you* plan on getting back out? Do you have a magic spell for that, too? No? I warrant a few dark, cold hours down here with no apparent egress—"

"'Egress'?" Clare interrupted him.

"*Way out*, you twit!" Morholt snapped. "And I'd hazard a guess that, after a few hours trapped down here, you lot would be *begging* for a couple of sticks of dynamite."

Clare thought about that for a moment. She turned to glance at Milo, who was frowning faintly. His eyes were cloudy and she wasn't sure how much of the conversation he—or rather Connal—had understood. It was true, they'd walked the path to get *into* the barrow. She wasn't entirely certain now that there even *was* a way out. Tombs were generally supposed to be one-way only, right? Maybe, once they'd returned the torc to its rightful owner, that would be it. Maybe they weren't ever meant to get out—

A stack of folded canvas bags landed with a thump at her feet.

"Now, ladies, gentleman, if you please ..." Morholt gestured at the bags. "Start with the gold, move on to the silver, and then, if we have room, choose a couple of the nicer bronze pieces. You can leave what's left of Boudicca's sword—in truth, I abhor violence—but don't forget her anklets and the gold belt. And that rather lovely silver wrist cuff sitting on the bier at her feet."

"Oh, *man.*" Al looked like she was trying to decide between getting sick or just plain fainting. "You want us to rob a *corpse?*"

"An historically significant corpse, yes." Stuart Morholt smiled coldly. "I'd pack *that* up too, if I thought Boudee's old bones could stand the journey. Alas, I'll have to settle for incalculable riches over academic worth."

Maggie's lips disappeared in a thin white line. She took a step forward, but Morholt just glared at her and held out the rosewood box. "Since you're the expert in handling antiquities, Maggie old girl, fetch me that neck ring."

"No. Shoot me if you want, but I won't desecrate that corpse."

"I think you will. Because if you don't, I'll shoot your niece." The gun swung to point at Clare. "And I am deadly serious this time. I'm very much done playing games with young Miss Reid."

"You really are a son of a bitch, Stuart," Maggie said. But she went and gently removed the torc without rattling a single bone. The golden neck ring was covered with a layer of dust, Clare saw, but otherwise looked exactly like the one that had lain in the box that Morholt held out to her aunt. Maggie placed it reverently on the velvet lining and Morholt snapped the lid shut.

"Put it over there, by the entrance, if you please." He indicated the tunnel through which they'd passed and then went about emptying a basket full of gold and silver torcs into the bag he held in his hand. Maggie set the box down in the shadowy mouth of the passageway and returned to Clare and the others.

"Good girl."

Maggie looked as if she was about to weep with rage.

"Now, Magda, no sentiment or misplaced notions of archaeological significance, I beg you." Morholt waved at the bier. "The old bird would never have been discovered in the first place without the profound historical meddlings of your delightful young charge. And I'm quite sure Boudicca herself, were she here, would be the first to tell you that *that*"—he pointed to the remains on the bier—"isn't her and has very little to do with her. Those are scraps. Mortal remains. Her spirit, I'm sure she'd say, lives on."

"Are you?" said a voice of smoke and ashes from the darkness of the tunnel mouth. "Are you really sure? Why don't you ask her yourself and find out."

24

Dr. Jenkins stepped out of the shadows and into the circle of light. There was something ... very *different* about her, and Morholt was the only one who didn't seem to notice it right away.

"Damn it, Ceciley," he said, barely glancing at her as he emptied another basket of ill-gotten booty into a bag and pulled the drawstring, stuffing it into his knapsack. "You were supposed to wait with the car and fend off any nosy locals. Can't you ever take direction?"

Ah, Clare thought. *So that's how Stu was able to steal the torc so easily in the first place. Inside job. That's probably who he'd been yakking on his cell phone to back at the warehouse.*

She looked back at the curator. Dr. Jenkins's glasses were gone and her lab coat hung from her shoulders in an almost cloaklike manner. Her hair, loosened from its severe updo, hung in waves past her shoulders, and in the light from the glowstick it looked redder somehow. She was barefoot. But the most notable thing about her appearance was that Boudicca's torc lay gleaming about her neck. The rosewood box lay open and empty at her feet.

"Oh, bloody hell," Maggie muttered. "Ceciley, you stupid, *stupid* wretch ..."

Smiling unpleasantly, Dr. Jenkins stood in a relaxed yet threatening stance in the mouth of the passageway. "Hello, Magda," she said in a low growl. "You're looking ... unwell. A bit pale. Perhaps it's the loss of all that smug superiority."

Suddenly the curator's face twisted even more grotesquely and she clutched at the torc around her throat as if it strangled her. She seemed to be going through what Milo had experienced when he'd slipped Connal's bracelet on. She panted like a wounded animal, gritting her teeth against the urge to scream, her eyes rolling white in her head.

After a moment her head fell forward and she looked as if she might sink to her knees. She thrust out a hand to steady herself against the wall.

"Ceciley?" Maggie took a tentative step forward.

Morholt finally interrupted his pillaging to look over at his accomplice. "What the hell—"

Dr. Jenkins's head snapped up, her gaze zeroing in on Stuart Morholt. "Thief ..." she whispered, the word slithering from her lips.

The air in the chamber seemed to be growing hotter and stuffier by the second and Clare wondered for a panicked moment if they were using up all the oxygen. The shadows leaping up the wall behind Dr. Jenkins looked as though they were too thick. *Shadows weren't supposed to be thick,* Clare thought. They seemed to have weight. Dimension. *Anger ...*

Suddenly the pitch torches on the chamber's walls—cold and dead for almost two thousand years—flared to brilliant, roaring life. Al yelped like a puppy and Clare dropped her candle, snuffing out its meagre flame. Morholt's glowstick exploded in a shower of green spatters that sputtered and extinguished—but it no longer mattered. The angry, writhing swaths of crimson and orange light racing across the domed roof of Boudicca's tomb cast more than enough illumination.

Morholt swung the barrel of his gun in the direction of the curator. Dr. Jenkins flung her arms wide and the weapon flew from his hand to shatter against the rough-hewn stone wall.

"Damnation!" Morholt protested. "That was an authentic film prop! I stole that!"

Anger momentarily trumped fear and Clare pegged him with a disgusted stare. "You mean that it wasn't even a *real* gun? Oh, I hate you so much."

"I told you," Morholt muttered. "I abhor violence."

"Well *that's* too bad," Clare snarled. "Because I'm gonna kill you with my bare hands."

Morholt's eyes hadn't left Dr. Jenkins's face. He nodded at the curator. "You may have to take a number."

"I've already got mine," Maggie said, glaring at him side-ways.

"Shut up, Magda!" Dr. Jenkins spat furiously. "You had your chance with him. You were just too blind and frightened to take up the mantle of the Druid Queen. You could have had everything—with Stuart at your side."

Morholt made a scoffing sound. "*She* would have been at *my* side, if anything ..."

"Oh, Ceciley." Maggie shook her head sadly. "Is that really it? All this time you've been jealous of my relationship with this ... this charlatan?"

"I'm hardly that!" Morholt said hotly. "You were there the night I opened that portal. You cannot possibly deny my power in the face of that. My abilities ..."

Dr. Jenkins's laugh was tinged with an edge of hysteria. "*Your* abilities. You had nothing to do with it. You don't even know how you managed it. But you are right about one thing. Dear precious Maggie here turned her back on the greatness of that achievement. And because of that, the sacrifice was in vain."

"Sacrifice!" Maggie was aghast. "You *intended* what happened to that poor boy?"

"What?" Morholt looked confused.

"Yes," Dr. Jenkins said flatly.

"No!" Morholt's complexion went ashen. "That was *not* part of the plan. It just happened. Magda—you know me better than that—"

"Which is why I never let you in on that part of the ritual, Stuart," the curator said. "You're weak. Sneaking. Power-hungry ... easy enough to manipulate. I may not have known exactly what would happen that night, but I knew something would. But we were never able to replicate the feat afterward—not without your participation, *Doctor* Wallace." The way she said Maggie's title made it sound like an insult. "But how ironic that this girl—this blood relation of yours—would be the one to cross over truly. The one to become our conduit and our guide. My path to Boudicca's vengeance ..."

The curator's head fell forward again, hair curtaining her features. Maggie took another uncertain step toward her colleague. Toward the woman who was *once* her colleague. The shadows roiled and coalesced, gathering around her. After long moments Ceciley Jenkins raised her head again, her dark eyes gleaming.

"For Andrasta ..." she hissed. Her voice held no trace of the curator's now—it was all Boudicca's.

She's transforming on a much deeper level than Milo did, Clare thought. She exchanged a worried glance with Al.

"Was I a pawn, too, my queen?" Milo took a step forward.

The curator's eyes flicked over to where Milo had spoken in Connal's voice. In the language of the ancient Iceni.

"A game piece in your schemes?" he continued.

"Connal. My. What a surprise." Boudicca's gaze went flat and serpentine. Full of an old rage as harsh and indelible as a dried blood stain. "Yes, you were." She too spoke in the Iceni tongue. "An ineffectual one. You were supposed to die that night and lead my spirit warriors to victory. Not live to watch our home and people go down under the sandal of the Roman. And there will be a reckoning for that. The spirit warriors will see to it."

Clare was assaulted once again with the image of Connal's remains in a glass case. "For the record? Their deaths didn't do you one damn bit of good," she said. "Neither did Connal's. It didn't make a difference—and so it didn't have to happen. And for another record? I was the one who helped him escape that 'fate.' Me and Comorra. Would you punish her, too?"

"She is my daughter," Boudicca said simply.

"She is indeed," Connal said. "And she followed close behind in your footsteps, my queen. She lies in the next chamber."

The shadow of a frown crept over Boudicca's face.

"She drank from your cup."

"No."

Boudicca spun on her heel and stalked toward the ante-chamber where Clare had seen Comorra's body and where dead torches now flared to life. A moment of weighted silence filled the dark air. Then a keening wail, almost inhuman, drifted back toward the main chamber. It raised the small hairs on Clare's arms.

"Well *that's* a bit distracting," Morholt said, stepping toward the archway. "Right. I'll just go take care of this unforeseen complication ..."

Maggie put out a hand to stop him. "I really don't think—"

"Magda." Morholt rolled an eye at her. "The poor woman is distraught. She needs comforting and, insofar as she is desperately in love with me, I dare say I'm the best party to offer it."

Maggie gaped at the utter brainless arrogance of the man. "To Ceciley, perhaps—although I have my doubts about that—but not to Boudicca."

"It's Ceciley's unrequited passion that's *made* her vulnerable to Boudicca in the first place," he said as if explaining the matter to a child. "If I can reach *her*, convince her she has a shot with me, I'm sure I could distract her long enough to get out of this mess before all the breathable oxygen runs out. Trust me. Love is all-powerful." He hitched up his utility belt and stalked down the corridor.

"And stupidity," Maggie shook her head, "knows no bounds."

"This is a staggeringly bad idea," Al murmured.

"Agreed," Clare said. "Let's go watch Stu get his pompous ass kicked."

"CECILEY—" Morholt put out a placating hand.

"Don't you touch me!" Dr. Jenkins turned on Morholt viciously, her face clouded with an anger that was more than just her own.

"Darling, it's *me*—"

"You stole my heart," she snarled. "Wretched thief ..."

"Ceciley, darling ..." Morholt tried again. "I really think you're just experiencing a touch of borrowed aggression. If you would just allow me to—"

"Worst smooth-talker *ever*," Al murmured to Clare.

"You stole my gold." The curator's fingertips brushed the sinewy contours of the torc around her neck.

"Er ... Boudicca?" Morholt peered at her closely.

"My husband. My daughters."

"Is Ceciley there?"

"You ... stole ... my ... land!" Boudicca's raven's-cry voice howled out of her wide-open mouth, louder than a full, crashing orchestra. The room grew even brighter and hotter, the air shimmered, and then she seemed to draw all the light and energy and heat back into herself. Beads of perspiration

shone on her forehead, her face looked gaunt and strained, her limbs shook. But in the light of the now-flickering torches her eyes still glinted almost red. Shadows licked at the dense air—Clare swore that she could almost *feel* them tangling in her hair like bats—swooping and diving, howling like wind through a tunnel.

The curator/queen stepped toward Morholt, hands splayed wide like the talons of some great bird of prey.

She did not see Stuart Morholt.

"Thieving Roman," she screeched. "I will make you pay!"

She saw Seutonius Paulinus.

"Good God, woman!" Morholt began to retreat down the passageway, and as she advanced toward him he turned and made a run for it. He barrelled past Clare and the others as Ceciley/Boudicca followed swiftly in his wake, looking for all the world like an avenging Fury.

They heard Morholt's screams. There was a flash of fire that sent them all scrambling away from the tunnel mouth ... and then there was darkness. Clare started to panic until she remembered the safety matches in her pocket. With shaking fingers, she struck one off the cavern wall. The sting of sulphur made her eyes water, but the bright little flame was enormously comforting in the absolute blackness.

At her side, Clare heard Al take a shaky breath. On her other side, she felt Milo—or maybe Connal, it was getting a little hard to tell—help her to her feet.

"Come," he said. "Come on. Take my hand."

He led her over toward the wall where he lifted one of the ancient torches out of a sconce. It was cold to the touch and Clare wondered at the fire that Boudicca had coaxed out of it. Before the match burned down completely she touched the flame to the brittle, pitch-crusted rag and it caught, giving off an oily light from pale sullen flames wreathed in choking smoke.

"Wait here."

Milo reappeared a moment later with another torch that he'd lit from the first. Now there was enough light to see their way back into the main chamber.

Maggie and Al fell in close behind her as Clare started carefully toward the tunnel. But when she glanced back, the sight of Milo's face as he stood looking down at Comorra's bier shocked and terrified her.

It's only the shadows, Clare told herself. *The shadows and your imagination.*

Maybe. But for a brief instant there, in the glow from the sputtering, smouldering torch, Milo hadn't looked anything like Milo at all. He had looked exactly like Connal ... and there had been a look of something like madness in his eyes.

BOUDICCA'S CHAMBER, when they got there, was empty. Both Morholt and Dr. Jenkins were gone. So was the knapsack full of looted artifacts. And most of the plastique.

"Mags?" Clare's voice was soft in the gloomy air. "This is bad, right?"

"I'm afraid it's not good." Maggie's voice was tight. "Even if there was a sufficient amount of C-4 left behind, we haven't a detonator."

"Can we dig our way out?" Al asked. Her teeth were chattering, but Clare didn't know if it was from fear or cold. It was starting to get awfully clammy.

"The barrow walls are probably ten feet thick at their thinnest point," Milo said in his own voice.

It was weird, because he was Milo again, but he was obviously drawing on Connal's knowledge. Clare moved closer to him, trying to get a good look at his face through the pall of smoke and darkness. His eyes were a little glassy and perspiration shone on his forehead and upper lip.

"Milo? You okay?"

He nodded tersely.

"How about Connal?"

"He's ... fine. A little pushy." Milo grinned a bit crookedly at her.

"Does he know where Boudicca has gone?"

"I ... I don't know. I think—he thinks—she'll try to raise her spirit warriors again."

"Then she'll have gone to find their bodies in the museum," Maggie said.

Milo nodded. "She'll probably try another sacrifice to provide them with a leader."

"You mean Stuart."

"He's the closest thing she has to a Druid now," Milo said.

Al's breath was starting to sound raspy and Clare was feeling lightheaded. "We have to get out of here," she said. "I mean—obviously—but does anyone have any bright ideas?"

"Tell him ..." Connal's cadences took over Milo's vocal cords again. "Clarinet. Tell him I need control. Tell ... Milo ... I need him to let me be fully free in order to work the magic."

"I ..." Clare hesitated.

A hand in the darkness gripped her arm above the elbow and Milo's face appeared close to hers. The shadows under his eyes and in the hollows of his cheekbones stood out in stark contrast to his pale skin. "You must. I can get us out of here. Tell him to set me free or we will all stay here trapped forever under this hill to keep my princess company."

"Clare." Al tugged her by the sleeve of her other arm, pulling her over by Boudicca's bier and out of Connal's earshot. "Do you think that's such a good idea? He's not exactly the poster boy for mental health stability at the moment. He's almost as off-the-rails as Queen Bee."

"Yeah. He is," Clare readily agreed. "Got a better idea?"

Al sighed so deeply it sounded as though she were deflating. "For the second time today—and I think this is a first for me—I'm ashamed to say I really don't."

"Neither do I ..." Clare glanced down and saw Connal's wrist cuff—the one he'd left lying on Boudicca's bier two thousand years earlier—on the stone between the queen's skeletal feet. "But I might have a backup plan if things go totally south." Putting on the leather gloves she'd tucked in her pocket, Clare picked up the cuff and pocketed it. Carefully—so that Connal wouldn't see. The air felt like it was growing thin and she hurried back over to the others. She didn't have much time left. Ironically.

"Okay, Milo," she said quietly. "Hand over the reins to Connal. It's not a sports car anymore, it's a war chariot. And he has to be the one driving."

25

Clare spent the ride back to London in the cramped confines of the convertible's backseat, trying not to stare worriedly. Connal had yet to relinquish his control of Milo, and he sat with his lanky frame folded awkwardly to fit behind the driver's seat and his shoulders pulled taut around his ears. His eyes kept darting about at all the unfamiliar twenty-first-century sights they passed as though seeing everything for the first time. Which he really was.

Clare had reluctantly agreed that, until they tracked down the vengeful warrior queen who'd hijacked Dr. Jenkins, Connal's consciousness should remain at the fore.

"Are you okay?" Clare now asked for the hundredth time. Connal had used his magic to transport them out of the barrow—and he'd almost collapsed at the base of the hill as a result. He'd managed the feat, but it had cost him.

"Connal?" Clare put a hand on his knee.

For a long moment he stared at her hand, his eyes fever-bright. Then slowly, methodically, as if trying to commit it to memory, he began tracing the contours of each of her fingers. Over and over again, all the way back to London. It seemed to calm him. Clare was afraid to withdraw her hand, but by the time they reached Great Russell Street at the edge of London's financial district, she was also just a little freaked out.

Having driven Milo's Bimmer like a maniac all the way back from Bartlow, Maggie now slowed to just over the speed limit. She drove past the ornate wrought-iron fence that surrounded the grand edifice of the British Museum and turned onto a side street that led to the entrance for staff parking. All the museum's windows were dark—the place looked deserted. Something was not right. Even in the dead of night there were always floodlights illuminating the stately marble faces of the building. But on this night the building loomed up in the darkness, a dim grey shape against the storm-tossed sky.

And it wasn't just the museum. The whole neighbourhood looked as though it had blown one gigantic fuse. Not even the streetlights shone. And no one was out on the streets complaining about it. High overhead the clouds roiled and scudded across the face of the sky as though driven by gale winds, but on the ground things were utterly still. Not a leaf stirring.

Something was *very* not right.

Maggie stopped near a service entrance at the back of the museum, where they found Stuart Morholt's Bentley parked at a haphazard angle. She went around to the back of the car while Al tilted her seat forward so that Clare could climb out. But Connal clenched her hand in an iron grip.

"It's okay," she said, gently prying his fingers loose as he stared at her with Milo's unblinking eyes. "I'm right with you."

Maggie reappeared at the driver's side door and tilted her seat forward as well. Then she held out Milo's cricket bat, retrieved from the trunk of the car. "I think, perhaps, our warrior prince might feel more at ease if he were armed with a weapon."

Connal looked at what to him must have seemed a good, stout wooden war club and smiled. He let go of Clare's hand and got out of the car. Then he took the proffered bat, testing its heft with the assurance of a trained fighter.

Maggie smiled at him and, nodding for the girls to follow, headed toward a set of utility stairs, fishing a security pass out of her pocket as she went. The indicator lights on the card reader were dark, though, and the door swung open on its hinges at a touch.

"Shimmer-fried," Al murmured, touching the dead panel with a fingertip. "I'll bet every electrical system in the building is toast. Boudicca must be pulling down some serious mojo."

Clare looked at her. "And you saw the sky outside, right?"

"Yeah. I don't like storms."

"Me neither, pal."

The air inside had a sepulchral quality to it. Intermittent shafts of moonlight spilled through high windows, cutting the hallway floor into alternating strips of light and dark. Maggie hesitated on the threshold as if her familiar world had become an alien, otherworldly realm.

An eerie wail suddenly echoed toward them from somewhere in a far-distant part of the building.

"We'd best hurry," Maggie said with calm determination.

They found their way in the near-darkness to the East Stairs and came out onto the upper floor's Ancient Near East Collection. Maggie led them at a clip through the Egyptian Collection, a series of connected rooms filled with sarcophagi, grave goods, and statues of long-dead pharaohs that stared at them with flat, dead eyes as they rushed past.

The room directly below the one that held the Bog Bodies display was home to an exhibit of medieval arms and armour. As they hurried through it on their way to the stairs, Clare noticed that one of the cases had been shattered and was empty. What had it contained? There was no time to stop and investigate.

They emerged onto the fifth level behind an information partition in the Bog Bodies display room. The four of them collectively paused and then slowly, silently, leaned around the partition.

At the far end of the room Stuart Morholt, duct-taped to an identification-plaque stand and dotted with taped-on bricks of grey plastic explosive, cowered before Ceciley/Boudicca, who held a detonator remote in one hand. The blinking light was alternating red and green.

The curator-turned-demon queen looked wild and weathered, thin and angular—as though the power she used was using *her*. Her feet were still bare, the soles now darkened with dirt. Her lab coat lay in a heap on the floor. Her pencil skirt was ripped up the side almost to the hip and she'd torn off the sleeves of her blouse at the shoulders.

Clare watched as she bent down to scoop up all but one of the dozen or more swords that lay at her feet—swords that must have come from the shattered medieval exhibit case. She stalked around the room like a prowling jungle cat, stopping to gaze hollowly at each of the Bog Body exhibits and to lay a weapon from her iron bouquet on top of every case.

Clare did a quick count of the glass cases in the room. And then she did it again. She was sure. Where there had once been thirteen, only twelve cases now held the spirit warrior remains. Clare really *had* changed history.

Connal hadn't died in the bog that night. Not in this timeline.

"This is what became of my spirit warriors," Boudicca murmured. "Ghosts trapped in glass cases. How I long to set them free ..." Her circuit of the room complete, she paced languidly back toward Morholt. Now she crouched down on her haunches before the last sword, her head tilted to one side and her eyes hooded like a snake regarding its prey in the moment before striking. "Do you know who I am?" She spoke as if she had no knowledge of Morholt's identity. Dr. Jenkins must have been completely buried beneath the queen's persona.

"Wh ... uh ... which one of you?" Morholt stammered.

"Do you know what I did?" The Iceni queen placed the detonator on the floor and picked up the blade. "How many lives I ended with the edge of my sword?" She drew her hand along the length of the antique weapon, leaving a bright, crimson smear on the iron. "Or with a word?" she continued. "Or a wave of my hand?" She waved her bloody palm at Morholt.

"I ... well, um, seventy thousand was the ... the official number ..." Morholt said weakly.

"Seventy thousand." From Ceciley's lips Boudicca's husky tones drifted like smoke. The smoke of burning Celtic villages. She rolled the words around in her mouth as though her mind was trying to comprehend the number by way of its burnt taste. "Seventy ... thousand ..." The queen reached up to her throat, ran the palm of her bloodied hand across the golden torc, and began to murmur words under her breath.

In his terror, Morholt began babbling. "Seventy thousand, yes! And 'jolly good' I say ... well done! Cracking efficiency. Take that, you bunch of pansy Roman gits!"

Clare winced and rolled her eyes. She ducked back behind the partition and glanced at her companions. "We're going to have to do something fast or Boudicca's gonna turn Stu into tomato paste." Unfortunately, she had no idea what that something was. Maggie didn't look as if she had any ideas either, and Milo/Connal didn't seem up to formulating cunning plans just at the moment. His eyes were unfocused behind his glasses and there was a sheen of sweat on his brow. He looked like it was a struggle just to stay upright.

Huddled beside Clare, Al tapped her on the shoulder. "Got the time?" she whispered.

"Yeah, it's ..." Clare automatically checked her watch. "No," she whispered back, holding up her wrist. "Shimmer-fried, remember?"

"Yup."

Clare waited for the forthcoming cunning plan.

"When you shimmer, you disrupt electrical currents, right?"

"Yeah ..."

"Boudicca-Doc's detonator is electronic and, with the batteries in, it's live. The torc around her neck is a shimmer trigger. All you have to do is get close enough to touch the torc. Then ..."

"Zot."

Al grinned. "*Zot*, indeed."

"We need a distraction—"

A howl abruptly rang out and the sound of shattering glass exploded in the room. Shards of display cases started shooting up like crystalline geysers from all twelve of the Bog Body display cases.

"*That's* fairly distracting," Maggie muttered, her voice bone-dry with something close to fear—well, as close to fear as Maggie ever got.

"Okay," said Clare, "our plan just got a lot more complicated."

Boudicca had raised both hands into the air. With a cry of summoning, she'd reclaimed her spirit warriors. Now, from within each of the demolished glass boxes ... *things* were stirring.

"Oh God," Al gasped in horror. "When I said 'bring on the bog zombies' a couple of days ago I was *kidding!*"

"Those poor souls," Maggie murmured, wide-eyed at the ghastly spectacle. The warriors' reanimated remains were barely recognizable as human. Hollow-eyed and leather-skinned, their faces were contorted with Boudicca's borrowed rage—as long-dead as they themselves were. They clutched their weapons with spidery fingers whose bones had long since been dissolved by the peat-bog tannins that had preserved their flesh and skin. The only thing that kept them upright was the power of Boudicca's blood magic that flowed through their desiccated limbs as surely as their own blood once had.

They heaved themselves out of the cases without muscle power or minds and, howling like banshees, began hewing about with whirling blades, smashing through the cases that contained the other, smaller artifacts and tearing through partitions and information boards. Laughing madly, Boudicca retrieved the detonator at her feet and spun in a circle, her face twisted in fierce, grotesque triumph.

Maggie went ashen. "If those abominations find their way out of the museum and into the city …"

"I have to get to Boudicca," Clare said. She didn't just need to *touch* the queen's torc, she needed to get it away from her. From Dr. Jenkins, whose own life force was powering the queen's magic. Just as Milo's was for Connal.

"My queen!" he hailed, his voice resonating through the gallery as he stalked past Clare into the room, swinging the cricket bat like a broadsword. "Boudicca!"

"Okaaay …" Clare threw a hand up in the air even as she fought down a panicked surge. "Change in plans …"

Her borrowed face a mask of fury, Boudicca turned on the intruder … and her lips stretched in a grim and welcome-less smile. "Connal."

"Andrasta bless you, Lady."

"She has not." Her voice was cold. "She was displeased with my last, incomplete sacrifice to her. I hope she looks more favourably upon this one." She turned to the shambling creatures gathering around her. "Kill him. Kill him and, for your reward, I will give you a new spirit warrior to lead you in death." She turned her flat stare on Morholt and then pointed the detonator remote at him.

"Boudicca. Do not do this thing," Connal pleaded as the first of the bog warriors charged him, sword swinging wildly with an uncanny power behind it. Connal dodged nimbly out of the way and the creature's sword shattered on the steel frame of a display case. Connal employed Milo's long limbs with the grace of a dancer as he brought the cricket bat around in a blow that sent the creature sprawling almost the length of the room. "You are a hero to thousands, Boudicca!" he shouted as two more of the bog men attacked.

And a cautionary tale to thousands more, thought Clare.

"You avenged the shame brought upon us by the Romans," he panted, parrying sword strikes as they came at him.

"I have brought more shame upon my people than the Romans ever could have," Boudicca snarled. "I sacrificed my honour. Mine ... my daughters' ... our entire tribe's." Tears, unheeded, welled up in her empty eyes and spilled down her cheeks. "So many ghosts hang upon my shoulders. Their voices haunt my sleep ..."

"I tell you again: you are a hero to many, Boudicca—" Connal whirled, and with a solid, sickening thump, smacked another bog man on the back of what passed for his head. The creature went down but struggled up again almost immediately. Connal couldn't keep it up forever. Clare had to do something.

As long as Connal could keep Boudicca talking she had a chance to get close. She just had to find a way to sneak over to where Boudicca stood, across the room and next to a staircase.

Clare ducked back behind the partition. "Mags," she whispered, "is there some other way I can get to that staircase?"

Maggie nodded quickly. "Go back down this one and through to the end of the medieval exhibit. There's a statue of an armoured horse and rider. It's just beyond that. You can't miss it."

"Good. You and Al should stay behind this wall. If Boudicca hits that button I don't want you anywhere near Morholt when he meets his explody doom." It suddenly occurred to her that she was giving her aunt orders. And Maggie was taking them without hesitation.

Without *much* hesitation, that is. "Clare, wait! It's far too dangerous. Your mother will never forgive me if I let anything happen to you."

"You didn't see the bill for cleaning the baby grand piano after the party, Mags. She'll probably look the other way. Al, stay with her." Clare kissed her aunt swiftly on the cheek and took off back down the staircase before Maggie could stop her.

Clare tore through the fourth level gallery, bounded up the far stairs, and poked her head around the corner. Connal must have disarmed one of the bog warriors, because now he and Boudicca were savagely going at it in a duel of flashing, ringing blades.

Boudicca had clipped the detonator to her belt—the red and green lights blinked steadily—but with all that lethal steel swinging around, there was no way Clare could get to it. Just then Connal looked over to where she was crouched. Their eyes locked—and for a flashing instant Clare thought she saw Milo gazing out at her. He smiled and, with his next swing, left himself wide open for a counterstrike. Boudicca saw the opening and lunged viciously, her sword slicing across his flank. Clare gasped and her brain screamed "NO!" as blood sprayed from the wound. In paralyzed horror she watched as Connal folded around Boudicca's over-extended weapon, wrenched it from her grasp, then staggered back and fell to his knees. He'd left himself vulnerable on purpose for a chance to disarm the queen.

"Milo!"

Clare heard Al scream her cousin's name from the other end of the long room. As Boudicca's head snapped around, Clare leaped at her from behind and grabbed hold of the torc.

In that instant the detonator exploded in a shower of sparks and acrid smoke and Clare felt herself starting to shimmer. But in the moment before the lightning flash hit that would send her hurtling back through time, she wrenched the gold collar off Dr. Jenkins's neck and threw herself backward, flinging the torc down the length of the hall. It hit a marble pillar with a resounding clang, harmonizing monstrously with the skirling howl that tore from the throat of the woman who had once been Dr. Ceciley Jenkins. And Boudicca the queen.

Clare hit the marble floor hard, sliding on one hip and skidding to a stop in a pile of glass shards at the base of a display case. All around her lay the defeated spirit warriors, deflating into piles of leathery skin and once more as empty of life as they'd been for the past two thousand years. A soft, whispering noise escaped from the desiccated windpipe of the tattooed abomination that had once been Macon, proud Iceni warrior. It sounded almost like a sigh of relief.

Clare turned her gaze away from the withered remains and hunched there paralyzed with horror as, in front of her, the possessed curator threw her arms up, clawing at the air with grasping fingers. Her ear-shattering screams built to a monstrous crescendo and swirling, sourceless light painted the walls and ceiling of the museum hall in red and purple swaths. Blood rushed madly beneath Dr. Jenkins's too-pale skin—a network of crimson maplines pulsing with fiery sparks. Her rigid limbs flailed wildly and the faint, flickering outline of a wild-eyed, red-haired Iceni queen appeared, superimposed on Dr. Jenkins's form—a phantom image in a double-exposure photograph. The ghostly apparition cried out in tandem with the cursed archaeologist and then it flashed like lightning and faded ... and the screams died on Dr. Jenkins's lips. Her eyes rolled back white in her head and she collapsed to the floor in a senseless heap.

26

Awash of dim blue shadows and silence settled once more on the museum hall.

Clare scrambled over to where Milo had fallen onto his side, his long body still curled around Boudicca's sword. He was panting and shaking, his hair plastered to his forehead and hanging in front of his eyes. Clare rolled him gently over onto his back and pulled the weapon out from under him. The long, shallow gash across his chest seeped blood through his Superman T-shirt, but it was nowhere near as bad as Clare had feared. His gaze was unfocused—wild still in the aftermath of the fight—but even as she watched, Clare saw that he was drifting back toward a lucid state.

Connal's lucid state.

"Connal," she said gently, helping him up into a sitting position. "Thank you. Thank you so much for everything. We did it. We got the torc back and Maggie will make sure it never falls into anyone else's hands ever again. I promise. Now we have to get Milo to a hospital." She reached for the silver cuff on his arm. "It's time for you to go—"

"No." His hand shot out and gripped Clare's wrist. "I will not go back, Clarinet."

Over his shoulder, Clare saw Al skid to a halt. Maggie, who was hurrying after her with a first aid kit, almost ran into her.

The grip on Clare's wrist tightened and Connal stood, hauling her effortlessly to her feet with him. His gaze had become flinty and there was a hard, determined set to his mouth.

Clare felt her stomach clench with apprehension. "Milo?" she said loudly. "Milo! Can you hear me?"

Connal shook his head. "He sleeps. Let him sleep forever so long as I can be with you." The silver cuff began to glow with a reddish light that pulsed in time to the blood Clare could see coursing beneath his skin.

A chill of dread flooded through her veins as the Druid prince stared feverishly out at her from Milo's eyes. Comorra had been willing to kill Clare so that she could have Connal. Would Connal be willing to do the same to Milo? It was somehow so easy to forget how different their world was. His was a place and a time where lovers' quarrels might be settled on the point of a knife.

A place where Connal had already lost so much. He must have seen things ... done things during Boudicca's rampage that had horrified him. And with the Iceni tribe in tatters, the queen gone, and Comorra—the girl he loved, even if he had barely begun to acknowledge it—dead ...

It was easy to understand how he saw this as the path away from all that misery. He could stay here. With her. In his desperation he would do it. It was madness, but everything Connal had been through may have put cracks in his sanity— and dragging his spirit into the present might have finished the job. It would be impossible to convince him to set Milo free.

Milo's mind—Milo's big, beautiful geektastic mind—would shrivel up and die, locked away in a prison made of magic. And it would be all Clare's fault.

"Miiilooo!" she shouted at the top of her lungs.

Suddenly, he doubled over with a cry of pure agony—his or Connal's, Clare couldn't be sure—and when he straightened up again his face was twisted in a snarl. His hands shot out and he gripped her by the shoulders, bringing his face down to hers and crushing his lips against her mouth. Searing heat bubbled up from deep in Clare's chest and waves of warmth flooded out to the ends of her fingertips. It was like shimmering but without the time travel. Every nerve ending in her body tingled and sparked, and the rest of the world seemed to vanish all around her. She kissed him back, hard, and as he stole the breath from her lungs she melted into the fierceness of his embrace. When finally Clare had to pull away she was gasping for air—wide-eyed, astonished, flushed, and weak-kneed—and dead certain that it hadn't felt *anything* like that when Connal had kissed her before ...

"Clare ..." he ground out between clenched teeth. "... de Lune ..."

Clare de Lune!

That *hadn't* been Connal kissing her at all! She knew it!

"Milo?" She took a hesitant step forward but he thrust out an arm, warning her away. She gaped at Milo's face as it twisted and contorted. "Milo—take off the cuff! Take it off *now!*"

Milo's long fingers gripped the edges of the knotted silver band as he strained to tear the bracelet from his arm. It wouldn't budge. "Too strong ... Clare ... help me ..." His body arched grotesquely as he fought against the presence that sought to overwhelm him.

That's it, Clare thought. *Time to play hardball.* Dodging his flailing limbs, she grasped the sides of his face with both hands. She ducked in and kissed him on the mouth again, inhaling sharply through her nose as his arm went around her like a vise and crushed her to his chest. Milo's lips moved hungrily over hers and Clare returned the kiss with an almost equal fervour. It was almost enough to make her forget what she had to do. Almost.

Until the second she realized that it was no longer Milo kissing her.

"You see?" he murmured in Connal's voice. "You want me. You know you want me."

Sure she did.

She *wanted* him ... to get the hell out of her prospective boy-friend. With Connal so passionately distracted Clare broke the embrace and hauled back with her fist, winding up to crack him across the jaw as hard as she could. She didn't have to. With a hollow thud Milo's head suddenly jerked to one side and he slumped to the floor.

Clare looked up to see Al grasping Milo's cricket bat in two hands.

"He'll be fine," she panted, hefting the bat. "He has a really hard head. Used to fall out of trees and land on it all the time when he was a kid ..."

Clare stared at her for a moment, eyes wide, and then dropped to her knees to make sure Milo was still breathing. He was. She checked his wrist and grimaced. The edges of the cuff's design looked as though they had begun to meld with the skin on Milo's arm. Boudicca's death-cursed torc had been powerful enough, but Connal's bracelet had carried the Druid's *living* spirit through time and poured it into Milo's body. And now it was trying its damnedest to stay there. Clare got up. She knew what she had to do.

She glanced over at Stuart Morholt, who was still taped to his information stand and staring at Clare and Al with something that might have been a measure of respect.

Then she turned to Al and Maggie. "Can you keep these two under control until I get back?"

Maggie eyed the bat in Al's hand and her mouth quirked in a half-grin. "I think we'll be able to handle things."

"What are you going to do?" Al asked.

"If Comorra never drinks the poison Boudicca left behind," Clare said, "if *that* Connal is there to stop her, then *this* Connal never exists. I'm going to go find him and make sure he gets to Comorra on time. *This* time."

"He won't be out for long, you know," Al said with a worried glance over her shoulder at the outstretched form of her unconscious cousin.

"I know." Clare nodded tersely. "Ten minutes. Give me that long and no longer." She thrust her gloved hand into her pocket and grabbed Connal's other bracelet—the one she'd taken from Boudicca's bier. He wouldn't need to leave it at the bier anymore—he wasn't going to *go* to the bier. He was going to take Comorra and run. Clare was going to make sure of it.

"Okay." Al checked her watch. It was a retro-cool vintage wind-up and had survived the shimmer trip to Boudicca's tomb just fine. "Ten minutes and then I'm calling it, pal."

"You bet." Clare nodded. She stripped off one of her driving gloves and placed her hand on the cuff. The cold, sinewy surface of the twisted silver bracelet sparked fire against her bare skin. Then the shimmering took over and she was gone.

IF SHE HADN'T been looking for him, Clare wouldn't have seen him.

Connal was a shadow. Just a shape in the gloom of early night, hunched and breathing heavily, clutching a shoulder wet with blood. He was crouched beside the bole of a mighty oak, his eyes closed and his face drawn tight with pain.

"Connal." Clare knelt beside him, shaking him gently.

His eyes snapped open, filled with animal wariness, and it took him a moment before he even recognized her. But then the ghost of his killer smile curved his lips and he murmured her name. "Clarinet ... Shining One ... have you come to take me to the Otherworld?"

"Actually, I came to ask your help so that I can keep Comorra *out* of the Otherworld."

"What?"

"She's on the verge of making a terrible mistake, Connal, and you have to help me stop her before she does."

The Druid's gaze sharpened and his mouth pressed together in a hard line. "Help me stand."

"Good. If you think you can make it, then we've got to go *now*." Clare got her shoulder under his arm and helped him to his feet. "How far is it to the village?"

"Not far. Just over that ridge. I was on my way there—"

"I know. Can you run?"

Connal nodded, fierce determination in his eyes. "I can try."

In fact, even though he was wounded, Connal could run a hell of a lot better than Clare could. She had to push to keep up with him as he fell into a loping, ground-eating jog. The terrain was a little rough but they made it to the Iceni town in probably just under five minutes. *This is cutting it close,* Clare thought.

The paths were deserted and most of the buildings in the village were dark. When they reached the Great Hall they saw that its doors gaped wide like the black maw of some huge, dead beast. Only a reddish flickering light shone deep within the shadowed roundhouse, the remains of what would normally have been a roaring blaze in the central fire pit.

Boudicca was draped over a low, backless chair beside the council fire. Still. Lifeless. Emptied of rage, elegant in death. At her feet, hunched and shaking, her hair hanging in front of her face, sat Comorra.

She looked up. "Hello Clare," she said, her eyes empty of all emotion. "Have you come to say goodbye?"

"Not exactly." Clare steeled herself and stood tall, knowing that Comorra was fragile and unpredictable in that moment. She didn't want her doing anything stupid. Like drinking from the poisoned cup she held in her hand. "I came to get you out of here."

"It's time to leave, Princess," Connal said softly. "I will take you over the mountains, to my home in the tribe of the Dyfneint."

"So that I may carry the blight of my mother's rebellion to another's door? I will not go." Comorra gripped the poison cup, her knuckles white. "My life would mean the deaths of hundreds more Celts, Connal. You know that. Maybe thousands. The Legions will not leave anyone alive who will stand as a rallying point for the tribes. I would live as one hunted and those around me would die."

Connal hesitated. A deep frown shadowed his brow.

"I don't have time for this," Clare muttered, automatically glancing at her fried, useless watch. She nudged the Druid sharply with her elbow. "Stop dawdling and say something!"

"He cannot." Comorra laughed mirthlessly. "There is nothing to say. He knows I'm right."

"Connal—" Clare was getting frustrated.

"The princess *is* right." Connal shook his head, his expression full of pain. "Our world is changing, Clarinet. It *has* changed. The Iceni are a proud people. We do not surrender without a fight—and usually not even then! *This* was a battle that the gods decided we were to lose and it will not end as long as Comorra lives. There would be no peace for the princess."

"But—"

"It is Comorra's decision, Clare." Connal's voice was harsh with leashed emotion. "One that I will respect."

"So she becomes just another casualty of war. A sacrifice to Andrasta." Clare tried but could not keep the bitterness from her voice. "And *you're* okay with that."

"Comorra is a princess." Connal said proudly. "And she is wise. And—"

"And you're in love with her, you dumb-ass!" Clare shouted. A thick, shocked silence descended on the three of them.

"He's ... what?" Comorra asked quietly.

"In love with you." Clare took a deep breath. "If you kill yourself, Comorra, it will wreck him. Utterly. Believe me on this one. So there you go—there's *another* casualty of war. And sure, in the grand scheme of things, whoop-dee-doo, who gives a crap about some dude's broken heart. But what about the *not*-so-grand scheme? Doesn't love count for something? Do you think all this ... this *carnage* would have happened if the Romans hadn't taken Prasutagus away from your mother? If she hadn't been so blinded by grief maybe she would have found a way to work things out with the governor instead of goading him to war." Clare shrugged helplessly. "I don't know. Maybe not. Maybe two people alone in the darkness can't generate enough light to drive it back. But maybe they can be a beacon for others. A candle in the window at midnight, you know? I mean, they can at least be there for each *other*, right?"

"Connal ...?" Comorra's expression warred with itself—as if she didn't dare to hope. But it also looked as though her grip on the cup might have loosened a little.

"And, by the way, she's in love with you, too!" Clare turned on the Druid prince. "And if you'd both take a second and stop being all noble and stubborn and ridiculous, you'd realize it. And you'd *do* something about it."

"But the war ..." Comorra protested weakly.

"To hell with the war! It'll go on with or without you two around to join in the fun. It's already ruined enough lives. Don't let it ruin yours." Clare glared at the Druid prince. "Connal, you once told me you'd die for Comorra—"

"No." Connal slashed the air with his hand and turned to Comorra. "I will not die for you."

Comorra stared at him, unshed tears rimming her wide blue eyes.

Clare held her breath.

Suddenly, in half a dozen strides, Connal was across the room and towering over Comorra where she sat hunched on the floor. He reached down, snatched the goblet from her hand, and hurled it across the hall. Then he grasped Comorra by her shoulders and hauled her to her feet.

"I will not die for you," he whispered fiercely, inches from her face. "That was what your mother wanted me to do. But she is no longer my queen. You are. And I tell you I will *not* die for you. But I will *live* for you. We will leave this place. We will run, hide, fight another day ... but we will live. Together."

Comorra stared up at Connal, speechless and flushed.

"Clarinet is right. I do love you." He smiled gently down at her. "I have loved you since I was fourteen years old, Princess."

Clare blinked in astonishment. So Milo wasn't the only one who carried a slow-burn torch.

"I never dared say it before, because I always knew my destiny was in your mother's hands." Connal took Comorra's hands in his and turned her palms upward. "It is in yours now. As is my heart. Come away with me."

In the next instant Comorra was kissing him and crying and Connal's strong arms were wrapping around her in a fierce embrace. Clare grinned and tried to find something interesting to look at in the pattern of the rug.

"Hey ..." she said after a few moments, "I don't mean to interrupt, but I have to get going. I just wanted to give this back to you first, Princess." With her gloved hand Clare reached into the pocket where she'd stashed Comorra's brooch. In all the craziness she'd forgotten to leave it back in the tomb. But as it turned out, this was a much better way to return it. She tossed it lightly through the air and the red stone of the raven's eye reflected the firelight, winking at her before Comorra caught it.

Outside, high above their heads, a raven perched on the peaked roof of Boudicca's Great Hall called Clare's name. At the sound of that harsh, imperative cry, Clare felt herself turning to stardust and shadows in front of her Iceni friends' eyes. She raised a hand in farewell and smiled as Connal put his arm around Comorra. She hoped with all her heart that he would never let go.

27

Milo's blond hair fell over his forehead as he sat against the base of a shattered display case. Connal's silver bracelet was gone, leaving only a fading red welt circling his wrist.

"It vanished," Al told her. "Just before you came back. That's how I figured you'd done it."

The one that had been in her pocket was gone, too. As if it had never existed.

Milo raised his head wearily and smiled at her. Clare dropped to her knees in front of him and threw her arms around his neck, sobbing his name into his hair.

"Hey ..." he murmured weakly as he pulled her close. "Hey, Clare de Lune ... don't cry. The guy had a point after all ..."

"What?"

He smiled at her, blue eyes clear and full of nothing but Milo. "I would have fought just as hard to be with you if I'd been him."

"You're not him."

"Well ... no. Not anymore."

"And you don't have to fight to be with me." She grinned and wiped the tears off her cheeks as she helped him to stand. "Just ask me out on a date."

A slow, shy smile spread across Milo's face, and for a second Clare thought he would back off a step, or maybe quip disarmingly. But then he bent his head and kissed her. Clare gasped and closed her eyes so she could watch the fireworks going off in her head at the touch of his lips against hers.

"Tomorrow night," he whispered in her ear. "I'll pick you up at seven o'clock. Dinner, dancing ..." He glanced down at where the wound Boudicca's sword had made still seeped blood through his shirt. "... *slow* dancing, and no Druids allowed. Deal?"

Clare suddenly, fervently wished she could travel *forward* through time. "Deal," she whispered back, and kissed him again.

"Right." Morholt's voice floated over to them, intruding *massively* on the moment. "How romantic. Lovely, yes. Look, can someone please cut me loose? I'm losing feeling in both major and minor extremities."

Al snorted. "I think we should leave him right where he is."

Clare sighed, seriously contemplating it. He was still damned annoying, but at least he wasn't splattered all over the gallery. She disentangled herself from Milo's embrace. "Let's cut him loose."

Maggie crossed her arms and glared balefully in Morholt's direction.

"He's just going to stand there and whine if we don't," Clare said, rolling an eye at him. "You're welcome."

They cut Morholt free and removed his plastique vest. Al stood watch over him with the cricket bat while Maggie patched up the gash over Milo's ribs and Clare slumped against a display case, exhausted. Dr. Jenkins was still unconscious and utterly unresponsive. Maggie thought she might have lapsed into some kind of shock-induced coma. Clare was struggling with feeling sorry for her. Or Morholt.

After they cut Morholt free, the five of them stood gazing around at the ruins of the Ancient Britain display room.

Milo kicked aside a shard of glass and picked up Boudicca's discarded sword, waving it at the devastation. "We're gonna have a hell of a time explaining this to Scotland Yard," he said.

Maggie shook her head. "Leave that to me. I'll tell them Ceciley's off her chump and has been displaying extremely odd behaviour lately. That she had some misguided notion that the Claxton Spectral Warriors exhibit was disrespectful to the dead. After all, she'll not be telling tales of demonic possession and Druid blood curses. And if she does? They'll find her a nice quiet room in a nice quiet institution, I dare say. I think we can safely convince the authorities that you lot were visiting me at work and that when she went on her rampage we just happened to be in the wrong place at the wrong time."

Clare winced at the turn of phrase.

"Sorry, duckling," Maggie patted her arm. "You know what I mean."

"Right!" Morholt suddenly smacked his palms together and rubbed his hands vigorously. He took a few steps in the direction of the exit. "Cheerio, then. Speaking of the authorities, I rather suspect that my presence here—seeing as how Scotland Yard considers me deceased—would only serve to complicate things. We don't want the police looking into this in any more detail than is absolutely necessary, don't you agree, Magda?"

Clare glanced at her aunt, who seemed ... conflicted. "Mags?" She would go along with whatever decision Maggie made. Clare suspected that, deep down, her aunt might still harbour some kind of feelings for Morholt, and she wasn't going to press her on the issue.

But then Milo glanced around and said, "Where's the torc?"

They looked over to see Morholt creeping away, his knapsack clutched tightly to his chest.

"Open that," Maggie said in a flatly accusatory voice.

"I will not." Morholt stiffened as if such a suggestion were an affront to his dignity.

"Al ..." Clare called over her shoulder.

With a look of pure delight Al hefted the cricket bat and strode toward Morholt with all the menace of a security guard advancing on a stoner at a rock concert. "You. Utter. Slimeball!" She yanked away the knapsack and pulled out the drawstring bag full of treasure from Boudicca's barrow. And the Snettisham Great Torc—Clare could clearly see its outline through the canvas. But now, with the swiftness of a striking serpent, Morholt snatched the bag right back.

"Drop it!" Clare snapped, reaching for it.

"I will *not!*" Morholt pulled out a bronze Iceni dagger and waved it at Clare. "I haven't been thwarted, attacked, kidnapped, plastique-wrapped, near-exploded, and generally abused by smarty-pants teenagers just to walk away from this nightmare with nothing to show for it. I'm leaving and I'm taking my little bag of souvenirs with me!"

Clare went rage-blind. She threw herself at Morholt, grabbing the canvas bag. The drawstring pulled open, the great torc dropped toward the floor, and without thinking Clare reached and caught it mid-air at the same time as Morholt did.

Clare's shimmering triggered the instant she grabbed hold of the torc. Only this time it was different. This time, she had company. Clare found herself hurtling through a stomach-churning, vertiginous maelstrom of sparkling darkness as she struggled to free the torc from Morholt's grip.

Suddenly Clare felt a jolt of pain, sharp enough to make her snatch her hand away. "Son of a—" she yelped, and in that instant—just as the lightning began to flare—the shimmering abruptly stopped. Milo lunged for her as if she stood at the brink of a precipice and pulled her to his chest.

"Clare!" Maggie cried out. "What happened?"

"He *bit* me!" Clare shook her hand and glared at the stinging, livid impressions of teeth stamped like tiny crescent moons into her flesh.

"Where's Morholt?" Al asked, staring at the empty space where the self-proclaimed Druid had stood only a moment before. He was gone. So was the bag of treasure. So was Boudicca's torc.

Clare cast her mind back to that instant just before she'd let go of the torc. What had she seen? She remembered a flash—a momentary impression—of moonlight glinting on water, far off in the distance. And the smell of the sea.

"Clare?" Al laid a hand on her shoulder. "Are you okay?"

"Yeah. I think so ..."

"And Stuart?" Maggie wondered.

"How far is Snettisham from the sea?" Clare asked.

"It's right on the coast," Milo answered.

"I think I know how Boudicca's torc got buried there," she said wonderingly. "I think that's where I left him."

Maggie and Milo exchanged a glance. Al patted her on the shoulder.

"I can't get him back." She shrugged helplessly.

No brooch. No silver cuffs. No torc. And although the Battersea Shield, safe in the restoration room in the basement of the museum, might still get her back, there was no sure way of finding Morholt if it did. Besides, Clare knew what had happened to the shield—and she definitely wasn't going to risk a one-way trip to the bottom of the ancient Thames ... not for Stuart Morholt.

She really hoped, for his sake, that Stu was as handy with his real Iceni dagger as he'd been with his fake James Bond gun.

OUTSIDE THE MUSEUM, dawn was breaking in a silent, pastel-soft sky. Maggie had called the police and the group went out onto the front steps to wait for them to arrive. Milo held Clare by the hand. Al walked at her other side. The two cousins were arguing over the top of her head.

"Seriously," Al was saying, "chaos theory is no laughing matter, Mi—"

"Oh, don't give me that line about 'the beating of a butterfly's wings,' cuz. It's poetic nonsense." Milo snorted. "And *Jurassic Park* was just silly."

"So ... what then?" Al countered. "You think this whole thing was a closed-loop event? What about ripple effect?"

"I was thinking more along the lines of quantum—"

"Guys!" Clare's head felt as though it were coming off her shoulders. "Really, are apes ruling the planet? Is it raining doughnuts? Are dinosaurs roaming the streets? No."

Milo and Al looked around as if wanting to confirm that assertion.

"Then let's leave it alone, shall we? Everything is the same as it's always ..." She looked up at Milo and frowned. "Have you always worn an earring?"

He put a hand up to the tiny gold hoop. "Yeah. Why? Don't you like it?"

"No ..." Clare murmured. "No ... I do." She shook her head and looked up into the sky. High above, a lone black shape was winging its way through the ruby-misted air, but it paid her no attention. It wasn't her raven. "Hey Maggie?"

"Yes, dear?" Maggie answered as she sank down to sit on the steps.

"I think I know what I want to do after I graduate."

Al turned and raised an eyebrow at her. This was news.

"I mean ... I know I've got a year left and there's always a slight chance I'll be able to pull off the grades to get into a university program, but I figured maybe I'd go the practical route instead. And I was hoping you could help me."

"What do you mean, duck?"

"Well ... I was wondering if you could maybe help me get an internship or apprenticeship or whatever on one of those archaeological digs you're always going on."

Maggie looked as though Clare had suddenly started speaking in tongues, but Milo smiled down at her and gave her shoulder a squeeze.

"Are you sure, Clare?" Maggie said.

Clare looked over at Al and grinned. "Yeah," she said. "I'd like to give it a try. I'm one of the smartest people Al knows, after all. And I think I might just have some useful insights into the past."

Maggie smiled at her wayward niece as they heard distant police sirens growing closer.

ACKNOWLEDGMENTS

This particular tale has been a long while in the telling. Now that it's out there, I'm thrilled to finally be able to properly thank those who made it all possible. First and foremost are the two people who made sure this actually happened: John and Jessica. John for (along with everything else) helping me bring Clare and Comorra's story to life in the first place. And Jessica for (along with everything else) never losing faith that we would find it a proper home once I did. Without both of you, I'm pretty dang sure I would still be typing into the void. Much love and gratitude. Much.

Massive thanks to Penguin Canada—to the lovely Jennifer Notman, who brought me into the fold, and to Caitlin Drake, my fabulous editor, who took such extraordinarily good care of me once I was there. I owe you. Large. Thanks to Mike Bryan, Lynne Missen, Nick Garrison, Mary Ann Blair, and Karen Alliston. Thank you to the design department for making this book look so good, and to Vimala Jeevanandam, my publicist, for making sure people see it. Much appreciation also goes out to Hefina Phillips for graciously accommodating my Celtic linguistic queries.

Thank you, as always, to Jean Naggar and the staff of JVNLA for continuing to take excellent care of me. You guys make me feel like part of the family. And it's an awesome family.

Thanks to my actual family, who are beyond awesome—my mom, my brother, Shelley, Janna, and Dayln. And thank you to all of my friends who continue to indulge me, help me, and put up with me: Mark and Danielle, Adrienne, Joanna, and Joe. Thank you Cecmonster for all sorts of inspiration.

And thank *you*, most of all, for reading.